Leech Girl Lives

Rick Claypool

LEECH GIRL LIVES
RICK CLAYPOOL

SPACEBOY BOOKS

Denver, Colorado

Published in the United States by:
Spaceboy Books LLC
1627 Vine Street
Denver, CO 80206
www.readspaceboy.com

First printed September 2017

ISBN-10: 0-9987120-7-8

ISBN-13: 978-0-9987120-7-9

To Uncle Kenny. The truckload of pulp sci fi I inherited from you changed everything. Your absence, and the impossibility of sharing this book with you, seems profoundly wrong. You are missed.

PROLOGUE: THE SPEECH, PART ONE

Before the attack, the leader of the revolution stood and spoke to her followers:

"All of us in the so-called 'civilized' world are brought up to believe human sacrifice is something that happened only in the distant past.

"We're taught that only savage, wild people who live in the wilderness and worship the sun or the soil or some pitiless god are capable of such cruelty.

"We're taught that the destruction of entire ancient cultures by the people who now rule is only slightly tragic. 'Look at the monstrous things those people we destroyed used to do each other,' we are told, 'and look at what they used to do to their neighbors. Yes, we're sorry they're gone. But if we're being honest, we're glad. And if we're being honest, we'd eliminate them again if we had the choice. Just look how much better we are than they were, with their blood sacrifices, their tribal wars. Look how much more human we are.'

"This is the great lie. It is the lie that we are better than the people who came before us. It is the lie that humanity has progressed. It is the lie the blinds us to our own cruelty and the cruelty of the society we were born into. It is the lie that makes the way things are seem the best they ever could be. It is the lie that makes change seem impossible.

"Of course you all know perfectly well that the practice of human sacrifice is alive and well. It is not organs ripped out from victims splayed on stone altars, but heads severed still screaming from our husbands and wives, our mothers and fathers, our sisters and brothers, as they are fed into to the Republic's monstrous Machine.

For what? Not security for their loved ones, though some may convince themselves that is why they offer themselves.

"No, the truly honest and aware know that what they purchase with their sacrifice is not security, but time—just a little more time—for those they love. A slight delay of the inevitable. A few moments of calm for their loved ones to savor their short lives. Until it is their turn.

"It is not changing the system that is impossible.

"What is impossible is that we should tolerate it for a single second longer.

"What is impossible is that this grave insult to humanity they have built their society upon should go unanswered.

"What is impossible is that we should suffer these sacrifices without standing up and crying out, 'ENOUGH!'

"What is impossible is that we should not rise up, now that it is OUR TURN, and demand the sacrifice from them."

BOOK ONE: THE FUTURE

ONE

Margo opened her eyes and realized she was sinking into a pit of carnivorous black muck and that a pair of giant leeches had enveloped her arms like the most disgusting pair of shoulder-length princess gloves.

The desire to give up and let the muck consume her alive was overwhelming. That's how the muck of despair gets you. First it saps your will to live. Then it devours you whole.

She remembered seeing the leeches slithering through the muck. She remembered reaching for them. She'd intentionally allowed them to envelop her arms. The leeches were her only chance.

The muck came up to her chest. Again her consciousness began to dim. She willed herself awake.

With the leeches enveloping her arms, she felt the leeches pulse with her heartbeat. Drinking. Yet with each heartbeat, her strength returned.

That's how the leeches win you, they want to keep you alive. So they grant their victims unnatural strength and an unwavering will to live. More than enough strength to overcome the despair the muck brings on.

Struggling, she reached up with her leech-covered arms and used the leeches to grab hold of a mushroom cap hanging overhead. She pulled with all her strength.

The muck pulled back.

Again her consciousness started to fade. But the suction cups at the end of each leech had a firm grip on the fungus. The leeches were going to pull her out whether she was aware of it or not.

Then everything went black.

When Margo came to, she was lying on the mold-fuzzy ground at the rim of the pit, coughing violently as gobs of the muck dripped off her clothes. As she watched, the gobs crept back into the pit.

She took a deep breath. The moist air of the wasteland stank of rot. Black clouds blocked the sun. Thumb-sized things scuttled underfoot.

She stood up and spat, then shouted "FUCK YOU!" at the Fungus Wasteland.

Using the leeches as her arms and hands was very odd. She knew she should want to remove the disgusting giant parasites as quickly as possible.

But she didn't.

She knew it was the same chemical mixture that the leeches released into her bloodstream to help her fight her way out of the muck that was altering her mind and making her want to keep them attached to her.

She knew she was stuck with them now. Part of her felt like it should bother her. But she didn't have a hard time convincing herself she had bigger concerns now.

Through the mist several hundred yards away, the mile-high geodesic dome of the Bublinaplex rose up from the mold and fungi that blanketed the Earth.

She had to get back inside.

But she couldn't remember how she got out.

Inside there were people she loved.

There were people she hated too.

And if she didn't get back inside and stop the people she hated, they would ruin everything for the people she loved. And everyone else too.

TWO

On a computer monitor, Margo saw a commercial for a new exhibit coming to the Museum of Genius. The commercial pissed her off. She hurled her yarn and crochet hook down to the floor and shouted at the screen.

"NO! No no no no no no GODDAMNIT NO!"

The screen was also the face of Margo's cyborg. Like all cyborgs it had a box-shaped computer monitor head with a screen where its face should be. The rest of its body was a modified human body covered in a skin of black plastic. In response to Margo's shouting, the cyborg backed away a little.

Today was the one-year anniversary of the day the guy Margo thought she might have been in love with was banished from the Bublinaplex. His name was Dr. Jasper Bearden. The Administration had found him guilty of High Recklessness. Margo thought that was bullshit.

Sometimes when she closed her eyes she could still hear the abrupt shriek he'd let out when the black pit opened under him. A second later, he was gone forever.

The Administration said people died because of what Jasper had done. Margo disagreed. Not about whether people died—people definitely died—but about it being Jasper's fault.

Margo's opinion apparently didn't matter to the Administration.

So today on the anniversary of Jasper's banishment she was determined to do nothing but mope around alone while watching dumb stuff on her cyborg's monitor. She would eat ice cream and get drunk on straight vodka. She would pass out by two o'clock and wake up feeling disgusting around seven. She would watch a stupid movie while eating buttered noodles and waiting for the headache pills to kick in. Then she'd consider combining the pills and the vodka. And she'd wear her pajamas all day.

It was supposed to be a pointless, wasted day.

The commercial ruined everything.

In the commercial the Executive Designer's head took up her cyborg's whole screen-face. The Executive Designer—whose name as far as anyone knew was simply "Fash"—was a thin old man with unruly white hair and a narrow jaw studded with white stubble. He had a pinkish complexion Margo disliked, mostly because it reminded her of her own ruddy skin. He was the chairman of the Administration. He did these commercials when he wanted to tell citizens of the Bublinaplex something important was happening.

The installation of a new work of art in the Museum of Genius was a momentous occasion in the Bublinaplex, where society was centered around the creation and appreciation of art. It was said that humanity's capacity for imagination was what had enabled humanity to survive. History's most significant works of art were on permanent display.

Executive Designer Fash's dark eyes widened on the screen and he said the work of art being added to the Museum of Genius was an installation by Lorcan Warhol.

That was when Margo flipped.

Lorcan Warhol was the author of the *Recklessist Manifesto*. He inspired a whole school of art that was devoted to making unsafe art.

By day, Margo was Inspector Margo Chicago, the Art Safety Inspector who had a way of staring down those who got in her way.

Art Safety Inspectors existed because of the Administration's policy of taking extreme precautions to protect the citizens of the

Bublinaplex—the last surviving human population in the world—from harm.

Until the Recklessists came along, the Art Safety Department's job consisted mostly of requiring wobbly, unbalanced sculptures to be secured so they wouldn't collapse onto anyone. Then the *Recklessist Manifesto* claimed safety was oppressive. Recklessists started making art designed to stab viewers in the throat, burn off their toes, poke out their eyes—or worse.

Artists making such things thrilled people who were bored with safety and terrified the Administration.

Except now, with a Lorcan Warhol installation coming to the Museum of Genius, the Administration seemed to be giving Recklessism its stamp of approval.

"End broadcast," she said to her cyborg. Its screen-face went blank.

"Call Sub-Chief O'Keefe."

Seconds later, O'Keefe's face filled her cyborg's screen-face. O'Keefe was bald with an orange moustache and a short goatee. He was Margo's boss and second in command in the Department of Art Safety.

"What's happening?" he said. "I'm busy, but show me a crab mandible and I'll open a pumpkin."

Margo said nothing.

O'Keefe was always saying things that didn't make sense. Margo figured this was his creative pursuit. She didn't judge. Her creative pursuit was crocheting little plush extinct creatures, mostly cats. For a minute she forgot what she wanted to say.

"You called for a reason?" O'Keefe said.

"The Executive Designer was on a commercial just now. Did you see it?"

He had not.

"Did you know Lorcan Warhol is putting up an installation in the Museum of Genius?"

Yes, he knew.

"Why didn't I know about this? Why am I not handling the inspection?"

"Too risky," he said. "Too risky for you or for anyone else."

"So you're handling it yourself then?"

"Syzygy."

"I don't know what that means."

"It's a kind of alignment of celestial bodies—"

"Nope, still don't get it," Margo interrupted. "Does it mean yes?"

"Yes."

"Where are you in the process? Have you met with Warhol? Have you been to the construction site?"

O'Keefe sighed, "Again, I'm very busy. Construction has only just barely begun. The same is true of my inspection." A finger entered the screen and he itched his nose. "And no, I have not yet met with Warhol or visited the site."

Margo couldn't stand it. How could she waste her day wallowing in self-pity while O'Keefe did nothing about Warhol building a monument to Recklessism in the Museum of Genius, the museum that displayed only the greatest art, art that was supposed to define eras and outlast generations?

"Give me the assignment," she said. "I'm not doing anything."

"Too risky," he said again. "What if you miss something?"

"If I miss something, someone might die and I will probably be banished," she said. "Then you can teach someone new to do the job better." She paused. "Please?"

O'Keefe gave in. "Come to the office," he sighed.

Margo hung up with O'Keefe and got dressed. For work she wore her Art Safety inspector uniform, a yellow button-up shirt and pants with diagonal black stripes. Before she left she glanced at the photo of Jasper by her bedside. Photography had been his creative pursuit. His wide-spaced eyes seemed to stare off at something above and behind her. His narrow nose and pursed lips were frozen in a crooked expression. He looked as if he was about to sneeze.

"Bless you," she said.

On her way out, Margo glanced at the bottle of vodka and the white container of headache pills on the counter.

"Come on," she said to her cyborg. "We're going to work."

The cyborg followed her out and closed the door behind her.

THREE

LATER

Black rain fell from the murky sky. Margo looked out from the hollow, cave-like carcass where she'd taken shelter. Water gathered in the tiny red cup-shaped fungi blanketing the ground around her. Scattered here and there were dark patches where she figured things had sunk down into the muck of despair and died. A small herd of slime grazers milled around on the hump of a nearby hill, apparently indifferent to the storm.

Seeing no obvious threats in the surrounding soggy slurry, she withdrew into the hollow. She closed her eyes and listened to the rain.

Her shelter was the body of a long dead tardigrade. Time had worn away its disproportionately small, pointed head and eight trunk-like legs. Where they'd once attached were now door-size holes. Only the empty shell of its oblong body remained.

Margo knew these nearly indestructible creatures used to be microscopic. They trundled along invisibly in the moss and soil, biding their time. Over the eons, the planet had become more and more hostile. The oceans evaporated. Dense fog filled the atmosphere. Radiation ravaged anything that survived, distorting every plant and animal left into a mutant version of its ancestors. Humanity retreated into geodesic domes, but the tardigrades thrived. They adapted and grew. Now, they were bigger than houses and were the dominant form of life on Earth.

Margo longed to hold a swatch of yarn and a crochet hook. Looking down, she saw the suction cups where her hands should be. She was unconsciously opening and closing them. They looked like weird eyeless puppets. She could not imagine how holding yarn and a crochet hook would be possible with her puppet hands.

She reminded herself she was lucky to be alive, and that reminder gave her strength.

She reminded herself *this* had been her choice.

Earlier, she'd fallen and bumped her head on a stone and passed out in the muck of despair. The muck of despair was no ordinary muck. It was a colony of carnivorous microbes that secrete powerful depressants into their prey.

When Margo woke up neck-deep in the muck, she'd *almost* let it take her. She hated that she was unable to outgrow her dumb teenage self-destructive impulses. She found that work was the best distraction when her thoughts turned self-destructive. Jasper, too, had been an excellent distraction. Life was better when he was around. She'd been in control. Things always got worse when she lost control. What she found power in was telling herself she had control over whether or not she went on.

When she was deep in the muck, not going on had been almost irresistible. Then she remembered a conversation she'd had with a former schoolmate and former friend, Thorsten Achebe.

Thorsten worked for the Pest Control Department. In the Bublinaplex, a Pest Control officer's job was to repel, expel, and exterminate invasive species any time they intruded into the dome. Pest Control officers were experts on the horrible things living in the Fungus Wasteland.

"If I ever got stuck in muck of despair, I'd find a sludge leech," she remembered Thorsten saying. They were sitting at a picnic table in Liminal Park. Thorsten was doodling one of his awful doodles in his sketchbook and Margo was crocheting a kitten's tail.

"Why would you find a sludge leech?" Margo had asked. She didn't much care, but she could tell Thorsten wanted to talk. She didn't mind indulging him.

Thorsten gave Margo a pleased look with his chubby, dimpled face. "The muck of despair puts chemicals in you that make you want to die," he said. "But a sludge leech puts chemicals in you that make you want to live."

"I thought a sludge leech just made it so you can't feel it when it's eating you."

Thorsten smiled. This was something he'd discussed with Margo before. "Sludge leeches do that too," he said.

He told Margo a revolting story about a worker from the Structural Safety Department who'd fallen off the side of the dome where he'd been working on repairs. The worker survived the fall but landed in a nest of sludge leeches. They rushed him to the Bodily Safety Department. The surgeons got the leeches off of him in time to save everything but his fingers and toes. But it didn't matter.

The chemicals the leeches put in him to make him want to live were so strong that when the leeches were removed and he wasn't getting those chemicals anymore, he didn't want to live without the leeches. He threw himself out of a fifth-floor window in the Tower of Safety. "And that's why they only let windows open this far now," he said, demonstrating with his index finger and thumb the maximum regulation size of an open window.

"That's how strong a sludge leech's pro-survival chemicals are?" Margo asked.

"Yes," said Thorsten, blinking his small eyes. He'd had a crush on Margo since forever. Margo politely pretended not to notice.

Margo chuckled and poked Thorsten playfully with a crochet hook. "So you really think that if you get stuck in some muck of despair, you're just going to feel around and there's conveniently going to be a sludge leech to save you?" she teased.

Of course, when Margo had found herself sunk in the muck of despair, she'd done exactly that and found not one but two sludge leeches.

The rain began to let up. Margo looked out from a hole where one of the dead tardigrade's legs had been attached. She warily watched the herd of slime grazers shamble closer. As far as anyone knew, these deformed descendants of domestic animals like cows, pigs, and dogs were the only mammals left besides human beings.

Their appearance repulsed her. They were vaguely human-shaped with their hairless pink and brown bodies with two front legs, two back legs, and a head. That's where the resemblance to a human stopped. What they used as their heads were actually their tongues. A patch of yellowish rasping teeth sprouted where a mouth should be relative to the two forward-facing eyes. A slime grazer's true mouth was the yawning, gummy hole between its shoulders from which its tongue-head protruded. From behind, the useless vestigial faces between their shoulders were visible just above the shoulder blades.

Nearly every member of the herd she watched had at least one leech in place of a leg. A few had leeches for all four legs. Margo was reminded again that things could be worse.

Her foot scraped against the floor of her shelter and the slime grazers froze, suddenly wary and distrustful of her presence. Several minutes passed, then a big member of the herd stepped forward and, from the gaping mouth around its tongue-head, released a horrifying bellow. It sounded like a yawn, a scream, and a guttural chant combined. It gave Margo chills.

Margo crept back into the dark of her shelter. She considered her next move. The slime grazers were harmless, she knew. But they might attract predators.

She did not want to be outside the dome when predators arrived.

FOUR

The Department of Art Safety occupied the top floor of the Tower of Safety, the ugliest building in the Bublinaplex. Too squat for something called a tower, it was shaped like an upside-down bucket. The walls were painted this sickly shade of green that always looked dirty.

And it smelled bad. The stink in and around the building had its source in the tower's lower floors, which were occupied by the Bodily Safety Department and the Bublinaplex's hospital. There, a mix of bathroom odors and the chemical attempts to kill bacteria lingered despite the best efforts of artists whose creative pursuit was to concoct pleasant smells.

Margo and her cyborg hurried toward the employees-only side door to avoid the worst of the smell and the sick people hanging around outside the main entrance.

Inside the Tower of Safety, there were several safety divisions between the Bodily Safety Department on the bottom floors and the Art Safety Department on the top. There was the main office of the Pest Control Department, which oversaw the work of the satellite offices around the inside edge of the dome. There was the Community Safety Department, which was responsible for stopping people from hurting each other or being reckless. Lastly, there was the Structural Safety Department, whose engineers kept the buildings standing, the electricity flowing, the water running and so on.

Margo and her cyborg rode an elevator to the top floor. Elevators bothered most of the people who worked in the Tower of Safety. After all, their job was to find risks where others might overlook them. The idea of an elevator breaking down was pretty much the first thing that came to mind for any safety inspector who stepped inside of one. So most took the stairs and claimed they needed the exercise.

As for Margo, her excuse for braving the elevator was her cyborg's limp. It had taken a nasty fall over a year earlier and broke its ankle. At the time she'd expected Jasper to be released from Community Safety's custody soon enough to mend it. Mending broken bones was among his medical specialties. But instead of being released he'd been banished and her cyborg's ankle had healed oddly. There was nothing Margo could do except live with a limping cyborg until she could replace it with an upgrade when they became available.

The Art Safety Department was a small, quiet warren of desks and chairs separated by graffiti-covered cubicle walls. Stacks of file folders containing inspection reports teetered on the desks where Margo's fellow inspectors hunched over their work. Some looked up to greet her with a smile and a nod but most kept their eyes down.

Like all good citizens of the Bublinaplex, the inspectors were trying to finish their work quickly so they could return soon to their studios, stages, kitchens, workshops, writing desks or drawing desks. Few allowed themselves time for workday small talk. Some were surely tempted to take hasty shortcuts in their paperwork in order to get through their work even faster. But the possible consequences of a botched safety inspection mostly prevented such temptation since the consequences would be severe. If a work of art hurt someone, it was the Art Safety Inspector who signed off on the safety report—not the artist who created the work—who would be held responsible.

Recklessists exploited this fluke in the rules to avoid any kind of consequence for creating dangerous art. Complaints about this lack of responsibility to the Executive Designer from the heads of Safety Administrators made little difference. The Executive Designer held firm. "We owe our survival as a species to creativity," he said in a broadcast speech watched by the people of the Bublinaplex on their cyborg's screen-faces. "I believe punishing artists because their creations are 'dangerous' or 'wrong' or 'reckless' will stifle creativity.

I will not, for any reason, allow creativity to be stifled, even for safety."

The power of the Art Safety Department rested primarily in its authority to insist upon changes to an unsafe work of art before it could be put on public display—changes that the artist would then be required to make. Despite the Executive Designer's rhetoric, an artist could, in theory, be punished for displaying an uninspected work of art or for refusing to make the changes requested by an Art Safety inspector. That didn't happen. Instead, Recklessists designed artworks so their dangerous qualities were hidden from inspectors. More and more, these artists even withheld their allegiance to Recklessism until after they succeeded in pushing a risky piece through its inspection and that piece had then slashed someone's face or stabbed someone's stomach or severed someone's finger. That is, when it was too late for the information to do anyone any good.

Since Lorcan Warhol had written the *Recklessist Manifesto*, more than a dozen Art Safety inspectors had been banished for High Recklessness and scores more faced lighter punishments for failing to detect a hidden danger some Recklessist purposely added to a work of art.

Margo's boss, Sub-Chief O'Keefe, had spent three months in the Community Safety Asylum for the Criminally Reckless. A statue he'd inspected was apparently sculpted by a Recklesisst. When a Shame Administrator stopped in front of it for a close look at the worksmanship, it reached forward and flicked his nose with a metal index finger. The finger didn't even leave a bruise but administrator was outraged.

One of the few fist fights Margo had ever seen had occurred in the aftermath of these new rules. She was drinking cocktails with her Art Safety colleagues in a nearby bar. One of them had become extraordinarily drunk. He was sure he would wind up banished. In a separate group, an apparent admirer of Recklessist art must have overheard. The Recklessist sympathizer said something loudly about how banishment was "too good" for those who would "repress" art in the name of safety.

In the end, Community Safety officers were called in to break up the quarrel by force.

Margo suspected O'Keefe had always kept her away from assignments involving Lorcan Warhol because of his fear of risking her banishment. He'd never admit protecting her, of course. And she'd never ask. But she resented him for it just the same.

After all, Margo hadn't acquired her reputation as the Art Safety Department's best inspector without dealing with her fair share of challenging inspections, including several inspections of Recklessist sculptures and an alarming pair of Recklessist trousers. She had an eye for detail. She was thorough. Possibly what most set her apart from the other inspectors was the sometimes terrifying sense of purpose she brought to her job. Her devotion to art safety, all her colleagues knew, bordered on an obsession, especially when she was dealing with what she suspected to be a work of Recklessist art.

The office beside O'Keefe's office was inhabited by the Chief Inspector, Tiff Austen. Through the crack in Chief Austen's door, Margo could see her rifling through an inspection report. The Chief was a broad-shouldered woman with hair the color of butter and a gap between her front teeth. Her left hand held the knob of a rubber stamp.

Margo knew the word UNSAFE was printed on the stamp. It rested in a red ink pad. Another rubber stamp with the word SAFE printed on it rested close by on a green ink pad. Chief Austen seldom used the UNSAFE stamp. Though the UNSAFE stamp was the stamp she seldom used, it was the one she kept in hand. A stamping error was a consequential mistake no matter what, but she'd rather accidentally stamp UNSAFE on a report declaring an artwork safe than stamp SAFE on a report declaring an artwork unsafe.

A curator once complained to the department about an inspection report incorrectly marked UNSAFE. Chief Austen explained it to him as if he was some sort of idiot child. He was livid. And powerless. Margo had overheard the exchange and savored the thought of what it must be like to put one of those smarmy curators in their place.

Margo knocked on the door to O'Keefe's office. "Come in," he said. The office was cramped and cluttered inside. O'Keefe looked up from his paperwork and smiled, "Sit down. Let's talk."

Behind him sat a cyborg that was at least twice as old as Margo's. Its square head hummed from the internal fan meant to keep it from overheating. On the bottom right corner of the front of its head, a tiny yellow light flickered.

Margo sat in the wooden chair across from her boss. Her cyborg stood behind her. "So?" Margo began. She recalled every other time she'd found out that Lorcan Warhol was working on a new exhibit. Each time, she'd asked to be assigned the inspection. "Pepperoni toes," O'Keefe had said last time, staring blankly. She'd known it was his way of saying no. The time before that, he'd replied, "Refrigerator carcass." The time before that, "Pine cone parabola." All denials, she knew. All without explanation.

O'Keefe leaned back in his desk chair and rubbed his eyes. His cyborg handed him a file. He took the file and slid it across his desk to Margo. "So you have an opinion about a work of art by our old friend Lorcan Warhol being immortalized in the Museum of Genius, eh?" he said.

"Opinion?" said Margo as she accepted the file and opened it. She thumbed through the file's contents. "I've got opinions about the color of hover cube I like to drive and the instruments I expect to hear on an electro-jazz record. This guy getting a spot in the Museum of Genius, right up there with the Old Masters and the Library of Literary Genius and the Archive of Musical Genius—in the same place where Andy Warhol's art is on the walls—it's a desecration of his descendant's genius." She closed the file. "It's bullshit, is what it is."

"I understand," O'Keefe said. "But Lorcan Warhol is probably the most influential and popular artist of our time. Like it or not, Recklessism would not exist were it not for him." He pushed his glasses up the bridge of his nose. "Just about everyone outside of the Art Safety Department admires his work. I don't think the Executive Designer could have ignored that if he wanted to."

Margo scowled. "The guy inspires a whole school of art that might be the single-most non-suicide cause of death in the Bublinaplex. But mister 'Genius' artist? He gets to live forever? How is that right?"

"Herringbone hand grenade," said O'Keefe. "You think I don't know what's at stake?" He drummed his fingers on his desk.

"Anyway, I'm giving you the assignment. You're the best inspector we've got. You're smart. You're resourceful. And there's just too much at stake for me to justify holding you back. Because the worst part of this isn't that giving Lorcan Warhol's art a place in the Museum of Genius legitimizes Recklessism. It's that it guarantees his vision will live on, inspiring future generations of Recklessists. Think of the mess today's Dadaists make, and multiply that by all the past generations of Dadaists. Say what you want about Dadaists, but at least when someone is maimed or killed by something they do, it's probably by accident. So what you've got to understand, Inspector Chicago, is that you must make sure the first work of Recklessism to appear in the Museum of Genius is safe enough for a blindfolded toddler on roller skates—and that is only half of the job you need to do here."

Margo gave O'Keefe a puzzled look. "What's the other half?"

"The other half," he said, "Is to make sure you do some inspiring yourself."

"I don't understand."

"Warhol's work of art will live forever. But so will the changes you require him to make." O'Keefe paused. "In other words, the first work of Recklessism in the Museum of Genius is also the work that the Department of Art Safety—that is you—will have the most influence in shaping."

That hadn't occurred to Margo. O'Keefe was right, of course. She began to doubt she was up to the task.

"You'll do fine," he added, seeming to sense her hesitation.

Margo wasn't sure, but she gave him a nod to show she understood. She stood up to go. "Thank you, Sub-Chief," she said, clutching the file containing the inspection paperwork against her chest.

O'Keefe nodded and waved her away. "You are our genius, Inspector Chicago. Make us proud."

FIVE

LATER

The starless night was darker than any Margo had ever known inside the Bublinaplex.

After the rain stopped she could hear things moving around outside her shelter. Shuffling things. Slurping things. Grunting things. She told herself repeatedly that the sounds were just the slime grazers. She wished they weren't there. They were so close she could smell the foul odor of their bodies even in the putrid air of the Fungus Wasteland.

She'd never been more exhausted but she could not sleep. Peering through a hole in the dead tardigrade's body, she could see the dim glow of the dome like a moon half-submerged in the ground. From the inside, the Bublinaplex's one-mile height and two-mile diameter seemed like the entire world. From the outside, Margo understood how small it really was.

Still, small as it seemed, traversing its circumference in search of a way back inside when she couldn't remember how she'd got out seemed like an overwhelming task.

She closed her eyes and tried to think about knitting.

She awoke with a start.

How long had she been sleeping? Could have been minutes. Could have been hours. It was still dark.

She heard a voice in the distance. The voice called her name. Who could be calling her name? Were her ears playing tricks on her? Was she dreaming? She scolded herself for falling asleep. She blamed the leeches for draining her strength.

Was it Jasper? Reuniting with him in the Fungus Wasteland was a fantasy of hers long before she awoke stranded there. The fantasy especially appealed to her when she considered the possibility of being banished after overlooking some Recklessist ruse. In the fantasy, her banishment would turn into a blessing when she found Jasper waiting for her in the wasteland. She imagined they would live a simple, primitive life together, hunting slime grazers and gathering edible mushrooms and cuddling from morning till night because there might as well be no one else in the whole world.

In the fantasy they didn't need the Bublinaplex. They didn't need anyone else at all.

She heard the voice again, closer this time. The voice was not Jasper's. She felt the sting of disappointment and was annoyed for allowing her imagination to tease her so. She reminded herself that the only place in the Fungus Wasteland she might realistically be reunited with Jasper would be in the belly of a hungry lobopod.

But she did recognize the voice.

She heard it again.

It was the Executive Designer.

Had Fash ventured out to search for her? That didn't make sense. Why would the most important person in the Bublinaplex care about her whereabouts, let alone risk his life to go looking for her?

She peeked out toward the dim glow of the dome.

She heard the voice again, closer this time. "Inspector Margo Chicago," it said. "Please come with me."

Eventually, she saw what she was looking for.

Trudging toward her through the muck in the dark was a cyborg, screen-face aglow with what must have been a recording of the Executive Designer.

The cyborg disappeared.

Margo figured it probably fell down in the muck. She stepped out of her shelter in order to retrieve it.

Then the glow of its screen-face reappeared.

And then it disappeared again.

Margo understood that the cyborg had not fallen into the muck.

She also understood that something large was moving in the dark between herself and the cyborg.

She took another step toward the cyborg and the large thing moved again in the darkness.

SIX

Margo sped up the hover cube as fast as she could, which was not fast.

She and her cyborg were heading toward the Museum of Genius. Probably she could have walked faster than its top speed. She fidgeted impatiently.

The hover cube had seats for two passengers and a hatch in the back for supplies. It had black and yellow diagonal stripes like Margo's uniform. On the side of the hover cube was the insignia of the Art Safety Department, a paint brush and a sculptor's mallet crossed over a sort of shield.

Hover cubes were made to be slow on purpose. They were safer that way. Layers of cushions padded them inside and out to protect passengers and passers-by if one should crash.

Margo looked down. Directly below was Liminal Park, a 200-acre expanse of fake grass and artificial hills. Elaborately costumed athletes were playing Field Pretend between spectator-crowded bleachers. For a second she wished she was in that crowd, kicking back with a beer and watching the game. Just a second. She hated large groups. If she was being honest, she'd rather watch the game from home. If she was being honest, she'd rather be doing what she was doing.

Ahead, the Museum of Genius rose up from the park. A jumble of sculpture gardens, open-air galleries, and food carts surrounded the immense building and a row of residential apartment towers stood nearby to the east. The museum's facade was an architectural mishmash. There were white marble columns and vast expanses of reflective glass and neon plastic statues, all crisscrossed with a network of artfully rusted wrought iron that climbed the structure like a kind of metallic ivy. Emerging from this mashup monument to aesthetic chaos was a spiraling 200-foot tower decorated with busts of the artists whose genius works were honored inside.

The top of that tower was where Lorcan Warhol's installation was being built.

Margo was about to dock the hover cube in the museum's elevated lot when a shrill buzzing sound came out of her cyborg's head. A message appeared on its screen-face: "Incoming call from Cuthbert Klimt."

Margo pressed a button on the cyborg's head. "Cuthbert!" she answered warmly. A chubby, stubbly face appeared on the screen.

Cuthbert had been her Primary Mentor. She always answered his calls. In the Bublinaplex, children were raised by mentors. No one knew their real parents' identities. The system was set up so parents' creative activities would not be disrupted by parenting duties. The work of child-rearing was left to mentors—educators tasked with teaching children everything they need to know in order to function and live full lives and sustain humanity for future generations and so on.

Cuthbert had raised Margo lovingly, and she loved him. "Sorry, you'll have to make it quick," she said to him through the cyborg. "I'm working."

"Working?" said Cuthbert, confused. "I thought today was your day off. Because of Jasper. That's what you told me, right? Or was yesterday your day off? Or tomorrow?"

She'd told him not to get in touch today because she wanted to be alone. Now that he'd caught her in her work uniform, flying a hover cube to the Museum of Genius, she felt guilty. "Something important came up," she said.

The hover cube approached an opening in the jumble at the base of the Museum. Hundreds of statues of genius Ancestors whose works were displayed inside covered the outside of the tower there. Out of habit Margo strained for a glimpse of the little bust of Judy Chicago, her wild curls and aviator glasses nestled among the stone and plastic heads near the north corner.

"I see," said Cuthbert. Margo sensed he was trying hard not to sound annoyed. He was sensitive. "Well, the reason I'm calling is because I thought you might change your mind about today, and I thought maybe you'd want to come over for barbeque and pie. But maybe you have other plans now?"

Barbeque and pie were Margo's favorites. "Barbeque and pie sounds perfect," she said. "But I don't know when I'll be done. Mind if I come late?"

Cuthbert hesitated. He did mind, but he would not say so. "The barbeque will get cold," he said. "I've got your favorite marinade on all these chicken thighs. Neither Belga nor I even eat chicken thighs. We never grow them unless you're coming over. Now we've got these mustardy chicken thighs, and the pie is on too."

"I don't care if it's cold," said Margo. The hover cube drifted into the museum lot. Margo blinked as her eyes adjusted to the dull electric light.

"Okay. Oh! I almost forgot to ask, do you have any feta cheese?" Cuthbert said. "I think feta would be nice on the salad I'm making, but I don't have any here and you know how it takes forever to grow a decent cheese. If you have any feta can you bring it when you come over?"

"I'm docking a hover cube at the Museum of Genius," Margo said. "I don't have any feta."

"Oh, that's right. Sorry!"

She and Cuthbert said goodbye. The hover cube meanwhile parked snugly between two others. Margo took the thick folder containing her inspection paperwork and she and her cyborg made a beeline for the Museum Safety officer's office. She had to stop and wait for her limping cyborg to catch up more than once.

The officer's name was Oliver Beckett. He was a gangly, easygoing guy who smiled so much Margo thought he must be a little bit stupid. She'd worked with him before, but never on anything so important.

Margo followed the narrow corridors until she found Beckett standing at his office door. He wore his blue and white striped Museum Safety uniform. He was holding the door open and smiling. The way he waited when she arrived bothered Margo. He oversaw the museum's surveillance systems so he could see any approaching visitors well before they arrived. He seemed harmless enough, but the idea of him thinking about her when she wasn't present gave her the creeps. "Welcome, Inspector," he said.

"Leave the door open," she said as she walked inside. A few minutes later, Margo's cyborg limped in to join them.

The office was dim. The sole source of light was a wall of monochrome monitors showing video feeds of every room in the museum. On the monitors were sculpture gardens and galleries and the museum's great atrium shown from various angles. There were people reading in the Great Books archive and huddled in listening booths, eyes closed, immersed in music. Some visitors could be seen wandering from room to room; others sat motionless for hours, studying and sketching individual works. Raucous flocks of mentees followed their Mentors. Cyborgs could be seen on some screens, standing motionless in corners and out-of-the-way recesses where they waited to be deployed while other cyborgs mopped floors and dusted picture frames.

Officer Beckett plopped down in the swivel chair behind his circular desk and swiveled around. He regarded Margo with an air of barely contained excitement. A wry smile crossed his boyish face. "You're here to meet him, aren't you?"

"Him?"

"The museum's newest genius," he said, knees bouncing. "Lorcan Warhol."

"Yep," she said, pretending Warhol being referred to as a genius didn't bother her. "I'm here for a first look at the installation. I'll need a pass to get through the security cyborgs."

Beckett spun around. He picked up a mug of something hot and took a long slurp. He started pressing buttons on the control panel on his desk. The images on the wall of monitors showing rooms throughout the museum disappeared. Replacing them were various views of the top of the tower, where Warhol's installation was being built. "There really is a fine view from this room here," he said. "Sometimes I even see Warhol himself up there directing his assistants. Once I think I saw him have a new idea, right there on the screen. He jumped up and sketched something out in his notebook and showed his assistants, and they burst into action. It must have been an inspiration. I must say, witnessing that was the most inspiring thing I think I've ever seen on the surveillance feeds. And I've seen a lot."

"I bet," Margo said, wondering how the guy who was in charge of safety in the Museum of Genius could be a fan of a guy who made art that was designed to mutilate museum visitors. She looked at the screens on the wall that were supposed to be her preview of the exhibit and was disappointed. Almost everything in the exhibit was obscured by an enormous blue cover that was draped over the work in progress like a tent. All she could see was that there were some things on the roof under a large piece of fabric. Not helpful.

"Alright," Margo said. "I need to get up there." She turned to her cyborg. "Come forward." When it started to take a step, it tottered momentarily as though it might fall. Margo held her breath. It regained its balance. "My pass, please."

"Of course." Beckett punched a few more buttons on his control panel. A scan code appeared on the wall of screens. "You know," he said, eyeing Margo's cyborg, "they're providing upgrades soon. This old fellow needs replacing."

Margo ignored Beckett's comment. Her cyborg leaned forward to scan the code on the wall with its screen-face. A sharp beep confirmed the scan's success.

She nodded at Officer Beckett, then turned to leave.

"Inspector," Beckett said before she could go. "Do you truly think Lorcan Warhol's art is undeserving of the title of 'genius'?"

Margo glanced over her shoulder at him. He was frowning like a disappointed child and nervously cracking his bony knuckles. "My opinion is that obvious, huh?"

"It is," he said meekly. "I just, well, you see—"

"What is it?" Margo said. She'd turned to meet Beckett's eyes, but his were downcast. He mumbled something. "What did you say, Officer Beckett?"

He gave Margo a wounded look. "I have a favor to ask of you. You see, I myself am not authorized to go past the security cyborgs I just gave you access to pass," he said. "And I am a very great admirer of Warhol's work. So, I was wondering if you could, when you're up there, ask him to autograph this t-shirt for me?" He held up a yellow t-shirt. "It would mean a lot."

Margo gave Beckett a look she hoped conveyed her disappointment that someone like him—a safety officer—would want an autograph from Warhol. "No," she said, and she turned and left Beckett's office. Her cyborg followed close behind.

They ascended the stairs that led to the roof. The walls were lined with obscure works by artistic geniuses whose greater works were honored in the main galleries. Eventually they met eight security cyborgs standing in a row with their arms linked to block the way.

One by one, Margo's cyborg walked up to each security cyborg, stood screen-face to screen-face with it, and beeped. In turn, each of the cyborgs blocking the way unlocked its arms from the others and stood aside to let them pass.

Once Margo reached the top of the stairs, she had to stop and wait for her cyborg again. She found herself pitying the biomechanical thing, the way its hands gripped the railing when it tried to bear weight on its bad leg as it unquestioningly followed her, its master.

For a moment she thought getting a new cyborg might not be a bad idea. But she quickly dismissed the thought. Maybe once this Lorcan Warhol assignment was over. Maybe after the assignment after that.

Why couldn't she just have its leg replaced? She'd asked several of the bio-engineers from the Cyborg Lab (they were regulars at Margo's favorite pub) and all any of them ever said was that growing individual limbs was impossible, and that when tissue was grown for cyborg bodies the process always was simply to grow an entire body. These answers never quite satisfied Margo, which was why she'd asked multiple bio-engineers this same question. The answer was always the same—but something about the absolute firmness of the bio-engineers' insistence on the finality of their answer struck Margo as disingenuous, almost evasive.

But what could the Cyborg Lab be hiding? She remembered the tour she took of their underground facility. The tour was part a course she'd taken in anatomy for artists. Walking through those corridors with a group had given her the shivers. Hundreds of headless bodies floated under odd-colored lights, immersed in some kind of nutrient soup. A highly choreographed staff of scientists meanwhile busied themselves with an array of complicated-looking medical instruments. The amount of manual labor it seemed to take to ensure that citizens of the Bublinaplex had a steady supply of cyborgs to do their manual labor for them had struck Margo as profoundly ironic.

An arched opening at the top of the stairs led out to the rooftop. It was at the center of the dome, the place where the steel and glass structure that protected humanity from the Fungus Wasteland was higher up than anywhere else in the Bublinaplex. The dome was so high one could almost forget it was up there at all. Clouds had moved to cover the sun outside and dusk was falling. The sky through the dome had a brown, overcooked look to it.

The rooftop looked like it had once been a café or a restaurant. Tiles arranged in a honeycomb pattern covered the floor. Artificial shrubs lined the waist-high ledge. But what dominated the space was the monstrous, tent-like cover that prevented outside onlookers from nearby buildings or passing hover cubes from seeing Lorcan Warhol's work in progress.

Margo understood the artist's interest in secrecy, but she didn't like it. As a safety inspector, she wasn't fond of surprises. Especially not from Lorcan Warhol. She could have forgiven a less thorough hiding of the work if it allowed her a better look. She got out her clipboard and pen.

About a dozen black-clad workers—Warhol's assistants—were quietly hurrying in and out from under the cover. One was lying sheets of rusty nails sharp-side-up on the floor. Another was gluing shards of broken glass to the shrubs. Others were cutting and placing nearly invisible, ankle-high lines of tripwire across the footpath through the exhibit. Others still were carving something into a stone slab that must have weighed several tons and which was placed precariously close to the edge of the roof.

Margo's cyborg's box-shaped head swiveled back and forth on its human neck, documenting all potential hazards.

Nearby, a tall assistant with a curly black moustache was supervising another assistant who was fastening down a heavy, steel tripod. Once the tripod was secure, the tall assistant then started attaching to it what looked to Margo like a prop out of a bygone era's science fiction movie: a high-tech laser gun.

Seeing the gun shocked Margo. Before this moment, it hadn't occurred to her that such weapons existed in real life. But of course they did—how else could the Pest Control Department fend off the worst of what crawled out of the Fungus Wasteland? But those weapons were supposed to be locked away in the Armory unless they were being handled by professionals.

Warhol's assistants, clearly, were not professionals.

The tall assistant finished fastening the laser gun to the floor. He then stepped briskly to the next tripod, where another assistant handed him another laser gun. He knelt down and started attaching it to the next tripod.

Lorcan Warhol was nowhere in sight.

Margo approached the tall assistant. "What are you doing?" she said as casually as she could, as if she was interrupting him hanging laundry out to dry. She didn't like stifling her rage, but she could do it when she had to.

The assistant stood up. He was nearly seven feet tall. He looked down at Margo and smirked. "I'm attaching laser rifles to this circle of gun mounts."

"Ah. I see." Margo rocked on her heels. Never before had she seen such a flagrant mockery of safety. She tapped her clipboard with her pen.

"You must be Inspector Chicago," said the tall man. He extended his hand. "Spreck Purcell, Mr. Warhol's Chief Assistant." They shook hands. "Mr. Warhol has been expecting you."

Margo ignored Spreck's politeness. "What's with the cover?" She asked sharply, pointing up to the massive thing. The cyborg's rectangular head pivoted to look wherever she pointed. "What are you trying to hide? Who are you hiding it from?"

"You'll need to speak with Mr. Warhol about that," said Spreck.

"Right." Margo crossed her arms. "Well right now I'm speaking with you about it. What's with the cover?"

"Yes, of course Inspector." Spreck smiled. "But I can't speak with you about that. You'll need to speak with—"

"Yes, of course. Mr. Warhol." Margo cleared her throat. "What about these, erm, 'laser rifles'? They're disarmed, I assume? You should know that even disarmed 'laser rifles' are unacceptable—it's always possible to re-arm them. When will you remove the laser rifles?"

Spreck's tone remained expertly calm. "They are not disarmed," he said. "And we can't remove the laser rifles. We're not even close to being done setting them up."

Margo uncrossed her arms. She gave Spreck a look she hoped expressed how completely ridiculous he sounded, telling the Art Safety Inspector he couldn't remove the laser rifles.

Spreck continued, "Listen, you and I both know the protocol here. You know the public won't be permitted to come see the exhibit without your department's approval. So there's no need to get worked up. I'm sure Mr. Warhol will be open to discussing any suggestions you might have."

Margo couldn't hold back an exasperated sigh. "Where is Mr. Warhol then?" She said. "I need to speak with him. Now."

"He's not here."

"But I thought you said he was expecting me."

"He is. Was. That's why I'm here, speaking to you now. You're here because you saw the advertisement, I assume?"

Margo didn't know how to reply to that. How did he know? Were Warhol's minions spying on her?

It was as if he'd read her mind. "We're not spying on you, silly," he said. "We've been micro-targeting the commercial for a few days now. Your cyborg here is the only place it's been airing."

Margo tried not to look annoyed and failed.

"Don't flatter yourself too much," Spreck said. "It's not like we made it special for you. Everyone will be seeing it in a couple weeks. Though you should know that opening day for the installation is more like a month away, not two weeks."

The extra time was good news to Margo. She tried to hide her pleasure from Spreck and succeeded. "When do you expect Mr. Warhol to return?"

"Eventually," Spreck said coolly as he knelt down to adjust the scope on the laser rifle.

Margo took a deep breath. She turned and walked back toward the stairs. Clumsily, her cyborg followed.

For the first time she started seriously worrying about what the consequences might be if she couldn't make this work of art safe.

"Stop recording," Margo said to her cyborg. Then, under her breath, "Time for pie."

SEVEN

LATER

The cyborg approaching Margo in the dark was stuck.

"Inspector Margo Chicago," called Executive Designer Fash repeatedly from its screen-face. "Please come with me."

Sometimes the cyborg would say, "You have nothing to be afraid of. Come with me and you won't be harmed."

Margo stepped out of her tardigrade carcass shelter and onto the soft ground outside. Carefully, she made her way toward the cyborg. She was skeptical of what the Executive Designer said. She had an impulse to question it, to argue with it, to give it a chance to convince her it told the truth, but she knew that wasn't going to happen. She would have to either trust the repeating loop of what the Executive Designer said, or not.

She approached the light of the cyborg's screen-face in the dark and considered the possibility that the cyborg and the Executive Designer could betray her. Simply being outside of the dome was an act of High Recklessness, punishable by banishment.

From the outside, the rule seemed stupid. Sure, she figured it discouraged adventurous types from getting out, exploring the wasteland, and coming back contaminated with who knows what. She was not an adventurous type. But with sludge leeches where her arms should be, there was no disputing that she would come back contaminated.

Worst case scenario, the cyborg's purpose was to lure her inside where Community Safety would try to cut off the leeches and then banish her back into the Fungus Wasteland anyway.

If that was what was going to happen she might as well drown herself in the muck of despair and be done with it. But she knew the leeches would not allow her to kill herself. Even when she simply thought about doing herself harm, she could feel the parasites tense. But she noticed such thoughts were scarcer now than they'd ever been. It was the leeches, she knew, working their chemical magic on her mind.

They didn't simply subtract her occasional self-destructive thoughts. It was as if they somehow actually made her love life more. She felt quick, light, and aware. Having not slept for days, she should be exhausted. The only discomfort she felt was a tingly not-quite numbness in her arms inside the leeches. She wondered, in a distant, detached sort of way, how much was left of them.

A few paces before Margo would have reached the cyborg, the huge shape again moved in the dark and seemed for a second to swallow the cyborg whole. An instant later the cyborg reappeared high out of the mud, dangling upside-down in midair. Margo's eyes had adjusted to the dark enough for her to see the long body of the creature coiled where the cyborg had been stuck in the mud and whose many pairs of claws now held the cyborg upside-down by its legs. It was devouring the cyborg's feet. "Come with me and you won't be harmed," said the upside-down Executive Designer's face, now blurred by the foamy slime that had oozed over the cyborg from the creature's toothy, circular mouth. She could hear the bones of the cyborg's feet crunch as the thing bit through.

A lobopod.

Lobopods resembled enormous, armored worms but with scores of legs that looked like smaller armored worms sticking out from their sides. Each leg ended in a deadly two-toed claw. A pair of thick, wormy antennae reached into the air from its head over its mouth.

As the lobopod consumed the cyborg, pushing it deeper into its mouth with its clawed feet, it gave Margo a gory reminder of the cyborg's biological aspect. Blood, black in the absence of light, poured from the wounds where the cyborg's legs now ended.

"Inspector Margo Chicago. Please come with me."

Margo could not see the lobopod's eyes but she could feel it watching her.

A second lobopod emerged from the muck and attacked.

EIGHT

Margo steered the hover cube away from the Museum of Genius.

The more distance she put between herself and the slow motion disaster on top of the museum, the better she felt. Cuthbert's barbeque and pie would make her feel better still.

Cuthbert had taught Margo almost everything she knew, from how to use a toilet to how to hold her crochet hooks.

Margo's Education had ended when she was twenty. Eleven years ago. Most mentors ended their relationships with their mentees after their Education was finished. That's not how it was between Cuthbert and Margo.

Of course there were other mentors who had contributed to Margo's Education. But as Margo's Primary mentor it was Cuthbert who provided Margo's home and taught her the basics of what she needed to know to get by in the Bublinaplex.

Secondary, Tertiary, Quaternary, and Quinary mentors schooled her in more specialized subjects like builder's geometry, hip hop dance, color chemistry, and experimental poetry. But at the end of each day it was Cuthbert and his home-cooked meals that Margo always returned to.

Margo loved Cuthbert's cooking. She did not love the lessons that had so often accompanied his dinners. Usually they were required lessons. Cuthbert always tried—and failed—to deliver the lessons as if they were a part of a perfectly natural conversation.

Between bites, he would lecture Margo about how the Founding Executive Designer set up their society to nurture humanity's creative spirit and explain how the only acceptable limit to any person's freedom was the possibility that one's action (or inaction) might harm another person.

The lectures bored Margo. She didn't give a shit about what had happened long ago and the morality lessons seemed like common sense. If there was nothing to distract Cuthbert, he could go on and on for hours with these lessons.

So Margo was grateful for Cuthbert's distraction when Belga Breugel entered their lives.

Belga started joining them for dinner when Margo was fourteen. Belga was unlike anyone Margo had ever met. Her skin was dark and her short black hair was braided into stripes that zigzagged across her scalp. She wore plain brown or gray dresses over her thin figure. She never wore jewelry. Margo thought she seemed like she'd stepped out of a painting of an ancient peasant village.

With Belga at the table, Cuthbert would talk about food he'd made instead of lecturing. He would prepare dishes for Belga that he'd never made before. He was always asking Belga if she liked what he had made. She always did. Cooking was Cuthbert's creative pursuit. With Belga around, he seemed newly inspired to show off his skill.

"It's the crushed fenugreek that gives the sauce that pungent sweetness," he would say, or, "The trick is to give just the right amount of water to the grocery protoplasm when growing strawberry spheres so they emerge as red and ripe as possible."

When Belga was late, Cuthbert would impatiently tap his fingers on the arm of his overstuffed chair as comedy programs played on his cyborg's screen-face. He would not laugh. He would keep glancing at the door over and over again until she arrived. She always eventually arrived. She would say she was sorry and Cuthbert would swallow his feelings and reply she had nothing to be sorry for.

But the fact was that Cuthbert became terribly anxious when Belga was late. He would get it in his head that whenever someone was late that he might never see them again. He knew it wasn't rational but he couldn't help it.

Belga worked in the Administration under the Executive Designer. She said she was a courier. Margo never quite understood what that meant. All she knew was that Belga occasionally would disappear for weeks at a time and then return as abruptly as she'd left. When Margo asked her why she had to go away, she replied, "Because I'm a courier." Cuthbert gently told Margo not to worry about it. Or ask about it.

Belga's absences was a topic Margo grew to understand she would not learn more about by asking questions. She was only very slightly curious. Her upbringing had made her accustomed to such gaps in information, gaps that were obviously intentional. From a very young age she was aware her natural curiosity would be, not so much discouraged, but redirected toward creating art.

One night over short ribs and fingerling potatoes, Margo asked Belga what her creative pursuit was. Cuthbert gave Margo a look that told her that was something else she shouldn't ask about.

Belga had just forked a bite of short ribs (really a cube of meat analog). She chewed thoughtfully and swallowed. She said, "I dream."

Margo eventually figured out that Belga had no interest in making art.

In the Bublinaplex, the idea of someone not being interested in making art was scandalous. This made Cuthbert's affair with Belga all the more fascinating to young Margo.

Growing up, Margo had never been as good at art as the other mentees. Her annual Creative Potential (C.P.) score was always on the low end of the spectrum. Thinking about it made her feel like a failure.

But Belga didn't care about art and Belga was just fine. She had her job. She seemed to like it.

The practical consequence of having a low C.P. score was that when Margo's Education was finished, she would be required to spend a greater proportion of her time working at her job than creating art. Before Belga, the idea of spending more time doing work than making art had seemed like a kind of punishment for her lack of natural talent. But now she could dream of growing up to be like Belga. She immersed herself in studying Art Safety and stopped worrying about her C.P. score.

Knowing full well Margo's devotion to Art Safety, Belga would sometimes tease her about taking up Structural Safety. Margo would reply by making an obnoxiously loud snoring sound. Supposedly there was a rivalry between the two departments where Structural Safety Inspectors were said to look down on Art Safety Inspectors as misguided busybodies who distracted themselves with "filing down sharp notes" while the engineers in Structural Safety were responsible for the real safety work. Art Safety Inspectors, for their part, were said to disdain Structural Safety Inspectors for their supposed "lack of imagination"—a serious accusation in this creativity worshipping society.

Of course, Margo never fully abandoned creativity. Even if she wanted to, such a decision would be perceived as a kind of artistic statement. She just made her crochet creatures and she never took them seriously. Making them was just what she wanted to do sometimes. No curators or gallery directors ever invited her to exhibit them, nor did she expect them to. The yarn-wrought beasts multiplied and filled her room.

Jasper had loved her crochet creatures. She'd given him a dachshund-shaped one and he'd carried it in his medicine bag everywhere he went.

If Cuthbert was disappointed in Margo, he never said so.

*

The last traces of diffuse sunlight shining through the dome cast a pinkish-orange glow on the white, cylindrical house where Cuthbert lived.

Margo landed the hover cube. Through the windows, Cuthbert's house seemed oddly dim.

Something was wrong.

The house was in the Culinary District. Savory aromas of simmering sauces and roasting meats and baking bread greeted Margo as she opened the hover cube's driver-side hatch.

Her cyborg struggled with the passenger-side hatch. Margo walked around to the passenger side of the cube and took the cyborg's hand to assist it as if it was an elderly person.

On the short journey between the hover cube and the house, the cyborg nearly fell twice. For a moment Margo glared impatiently at the cyborg, caught herself, and then felt silly. It was like catching oneself thinking mean thoughts at an appliance.

Was her cyborg getting worse? She wondered. Or was her patience wearing thin?

Cuthbert greeted Margo on the front stoop with a tremendous hug. He was a pudgy, unwieldy man with big meaty arms and a round face with a deep dimple in the middle of his chin. "Oh, Margo!" he moaned, his face still buried in her shoulder, "I was afraid you weren't going to make it."

"I made it," she said. She didn't ask Cuthbert why he was crying. Sometimes he just cried. Sometimes it was better not to ask.

Inside, the piquant smell of Cuthbert's barbeque chicken and apple pie started to dispel the lingering feeling of frustration from Margo's thwarted inspection attempt. Food in her stomach would finish off the frustration for sure.

Cuthbert closed the front door behind Margo's cyborg. "Sit down," he said warmly. "I'll make you a plate." Margo sat at the dinner table—a mighty expanse of smooth, dark wood Cuthbert had planed himself. Where the wood came from was another one of those questions he avoided answering.

An empty pint glass with dry foam along the rim and a used fork and knife had been left where Belga normally sat. Margo had half-expected to interrupt the two of them here, bantering over drinks and playing cards. Where was Belga?

Cuthbert meanwhile was being a little too quiet in the kitchen. He reheated her a plate of chicken ribbons and sweet potato slats (which were never very good reheated) and bitter greens mash (which was strangely even better reheated). "Bon appetit," he said as he joined Margo at the table.

"Thank you," Margo said, taking a bite. "It's perfect."

She looked up to meet his eyes. Tears were streaming down his face. He sniffled and wiped his eyes. "Enjoy," he said, his voice wobbling to stifle a sob.

She put down her fork. "Cuthbert, what's going on?"

His mouth moved but he didn't say anything. His hands opened and closed, grasping for something but not finding it. The tears kept coming.

Margo's stomach growled. She looked down at her plate. She was so hungry. She was also terribly worried and confused by Cuthbert's behavior. She didn't know what to do.

"Please," Cuthbert said, gesturing with his pint glass. "Eat."

Margo ate. She felt awful, stuffing her face while Cuthbert was so obviously upset about something, but she couldn't help it. She knew she eventually would find out what was bothering him and help him feel better. She convinced herself she wouldn't be much help to him as long as hunger distracted her.

Cuthbert had quieted down. He opened a can of beer and placed it in front of Margo. He opened another can and raised it as if he were toasting something. Margo picked up her can and knocked it against his and they drank.

Cuthbert gulped down nearly half the can. "Belga is leaving me," he said.

The news stunned Margo. After what felt to her like too long of a pause, she asked, "Why?" then immediately regretted the question. The reasons would be painful. Explaining right then would upset him even more. Better to say she was sorry or that Belga was being ridiculous or that if he kept making chicken the way he made chicken, someone else was bound to come along.

Cuthbert took another swig and answered the question. "She says it's my mentees. Can you believe it? She says she can't cope with me being a mentor anymore." Cuthbert told Margo how Belga said she suddenly and unexpectedly started hating the mentees who came over. It didn't matter that nowadays Cuthbert was no one's Primary Mentor and that what Mentees he had just came over for lessons in growing and grilling synthesized meat, pickling vegetable spheres, and things like that. The fact was she said she hated him being a mentor, and that was that.

Cuthbert's creative pursuit was cooking, but mentoring was what he really loved.

He finished his beer. The can made a hollow sound when he set it on the table. "I don't know what to do," he said. "I really don't know what to do." He looked at Margo with his moist, puffy eyes.

"Where is Belga now?" she asked.

"I don't know. Gone. We tried talking about it. She wouldn't listen. She told me she wouldn't make me choose. She knows how much I love mentoring. So she's just going. For good. And she insists there's nothing I can say or do to change her mind."

Margo sipped her beer. She was looking down at her empty plate. "You know you'd eventually start hating her if you let her take being a mentor away from you."

Cuthbert sighed. "I know."

Margo got up and fetched him another beer from the kitchen. She could have told her cyborg to get the beer but she wanted to leave the room for a minute. She got herself another beer too. Back in the dining room she asked, "So do you know when she'll be gone for good?"

"Next week is what she said. She told me not to bother trying to find her. She keeps saying she's sorry. I keep telling her we can work it out. But she says its final." He opened his new beer and took a long drink.

Margo decided she couldn't leave Cuthbert by himself tonight. Not like this. She'd spend the night. His devastation reminded her how she was after they banished Jasper. It reminded her of Cuthbert's kindness then.

Margo reached out her hand to Cuthbert's hand on the table. He smiled and looked at her through his red-rimmed eyes. She smiled back. She hoped the smile looked reassuring.

They sat together in the quiet dining room, drinking beer until neither was able to walk straight.

*

Margo awoke in the middle of the night on the couch in Cuthbert's living room. The room was spinning.

Under her legs she felt the knees of someone sitting on the couch and in her sleepy, drunken fug she thought it was Jasper. She reached for his hand and touched the plastic-coated skin of her cyborg.

Margo remembered where she was. Her mouth was dry and she had to pee but the way the room listed in the dark made her not want to move.

She remembered Jasper's banishment one year ago.

She thought about that day as Cuthbert's living room kept spinning.

The Shame Administrator wore ceremonial robes. He stood high on the dais before the large crowd gathered in the Temple of Shame.

The Temple of Shame stood near the west edge of the Bublinaplex. There, the Shame Administration performed the Banishment

Ceremony. It was a terrifying and in Margo's opinion savagely primitive ritual. The ceremony began at sunset. A large window looking out into the Fungus Wasteland took up most of the wall behind the dais. By the time the shamee was to be expelled, nothing but darkness could be seen outside.

"Shame," said the Administrator. "Shame. Shame. Shame. Shame." He knocked his heavy wooden staff against the marble floor each time he said "Shame." The knocking reverberated through the Temple like the beating of an immense, hollow heart.

The crowd picked up the Administrator's chant. "Shame. Shame. Shame." Spectators stomped their feet in a steady, brutal rhythm. "Shame. Shame. Shame."

A recessed aisle cut through the chanting crowd. When the door at the far end opened, the audience looked to the dark opening and waited for the banishee to appear. When Dr. Jasper Bearden finally stepped out, he was naked and shaking. He covered himself with his hands, his tired eyes fixed downward.

The crowd's chants grew louder. The rhythm quickened. "Shame. Shame. Shame."

A cyborg wearing a hood and ceremonial robes appeared and draped a cloak made from tardigrade hide across Jasper's shoulders. Another ceremonially garbed cyborg stepped forward and strapped a respirator over his face.

Then, as Jasper began his march to the altar, where the Shame Administrator now stood, the spectators fell silent just for the briefest instant.

At the Shame Administrator's signal, the crowd erupted in a roar of derision, then started pelting Jasper with the various objects they'd brought with them to the ceremony for that purpose.

At Banishment Ceremonies, spectators traditionally throw at the banishee things that would be useful for someone attempting to survive in the Fungus Wasteland. Also traditionally, they throw the things hard enough to hurt.

A leather boot smacked against Jasper's head. When he leaned over to pick it up, the other boot struck his bare ass (which the tardigrade hide did not quite cover).

Near the altar, Margo noticed a number of small children in the crowd carrying fourteen-ounce cans of raw nutrient paste in their arms. As soon as Jasper was so close that they couldn't miss, they volleyed the cans at him with appalling glee. The dull thumps of the cans against Jasper's skinny arms, his heaving chest, his pale stomach, nauseated Margo.

It was too much. Jasper collapsed onto the floor. He lay still, then continued crawling forward, leaving a trail of smeared blood on the white marble as he went.

The thought of Jasper's blood on the white marble made Cuthbert's living room stop spinning. She felt sick. Remembering what happened next always made Margo feel sick.

Margo was trying to fight her way to the front of the crowd. She'd crocheted a pair of pants to help him keep warm at night in the wasteland. The pants were balled up in her hands. She wanted to get as close as possible to him to throw him the pants. At that moment it seemed like the most important thing in the world. But she couldn't make it to the front.

So Margo threw the pants as hard as she could from where she stood. She let out a little grunt as she did so. The airborne pants grazed the arm of a man who was pointing accusingly at Jasper to the rhythm of the crowd's chants: "Shame. Shame. Shame."

And the pants fell to the floor, beside the pointing man's feet.

Maybe Jasper might have seen the pants and still reached for them if he wasn't wearing that respirator.

Margo called his name. If he heard her, he didn't show it. But the crowd was in such a frenzy and chanting so loudly she was sure he didn't hear her.

She called his name again. He didn't hear her.

Jasper's march of shame ended at the front of the Temple, where the Shame Administrator stood. The Shame Administrator raised his hands and the crowd became quiet. Then he spoke. "You, Jasper Bearden, have been found guilty of High Recklessness," he said in a cold, authoritative voice. "For shame!" he bellowed. As the chanting began anew, another cyborg emerged and placed the Helmet of Shame on Jasper's head.

The Shame Administrator raised an immense club high over his head, then hammered it down on Jasper's helmeted head. Jasper fell to his knees.

The Shame Administrator raised the club and brought it down again. Jasper shook his head and looked up at the Administrator, who brought down the club a third time and punctuated the blow with a final "Shame!" as a trap door opened under Jasper.

He fell into that black pit in the floor. He let out an abrupt shriek. Cans of food and other supplies could be heard clattering against what must have been a metal chute below.

And Jasper was gone.

A Community Safety officer with a push broom shoved the boots and more cans and other items in the aisle that the crowd had thrown at Jasper after him into the hole.

The pants Margo made for him remained on the floor.

She left them there.

That night on Cuthbert's couch and any other time she thought about it, she wished she hadn't left them there.

NINE

LATER

The second lobopod lunged forward. Margo hopped out of its way. It reared up and squirted slime at her from a pair of nubby appendages on either side of its open mouth. Her attempts at dodging the slime were clumsy, but the creature's aim was poor. What little slime glopped onto her clothes was only dangerous in so far as it was a sticky distraction from the curved claws of razor-sharp chitin at the ends of the creature's numerous segmented legs.

Meanwhile the other lobopod was holding the cyborg with the Executive Designer on its screen upside-down. It tore the cyborg's leg from its socket with an ugly popping sound. Margo cringed. Either unfeeling or unable to communicate its pain, the cyborg kept broadcasting the Executive Designer's message: "Please, Inspector Margo Chicago, if you can hear me, follow me."

NOPE, thought Margo.

Margo's leech-arms reared up in a posture of counter-attack. She had the strange feeling of not being sure if the leeches were doing what she wanted them to do or if they were acting on their own. The lobopods terrified her, but the prospect of fighting them made her feel oddly excited. An inward tingling tickled her shoulders where the leeches were attached and crept down her spine. The leeches bent and wriggled in ways that reminded Margo there was by now not much left of her arms inside them, that her bones were little hindrance to however the leeches might bend and knot themselves.

With her leech arms she reached out and grabbed of one of the lobopod's legs with her suction cup hands. With surprising strength, the leeches yanked the leg away from the lobopod's body. The creature coiled up and writhed. Its claws slashed at the air in every direction. Now it was angry.

The severed leg twitched and jerked in Margo's grasp. She raised the leg up like a kind of grotesque half-living weapon and used the claws to slash at the lobopod's thick, chitinous body. At first, hitting the lobopod with the severed leg had no effect but she didn't know what else to do and doing so repeatedly did not tire her out. It was the leeches doing the work. Eventually the claws gained purchase between a pair of segments just below the lobopod's head. Margo pulled back on the leg, prying away a section of the lobopod's hard outer shell and exposing bloodless white flesh underneath.

The leech arm that held the lobopod leg in its suction cup snapped back like a whip, then with the force of the recoil stabbed the lobopod claws deep into the open wound. The creature shrieked and bucked, dislodging the claws and throwing Margo yards back into a heap of fungal goo.

She got up quickly but it didn't matter. The wounded lobopod was retreating. It veered toward the other lobopod, which was still feasting on the partially dismembered cyborg, and reared up and tore away one of the cyborg's arms, then plunged into the mud and disappeared. The other lobopod dropped what was left of the cyborg and followed.

"You have nothing to be afraid of," said the Executive Designer through the cyborg's mutilated remains. "Come with me and you won't harmed."

Margo felt exhilarated. She supposed it was the chemicals from the leeches racing through her system. She realized she was still holding the severed lobopod leg. She raised it up in the air and yelled like an animal. When she finished yelling she dropped the leg and approached the what was left of the cyborg. It was a legless, one-armed mess of blood and slime. Its cracked screen-face flickered. She hoped she was right about her belief that cyborgs can't feel pain.

She wasn't following this cyborg anywhere, but still, it could be useful. Maybe she could use it reach the Executive Designer himself, or someone from his office, to get more reassurance about what would happen to her if she had been able to follow the cyborg. She would just have to find out where it was supposed to take her.

She did not trust the Executive Designer, but she did not see another option. Her tussle with the lobopods reminded her that she could put up a fight if she didn't like what the Administration had planned for her.

A small smile creased her face. There was something funny about she, an Art Safety Inspector, now factoring in the possibility of physical violence when weighing the options of what she would do next. She still didn't want to hurt anyone. But she would not allow anyone to hurt her. She knew the leeches' self-preservation instincts were having an effect on her and she didn't fight it.

Dawn, meanwhile, had arrived around her. The sun was an orange blur through thick knots of gray cloud cover. A fine mist swirled over the muddy ground.

The moment Margo knelt down to better see the cyborg, its damaged screen-face went black. Then it blinked back on. Fash's face reappeared, blurry and with the colors all wrong. His voice was a distorted, staticky rasp. His words were unintelligible. She shook the cyborg. Shaking it did not help. She watched it blink out and then blink back on again. She would have to hurry.

She could not believe she'd encountered two lobopods and lived. She understood she owed her life to the leeches but she felt no gratitude. They needed none. What the leeches needed, they took already.

Margo decided she'd had just about enough of the Fungus Wasteland.

Nearby the dome gleamed in the pink and orange dawn light. The city inside was a vague, blurry silhouette.

She picked up what was left of the cyborg and slung it over her shoulder. She started searching for a way back in.

TEN

EARLIER

In the lamplight of her bedroom, Margo sat on her bed, humming a tune she made up as she went along while crocheting from a ball of gray yarn that her cyborg was holding. The cyborg was sitting in the chair beside the bed, feeding thread between its plastic-coated fingers toward Margo's stitching and looping hands.

Gradually, the yarn took the shape of a cross the size of Margo's forearm. Once folded and stitched together and stuffed with cotton, it would become a plush cube. Her handiwork rested in the palm of her hand and she wondered whether anyone else would think her end product would be as funny as she thought it would be.

There was a knock at the front door.

Over the past three and a half weeks, Margo had tried multiple times and failed to meet with Lorcan Warhol. Each time, she instead had been met by Warhol's assistant, Spreck Purcell, whose condescension and cloying dismissals irritated the hell out of her. Every time, she would try to hand Spreck the file of her required changes to make the installation safe, and every time he would back away with his hands behind his back to avoid touching the file Margo shoved at him. "I'm sorry," he would say, "You'll have to give that to Mr. Warhol." Fed up, she'd simply left a copy of the file on the floor in the middle of the unfinished exhibit.

The odds that Warhol would have enough time to implement Margo's ambitious changes—changes she hoped would exceed Sub-Chief O'Keefe's expectations—before the scheduled opening diminished daily.

Drawing up the schematics and writing her recommendations had taken Margo a full week. The changes detailed in that file went far beyond anything she'd ever done. Every sharp corner or hard surface needed padding. Whole sections of the exhibit needed to be walled off behind shatterproof glass. The laser rifles needed to be replaced with plastic squirt guns.

Complicating matters further was the gigantic balloon that had appeared on top of the Museum of Genius as part of the exhibit. It was attached to the roof by a long black cord in the center of the ring of rifles. In an appallingly flamboyant gesture of outrageous recklessness, the cord connecting the balloon to the rooftop stank of gasoline. The balloon was as big around as the entire roof of the building itself. Margo was sure the balloon was made to float using hydrogen or some other explosive gas. What looked to Margo like a half acre of blue material covered the balloon. What it really looked like, no one on the outside could see.

Margo had instructed Spreck how to make the balloon safe. Again, Spreck told her she would have to speak with Mr. Warhol about that.

Now the installation's opening was three days away.

There was nothing more Margo could do. Warhol was avoiding her. She'd tried to meet or speak with him again and again until she was sick of trying. After each failed attempt, she distracted herself with her crocheting.

The knock at the front door came again. Through the door, Margo heard a familiar voice call to her.

How dare he come here.

"Um, Margo?" called the voice. "I know it's been a while. Can we talk?"

How dare he ask to talk.

It was Thorsten Achebe. Margo had known him since she was a kid.

Once, when Margo was eight and Thorsten was seven and they were getting ready to play a game with a bunch of other kids, he farted so loudly it was almost unbelievable. The other kids thought it was hilarious. Afterward they teased Thorsten about it every day until he cried, then tormented him for crying for what seemed like years. He cried a lot.

Margo didn't react to the fart. In her head she thought "gross" but she didn't say anything out loud. She kept on playing with him like nothing had happened.

Since that day Thorsten would do just about anything for Margo. When she'd wanted to find out if a boy that she liked also liked her, she would get Thorsten to find out. When she'd wanted something to drink but didn't want to stand up to go get it herself, she would ask Thorsten to get it for her. When she'd wanted to hear someone say nice things about her creative projects, she would tell him she wanted positive feedback, and he would give it. His subservience was so obvious the other kids nicknamed him "Margo's cyborg."

Now Margo hated him.

She hated him because she blamed him for Jasper's banishment. She believed Thorsten, not Jasper, was the one who had been reckless. She believed it was Thorsten, not Jasper, who should have been banished.

He knocked again.

*

One night two years earlier, Margo and Jasper were celebrating. They each probably had drunk a whole bottle of wine. They were leaving a small gallery in the Sculpture District. They were going to get something to eat. Their cyborg helpers followed several paces behind.

Jasper had just finished his medical exams. In less than a week, he would, officially, be a licensed physician. He would be the youngest surgeon in the Bodily Safety Department.

With their arms over one another's shoulders, Margo and Jasper ambled through the cluttered streets between the gaudy facades of buildings in the Sculpture District toward the more utilitarian structures of the Culinary District. Playfully they argued over which restaurant they would go to. Jasper wanted pasta. Margo wanted steak.

Suddenly the cyborgs stopped. Together they started blaring out a shrill, barking alarm. A Danger Alert. Like everyone else out on the streets, Margo and Jasper stopped what they were doing and turned to their cyborgs' screen-faces. The screens pulsed yellow and red with the alarm until an unsmiling woman wearing the blue and black striped uniform of a Community Safety officer appeared.

The officer said a five-year-old boy was missing. A breach in the Bublinaplex dome had been discovered near where the child had last been seen. The breach was near where the Sculpture District and the Culinary District met. Citizens of the Bublinaplex were advised to avoid the area and to keep a close eye on children and the elderly. Anyone in either district was advised to remain indoors until the breach was closed and any threat isolated. The officer also said it was unknown whether the boy merely had wandered through the gap in the dome or if something from outside had found its way inside the dome and dragged the child out. The Pest Control Department, the officer assured viewers, had been deployed.

"Damn lobopods," cursed Jasper. Any time there was some risk of someone being attacked by something from outside the dome, Jasper immediately expected the worst.

But it was not unheard of for a lobopod to drag a child away through a breach in the dome. Because of his medical training, Jasper knew what a lobopod could do to a person. Their bites made wounds he hoped he'd never see again but knew he would.

"You don't know it was a lobopod," said Margo. "You don't know the kid isn't just lost."

Jasper walked quickly ahead of Margo and changed direction. His cyborg trailed behind. Margo jogged to catch up. "What are you doing?" she said.

"I've been trained to take care of a lobopod bite," he said. "I have a responsibility."

Margo didn't argue.

On the inside, the edge of the dome was a flat, empty space and the ground was carpeted with artificial turf. When they found the breach they were surprised to see their old friend Thorsten standing beside it and wearing the green and black striped uniform of a Pest Control officer. Beside him, salty mist and the wet stench of acrid rot seeped through the jagged, triangular opening. A few feet away, on the opposite side of the crack, stood Thorsten's cyborg.

Margo no longer saw Thorsten as often as she did before she started seeing Jasper. The reunion at the edge of the dome was awkward. "Oh, hi," said Thorsten, looking up from his sketch pad. He was doodling as he was supposed to be guarding the breach.

Margo wasn't surprised by his divided attention, but Jasper was outraged. "What are you doing? Where's your weapon?" demanded Jasper. "Have they found the boy?"

"Weapon's right here," Thorsten mumbled, raising the low-voltage electric prod—what Pest Control officers used to zap anything that might try to enter the dome—that hung from his hip. He didn't meet Jasper's eyes. "Boy's still lost."

"Is there a search party out there?"

"No."

"Is one on the way?"

"Not sure."

Margo bit her lip. She knew Thorsten cared about saving the boy, but he was just doing his job. Standing guard by the breach, making sure nothing came out and no one went in, was his job. He could doodle while doing that. Anyone could. The problem was that Thorsten didn't make any effort when he spoke to Jasper to sound like he cared. And this, Margo knew, would enrage Jasper.

"I can't believe this," Jasper snapped. He looked at Margo. "Wait here," he said, then dashed off. His cyborg followed close behind.

Margo and Thorsten stood there quietly for a few minutes. Thorsten's attention returned to his sketch pad. "What are you drawing?" Margo asked. Thorsten showed her. In the picture were a couple of characters Margo guessed were supposed to be superheroes because they wore capes. One was a guy in karate pants with anatomically incorrect bulging muscles and one was a woman with weirdly large boobs and almost no clothes. The superheroes were punching a thing that could have been half dragon, half bear. "Cool," Margo said, unconvincingly. She'd forgotten how bad Thorsten's art was.

After a few minutes Margo asked her cyborg, "Where is Jasper?" A map of their immediate surroundings appeared on the cyborg's screen-face, and a blinking black dot indicated Jasper's cyborg was inside a small sculpture gallery they'd passed on the way.

After several minutes longer standing there with Thorsten and not saying anything, Margo noticed something moving on the ground outside the breach. She tapped Thorsten's shoulder to get his attention. Then he saw it too. A baby tardigrade, the size of a loaf of bread, was poking its pointy head through the opening. Thorsten knelt down and zapped it with his prod. The little tardigrade squealed and waddled away.

"Poor little guy," said Margo.

"Nothing in, nothing out," said Thorsten. He gave Margo a blank look, replaced the prod in its holster, then resumed doodling.

Jasper returned almost an hour later. A posse of five hard-faced men arrived with him. Their cyborgs followed after them. The men carried shiny, oversized weapons, swords and scimitars and axes, all with ornamental serrations and rows of spikes.

Margo recognized Ulrich Van Gogh standing beside Jasper. It was relatively well known that Ulrich was a maker of illicit weapons. He curated a small gallery, the location where Jasper had disappeared to. Through Ulrich's dense blond beard, his expression was unknowable. Margo supposed he must have been relishing this opportunity to bring out the weapons he'd made and maybe even use them.

A loophole enabled Ulrich to get away with forging the deadly blades despite the rules against unsafe art. The rules simply forbid him from publicly displaying his creations. So he made them and kept them in a cache in his cellar. Occasionally, he gave them as private gifts to his neighbors. Displaying the weapons was never Ulrich's intention. He considered his weapons, and the weapons he made for his neighbors, a more trustworthy line of defense than what the Pest Control Department provided.

Jasper's hand clutched the hilt of the dagger at his hip. "Has anyone arrived to search for the boy?"

Thorsten looked up from his sketch pad "Not yet."

"Then step aside." Jasper glanced at Margo. Margo thought she saw him seeking her eyes for approval. He found only Margo's frown. She glanced anxiously at their weapons. She was a safety inspector. She didn't like this.

"I can't let you go out there," said Thorsten. He sounded like someone confessing a personal shortcoming more than a guard imposing his authority. He shuffled sideways to stand in front of the opening.

"Let us pass," growled Ulrich from behind Jasper, "or the boy's blood is on your hands."

"That's not how it works," pleaded Thorsten. "You don't even know he's out there."

"We know nobody is looking," said Jasper. "And you, a Pest Control officer, know better than anyone what kinds of things he's likely to meet out there. You know for every minute we wait, the odds in favor of that boy's survival plummet. And here I am, a physician, ready to find him and give him whatever medical attention he needs. And here we are," he said with a gesture to the others with the blade in his hand, "six strong citizens willing to risk going out there to make sure the boy is safe. The risk is ours." Jasper stepped forward. His face was uncomfortably close to Thorsten's. "What do you risk?" He asked, punctuating "you" with a poke of his finger in Thorsten's chest. "We're not asking you to go out and look with us. All we're asking is for you to step aside. Is that too much to ask? Let us save that boy before it's too late." Jasper shoved Thorsten, who lost balance and fell to the ground. The physical violence, mild as it was, shocked Margo.

The violence shocked Thorsten too. For a second his face knotted up like he would cry. Margo knew it wasn't the first time he'd been pushed to the ground.

What Thorsten did next didn't surprise her, but it did disappoint her.

"Fine," he said, standing up and stepping aside from the breach. He brushed the dirt off his pants. "Have it your way. Go on out there. All of you." It was Thorsten's job to stop them from going out of the dome, Margo thought. She knew Jasper was making things difficult, but come on. Couldn't Thorsten do this simple job?

Margo stepped forward. "Don't go out there," she said to Jasper. "You know he's guarding this breach for a reason. Do you have any idea how dangerous it is out there?"

Jasper touched Margo's hair and the side of her face. He made a face that she guessed was supposed to look reassuring but came off as condescending. "Don't worry, babe. We'll be alright," he said. "We won't go far."

One by one, Jasper, his blade-wielding posse, and their cyborg helpers crouched down and crawled through the crack in the dome. Spores and filth from the Fungus Wasteland coated the dome's exterior, making its supposedly transparent surface mostly opaque. From the inside looking out, the search party was impossible to see.

Margo and Thorsten waited together for the search party to return. Thorsten stared at the ground. Margo used her cyborg to search for updated information about the missing boy. She found nothing new or helpful. She also tried to pinpoint the location of Jasper's cyborg, but the tracking function didn't work outside of the dome. Margo and Thorsten didn't speak.

Something like two hours later, Jasper returned. He was covered in blood. He was breathing hard, ragged breaths and speaking too rapidly to understand. He was alone.

He was about to duck back inside through the breach when Thorsten's cyborg stepped forward. It held him back with surprising strength. Jasper screamed. He tried scrabbling around the cyborg on his hands and knees, to no avail. It would not let him back inside the dome.

Thorsten frowned at the screaming man.

"Damnit Thorsten let him back in!" said Margo. "Let him back in right now!" Thorsten's expression didn't change. Jasper's speech had dissolved into terrified sobs. Only fragments of sentences about what had happened to the others could be understood. Something about no trace of the child. Something about a tickle swarm.

Jasper fought Thorsten's cyborg until he was exhausted. Thorsten said nothing and didn't intervene. His cyborg's job was to stop anything outside the dome from coming in. Apparently it was better at its job than he was at his. Margo pleaded with Thorsten to make his cyborg let Jasper back inside. It was the first time he'd refused to do what she asked him to.

Three more Pest Control officers eventually arrived. They wore protective suits and face masks and they'd brought a quarantine bubble, a glass sphere on wheels that was filled with fungicide and chemicals to kill any tickle swarm mites Jasper might still unknowingly be carrying. They put him inside the glass sphere immediately after allowing him back through the breach.

Much later, when Jasper gave his official testimony, he said it had started when one of the search party members chuckled to himself after making a bad joke. Tyler Kahlo was his name. Margo remembered his broad face and tiny nose. No one else had laughed. Minutes later, the joker started giggling, first quietly, then with more fervor and then, fully, hysterically. He was wiping tears from his eyes and having a hard time breathing.

Tyler fell on the ground. He clutched his stomach. He wiped blood from his eyes. The others stepped back but by the time they realized they'd stepped into a tickle swarm, it was too late. Thousands of bloodthirsty mites, each no bigger than the period at the end of this sentence, were already clambering between toes, behind knees, under armpits and anywhere else they could crawl and elicit laughter, releasing the serotonin the creatures craved into the bloodstream of their victims.

The only explanation for Jasper's escape was luck.

Once discovered, the desiccated bodies of the others were immersed in chlorine to destroy the microscopic eggs that would have been laid in their mouths, lungs, and intestines.

For defying Thorsten's timid attempts to forbid the posse from leaving the dome, Jasper was found guilty of High Recklessness.

Thorsten was given a mild reprimand for allowing Jasper and Ulrich and the others to leave.

Weeks after the failed search, the missing boy's body was found in a ceramics gallery at the bottom of an unusually large vase.

Margo meanwhile tried to keep up her normal working and crocheting routines as much as she could while Jasper faced banishment.

One day she was about to start a new project and she told her cyborg to bring her a swatch of red yarn from a peg on the wall. The cyborg picked up the yarn and then slipped on the cluttered, clothes-strewn floor of Margo's bedroom. The fall broke its ankle. Embarrassed about the apparent lack of safety of her own bedroom, Margo told no one. She made a conscious effort to keep her bedroom floor a mess for fear of being asked why she'd started keeping it neat. Over the years, Cuthbert had repeatedly told Margo that the mess on the floor of her room was a disgrace. Jasper had never made any comments about it.

She convinced herself Jasper would eventually be released and she would soon be able to ask for his help with the cyborg's ankle. He was never released and the cyborg's ankle healed weird.

*

"Please, Margo. Let's talk," said Thorsten again from outside Margo's apartment door.

Margo said nothing. She knew Thorsten wouldn't wait all day.

He called through the door a few more times.

As quietly as she could, Margo waited in her bedroom. He left eventually.

She knew she should return to the Museum of Genius. She should try again to confront Lorcan Warhol. But dealing once more with that smarmy Spreck was simply too much. Now that her thoughts had turned to Jasper and Thorsten and that poor dead child and other depressing past events, she felt a familiar sense of hopelessness setting in.

She knew if she didn't do something right away, she'd sink fast into an immobilizing depression.

"Come on," she said to the cyborg. "Let's get a drink."

ELEVEN

LATER

It was morning. The cloudy sky over the Fungus Wasteland turned from ash gray to bruise blue. Margo carried the cyborg's limp carcass toward the dome. A steady stream of staticky hissing mixed with Executive Designer Fash's voice gibbering incoherently came out of its head.

The Bublinaplex rose up from the muck and rot of the Fungus Wasteland like an immense, misty blister. From the outside, it looked like it could be a ruin, the way mold stained its surface and tendrils of fungus curled around the beams that formed its honeycomb structure of repeating hexagons.

She was trying to get back inside. The problem was she didn't remember how she got out in the first place. She resigned herself to searching the perimeter for an opening. It was a task she knew might take days and the days would likely be punctuated with more lobopod encounters and encounters with who knows what else.

She trudged through mud and into thick patches of reedy fungi growing around the dome. In some places the growth was so dense and high it was like walking through a tunnel. The idea of being inside a rib cage came to her mind.

A twenty-foot steel and concrete foundation formed a wall that surrounded the dome most of the way around. Deep trenches had been dug most of the way around the outside to prevent a repeat of what happened to Jasper's search party.

To see where she was in reference to structures inside the dome, she had to leave the cyborg on the ground and climb up the wall.

Climbing the wall would have been easy if she'd been able to use the suction cup hands at the ends of both leech arms, but, she learned the hard way, she had to climb with one suction cup hand and carry a stone in the other. Lacking fingernails, she had to use the stone to scrape away the filth covering the glass to see inside well enough make out the faint outlines of buildings.

SHIT.

Now that she knew where she was, she doubted whether she'd get to where she needed to be by nightfall.

She did not want to spend another night in the Fungus Wasteland.

She made her way back down to the ground, gathered up the mutilated cyborg, and tried to make as much progress as she could as fast as she could.

Around midday as she was making her way through a particularly tough patch of mushroom stalks, she felt the ground beneath her tremble. Something massive was on the move. The cyborg's noise must have drowned out the sound of whatever it was until it was alarmingly close. Now there was a low rumble like breathing and regular booming thumps of tremendous footfalls and the sound of thousands of mushroom stalks snapping and being crushed into the mud.

She listened. She knew she could silence the cyborg but she feared if she shut it down she might never be able to switch it back on. The cyborg had given her an idea that she thought might be her ticket out of the wasteland. She needed it to still function somewhat for her plan to work. She held her breath, waiting.

Ahead, the vast animal rose up from the fungi.

It was an ancient tardigrade, one of the old survivors, trundling along in its slow way. The creature was breathtakingly immense. Maybe fifty feet high, maybe two hundred feet long. Without buildings around for comparison, it was hard to be sure. It was definitely bigger than Cuthbert's house. Eight thick legs ending in a row of curved claws carried its preposterous bulk. Sensory tendrils emerged from between the legs, feeling the ground for food and testing for poisons. It must have found something interesting on the path in front of Margo, because its disproportionately small, cone-shaped head dipped down into the mud, where it snuffled and shoved at the semi-solid ground and stopped, presumably to feed.

Margo stood awestruck as she watched the creature. It gave her chills. Nothing she'd ever seen inside the Museum of Genius had ever given her the sense of wonder and terror she now felt looking at this animal that was, she knew from biology lessons as a mentee, almost certainly centuries old.

Whatever had happened to eliminate the human race from most of the planet had, over the millennia, allowed these mutated microorganisms to grow and spread and become the Earth's new rulers. The oceans had evaporated into the salty haze that now filled the atmosphere, most plant and animal life had perished, and mold and fungus covered the swampy, ruined world. Tardigrades, using their singular ability to shrivel up and survive the harshest conditions in a dormant, almost mummified state, survived, then thrived.

Human beings now might as well be microorganisms to the tardigrades, Margo thought.

The immense foot of another tardigrade sunk into the ground not ten feet away. Margo scrambled backwards to escape the wave of mud that surged toward her from the footfall. She stared up at the creature. A hairlike tendril as thick as a finger brushed her face. Gently it ran along her jawline and under her chin and then was gone. The beast was moving away from her in the direction she was going.

She noticed that even though the creatures appeared to move slowly, their size meant that their steps carried them a relatively long distance. The tardigrade, in its vastness and its indifference to obstacles, progressed along the path much faster than she was managing.

Margo had an idea. At first she dismissed it as ridiculous. It wouldn't be safe. Then she dismissed her dismissal. Anything that would speed up her efforts to get back in the Bublinaplex would be safer than another night in the wilderness of the wasteland.

She tucked the cyborg torso under her leech arm and coiled the leech arm around so she was sure she wouldn't drop the battered thing. She took a deep breath, counted to five, then sprinted toward the closer of the two tardigrades. She jumped and reached out her other leech arm and got her suction cup hand to hold fast to one of its legs. Then she climbed, counting one-two-one-two, while still holding tightly to the cyborg and trying to catch a foothold to propel herself forward.

She pulled herself up and onto the creature's armored back. She looked around. Her pulse thumped hard in her ears. From her perch she could tell the tardigrades were indeed following the circumference of the Bublinaplex in the direction she wanted to go.

If the cyborg torso under her leech arm stayed just alive enough for her to carry out her plan, she could be back inside before the day's end.

Every time the tardigrade seemed to consider veering away from its path around the Bublinaplex but then chose to stay close to the dome, Margo thanked it.

Every time the cyborg seemed about to shut down for good but stayed on, she thanked it too.

TWELVE

EARLIER

The Bestiary was a dim pub nestled on the edge of Liminal Park, not far from the Museum of Genius. Preserved bodies of animals that no longer existed hung from the walls and ceiling.

Margo sipped her martini. Stuffed and mounted house cats surrounded her favorite booth. There was a big fat fluffy striped cat next to a tiny little baby orange cat and a skinny spotted hairless cat. They were all posed in various catlike positions, batting at each other's tails and climbing the walls and cocking their heads. One cat hanging on the wall was posed baring its teeth and claws withbulging blue glass eyes and its nose was all crunched up in a snarl. Margo wondered if it died like that, howling and spitting, or if somebody just posed it that way.

Looking at the angry cat made Margo wonder what had happened to the last cat in the world. Was it here on this wall? Did it outlive its owners? Did it die alone in the Fungus Wasteland?

Years earlier it was the cats that had inspired Margo to pick up crocheting. She started out with two-dimensional cat-shaped pieces ("flat cats," she called them), then moved on to cotton-stuffed plush cats. Eventually she started crocheting other cute extinct things too.

She closed her eyes. She took a deep breath. She took out her current work in progress—the fuzzy gray cube that would become the head of a little plush cyborg. She thought it would be funny to have her cyborg carry it around. Any time anyone asked her about getting a new cyborg, she'd have her cyborg pull it out and she'd say. "My new cyborg is my cyborg's cyborg." She took the olive out of her glass and ate it.

Her cyborg sat across from her. She offered it the can of raw food paste she'd ordered for it. The cyborg opened a door in the side of the rectangular box that was its head. With one hand, it reached in and pulled out an empty, crushed food paste can. It placed the empty can on the table, then took the full can and put it where the empty can had been and closed the door.

From her shoulder bag Margo removed a shiny black case and placed it on the table. Inside were crochet hooks of various sizes and a ball of yarn.

In her favorite booth in her favorite pub, she resumed her creative work in peace.

As she finished her martini, she made a pair of arms and a pair of legs for the little plush cyborg. She asked her cyborg to get her another one. Then as she watched it limp toward the bar she regretted not just getting up and ordering it herself. Despite her empathy, ordering cyborgs around seemed natural to her, as it did to all who were raised in the Bublinaplex. It was only after she noticed how performing tasks for her worsened the cyborg's suffering—as if it could feel anything at all—that she felt bad about doing it.

When the cyborg returned with her martini, it was not alone. "Good afternoon, Inspector Chicago," said Spreck Purcell. He stood beside the table as the cyborg handed Margo her martini and took its seat. Spreck stooped a little, unable to stand straight up to his full height because of a stuffed bat, wings outstretched, hanging from the ceiling. She'd never noticed the bat before.

Spreck held what must have been a thirty ounce glass filled with something blue and with a tiny umbrella poking out over the rim. "May I join you?"

Margo nodded. The cyborg scooted into the corner of the booth and Spreck sat down beside it. Spreck placed his drink on the table, then leaned forward and started slurping it through a straw. "I have a message from Mister Warhol," said Spreck, folding his large hands together in front of him. "He wants you to meet him. Tonight." Spreck slid a small piece of paper across the table. Margo picked it up.

Cardstock, Lorcan Warhol's personal stationery, apparently. Scrawled on it was an address and a time—"6 p.m. sharp"—underlined three times.

Margo knew the building. It was a skyscraper beside the Museum of Genius with galleries on the lower floors and apartments through the rest. It was the kind of building where curators lived. The card said "top floor."

She wondered what was up there but she was too relieved that the meeting was finally happening to give it much thought. "What took so long?" she asked Spreck.

"Mister Warhol is a perfectionist," Spreck said, seeming sincere. "Before, when you came to the exhibit, he wasn't quite ready, and his masterpiece, Hazard no. 457, wasn't quite ready either."

"Now it's ready?"

"Now it's ready."

*

It was 5:58 when Margo and her cyborg arrived at the address. There was a little café with its name on a lighted sign over the doorway, "The Rubber Spike." As soon as Margo saw the café's customers she understood the sort of place it was.

Margo sighed. Lorcan Warhol had an obnoxious sense of humor.

She scanned the room to find him. Lots of young people and lots of padding, fake weapons, and, of course, rubber spikes. Just about everyone was either wearing a helmet or had a hairdo that looked like it was messed up from being under a helmet. At one table sat a young couple who were so heavily padded they looked to Margo like overstuffed pieces of furniture with tiny human heads on top.

She noticed a few newer-looking cyborgs. The new models must have come out.

Margo could tell from the squeaking sound coming out of the guy next to her at the bar that he wore something inflated under his clothes. She tried not to stare but she couldn't help it. She was fascinated. He was having a difficult time trying to drink his drink. His inflatable undergarment made it nearly impossible for him to bend his elbow.

Warhol had asked her to come to a SafetyPunk bar.

Then she saw him. He was way off on the far side of the room, sitting at a table for two against the plate glass window that made up the wall on that side of the room. He was waving his arms to get her attention. He had spiky black hair and a big bushy beard. Margo didn't remember a beard in any photos of him she'd seen but she was sure it was him. She made her way between the tables, chairs, and padded people. It was a tight squeeze. She received annoyed looks from under helmets and through safety goggles. Her cyborg struggled to keep up.

Warhol stood and made a little bow to her when she got the table. "Inspector Chicago," he said, "we meet at last." He was a small, young-looking middle-aged guy with pale blue eyes and a receding hairline in front of that spiky hair. His suit looked like what she imagined an undertaker in Victorian London might have worn. Up close, his bushy beard obviously was fake. He made no effort to conceal the black elastic band that stretched across the back of his head to hold the beard in place.

Margo sat. She noticed that the view through the window was of the Museum of Genius' rooftop—where the installation, Hazard no. 457, was still covered. There wasn't a seat for her cyborg so it stood behind her chair, leaning a bit so it's good leg bore most of its weight. "I was surprised when I realized you set up our meeting at a place like this," she said. "It doesn't seem like your style."

"I suspect you know very little about my style," Warhol said. He gestured toward the room. "I love SafetyPunks. You know why?"

"Why?"

"Because they know that they are precious. They just don't know how precious they are, or to whom."

A waiter wearing protective headgear that completely covered his face set down a plate of warm pita bread with hummus and baba ganoush on their table. The waiter turned to Margo. "Can I get something for you?"

"Well, I assume a martini is out of the question."

"A what?"

"A cocktail," she said. "Mostly gin."

"Sorry," the waiter said. "No, the closest I can get you to gin is ginger tea."

"No ginger ale?"

"No ma'am. Too sugary."

"Can I get some honey or sugar in my ginger tea?"

"Sorry, ma'am."

"A lime wedge?" Margo asked, "a lemon wedge?"

"Worse for your teeth than sugar, ma'am."

The waiter stood there, waiting. "Ginger tea," Margo said.

The waiter withdrew.

"The SafetyPunks suspect they are even more precious than they themselves can possibly imagine," Warhol was saying, "so they do everything they can to protect themselves. From what? Don't bother asking. They can't really say. But they think they are smarter than their mentors, people my age who are constantly telling them just to forget the padding and just go out in a t-shirt." He dipped a triangle of pita in the hummus and took a small bite. "But they don't listen, of course. People who are convinced they are right never listen. They just wait for their turn to speak."

Margo gave a curt nod. She wanted to ask about inspecting the installation. She wanted to get this meeting over with. Of course if she brought it up now it would prove to him she was in fact just waiting her turn to speak and for some reason right then she felt like it was important for him to think she was really listening. He was still going on about SafetyPunks and their mentors. "On some level, mentors must realize that what makes them so uncomfortable with the way their SafetyPunk mentees dress is that the SafetyPunks are not really wrong. The foam padding and the helmets and everything, all the SafetyPunk gear, it reminds the mentors and everyone who isn't wearing protective gear that, by not being as cautious as they can possibly be, they are placing themselves at risk. It's an uncomfortable thing to be reminded of. And who knows, everyone in the Bublinaplex could slip and fall. All at the same time. And everyone who isn't protected might break their necks. And then the SafetyPunks would have been right all along."

The waiter returned with Margo's tea. She took a sip. The tea was cold. Of course it was.

Margo was sure she saw where Warhol's speech was leading. He saw himself as the antidote to the SafetyPunks' safety fanaticism. She understood what he was saying but she thought he couldn't have been more wrong. When Margo saw SafetyPunks, she didn't think of the existential anxiety of the world or whatever. She thought, here are some self-indulgent kids who spend way too much of their creative energy on their own appearance.

Still, Margo resisted interrupting with her disagreement. All this stuff about SafetyPunks wasn't what she was there to talk about. All she needed was for him to review and approve the file of changes to his installation that she was proposing. She had erred on the side of asking him to change too much. Her strategy in being over-comprehensive was to let him refuse some of her changes so she could relent without really giving in. It was a gamble. Some of her changes were non-negotiable. Others, she knew, went a bit overboard in terms of what actually needed to be done to make the exhibit safe. She expected him to refuse most of these. Still, she couldn't help hoping Lorcan would accept a few of these overboard suggestions. Sub-Chief O'Keefe had insisted that she make the exhibit as safe as humanly possible and leave a mark on the exhibit on behalf of the

Department of Art Safety. Maybe her changes would inspire future generations of Art Safety Inspectors. Maybe her changes would demonstrate she could live up to O'Keefe's expectation that she was the Art Safety Department's genius.

"Do some of them wake up in bed wearing a helmet?" Warhol was saying. "Sure, I'm sure some do. And good for them, I say. But I don't want to be forced to wear a safety helmet to sleep. Do you?"

Eventually Margo decided it was her turn to say what she wanted and she didn't care if Warhol didn't think she was listening to him, because she wasn't. "That's very interesting Mister Warhol," she said, "But we're here to discuss Hazard no. 457 and my inspection report." She pulled a clipboard with an inch-thick stack of paperwork from her shoulder bag. "This is for you."

"Of course, of course," Warhol said, accepting the report, which was identical to the one she'd left for him on the roof of the Museum of Genius. He leafed through the pages then ceremoniously set it down on the table. He stood up. He started clapping his hands loudly. "Bravo, Inspector Chicago! Absolutely perfect. Well done! Bravo!" People sitting nearby were looking at him. "Are you proud of this?" he said and jabbed his finger down at the stack of paper. "You should be proud, Inspector," he cackled, still clapping. "Be proud!"

Margo didn't know what sort of reaction she'd expected from Warhol but this was not it. The confusion on her face must have been obvious. And the annoyance. Her patience was wearing thin.

Warhol sat back down. He put his elbows on the table and rested his head in his hands and gave Margo an impish look. "Tell me about your inspection."

"Alright," Margo said, taking a piece of pita. Everything she was about to say, she'd already said to Spreck. But while Spreck seemed determined to dismiss or ignore what she said, Warhol was a parody of someone giving her his rapt attention.

"To be honest, I thought your installation was a pretty obvious exercise in flagrant risk. You just figured out what was the opposite of something safe and you made that. So you have a dozen laser rifles arranged in a circle, all aiming toward the middle. A circular firing squad. It would be easy for anyone to walk up and pull the trigger on one of those. It would be easy to shoot straight across and accidentally, or purposefully for that matter, shoot the person standing at the laser rifle on the opposite side. But that's not really the point."

"Tell me, what is the point?" He batted his eyes coyly.

"Well, the point of the rifles isn't to shoot the other visitors. It's to light the fuel-soaked fuse in the middle. That's what that black rope is, right? It's a fuse leading up to that big balloon." Margo looked out the window. They had a clear view of the huge cover.

"And inside of the balloon?"

"Inside of the balloon I suppose is some sort of lighter-than-air gas. And if I wanted to fill a balloon with an unsafe lighter-than-air gas, I'd fill it with hydrogen. That's what's inside, isn't it?"

Warhol fidgeted in his seat and grinned. He was like an impatient child expecting a promised treat.

"Therefore?" he asked.

"Therefore, anyone could walk into the installation and shoot the fuse. The fuse would burn straight up to the balloon. I don't know if the laser is supposed to burn completely through the fuse and release the balloon or not. If the laser shoots the balloon loose, maybe it floats up and scorches a section of the dome or the fireball drifts somewhere else like into this building. If the balloon stays attached, once the flame travels up to the fuse and gets to the balloon, maybe the whole thing bursts into a fireball and comes crashing down on the museum, killing everyone in the exhibit and burning probably the top several floors or so. Either way, hundreds die. Irreplaceable works of art are lost. I'm held responsible and banished. The end."

Warhol leaned back in his chair. "Doesn't it feels good to be responsible for stopping all of that from happening?" he said. "If I accept your changes, if I allow your preoccupation with safety to utterly destroy the work of 'genius' I've envisioned, I make you a kind of a hero, don't I?"

"Do you?"

"I do," he said. "And I will. I accept each and every last one of your changes. They're perfect. They're brilliant. Thank you."

"Wait, what?"

Warhol turned around and tapped the person sitting at the table behind them on the shoulder. The person wore a ridiculously large helmet. When the person turned around, Margo saw that it wasn't a person at all—it was a cyborg. On its face-screen were the words "recording audio."

Warhol smiled and said, "Play back 'fireball' quote." The cyborg played back Margo's voice, "the whole thing bursts into a fireball and comes crashing down on the museum, killing everyone," click.

"Listen to you," Warhol says. "Such outrage. Such righteous indignation. This recording here will make a lovely background music for when people are walking around, looking at Hazard no. 457—or at least, your dementedly safe vision of what it's allowed to be."

"What?" Margo was confused. Why would he be adding audio of her voice railing against his recklessness to his work of art? Why would he go out of his way to give the Art Safety Department even more of a voice—literally—in the work of art that was supposed to be Recklessism's Museum of Genius debut? "What do you mean my dementedly safe vision?"

"Don't you understand?" He picked up the inspection report and waved it theatrically. "Your words. Your changes. Your inspection. These are what Hazard no. 457 is really about," he said.

"You see me as some sort of monster intent upon destroying the 'safety' that you work so hard to maintain. But my work, the reason that it's so important, is that the sense of security that all of you hard-working safety inspectors lull us all into is an utter sham!" Warhol raised his voice and pounded his fist on the table. "The people here in this city live in a bubble, literally and figuratively. They're not safe. Not really. The true threats lurk between the cracks. The true threats are what we can't see."

Margo massaged her temples with her thumb and index finger. "And you intend to send people this public service announcement of yours by giving them laser rifles to point at each other?"

"Right, right. The laser rifles. Listen. I know you want me to take them down. I knew you would insist I take them down before my team even started setting them up. And, to be honest, by now they're probably already down. Understand? And the gas-soaked fuse has probably already been removed. All of your proposed changes are in the process of being made. After all, Hazard no. 457 is a tribute to you, Inspector Chicago. You haven't figured that out?"

"What?"

Warhol tapped the cyborg sitting behind him on the shoulder again. It leaned toward him and he whispered something to it. Margo realized he was making a call. "Spreck," he said into the side of the cyborg's head, "It's me. Do it now. NOW." He turned back to Margo and smirked. "Watch," he said.

Through the window Margo could see that something was happening under that massive cover. It rippled and shifted like a choppy fabric lake. She saw that Spreck and the rest of Warhol's assistants and their cyborgs were pulling it away. She realized the view from where they were sitting at the window would make them the first to see the exhibit unveiled. The cover fell away in big wrinkled piles. The balloon bobbed up, jiggling at the end of its rope. It was shaped like an enormous egg. It was even bigger than Margo thought.

The balloon turned and Margo saw that a face was painted on it. It was a massive head. It rotated around to face her.

She saw it and understood immediately what it was. What could she possibly say? Lorcan Warhol could hardly contain his giddiness. He grinned ridiculously. His eyes studied Margo's face for her reaction.

Her awareness of Warhol's cyborg probably recording her made her squirm. "Really?" she said.

The balloon was a grotesque and unflattering caricature of Margo's face. It was large enough to be visible from nearly everywhere in the entire Bublinaplex.

"Ta-da!" Warhol shouted. He was clapping again. "I'll cover the walls of the exhibit with copies of your forms here detailing all your changes. I'll have Spreck rig the audio so your little speech is on a loop up there. And of course I'll make sure each and every one of your little requests is filled. For the sake of safety, of course."

Margo felt nauseous.

She realized Warhol's plan had been basically the same as Sub-Chief O'Keefe's—to make her a celebrity for safety. O'Keefe had thought putting the Department of Art Safety's mark on the installation would somehow transform Lorcan Warhol's Recklessist masterpiece into a monument to safety. But now it seemed like that had been Warhol's plan all along. Warhol had correctly anticipated how Art Safety would react to an extremely dangerous work of installation art on top of the Museum of Genius and successfully set her up for total humiliation.

Admirers of Warhol's work would be outraged when they saw what the Art Safety Department had done to his 'vision.' They would mock Margo's words and they would mock her report and they would mock her face. They would accuse her of destroying the vision of a "genius."

Warhol had made his own installation, the work of art that would live forever in the Museum of Genius, into a martyr for Recklessism. Considering his lack of subtlety, she supposed the huge stone slab standing at the edge of the exhibit—which she now saw stood a few hundred feet directly over the main entrance to the museum—was probably carved like a gravestone for the work of art that would have been had she not intervened.

Generations of Recklessists will be inspired. And generations of Art Safety Inspectors will be ashamed. Margo's lack of restraint, her absolute disrespect for the art will become a textbook example of what not to do when inspecting an exhibit.

Margo imagined these consequences falling one after another, chapters in an already written book, as real to her as a Danger Alert.

The odds she would be banished because of someone being hurt in the exhibit had vanished. But facing hungry lobopods for the moment seemed preferable to the life of shame Warhol had created for her inside the Bublinaplex.

Margo reminded herself it was Sub-Chief O'Keefe who had so wrongly predicted the outcome of her inspection. O'Keefe would not blame her. He would take her side. Still, it was she who had performed the inspection and it was her face on that balloon. Would she ever again be able to step inside the Museum of Genius with that grotesque caricature floating on top?

Warhol meanwhile had climbed up onto their table. It wobbled slightly off-balance under his feet. He winked at Margo and smiled. "Not terribly safe, eh?" he said, arms outstretched. "See, I could fall and break my neck here, in the safest café there is." The plates of hummus and baba ghanoush rattled against his black shoes. Gleefully he kicked a plate off of the table. It flew through the air toward a tea-drinking SafetyPunk, who ducked fast enough to avoid it. Warhol laughed.

Everyone was now staring at Warhol. He waved at the SafetyPunks looking at him. "Hey! Hi! How are you?" Some of them waved back.

The waiter appeared. Politely, he asked Warhol to please step down from the table and to please leave. Warhol ignored him. The waiter turned to Margo and implored her to get her friend off of the table.

Before Margo could say anything, Warhol removed his false beard with a theatrical flourish. "Don't you people know who I am?" he said. A few of the staring diners nodded. And then something seemed to click—the shocking nature of his presence, the potential for catastrophe that he, the Chief Recklessist, represented.

"For all of you who don't know who I am," he said, his voice booming. "I am Lorcan Warhol!" The people sitting close to Margo and Warhol stood up and backed away. "That's right! Flee in terror," he said, quietly.

Then he shouted, "Flee in terror!"

The SafetyPunks fled. They leapt from their chairs and clambered over and under tables in a desperate effort to put as much distance as possible between themselves and Lorcan Warhol.

Margo got up and backed away from the table.

As the SafetyPunks trampled one another trying to flee The Rubber Spike, Warhol jumped down from the table and rushed at them, hands over his head like a child pretending to be a monster.

Probably the helmets and padding they wore protected a few from being trampled, though the bulky, unwieldy costumes they wore made it impossible for anyone to escape quickly.

Before long, Margo and Warhol were alone with their cyborgs.

"We really must do this again some time, Inspector Chicago," Warhol said. "But now I must go." He motioned to his cyborg. "I have work to do."

"You do," said Margo. "So when can I come up to conduct the final inspection?"

"Give me a few hours. I'll call you."

Margo didn't want to leave with Warhol so she stood there while he and his cyborg left. She picked up her mug of cold tea and took a sip. It was gross. On the floor she noticed he'd left his beard behind. She turned to her cyborg. "Is he an ASS or WHAT?" she said. The cyborg said nothing.

THIRTEEN

LATER

Margo clung to the tardigrade's back with one of her suction cup hands. The immense creature was crawling around the Bublinaplex. With the other suction cup hand she worked on the dying cyborg, trying to bypass the repeating recording of the Executive Designer.

"Shit," she would say as the cyborg's screen-face blinked off. Then it would blink back on and the Executive Designer's face would still be calling for her. Each time the cyborg rebooted, the Executive Designer's face was more pixelated and blurry and his voice became more distorted and down pitched. Thick blood still oozed from the cyborg's wounds where the lobopod had ripped it apart. Margo was surprised it still had blood left to bleed.

If she could access the cyborg's command line interface, she was sure she could make it do what she wanted with what limited capacity it had left.

Against the tardigrade's bumpy skin Margo's suction cup hand held fast. She could feel her sense of touch returning through the suction cups somehow. The coolness of the animal's plodding body beneath her was the first thing she noticed. Inside the leeches, her arms would be almost fully digested by now. She hadn't imagined that the feeling in them might return. She thought about how Thorsten would rationalize it. "It makes sense, from a survival perspective," he might say. "The better they mimic real appendages, the likelier their host will accept them. And if the leeches get hurt, I bet you feel the pain. So you protect them like you would the arms you were born with."

After several failed attempts, Margo reached the cyborg's command line interface. As a mentee, she'd learned that at the core of each cyborg's programming was a simple set of instructions and that these instructions formed the basis of every task a cyborg could perform. With basic knowledge of the cyborg's program language, a cyborg can be made to do practically anything.

"Record message," she said to the cyborg. The word "recording" flashed on its face-screen. "I'm stranded in the wasteland. I'll wait for you at the kennel door. Please let me in," she said. Then, "End recording." She sighed. Even in her desperate state she hated the idea of asking Thorsten Achebe for help, but she didn't see any alternative. She told the cyborg to send the message.

If the dying cyborg worked the way it was supposed to, the message would go to Thorsten's cyborg. She was pretty sure the cyborg would not last long enough for her to receive a reply from Thorsten, so she couldn't be sure that the message transmission actually had worked.

Soon the cyborg's screen-face went black and refused to turn back on. After several failed attempts to reboot the cyborg, Margo let its limp remains slide off the tardigrade's back and into the moldy ooze below.

The tardigrade continued to trundle around the dome. With the cyborg gone, Margo felt truly alone on top of the beast. The feeling was oddly exhilarating. Again she entertained the fantasy that maybe she could survive out here, that maybe it was possible that Jasper wasn't dead, that maybe there were others living free and savoring the wilderness.

She knew such ideas were nothing more than toys for her mind. For the moment they helpfully distracted her from thinking about what might happen if Thorsten failed to answer. She was well aware that such ideas could become dangerous if she let herself take them too seriously.

She tried not to take them too seriously.

FOURTEEN

EARLIER

Margo waited in her apartment while Warhol was supposed to be finishing her recommended changes to his installation.

She dwelled on the humiliation she would face because of Warhol's art. She thought about that big grotesque balloon parody of her face and the way he was going to incorporate her voice and how he would undermine her inspection by incorporating everything she'd asked for.

Would she ever again be able to perform another inspection?

It made her want to quit. Hell, it made her want to die.

Did he know it would make her want to die? Did that make the work unsafe? Could she insist on more changes, starting with the removal of that balloon, if the life the changes were intended to protect was her own?

But no. He would find a way to ridicule her for that too. And it would force her to admit her suicidal feelings to Warhol, of all people, who she could only imagine would use that information against her.

She couldn't help but smile a sad, hopeless smile when she realized that even if Hazard No. 457 did drive her to kill herself, it would be she, as the Art Safety inspector, who would be considered officially responsible for her own death, not Warhol, the artist.

She hated him so much. She'd done all she could to stop him, exactly as he'd known she would, and now she felt completely powerless to do anything more.

She knew she should contact Sub-Chief O'Keefe. He would want to know about their grave miscalculation, to hear her impression that her aggressive inspection was actually what Warhol had expected—what he'd wanted—and that the result was going to make Recklessists look like the victims of the Art Safety Department's creativity-stifling oppression.

O'Keefe would be so disappointed and his disappointment was the last thing she felt like dealing with right now. She decided not to call him. He'd find out soon enough anyway. Knowing sooner wouldn't change anything.

She decided the only thing to do now was distract herself until Warhol called for her to come perform her final inspection. She told her cyborg to sit across from the living room couch, where she settled in to watch a movie while she waited.

In front of the cyborg was a wide rectangular magnifying glass positioned so when it sat down, its screen-face was magnified. On either side of the seat were speakers that connected wirelessly to the cyborg's audio.

"Menu," said Margo, now curled up under the blanket that had rested on the back of the couch.

She narrowed her options from among the thousands of films, both new and archival, that were broadcast out of the Film District. She wanted to watch either a romantic comedy or a horror movie. Love or death.

"Browse horror."

Margo found a movie called *Pointy Teeth*. During the opening credits she went to the kitchen for a snack. She told the Cuisine Printer she wanted pizza rolls. The machine rattled and beeped and made rapid clicking noises as it constructed the pizza rolls from raw food paste.

Margo took the pizza rolls back to the couch and finished them as she watched the beginning of *Pointy Teeth*.

Pointy Teeth was a vampire movie. In the movie, vampires were attacking people in the Bublinaplex. The vampires came from somewhere in the Fungus Wasteland. They crept on all fours through cracks in the dome. Margo appreciated that the vampires in this movie were different from most movie vampires. Instead of sucking peoples' blood, these vampires sucked creativity. So their victims were still alive after being attacked, but they were left as pale husks of their former selves, capable only of eating, sleeping, and performing dull repetitive tasks. The people in the movie didn't call them vampires. They called them ghouls.

The pizza rolls were awesome.

Margo got bored with *Pointy Teeth*.

"Browse rom-com."

She found a romantic comedy called *Verses*. It was about a poet and an opera singer. The poet needed complete silence in order to write. But because of some sort of bureaucratic mix up, he'd wound up living next door to this opera singer who was always rehearsing very loudly. The poet would bang on the opera singer's door and yell "Please be quiet! Please!" Of course, they overcame their mutual annoyance and fell in love.

Margo got bored with *Verses*.

She lay down and let it play and closed her eyes and tried to let the sound of the movie distract her from her self-destructive ruminations as she waited.

*

Margo awoke on the couch to the buzzing sound coming out of her cyborg. Someone was calling her. "Answer," she said. Lorcan Warhol's face appeared on the screen.

"Rise and shine, Inspector Chicago," he said. "At long last, my masterpiece is finally ready for you."

Margo rubbed her eyes and yawned. It was past two in the morning. She mumbled something at Warhol to let him know she understood what she was supposed to do and that she would be on her way to do what was expected. Warhol hung up. She told her cyborg to make coffee and find her a clean Art Safety uniform. When she was dressed and caffeinated, they left.

Outside the night was as cool and dark as it ever got under the dome, which was not very. High above, artificial stars twinkled on the dome's inside surface. Margo and her cyborg followed a walkway to the nearest transport station. Streetlamps cast diffuse cones of light ahead.

The transport station platform was empty except for a woman wearing a large hat. She stank of avant garde perfume. The pungent mixture reeked of citrus, burnt cedar, and rotten eggs. Margo felt cold and annoyed.

When the transport capsule arrived she made sure board as far from the odorous hat-wearing woman as possible. Her cyborg followed close behind. The capsule jolted forward before it could take a seat and the sudden acceleration knocked it off its feet and onto the floor with a crash. It struggled to get up until Margo took its hand and helped it into the seat beside her. Its chest rose and fell rapidly from the exertion. The capsule wormed through the city.

She looked out the window. The capsule passed light sculptures and pedestrians wearing glowing clothes. Then she noticed her reflection. Her hair was a tangled mess. Deep rings underscored her eyes. She took a sip of coffee from her thermos.

Her groggy mind started second guessing the trust she'd placed in Warhol. He said he would make all of the changes she'd asked for. She'd believed him. Why did she believe him? Because he'd somehow managed to turn cooperation into sabotage? She was beginning to think she'd been very stupid. What if it was his plan all along to take advantage of her trust and leave behind something glaringly unsafe? What if his intention had been to lull her with a lie into a sense of everything being taken care of? What if giving her the impression he thought he would still win by losing, by letting her think he would allow his masterpiece in the Museum of Genius to be made safe, was the real deception?

Her imagination ran wild with the worst worst-case scenarios she could think of. What if she was walking into a trap? What if his plan was to kill her? What if there was something like a giant, spring-loaded spear set up to stab the installation's first visitor through the heart, and, by being that first visitor, the irony would be that Margo would make it safe by triggering the mechanism, at the same time becoming a literal sacrifice for safety. Maybe the giant, dumb-looking balloon caricature will become a ridiculous memorial to her. Maybe that was what the big stone slab was for. Maybe what the piece was really about was the death of safety and that was why it was so important to make it about her, and that was why she must die.

She tried to tamp down these thoughts. She took a deep breath and resolved to make her final inspection of Hazard no. 457 as thorough and rigorous as possible. That was all she could do and she insisted to herself that it was enough.

The transport capsule stopped and Margo and her cyborg got out. A footpath led out of the station and through Liminal Park to the Museum of Genius. Along the path were carts where cooks were whipping up sweet and salty snacks for anyone still out at this late hour.

Margo was tempted by the smell of sugar and fried dough. She nevertheless pressed on as fast as she could. She decided she'd treat herself to a beignet after the inspection. The positive reinforcement urged her onward.

"Time?" she said to the cyborg closer to the Museum of Genius and she realized she was walking by herself. She looked back. Her cyborg was a good distance behind now but limping steadily forward. Definitely too far behind to hear her request for the time or for her to see its answer displayed on its screen-face. She decided not to wait for it. It knew where they were going. It would catch up. She continued to the museum entrance.

A wide front staircase where sculptors and painters and writers and actors loitered in the dead of night with greasy snacks and carried on noisy conversations marked the ground floor entrance to the Museum of Genius. A busker serenaded them with a green plastic synthesizer he held like a guitar. At all hours the steps were a popular hangout. Among the artists was a poet Margo vaguely remembered being mentored with. He urged her to join their impromptu party. Climbing up the steps she forced a smile and a wave and pretended she didn't realize what he was saying.

The museum's heavy, ancient-looking wooden doors occupied a series of stone archways at the top of the steps. Margo approached a door and pushed. Usually the doors were locked at this hour, but they opened. She assumed Officer Beckett must be on duty and that it was he who'd unlocked the doors for her. She turned around to see where her cyborg was. It was farther back than she would have thought and struggling to catch up.

She stepped into the museum. An odor of old things hung in the air, of things drying out and slowly rotting and ever-so-gradually becoming dust. In the dim auxiliary lights, it wasn't hard to imagine the ancient masterpieces sleeping, as Cuthbert had long ago told Margo was the reason for the museum closing at night.

As she approached the central atrium the sound of her footsteps against the marble floor echoed throughout the vast, dark space. A forest of sculptures rose up from the floor. What little light was present cast jagged shadows against the strange forms to create suggestions of immense but not entirely immobile angular shapes. Paintings and drawings covered the walls to make odd juxtapositions like windows to different worlds from the same wall. Great multicolored mobiles hung suspended from the vaulted ceiling. At the far side of the atrium was the metal box containing the elevator that would take her and her cyborg to the rooftop.

Tonight she'd make an exception to her practice of avoiding elevators. She stepped up to the metal box and pressed the UP button and glanced at the listings on the building directory: Floor 3, Postmodern Paintings. Floor 6, Indigenous Sculpture. Floor 7, Library of Literary Genius. Floor 11, Archive of Musical Genius. Floor 15, Medieval Architecture. Floor 22, Realistic Drawings. Floor 37, Folk Sculpture. Floor 45, Statuary. And so on.

The elevator arrived. Her cyborg still had not. She looked back toward the museum doors. Maybe it really was time to consider a replacement.

At that moment, when she was about to walk back to the doorway to check on her cyborg's progress, a thunderous crash shook the building. Statues and sculptures toppled all around Margo and paintings fell from the walls. She lost her footing and fell. Debris crumbled from the walls. A cloud of dust engulfed the atrium.

Total confusion and panic gripped her. A crack ripped through the white marble floor like a bolt of black lightning from the doorway to where she lay. She was gasping and choking on the dust and she didn't know what was happening.

She didn't know how long she was trapped in there. It must have been hours. Then a woman wearing the red and black striped uniform of the Structural Safety Department pushed through the rubble of what remained of the entranceway and shouted back to unseen colleagues, "There's someone in here!"

FIFTEEN

LATER

Margo climbed down from the tardigrade's back. Indifferent, it shambled away.

She'd arrived at her destination: The pair of twenty-foot steel doors that led into the Pest Control Department's temporary holding pens for things that had been caught in the Bublinaplex.

Around the doors was a clearing. Margo remembered from Thorsten's descriptions that on the other side of those steel doors was a sort of anteroom to the Fungus Wasteland.

When creatures from the Fungus Wasteland were captured in the Bublinaplex, they were brought to the Pest Control kennel. Sometimes they were kept for study. Sometimes they were killed and dissected. Sometimes they were released.

When a creature was to be released, its cage was opened into the vestibule where the steep downward slope of the ground urged the animal down and out through the twenty-foot doors Margo now faced from the outside.

Seeing the doors, Margo felt she should be thrilled. This was the way back home. On the other side was her life and the people she loved, not to mention a hot shower and a comfortable bed. And a sandwich. She was desperately hungry but still not desperate enough to start sampling raw mushrooms.

But she hesitated. This was the moment when she had to give up on the dangerous fantasy of reuniting with Jasper in the wasteland. She'd survived this long, hadn't she? He could be out there, surviving all alone, living day by day on mushroom meat and rainwater, wanting nothing more than to be reunited with her and here she was, scrambling to get back inside the Bublinaplex for a sandwich.

He could be the chief of a tribe of the banished. They could have found a way to live off the land together, to build a new society where there are no Recklessists or safety inspections, just foraging and sleeping and sex and wild dancing. And predators.

But what would he say when he saw the leeches?

This was the point where she dismissed the thoughts as fantasy. She told herself it didn't matter what Jasper would say if he saw the leeches. The leeches' chemical bond with her now was too strong to break. And anyway in reality, Jasper would be too full of maggots, or the maggots would be too full of him, for her to be judged over the leeches.

In the clearing Margo's attention was drawn to a sound like someone yelling something in a language she couldn't understand. Something was half-hidden in the reed-like mushroom stalks surrounding the clearing. She took a few steps closer, then stopped. She stood completely still. There in front of her was a big slime grazer lying on the ground. On top of the creature was a spiral red and white striped shell the size of a beach ball.

The shell belonged to an arachnimonite. Inside the snail shell was a thing like a squid with eight armored tentacles it used for walking like spider legs. The nimo was feeding on the slime grazer's insides, butchering it alive with knife-like blades at the ends of its tentacles.

The slime grazer shrieked in agony for what seemed like a long time as the nimo buried itself deeper and deeper into its victim's torso, hollowing it out and soaking the surrounding dirt with blood. Attracted by the blood, beetle-like things scurried out from the densely grown fungus toward the now barely moving but still-living carcass.

Something about how easily those spidery tentacles sliced the slime grazer's flesh made Margo more afraid than she felt when she'd encountered the lobopods. Somehow she knew those tentacle blades could make short work of the leeches.

Margo wanted to help the slime grazer, even if helping it meant simply killing it to end its suffering, to end the almost human-like sounds coming out of the "mouth" in the middle of its vestigial face and into which it had withdrawn its tongue-head.

She wanted to help, but she didn't.

The slime grazer's shrieks eventually stopped. Margo still could hear it breathing. And she could hear the nimo's beak crunching on innards and connective tissue and bones.

She wished desperately for some sign that Thorsten had received her message. She looked longingly at the cold steel of those huge airlock doors. Inwardly she repeated, "Please open. Please open. Please open." In the clearing she felt exposed, like she should be hiding from the tentacled creature in case it was still hungry after it finished its meal.

She wanted to hide but she wanted Thorsten or anyone really on the other side of the door to see her and let her in.

The slime grazer died. The nimo moved on.

And after what seemed like hours, the airlock doors slid open. Margo took a step forward. A cyborg emerged. Thorsten Achebe's face was on the cyborg's screen-face. She sighed, relieved her message had been received. She waved a leech arm and said, "Hey." By this time Margo was too exhausted to rejoice as much as she felt like she should at the sight of him.

"Hey," said Thorsten through the cyborg. Then, "You see that dead slime grazer over there?" The cyborg pointed at the dead slime grazer.

Margo didn't bother looking. "Yes."

"I'm sorry," said Thorsten. "But I have to ask you to get inside of it."

Now she looked at it. Was it still twitching? "What?"

"There are surveillance cameras everywhere inside" Thorsten explained. When he'd got her message he'd had to think fast about how to sneak her in. So he released a wounded slime grazer along with a hungry nimo and hoped what he thought would happen would happen. And it did. And now there was a hollow slime grazer for her to get inside. "So, I'm sorry, but if you want to come in here you'll basically have to wear what's left of the slime grazer." he said. "My cyborg will drag it in."

There she'd been, standing there waiting for a sign that Thorsten had received her message and wondering if she'd be stranded for another night in the wasteland, and it turned out the gory scene playing out beside her was in fact the sign that Thorsten received her message.

And as repulsive as the idea of squeezing into that dead slime grazer was, she thought it would be worse to allow its death to go to waste. After all, it died for her. And anyway it wouldn't be her first time inside a dead thing during her time in the Fungus Wasteland. Though she now appreciated the spaciousness of the dead tardigrade carcass compared to this. To fit inside she had to tuck her head behind the slime grazer's rib cage and hug her knees to her chest.

The cyborg took the dead animal's forelimbs in its hands. With surprising strength, it started to pull.

Even compared to the stench of the wasteland, the bloody reek inside of the slime grazer was foul.

As the cyborg dragged the slime grazer's body into the Bublinaplex, Margo concentrated very hard on trying not to vomit.

SIXTEEN

EARLIER

First there were hundreds of mourners gathered outside the museum.

Then there were thousands.

The mourners wept and carried candles and put their arms around one another and left tokens to the memory of the eleven who'd been killed the night before.

What had happened that night soon became known simply as "The Tragedy."

Photos, paper flowers, tiny angel sculptures, various seemingly random tokens, and belongings associated with the dead were assembled around where the front of the museum used to be.

Hundreds of security cyborgs were sent to seal off the Museum of Genius to all—all but the Structural Safety officers assessing the building and the Community Safety officers investigating what had happened.

The prime suspect, Lorcan Warhol, was already locked inside the Community Safety Asylum, awaiting his judgment.

Some Recklessists meanwhile were starting to gather off to the side of the crowd of mourners. They carried signs with slogans written on them like "Free Lorcan Warhol", "Life is risk", "Open Hazard no. 457," and "Death defines life." At first, there were only a dozen or so. But Warhol was popular. His influence was strong. As that long day wore on, their numbers increased.

The opening of Warhol's installation in the Museum of Genius was supposed to be the pinnacle achievement of their movement. The turn of events had thrown the timing of Hazard no. 457's opening into chaos. The Executive Designer had declared a day of mourning and mentioned only that the opening of Warhol's exhibit would not be that day, as had been planned.

Seeing its opening delayed, no matter the reason, sent some Recklessists into a self-righteous rage. Accusations of a conspiracy to suppress the exhibit and persecute Recklessists emerged as a matter of course (conspiracy theorizing, after all, was fast becoming a popular creative pursuit among writers who sympathized with the Recklessist cause).

The raging Recklessists were impossible to ignore. As for what the Administration was prepared to do to in response to their demands, no one seemed to know. The chiefs of the various safety departments tried to counter the Recklessists' demands by insisting to the Administration that a thorough safety inspection of the whole Museum of Genius would be necessary before it could be reopened, and that a thorough safety inspection, by definition, would take time.

Inspector Margo Chicago woke up in a daze in the middle of the day. She was on Cuthbert's couch. She couldn't remember how she got there and for an instant she startled herself with the thought that she must have slept through Warhol's calls to let her know the installation was ready for her final inspection.

Then she remembered answering Warhol's call. She remembered traveling in the middle of the night to the museum and she remembered waiting for the elevator. She remembered the crash.

Her head throbbed. The sunlight shining through the windows of Cuthbert's living room seemed brighter than normal. "Get me some coffee and headache medicine," she said, intending to speak to her cyborg.

Cuthbert replied, "You're awake! Thank goodness. I'll get them for you right away. Do you need anything else?" From the quaver in his voice she knew he'd been crying again.

"No," she said and winced at his overbearing kindness. She sat up and rubbed her eyes. "Actually, since you asked, can you draw the blinds too?"

After Cuthbert fulfilled her requests and Margo washed down the headache pills with her Mentor's strong, black coffee, she asked, "What happened? And where's my cyborg?"

"Oh Margo!" he clasped his hands together. "I thought you'd been killed."

"You always think that."

"No, I know. But this time, it was a perfectly reasonable fear," he said, and he told her what he knew about The Tragedy, that a twenty-ton stone slab, part of Lorcan Warhol's installation, had come loose and fallen from the top of the museum directly onto the front steps. The eleven people gathered there were crushed instantly. Structural Safety officers were clearing the rubble and removing remains when one found her inside the museum. "You're lucky to be alive," he said.

"And my cyborg?"

Cuthbert shrugged. "Crushed too, I guess." He seemed to think it was an odd question. He took a piece of tissue from a box and wiped his eyes. "Yes, I guess everyone who died probably had a cyborg with them too. None of the Administration's announcements mentioned the cyborgs. I suppose you'll have to get a new one."

Margo stared into her cooling cup of coffee. Right then she knew she didn't want a new cyborg. She wanted her reliable old limping cyborg. The thought of it being crushed under that stone slab left her with an empty feeling she knew she wouldn't soon shake. She was aware of herself feeling more sad about the death of her cyborg than the real human beings who'd also lost their lives. She scolded herself. A dead cyborg was no more a thing to be sad about than a dead toaster.

But the fact was that her cyborg's brokenness had been a constant reminder of Jasper. She didn't feel ready to move on from this reminder but she told herself maybe it was better now that she had no choice. She told herself this, but she didn't quite believe it.

And then she remembered she hadn't yet inspected Warhol's installation. She sat up bolt upright. "I have to go," she said, throwing the blankets off herself. "I have an inspection to perform." She was wearing an ill-fitting pair of pajamas, a present from Cuthbert and Belga from nearly fifteen years ago. The pajamas bore the same yellow and black stripes as an official Art Safety uniform. Could she perform the inspection wearing these pajamas? If she had to, she would.

And then she realized the trouble she was in. A work of art she was responsible for inspecting had killed eleven people.

Eleven. People.

The room began to spin as it had when she was drunk.

"Slow down, dear," said Cuthbert. "Slow down. Relax. Everything is taken care of."

"What?" Margo said. Everything was suddenly so confusing again. And the headache was getting worse.

"You don't have anything to worry about. The Tragedy wasn't your fault. No one blames you. I had a word with Euclid. He says you can't be held responsible for anything. The exhibit wasn't yet open to the public. Plus what happened, technically happened outside of the Museum of Genius. Community Safety has Warhol in their custody and they're holding him fully responsible. Euclid has generously offered to finish your inspection so the exhibit can open with as little delay as possible." He rested a reassuring hand on Margo's shoulder. "All you need to do is relax."

Thanks to Cuthbert's words, Margo's panic lessened—then turned quickly into anger. O'Keefe would finish her inspection? Not if she had anything to say about it. "I need to speak with O'Keefe," she said. "Can I use your cyborg?"

Seeing Margo awake thrilled O'Keefe, but his insistence on taking over the inspection was absolute. He informed her that the exhibit's opening had been delayed only 24 hours—it would open tomorrow. There had been too much chaos for him to trust that every issue she'd raised about Hazard no. 457 had been resolved. If anything went wrong now, he would take responsibility. He insisted he would not have stepped in if he didn't have absolute faith in Margo's abilities, and that, as soon as Structural Safety signed off on the integrity of the building, he would go up to the installation and have a look for himself. "Aardvarks and escarole," he said. "I'm relieving you of your responsibility for inspecting Hazard no. 457, and that's final."

Margo protested. She knew the exhibit from top to bottom. She knew what was potentially dangerous about it and what should be done to make it safe. She knew the fact that it would seem safe made it so risky. And she reminded O'Keefe that it was a caricature of her face on the balloon floating over it.

O'Keefe wouldn't hear it. "Take some time off. As long as you need. I'll deal with everything from here," he said. "Rest. Relax. Even a sad clown gets a flower in his buttonhole."

Margo would let O'Keefe have his way. She would relax. Or at least go through the motions. She decided not to stay at Cuthbert's for long. She knew she'd soon lose patience with his doting and before long wind up snapping at him for no reason other than to get him to back off. Despite his protestations, she was better off leaving for both their sakes. She needed to be alone. She changed into an old, unfashionable outfit that had been long forgotten in a box at Cuthbert's and left.

She opted to walk instead of taking a transport capsule. She took the long way to avoid passing the Museum of Genius with its crowd of mourners and Recklessist protesters. She saw them on a broadcast Cuthbert showed her and for her that had been enough.

Even from a distance the balloon with the caricature of her face could be seen floating over the Museum of Genius. It made the tower where it was attached look like a huge lower-case "i".

Her route home through the Bublinaplex meandered through the Literary District, past quiet libraries, stationery galleries, pubs, and small groups gathered for more-somber-than-usual impromptu poetry readings. From the nearby Music District, pianists, violinists, guitar players, and drum machine programmers could be heard expressing their anguish about The Tragedy with elegiac instrumentals.

The Nursery District, as Margo passed through, seemed unaffected by the funereal mood. By then it was late enough to be dinner time, maybe even bedtime for the little ones. The playgrounds were empty. Abruptly abandoned toys lie forgotten for the moment on sidewalks, in sandboxes, and in patches of artificial turf. Margo could hear babies crying, a typical sound in this district on any day. Not as loudly, but just as clearly, she also could hear laughter. The joyous sound failed to lift her mood. On the contrary—she found an almost malicious quality to the gleeful, muffled chuckles coming from inside the walls of the nursery facilities.

As she walked she found herself turning over recent events in her mind. She began to suspect something wasn't quite right. Specifically, there was something off, in her opinion, about Cuthbert and O'Keefe's explanations for The Tragedy.

What bothered Margo most, and she hated to admit it, was that The Tragedy didn't seem to her like something Warhol would do. Not because she didn't think Warhol wouldn't really make art that would kill people. But because he was so obsessed with the spectacle of his art, The Tragedy seemed downright unimaginative by his standards. If he was going to arrange an event that would kill people, why would he time it to occur in the middle of the night, when practically nobody was paying attention? If the stone had fallen the next day, when crowds gathered for the opening of his new exhibit, there would have been many, many more witnesses and many, many more than eleven victims.

Before Margo was halfway home, she began to regret her decision to walk. She was tired. She needed a shower. If she had rode a capsule, she'd already be in bed.

In the Architecture District she dodged through the loose gravel of construction sites and hurried down the Thoroughfare of Monuments. Great structures of stone, steel, and glass lined the street. Margo felt small in the shadows of obelisks, towers, arches, and statues. She took some comfort in her insignificance, here where these structures, some ancient, some new, blocked the view of the immense balloon with her face on it.

This was when she realized she'd forgotten to tell O'Keefe about Warhol accepting all of her changes to Hazard no. 457. She'd also kept her understanding of its true purpose—to humiliate Art Safety and enrage Recklessist sympathizers—to herself.

She told herself it would be okay. O'Keefe would draw his own conclusions. She told herself that was just as it should be.

When finally she was turning the doorknob to open her apartment door, she was struck at that moment by how relieved she felt by her cyborg's absence. It was the first time in a long time when she'd arrived at her own front door without having to stop and wait for it to catch up. Her relief made her feel guilty. She really did miss her cyborg and mourned the loss of it. But now she would no longer be delayed waiting for it to catch up. The need to get its foot fixed would no longer be a reminder of the need to find the cyborg a doctor who wasn't Jasper. A reminder to move on from Jasper. The truth was, she had allowed her cyborg to become an emotional burden. The absence of that burden was freeing, even if the circumstances were tragic. She vowed not to shop for a replacement cyborg for a long time.

She entered her apartment. Sleepiness overcame her as she stepped into the living room and collapsed onto the couch. She closed her eyes.

A man's voice came out of her kitchen.

"Finally!" he said. "I thought you'd never get back."

Margo sat up.

Warhol's tall assistant, Spreck, was standing in the kitchen doorway. In one hand he held a bowl of what looked like spaghetti and meatballs. In the other, a forkful of dangling noodles.

SEVENTEEN

LATER

Inside the Pest Control Department's kennel the walls were smooth and clean. The floor of the pen that the slime grazer containing Margo had been dragged into was packed dirt. Through his cyborg, Thorsten told her that he would take care of the camera in the corner of the ceiling so she could come out unseen from the slime grazer carcass. He confessed there was nothing he could do about the smell.

Margo emerged from the carcass gagging and spitting. She could taste the revolting stench of the dead creature in the back of her mouth. Thorsten's cyborg had left her sitting on the dirt floor covered in visceral goo and feeling disgusting. She stared for a moment at dust motes drifting in the light that came in through a barred window high on the wall near the ceiling.

There was a water trough in the corner. Desperate to be clean, Margo made a hasty and clumsy attempt to use it to wash herself. A skin of grime quickly coated the surface. She considered undressing, then quickly realized using her suction cup hands to unbutton her shirt would be almost impossible and that even if she did succeed she'd never button it back up. She resigned herself to washing up with her clothes on.

When she was done she felt cleaner but hardly as clean as she wanted. The trough water was black with filth. She should have taken a drink first. Her clothes were wet, cold, and heavy.

She wanted to get a good look at the leeches so she ripped her sleeves off of her shirt. Until now she'd avoided looking closely at them. Twisting her neck to look down at each shoulder where each leech attached, she was surprised by the neatness of the seams where the tops of her arms ended and the leeches' mouths began. For some reason she'd expected ragged, oozy wounds. But no. They fit. That's the word she couldn't help thinking, as if the leeches were a pair of tailored gloves.

A puddle formed under her as she stood drip drying in the corner of the cell. The dirt floor became sticky.

She wondered if, after this was over, she would still hold a grudge against Thorsten. Maybe, maybe not. She couldn't say she'd forgiven him for letting Jasper do what got him banished. But at the moment it didn't seem to matter.

And as she stood there, locked in the cell with a dead slime grazer, cold and sopping wet and looking at the leeches that had devoured and replaced her arms, little that had seemed important before mattered now.

Yes, Thorsten's role in Jasper's banishment certainly seemed to matter less now. If Margo was being honest with herself it was at least in part because by not staying out in the Fungus Wasteland to search for Jasper, she felt she bore some responsibility for his banishment too. This was because there was a part of her that whispered: if she'd truly cared about him, she would have tried harder to find him out there in the wasteland. But she really didn't try at all. Now this part of her was regretting it. It was telling her maybe it would have been better if she'd died out there in the wasteland desperately searching for him instead of giving up like she did on the possibility of him being alive.

The truth was, she didn't even try to find Jasper.

Now her mind wandered to the question of whether her having leech arms meant Thorsten would no longer look at her with that secret crush look he always gave her, and which she always done her best not to reciprocate. It was a thought that made her hate herself. How Thorsten saw her was something else that didn't matter now.

Margo knew she had to distract herself fast or risk spending the rest of however long she would be stuck in this cell ruminating on depressing things.

She decided to try coming up with names for the leeches.

The leech on her right was a little thicker than the one on her left, and the one on her left a little longer than the one on her right. The right one was a lighter shade of dark green than the left one, or that might just have been the poor lighting in her cell. Other than that she couldn't see much to distinguish one from the other. Definitely not much to go on in terms of either leech having a distinct personality.

Lefty and Righty? That felt lazy. So did Shortie and Longie. But she figured she might forget which name went with which leech if she didn't employ some kind of mnemonic device, like naming the one on the left Lulu and the one on the right Rita.

Before she'd selected a name for either leech, the cell door opened. Brilliant sunlight framed the intruder's silhouette in the doorway. She recognized the square head as belonging to a cyborg. The cyborg stepped forward, shoved something heavy into the cell, then immediately retreated and closed the door behind it.

For a minute the heavy thing lie there like a stone.

Then in a terrifying instant it sprung into the air at Margo, all tentacles and mandibles clambering for her face. It knocked her to the ground and tried to pin her down as its countless stabbing appendages sliced at her.

This was an unusually large nimo, she realized with horror.

Margo screamed. The leeches flailed.

She shoved the nimo away and picked it up by its shell with her suction cup hands and let out a rage-filled yell as she threw it down on to the dirt.

It landed on the pointed tips of its armored tentacles and clambered right back at her. It jumped and wrapped itself around her torso and she could feel the serrated beak trying to bite her stomach.

With an angry grunt, Margo's leech arms again wrenched the nimo away. She threw it against the wall where it hit with a revolting crack. Its shell split open. Its insides were oozing out but still it reared up as if about to attack again. But it was weak and slow now and Margo jumped on top of it and stomped and stomped and stomped on it until its tentacles ceased their twitching.

When she stopped she noticed the cell door was open again. Two cyborgs now stood in the doorway, watching her.

She was knee-deep in nimo innards.

She supposed washing up in the trough had been pretty much pointless.

EIGHTEEN

EARLIER

Margo was sitting at her kitchen table across from Spreck as he consumed his second bowl of spaghetti. There was enough spaghetti for Margo to be having a bowl too. Spreck's cyborg, a newer model, sat at the head of the table. "Let me get this straight," she said with utter exasperation. "Community Safety is looking for you. When they find you, they'll throw you and anyone who helps you in the Asylum. You're sure they're dead set on banishing you along with your boss and your accomplices. AND YOU CHOSE TO COME HERE, TO MY APARTMENT?

"Inspector Chicago, listen, I'm sorry, I ... "

"WHAT THE FUCK, SPRECK."

"Please, if you'll just hear me out ... "

"WHAT. THE. FUCK."

"Please, I ... "

"Fuck you."

"Please."

"FUCK. YOU."

Shouting at Spreck felt better than anything Margo had done in a long time. She fully intended eventually to let the conversation move on, but this moment was one she wanted to savor. She allowed the silence between them to stretch on for another minute, then acquiesced. "FINE. TALK."

"First, I'm sorry about giving you such a hard time when you were trying to inspect Hazard no. 457." He stretched and said through a yawn, "You understand I was just doing my job, right? I mean, it was my job to be in your way. You get that, right?"

"Come on, Spreck," Margo said. "You didn't get away from Community Safety and break into my apartment to apologise." She scooped up a forkful of noodles. "The sooner you tell me what you really need to tell me, the sooner you can leave."

Spreck looked down into his empty bowl.

"Okay, how about this," Margo said. "I ask you a question. You answer. Question one, did you purposely drop that rock on those people?"

Now Spreck shot her dagger eyes. "Don't be stupid," he hissed. "Of course I didn't. And neither did my boss for that matter. But that hasn't stopped Community Safety from locking up Mr. Warhol. He's as good as banished. They'll lock me up too, as soon as they find me. Banish me too." He sighed.

"And you're here because... ?"

"I came here because I think you can help me."

"Why would I help you?"

"Because I can help you."

"How?"

"First things first," said Spreck. He turned to his cyborg. "Show the inspector what you saw last night. Play from three oh nine and thirty seconds." Eyebrows raised, he turned toward Margo and gestured toward the cyborg's screen-face. "Watch this."

The cyborg's screen-face displayed in green and black night vision the view from the top of the Museum of Genius looking down on Liminal Park. A person appeared in the distance following the footpath toward the museum. A minute later, another person appeared following the first person. The second person moved in an awkward, lurching manner. Margo recognized that the second person was not a person, but a cyborg—her cyborg, limping along. And the first person was herself, she now could see.

Margo looked at Spreck. "You were spying on me?"

"My cyborg here was looking out for you," Spreck said with a dismissive gesture. "Just watch."

On the cyborg's screen-face the view panned around to show the Museum of Genius rooftop. In the foreground, Spreck could be seen talking to Warhol. Behind them were the silhouettes of Warhol's other assistants moving around under the floodlights that enabled them to work at that late hour. The immense stone that would soon crush the people on the museum steps loomed over the scene, blocking the artificial starlight.

"He's going over the checklist of your safety measures," Spreck said. "He really was trying to do everything right."

"Right," said Margo. "In order to humiliate me and discredit the Art Safety Department."

Spreck gestured back to the screen. She was right. There was no point arguing with her.

Soon an explosive ripping, cracking sound dominated the cyborg's audio and the video became a shaky jumble. When the video resumed Warhol and Spreck were in the foreground and exchanged looks of fear and confusion and the black-clad assistants scrambled away from the stone. "No!" cried Warhol as the stone could be seen breaking free. "No no no no no no!"

A second later, the immense thud of the stone against the museum steps could be heard and for an instant the image on the screen once again blurred, presumably as the tremor of the stone's impact shook the rooftop.

"Stop," said Spreck. The cyborg's screen-face went black. Margo stared at the empty screen and gnawed a fingernail. "Next thing we knew, Community Safety hover cubes were descending on us. Mr.

Warhol walked up to talk to them. The nearest officer cuffed him and took him away. The other officers went for the other assistants. Lucky for me, my cyborg and I were standing next to the big cover we'd had over the installation. We hid in its folds for the rest of the night. Community Safety didn't find us, and we slipped out before dawn."

Margo bit off a piece of her fingernail and said nothing. So she was right. The Tragedy wasn't Warhol's style. He didn't do it. At least, not intentionally. The video convinced her of that.

Spreck was saying, "So you see the falling rock, it's not something we did. You see that, right? It's obvious from the video, right?"

Margo shook her head. "It's obvious that it wasn't intentional. That doesn't change anything. It's still High Recklessness. You and Warhol and the rest, you're still responsible."

"No, you're not understanding what I'm trying to say. I think the falling rock was intentional." He leaned forward. "I think we were sabotaged. And whoever did do it is still out there."

"But Spreck," said Margo. "All your enemies are Safety people." She rubbed her eyes. "Do you really think someone wanted to see Warhol banished so badly that they were willing to kill almost a dozen people to do it?"

"I didn't say it makes sense," he said. "I thought you could help me figure it out."

Margo sighed. This was not her idea of relaxing. But then again, O'Keefe had relieved her of her official duties. She had time to spare, and if she wanted a task that might undo her feeling of failure with the Warhol inspection, there would be nothing better than finding out who really caused The Tragedy.

"Okay," she said. "I believe you. If you're right, and this wasn't an accident, it means there's someone on the loose in the Bublinaplex who could get away with murder if Community Safety pins everything on Warhol and we do nothing. So I'll try to help you figure this out. No promises. But I'll try."

"Outstanding!" Spreck said. "How do we start?"

"First things first," said Margo. "You said that you would be able to help me. What did you mean?"

"Can't we talk about that tomorrow?"

"We'll talk about it now.

Spreck took a deep breath. "I can help you prevent the next Tragedy."

Margo fixed her eyes on him. "What do you mean, 'the next Tragedy'?"

"You promise me you won't be mad?"

"No."

"But you're going to help me prove my innocence, and Warhol's innocence, of involvement in what happened, right?" The look on Spreck's face was desperate.

"Yes," Margo said, though she wasn't sure finding that someone else was responsible was the same thing as proving Warhol and Spreck's innocence. "If we prove there's someone else out there who purposely killed those eleven people, yes, that will help prove your innocence," she said anyway.

"Okay, here's the situation," he said. "The exhibit, Hazard no. 457, does include one modification you did not ask for. Something you would have had no way of knowing needed to be altered until you arrived in person to do your final inspection. Which, of course, you never had a chance to do."

"What the, you added something?" Margo felt betrayed—and angry with herself for trusting Warhol as much as she had. "You added something that'll leave it unsafe, didn't you?" She told herself to keep calm, that whatever Warhol and Spreck might have done, O'Keefe would be able to handle it. "What did you add?"

Spreck looked down at the floor and confessed, "Goblin polyp spores."

Margo's first thought was that she was going to be banished. Then she remembered that whatever happened with the exhibit was now O'Keefe's responsibility. Her next thought was that O'Keefe was going to be banished. She tried hard to seem calm as she asked, "Where are the spores, Spreck?"

"In one of the squirt guns we set up to replace the laser rifles. In the water. They're somewhat powerful squirt guns. Shoot thirty feet, maybe."

Margo was stunned. "You put goblin polyp spores in a squirt gun?"

Goblin polyps were a kind of lumpy, slimy fungi. Their spore-covered, sticky stalks grew about as tall as a small child. They were ugly and invasive, and they could grow and multiply at a terrifyingly rapid rate.

What worried Margo was what the spores did to peoples' brains.

Hallucinogens were by no means unknown inside the Bublinaplex. Some of those who were frustrated by the limit imposed by the dome on the possibility of exploring the physical world opted to explore what some called a "metaphysical dream world" they could open up by consuming synthesized psychotropic chemical cocktails. Officially, such drugs were forbidden. But being forbidden didn't make them completely unavailable, nor did it keep sympathetic Community Safety officers from turning a blind eye unless users' drug-induced recklessness posed a physical threat to themselves or others, which was almost never.

Goblin polyp spores belonged to a category of hallucinogens far more dangerous than even the most powerful recreational drugs. The hours of monstrous visual and sensory unrealities that overwhelmed anyone exposed to just a small amount of the spores were only one of the spores' dangerous effects. The other, arguably more dangerous effect, was the overwhelming fugue compulsion that consumed spore victims, driving them to run as fast and as far as possible from the place where they first came in contact with the spores.

For the fungus, it was just its way of dispersing its progeny as widely as possible. But it meant that people exposed to the spores in Hazard no. 457 wouldn't simply freak out and see crazy things.

They would freak out and see crazy things and then quite possibly run and take a flying leap off the side of the building. Or they might run off throughout the Bublinaplex, potentially contaminating Liminal Park and neighboring districts with spores. Or they might run to the edge of the dome in desperate search of a way out and injure themselves by throwing themselves against the glass in an attempt to escape. Or they would succeed and wind up lost in the Fungus Wasteland. Margo wasn't sure, she wasn't an expert on these things. Thorsten was, but talking to him now was the last thing she wanted to do.

Margo stood up. "When you got here, why wasn't that the first thing you told me?"

"I'm sorry," Spreck said, "but I wanted to make sure you understood that Warhol and me and the other assistants are innocent before telling you about the spores."

"But you're not innocent!" Margo started nervously pacing back and forth in her kitchen. "The spores make you not innocent!"

Spreck gave Margo a thoughtful look. He apparently hadn't thought of it that way. "But still, innocent of the crime that Community Safety wants to blame us for," he said. For someone who'd just said he was sorry, Margo found his tone oddly guiltless. "Anyway we were sure you were going to notice the spores right away and make us remove them when you conducted your final inspection. At the time, Mister Warhol and I, when we added the spores, we really thought of it as a gift to you. You were supposed to discover them and you were supposed to feel like you defeated us. It was kind of our way of saying sorry for everything else about the exhibit, like the balloon, which I admit, yes, was a bit mean spirited. And yes, of course, we were simultaneously setting up the victory for you, for safety, to look like a tragedy for Recklessism, with all our original plans that you made us dismantle on display and the recording of your voice testifying about how awful it would have been— "

"Shut up," said Margo. "Let me think."

She couldn't believe she was having this conversation. She didn't think Spreck understood the seriousness of the mess he'd made with the spores. To be honest, neither did she. "Do you realize how fast those spores grow? How fast the fungus will spread?" He scratched his head. The question seemed to puzzle him. Clearly, he did not. "Fast," Margo said, and she was about to start lecturing him about how she was pretty sure it would be maybe just a few hours before anyone who entered the Museum of Genius would be susceptible to inhaling the spores when she realized the person most at risk right now was Sub-Chief O'Keefe.

Margo turned to Spreck's cyborg. "Contact Sub-Chief Euclid O'Keefe." She waited. It was taking O'Keefe longer than usual to answer.

When O'Keefe eventually answered, his face at first did not appear on the screen at all. The screen just remained black and silent. For a moment Margo thought Spreck's cyborg must have been broken. Then the bottom of the enormous balloon with the caricature of her face on it came into view. The cyborg was looking up at the night-dark dome. The cyborg and O'Keefe were on the roof of the Museum of Genius, which was what she was afraid of.

"Hello?" she said into Spreck's cyborg. "Sub-Chief? Are you there?"

"Inspector Chicago!" she heard O'Keefe's voice yell. "I am under siege! Ghost heads in my ears! Ghost heads in my nose!"

For a moment Margo thought this might be O'Keefe's usual nonsense. Then his crazy-eyed face wheeled into view. He was on his back on the ground. The cyborg was trying to hold him down.

The cyborg was preventing him from running.

"Let me go!" O'Keefe shrieked, "It's raining teeth! It's raining tongues! Aaaaah!"

Margo narrowed her eyes at Spreck. Now he looked sorry. "Well we can forget about 'preventing' the next Tragedy," she said. "The next Tragedy is happening. It's happening right now."

NINETEEN

LATER

Margo was still agitated from the nimo attack. Now the two cyborgs in the doorway had cornered her. Her breath quickened and her heart throbbed. She had to stifle the impulse to tear off the cyborgs' heads with her suction cup hands.

Instead, she whipped her leech arms at the cyborgs, grabbed each by the chest with her suction cup hands, and pulled them in close. Then with a shout she shoved both of them down on their backs on the ground. She stepped on them, a foot on each of their chests, and looked down at their screen-faces.

On one screen was the blank face of a woman with thick eyebrows and long, wet-looking hair. On the other screen was Thorsten, his eyes wide with disbelief. They looked up at Margo. Margo looked down on them.

"Sorry about putting the arachnimonite in the cell with you," said the woman in a deadpan voice. "I didn't know you were in here."

"You killed it," said Thorsten. "I've seen what a hungry nimo can do to a person. I've seen what's left. What's left after a hungry nimo half the size of that one gets hold of a person twice your size. Holy shit, Margo. HOLY SHIT."

"I'm Cola Dubuffet," said the woman. "Professor Cola Dubuffet. I work here with Thorsten. This cell is disgusting. You don't need to stay in here. Come on out. Let's get you cleaned up."

Margo stepped off of the cyborgs' chests. She considered helping them up but let them get up on their own. It wasn't like it made any difference to Thorsten and Cola who were physically elsewhere.

Margo felt like she was getting away with slighting them intentionally, which made her smile. Serves them right, leaving her there to fend off that thing. Then, slowly, Cola's words sunk in. After a minute, Margo asked, "I can get cleaned up?" Then, "I don't have to hide?"

"Thorsten told me about how he made you hide in the slime grazer carcass," said Cola. "Sorry. I think he overstated how sneaky you need to be to get through security here. It's just me and him, and I don't care. No one else is here. No one else is paying attention."

"I still can't believe you killed it," Thorsten went on. "Just with, I guess with those sludge leeches. Wow. Holy shit Margo."

Margo crossed her leech arms. She was tired. There was something about Cola that she didn't trust.

"Why don't I have to hide? I'm a fugitive. Community Safety is after me for I don't know how many counts of High Recklessness. How do I know one of your other work buddies won't be as casual as you are about letting me hide out here?"

"Like I said, no one else is here," Cola said in her deadpan voice. "Everyone else in Pest Control is out dealing with the goblin polyps."

"They still haven't been contained?"

"We'll talk about it later," said Cola. "In the war room."

Thorsten didn't say anything when Cola brought up the goblin polyps, and he didn't meet Margo's eyes.

Cola said, "Let's get you a shower."

TWENTY

EARLIER

How long could O'Keefe's cyborg prevent its hysterically hallucinating master from bolting, possibly off the rooftop and into oblivion? Margo didn't know.

He was up there because of her. And she couldn't shake the thought that it should be her suffering the consequences of her botched inspection. Now she was responsible for saving O'Keefe and preventing anyone else from being exposed to the spores and she was scared beyond belief of screwing up her rescue mission.

She was sitting at her kitchen table with Spreck and calling Thorsten on the screen-face of Spreck's cyborg. Spreck carefully sat far enough off to the side of Margo that he remained off screen.

"Margo?" said Thorsten, blinking and rubbing his eyes, thoroughly confused because the message on his cyborg's screen-face would have told him the identity of the caller was unavailable, thanks to Margo's quick adjustments to Spreck's cyborg's security settings. Margo's vehement avoidance of him since Jasper's banishment probably put her face among the last he'd expect to see staring back at him on his cyborg at this late hour, or any hour at all.

"I haven't forgiven you," Margo said. "I need your help."

She told Thorsten about the goblin polyp spores in Hazard no. 457 and O'Keefe's stranger-than-usual gibberish. Thorsten made a face like someone with a mouthful of something revoltingly bitter. He didn't say anything. "What do you think?" Margo prodded. "How much time do we have?"

Thorsten held back his reply. He seemed to be thinking, and his thoughts seemed to pain him severely. When finally he broke his silence, all he said, preceded by a heavy sigh, was, "Oops."

Margo repeated it back to him. "Oops? Yeah, oops." Then, "Wait, what do you mean oops?" Thorsten started to speak. Before he said much, Margo told him to shut up. Now she was having thoughts that pained her severely. She looked at Spreck. "Where did you get the spores?" she said. "Who gave the spores to you?"

Spreck didn't say anything. He refused to meet Margo's eyes. She looked back at Thorsten on the cyborg's screen-face. "Does the name 'Spreck Purcell' sound familiar?" she asked. Reluctantly he returned Margo's look and nodded.

Spreck meanwhile had stood up beside the table. He was silently freaking out, frantically gesturing to urge Margo against this line of inquiry. Margo knew full well what he was trying to do, but she pretended she didn't understand.

"Thorsten," she said, looking back to her former friend on the cyborg's screen-face. "I need to ask you a question. I need you to be honest. This is a potentially catastrophic, life or death situation. Answer simply yes or no. Did you give goblin polyp spores to Spreck Purcell to use in Warhol's installation?"

Hesitation. Then, "Yeah, kind of, but— "

"Stop talking," interrupted Margo. She was furious. She grabbed Spreck's cyborg's head and forced it to turn so the screen-face was aimed at Spreck and he and Thorsten could now see each other.

"Allow me to re-introduce you," she said. "Idiot who is making my life miserable number one, meet idiot who is making my life miserable number two."

She sat back in her chair with a huff. "We just need Warhol here and you jackasses can have a We Make Life Miserable for Margo convention."

Spreck and Thorsten didn't say anything to each other.

"Margo, please," Thorsten pleaded. "I was assured that every precaution would be taken to keep the spores under control. They insisted that the inspector—you—would catch the spores before they posed any risk."

Margo stopped, "They?"

"Him. Spreck."

She smirked at Spreck.

"It's just, my C.P. score is so low," Thorsten went on. "My art, my drawing, everyone thinks it's terrible. So I thought maybe this was my chance. A way to make my mark, you know? Lorcan Warhol, an artistic genius, needed my help. How could I say no? I mean the whole point of having the spores in the installation was so they could be taken away, right? That was the point, is what I was told." He was talking too fast. The realization of what he'd done had hit him and he was panicking. "I thought, after the exhibit opened, I could go up to the Museum of Genius and visit it and know the little part I played in it, think about the thrill of the risk I took just by providing the spores, you know? Of course I would never be able to tell anyone about it unless I want Community Safety coming after me." He stopped for a few seconds. "Oh god. I've told you about it."

Margo had no patience for Thorsten. O'Keefe needed rescuing. Goblin polyps were growing and multiplying and spreading spores in the museum. She turned the cyborg's screen-face back toward herself and stood looking at Thorsten's pathetic face. His eyes were red. Was he going to cry? "What happens next to you doesn't matter," she said. "What matters is fixing this. So please, tell me. How much time do we have?" Spreck, standing beside Margo, didn't move, as if by not moving she might forget he was there. Again Margo asked, "Thorsten, how much time?"

Thorsten wiped his nose and mumbled, "If you have any time at all, you don't have much. In the right conditions, a spore can grow into a full-grown polyp in less than twenty-four hours. The ventilation system in the Museum of Genius is probably the right conditions. So you have less than a day until there's a pretty big risk of inhaling spores as soon as you walk into the museum, with the highest risk on the roof and upper floors." He sighed. "And you have just a couple days before the spores floating in the air start growing polyps all over the inside of the museum and crusting over the art with their fungal slime. Works of genius will be destroyed. And if nobody does anything about it, it'll be a week, maybe less, before the polyps spread out into the rest of the Bublinaplex."

Thorsten's predictions shocked Margo. This was worse than she thought. Way worse. How could he or Spreck or ~~Warhol or Thorsten~~ anyone with a brain have thought the potential slime-borne destruction of the Bublinaplex and quite possibly the end of humanity in a frenzy of spore madness was worth the risk? For some sort of artistic statement? She forced herself to seem calm and asked, "Has anything like this ever happened before?"

"There have been goblin polyp infestations before, sure," Thorsten said, "but nothing on this scale. The usual procedure is to evacuate then isolate and then exterminate. Usually it's just Pest Control needing to eliminate the polyps from some Structural Safety officer's house because the spores got stuck on a boot or something. Quarantining the whole Museum of Genius will take every Pest Control officer there is and then some, plus a mountain of paperwork, and that's if the Executive Designer's Administration decides to help rather than of get in the way. And that's a huge if."

Margo thought of O'Keefe hallucinating on the rooftop. "We don't have time to do this the way it's supposed to be done," she said. Looking at Spreck's cyborg, she got an idea. "I think there's a way to rescue O'Keefe and keep the public out of the museum, at least for long enough to give Pest Control time to exterminate the goblin polyps."

"Wait," said Spreck. "Keep the public out of the museum? What about Hazard no. 457's opening tomorrow?" He made a droopy face at Margo and chewed his lip in a way that she supposed was supposed to convey the seriousness of his concern. "The Recklessist community will be deeply disappointed."

Margo glared at him. "Do you really think I care?"

Thorsten piped up. "What can I do to help?"

Margo told him to get Pest Control moving on its extermination plan as fast as he could.

Spreck asked how he could help.

"Do nothing," said Margo. "Stay in my apartment. Don't talk to anyone. I'm taking your cyborg."

Margo wanted to tell Spreck he should do what she intended to do herself. Because the truth was, her plan was reckless and she imagined a Recklessist would be more comfortable doing what had to be done than she would. But she didn't trust him. And she reminded herself it was other people's lives he was in the habit of risking by assisting Warhol with his art, not his own. Could she depend on him to risk his own neck? She didn't want to find out.

Thinking about what she was about to do, she figured the odds were good she'd wind up caught and caged and eventually banished— possibly before she even had a chance to do any good. But if she wanted to save O'Keefe, she didn't have any choice.

She ended the conversation with Thorsten, then used Spreck's cyborg to reach Oliver Beckett, the Museum of Genius' Safety Officer. Unbelievably—and fortunately for Margo's plan—he was still in his office in the museum when she called. "Stay put," Margo told him. "Unless you start feeling crazy. I'll be there soon. I'll explain. Just don't breathe any more than absolutely necessary."

TWENTY-ONE

LATER

At first, Margo thought the leeches seemed to enjoy the hot shower. Then the antiseptic chemicals in the water must have started to irritate them. To Margo, the sensation felt like a burning itchiness in her leech arms. The feeling would not have been so terrible if she still possessed fingernails to scratch with. She cut the shower short.

Cola had provided her with a green and black striped Pest Control uniform. Thankfully it had no buttons and no zipper. She put it on and then followed Cola's directions through the building's yellow-walled halls to the so-called war room.

She found Thorsten and Cola seated near the end of a long table. Their cyborgs stood behind their chairs. Covering the wall on one side of the room was a screen with a map of the entire Bublinaplex. On the opposite side of the room, a large window offered an expansive view of the city. In the distance, where Margo expected to see the Museum of Genius and the grotesque balloon with her face on it, an immense tube of some kind could be seen completely covering the museum and extending all the way up to the mile-high ceiling in the center of the dome.

Thorsten sat up in his chair. His face was blank. He'd been scribbling in his sketch book. Hastily he closed the sketchbook and put it away. Margo stood in the doorway as Thorsten and Cola sat there looking in her direction.

"So you have sludge leeches on your arms?" Thorsten said, as if this statement of fact were a question.

Margo gave Thorsten a look. She was thinking that hearing him talk so matter-of-factly about the leeches that had replaced her arms should make her feel awkward or embarrassed or angry. Like someone just coming out and saying something about her weight or her height or weird things about her body like the shape of her head or the size of her boobs. But she felt nothing, and without hesitation replied, "Thorsten, you should know very well that, at this point, the leeches are my arms."

"Yeah," he said meekly. "I know." Then, "Do they hurt?"

"No."

He glanced across the table toward Cola. "Do you want us to remove them?"

Margo shifted uncomfortably. The leeches were mostly hidden in the sleeves of the Pest Control uniform, but her suction cup hands and segmented wrists were plainly visible, and the way they bent to form semi-circular arches when she folded them across her chest was entirely different from the way regular human arms bend at an angle at the elbow. "No," she said, then looked up at the ceiling, thinking for several seconds. Then, again, she repeated: "No."

Thorsten wasn't meeting her gaze. It was like he was looking at something on the floor. The floor was white linoleum tile. "It's hard not to look at them," he said.

"I know," said Margo. "It's fine. Go ahead. Look."

Thorsten, seeming embarrassed by the invitation, looked away. But Cola stood up as her cyborg helped with her chair and she walked up to Margo. She stood taller than Margo thought she should for some reason, and Margo realized that reason was that, in contrast with Cola's height—she wasn't even that tall—her cyborg, which followed her, was especially short. "Let me see," she said.

Still, she saw no reason not to cooperate. She used a suction cup hand to pull back a sleeve and extended her left leech arm for Cola to see. Cola put both hands on the extended leech. She ran her fingers along its segmented surface. "Fascinating," she said, cradling Margo's leech arm. "It's not as slimy as I thought it would be." She seemed about to bend down and rub against the leech with her cheek.

Margo withdrew her arm and Cola shot her a wounded look. This woman's strange intimacy with the leech was making her uncomfortable. Was it jealousy? As if Cola might somehow charm the leech away from her? Margo didn't dwell on it. She gestured toward the multicolored map of the Bublinaplex. "What do the colored dots mean?" she asked, hoping to shift attention away from the leeches.

Cola took a step back. "This map is why we call this room the war room," she said. "The dots represent sightings of Invasive Organisms. 'Pests,' as our crudely named department would label them."

"That bright pink color around the Museum of Genius," said Margo. "Goblyn polyps?"

"Correct," said Cola.

Margo scanned the map. Multicolored dots decorated much of the city, especially near its edges. The map lacked any discernible key. What most of the things that had crept in from the outside were, she could not tell.

"Nimos, slime grazers, lobopods," said Cola, helpfully. "A variety of molds and fungi. Now and then they all find their way inside. Last month we even had a patch of muck of despair show up in the Theatre District." She shrugged. "It's impossible to know for certain how all these things get in. We try to figure out as best we can, but our main priority always is making sure they are contained and removed." Staring at Margo's leech arms again, she said, "May I take a sample?"

Margo couldn't hide her discomfort. She ignored the question. "Why don't you tell me more about what's happening with the goblin polyps?"

Now it was Thorsten who piped up. He told Margo that a task force made up of staff from Pest Control, the Administration, and the Museum of Genius came up with a plan to use the vast tube she saw out the window to completely seal off the museum from the rest of the Bublinaplex. "Powerful fans are supposed to blow the spores out of the building and up through the tube and out a narrow hole at the peak in the dome. Meanwhile, Pest Control is supposed to get to work scraping the slimy, sticky fungi off the inside of the museum."

"Sounds like a good plan," said Margo.

"Doesn't it?" Cola said. "Except it's not working. Workers from the Structural Safety Department who were supposed to finish installing the tube keep inhaling spores. Most of them wind up tangled in the safety nets below their work areas, wriggling and hallucinating. It's a disaster."

"So what are you going to do?"

Cola took another step back from Margo, then walked toward the window. "Funny you should ask," she said. Though Margo couldn't see Cola's face, from the tone of her voice, Margo knew she was smiling. "I have a plan. It's been hard to convince some of our superiors that it will work. But, if you want, you can make things much easier for me ..."

"Cola, don't," said Thorsten, more firmly than Margo had ever heard him speak. "I already asked her. She said no. Leave it."

"No, you didn't ask her," Cola snapped at Thorsten. "Not in a way that helps her understand what's at stake, anyway." She turned to face Margo, who was still standing on the other side of the room, unsure of what exactly she was doing there and what these two expected of her.

Margo wanted to sit. Why didn't they invite her to sit? Why did she feel like she needed to be invited to sit in order to sit? She shook her head. "Do you guys have anything here to eat?" she said, then walked up to the table and sat down. "And she's right," she said with a nod in Cola's direction. "I have no idea what you two are talking about."

Cola turned away from the window. She walked back to the table. With her hands resting on the back of a chair, she looked down at Margo and replied, "Thorsten asked if you want us to help you get rid of the sludge leeches that have eaten your arms and attached themselves to your shoulders and are now serving as your arms. The leeches will be there, feeding on you, for the rest of your life. And they'll secrete chemicals into your body that, among other things, essentially supercharge your will to live." Cola paused and looked at Thorsten, who had stood up and was now nervously leaning against the table with both hands. The way they were bent toward each other it was as if they were part-way bowing to one another, as if they were about to engage in a duel.

"I know all this," said Margo. "From before, I mean. Thorsten told me all about sludge leeches a long time ago."

"You don't know all of it," Cola said. "Thorsten didn't know—in fact no one knew until I figured it out a few days ago—that the chemicals these leeches inject into their hosts also demonstrate powerful anti-hallucinogenic properties." Cola walked around the table so she stood behind Margo. She rested her hands on Margo's shoulders. Margo resisted slapping her away with a suction cup hand.

"If you let us take the leeches, I think I can isolate those chemicals, create an anti-hallucinogenic mixture and give it to the workers who are supposed to be helping purge the goblin polyps from the museum. I might even be able to synthesize an anti-hallucinogen for everyone in the Bublinaplex—rendering the goblin polyp infestation a minor annoyance instead of an existential threat." She paused. "Think about it, Margo. These leeches that you brought us can save the Museum of Genius. They might save us all." She started squeezing Margo's shoulders.

Margo did not reply.

"You don't have to say anything," said Thorsten. "You don't have to do anything."

Margo stood quickly and shoved Cola backward in the process. The thought of removing the leeches must have triggered something in them. Margo could feel her mood changing. The mere thought of losing them suddenly flooded her with panic, as if losing them would be as painful and traumatic as losing Jasper. She knew the leeches were somehow exuding chemicals to alter her thoughts and feelings, but she was powerless to stop them. Maybe she would have sacrificed the leeches if they weren't manipulating her, and maybe she wouldn't. She didn't know. All she knew now was that in that instant she could not willingly sacrifice the leeches. It took all the self-control she had to stop herself from either running away from Cola or attacking her.

Margo walked around the table and approached the window. The sun as seen through the dome was a bright yellow blur on a hazy orange plane. It was the middle of the afternoon. It was as much natural light as anyone ever saw in the Bublinaplex. "I do have to do something," said Margo.

"Wonderful," said Cola, and though her voice kept its monotone she was clearly pleased. "I'll help prep you for surgery."

"No," said Margo, turning. "You're not touching Leo and Randi." She winced. Those names had sounded better in her head. "You're not removing the leeches."

"So you're going to let that fungal slime ruin everything inside the Museum of Genius? You're going to let the air inside the museum, maybe inside the whole Bublinaplex, be filled with airborne hallucinogens? You're not going to help?" Cola said.

"No," said Margo. She wanted to scream. Instead she took a deep breath and said, "I'm going to deal with this myself."

TWENTY-TWO

EARLIER

It was night again by the time Margo began her mission to rescue O'Keefe from the spores that were driving him mad. She took a transport capsule to the Tower of Safety. Spreck's cyborg rode by her side.

On the way, she tried to stop herself from thinking about what she was about to do. The risks she was about to take, even if the were for safety's sake, would have consequences she wasn't ready to meet.

She tried desperately to imagine alternate courses of action. She really tried. But her terrible idea was the only idea she had that stood any chance of saving O'Keefe and containing the goblin polyps as quickly as was necessary.

She had hardly any time at all.

Would she wind up banished because of what she was about to do? Maybe. She tried to let herself be okay with that, even tried embracing the idea of banishment by letting herself think about the possibility of being forced out of the Bublinaplex resulting in a reunion with Jasper in the Fungus Wasteland.

It wouldn't be the last time she used this fantasy to drive herself forward.

She and Spreck's cyborg arrived at the Tower of Safety and took the elevator up to the Art Safety Department. Unlike the twenty-four-seven frenzy of activity in the Bodily Safety Department that took up the tower's first several floors, Margo expected the Art Safety Department to be dark and empty.

All she had to do was walk in and take what she needed and get out.

Stepping out of the elevator she imagined what her colleagues might say to her if she'd arrived during the workday. They would ask questions, questions like, "How did it go, making Lorcan Warhol's so-called 'genius' installation safe?" and "Where were you when the Tragedy happened?" and "How does it feel to have a giant inflatable caricature of your stupid face floating over the Museum of Genius?"

She was grateful the department was empty at night.

Margo walked the dark halls. The cyborg followed behind quietly. She supposed she also should be worrying about how Lorcan Warhol was being wrongly held responsible for The Tragedy and how his assistant Spreck was hiding out in her apartment. She would have to deal with those two too, and soon. Or would she? Seeing Warhol and Spreck banished should seem like a blessing. But no one seemed to be looking for whoever was really responsible for The Tragedy. Next to them, Warhol and Spreck seemed about as dangerous as a wet slice of cake. As far as Margo could tell, nothing was stopping whoever was responsible for The Tragedy from striking again. No, she didn't want to see Warhol unjustly banished, and she couldn't let Community Safety convince themselves the problem already had been solved while the true killers still were unaccounted for.

Artificial starlight coming in through the windows helped Margo find her way around the dark office. She walked past her cubicle, toward O'Keefe's office. His door was closed.

She tried the knob. It turned. She slipped inside and, not thinking, almost flipped on the light. But her eyes had adjusted and there was light enough coming in through O'Keefe's window for her to see what she needed to see. The room was small and she thought she knew exactly what she needed and where to find it. In the top drawer of O'Keefe's desk, she found a blank inspection report. She picked up the blank report and then quietly slipped back out into the hall.

At her cubicle, she filled out the report. It took her only a minute.

Next she went around the corner to Chief Inspector Tiff Austen's office. She was less sure where to find what she was looking for in the chief's office. She would have to be careful. If she was caught, the woman in charge of the Art Safety Department would not be forgiving.

The hallway was oddly less dark near Chief Austen's office. Light was coming out from under the crack between the floor and the office door.

It was night and it looked like Chief Austen was inside her office.

Margo hadn't planned for this.

Now Margo's plan seemed worse than reckless. It seemed stupid. She hesitated. This part, where she did a little bit of sneaking around the Art Safety Department, wasn't even supposed to be the reckless part yet. But she didn't know what else she could do. She needed to save O'Keefe.

Maybe Chief Austen being in her office didn't totally ruin her plan. She supposed it really depended whether she cared about being caught. She didn't have time to think up another plan. She would just have to not care about the consequences of this one. To think that was a helpful shortcut, though it also seemed to Margo like yet another kind of recklessness. She would need to accustom herself to the idea that the Fungus Wasteland would not be such a bad place to wind up.

Margo opened Chief Austen's door.

"What is it? What do you want?" Chief Austen said. Margo stepped inside. The Chief was sitting behind her desk and looking upset in the light of her desk lamp. She held the UNSAFE stamp, its bottom shiny with red ink. She recognized Margo and sighed, "Inspector Chicago? What on Earth are you doing?" Then, after composing herself, "Get out, Inspector. Get out right now, Inspector. Please."

"I'm sorry Chief," said Margo, stepping forward into the room. Spreck's cyborg blocked the door behind her. "I need you to know that what I'm doing, I'm doing for safety's sake. I'm doing what I'm doing because lives are at stake."

"Are you drunk, Inspector Chicago?" the Chief asked. "Are you not feeling well?" Margo didn't respond. The Chief shrugged her broad shoulders. "Whatever's going on with you, let's talk tomorrow, alright? I'm just finishing up here." She paused. "And I think you'll be in a better frame of mind to discuss what's bothering you after you get some sleep." As she said this, she placed the UNSAFE stamp in its inkpad, then clasped her hands together under her chin.

Margo seized her chance. She lunged forward and snatched the UNSAFE stamp off of the Chief's desk. Chief Austen tried to stop her but she wasn't quick enough. "You give that back at once," the Chief shouted.

"I only need it for a second," Margo said. She turned and spread the inspection report she'd just filled out flat against the wall beside the Chief's doorway. But before she could stamp "UNSAFE" onto the report, Chief Austen had leapt out from behind her desk and with both hands had taken hold of Margo's arm. The Chief was strong. Margo turned around, trying to wriggle free, to face the Chief. The Chief hurled Margo down to the carpeted floor, where she landed on her elbow and banged her head against a little table with some books on it. As Margo lay on her back, the Chief crouched down on top of her and started prying Margo's fingers off the stamp.

The Chief pulled back Margo's pinky finger until tears came to her eyes and waves of pain shot through her arm and throbbed with the rhythm of her pulse. But then the Chief's grip loosened and Margo was able to flip herself over and get up onto her knees. Using one hand she flattened out the inspection report on the floor. She pressed the rubber stamp against it. She pressed as hard as she could so the word "UNSAFE" was as clear and red as it could be. Then she let go of the stamp and Chief Austen took it back.

Pain shot through Margo's throbbing finger. She thought Chief Austen might have broken it. In an instant Chief Austen was back behind her desk, frowning darkly and looking down at Margo panting on the floor.

Margo thought she could probably make the Chief understand what she was doing. She could show her the video on Spreck's cyborg to demonstrate Warhol's innocence. She could have explained that Sub-Chief O'Keefe's life was in danger.

But there was no time. "Please," Margo said, "Trust me." She stood up with a grunt and held up the inspection report she'd just stamped. "It's for safety."

And with that, Margo backed out of the Chief's office. She and Spreck's cyborg got out of the Tower of Safety as quickly as they could. Repeatedly she looked over her shoulder to see if Chief Austen had sent her cyborg after her. Nothing followed. Spreck's cyborg kept up fine.

At the nearest transport station they caught a capsule just before its doors closed. Margo sat down, still breathing fast, and she saw Spreck's cyborg's chest was rising and falling rapidly too.

The first thing Margo noticed as the capsule approached the Museum of Genius was the light. Hundreds, perhaps thousands of artificial candles held up by mourners were twinkling outside the museum. Mourners had gathered for a vigil to memorialize the eleven dead.

She clenched her teeth and steeled herself for what came next in her reckless plan to prevent O'Keefe from becoming the twelfth death.

Around the front steps of the museum the crowd stood at least ten rows deep. Margo and Spreck's cyborg squeezed their way through to what was left of the front steps. The shattered stone slab that fell had been cleared. What was left of it remained in a fenced-off pile. The pile now seemed to serve as a kind of shrine and was almost completely buried by small works of art and everyday objects left by mourners.

At the top of the museum's damaged front steps she met a line of cyborgs. Linked arm-in-arm, they formed a barrier at the door to keep visitors out. Across their screen-faces flashed a message that read, "Temporarily closed. Investigation ongoing. Warhol opening rescheduled for tomorrow."

With the illicit inspection report in her sweat-slick hand, Margo turned to Spreck's cyborg. "Call Oliver Beckett," she said.

"Damn it all, Margo," said Beckett when he answered. "What the hell is happening? Where have you been? I've been trying to call your cyborg for the past hour."

His surly tone took Margo by surprise. "Sorry," she said. "My cyborg was destroyed in The Tragedy."

"Oh," said Beckett. "I see." He relaxed his scowl. "Sorry."

"Apology accepted," said Margo. "Though I don't know what you have to be sorry for. I'm out here in front of the museum, at the top of the front steps. Can you let me in?"

Beckett ignored her question. "What the hell is happening?" he repeated. "I've got surveillance cameras on the rooftop showing a guy who looks an awful lot like your boss wrestling with a cyborg."

"Don't go up there," said Margo. "Let me in."

"Tell me what's going on," he insisted.

"I don't have time to explain. If you don't let me in, people will die. Let me in!"

Beckett's face twisted into an expression Margo didn't know how to read. Was there a hint of a smile? No matter. In an instant his face on the cyborg's screen disappeared and replaced by a pixelated jumble of black and white lines and squares.

Margo directed Spreck's cyborg toward the line of security cyborgs, where the code on the cyborg's screen-face instructed the security cyborgs to stand aside.

Oliver Beckett met Margo and Spreck's cyborg in the atrium. "Inspector Chicago," he said flatly. "I suppose you're happy with how things have turned out." He crossed his arms.

"What?" said Margo, not understanding what he meant and not interested figuring it out. "Listen. I need your help."

"Oh right," said Beckett, "Remember what you said to me last time I asked for your help? 'No' is what you said. Remember?"

"I don't know what you're talking about, Oliver," said Margo. "Can we go back to your office so I can show you what we need to do?"

Beckett gave Margo a snotty look. "No," he said.

Suddenly Margo remembered what Beckett have felt slighted about, and she laughed. She didn't have time for this. "Seriously?" she said. "You're going to let someone die—actually, potentially, lots of someones—because I wouldn't ask Lorcan Warhol to sign your stupid t-shirt?"

Beckett said nothing. He looked at the floor.

"That's what I thought," said Margo. "Let's go."

They withdrew to Beckett's office. The surveillance cameras displayed the museum's emptiness save for several Structural Safety officers, some standing around and talking and some inspecting the building's foundation from inside the basement. In most rooms, cyborgs could be seen working tirelessly, sweeping the floors and dusting precious objects.

A monitor displaying a view of the rooftop clearly showed O'Keefe and his cyborg struggling with each other on the floor.

Beckett stood petulantly beside the wall of monitors with his arms folded. "Okay Inspector Chicago. Here we are. Tell me what you want."

"First, a question. Can you tell from your surveillance recordings what really happened here last night?"

"Probably," he said with a shrug. "Community Safety confiscated the recordings before I could watch them."

Margo let out a sigh of relief. If Community Safety had taken the surveillance recordings, it was only a matter of time before some officer watched the tape and realized that Lorcan Warhol, Spreck Purcell and the rest were innocent. Of course, she supposed they could suppress the evidence. But that was out of her hands now. Finding a way to get the video evidence to Community Safety was one less thing for her to worry about. She could focus on saving O'Keefe. After that, the best thing she could do for Spreck and Warhol was find out who sabotaged the installation.

Margo told Beckett about O'Keefe and the spores and her plan to save her boss and prevent a goblin polyp epidemic.

"That's insane," he said. "You'll be banished for recklessness. Hell, I'll be banished too."

"I won't admit you helped," she said. "But I do need your help. I need you to show me what to do with this." She handed him the inspection report.

It was an extremely simple report. On the blank line where the work of art to be evaluated as Safe or Unsafe is supposed to be written, Margo had written "Museum of Genius." The word "UNSAFE" was stamped across it in bright red ink.

Beckett gestured toward a slot in the wall opposite the surveillance monitors. "Feed it in here," he said. "But you know people saw me come back here with you. For all I know, you could be recording everything we're saying on that thing," he motioned toward the cyborg.

"I'm not recording anything," she said. "And you can just tell Community Safety that I threatened you."

"They would believe that?"

She made a fist and slugged him in the jaw.

"Ow," they both said. Beckett rubbed the side of his face. Blood trickled out from the corner of his mouth. Margo rubbed her knuckles.

"Okay then," Beckett said after a minute.

Margo fed the inspection report into the slot. The machine in the wall made a small scraping sound as it scanned the report, translating it into instructions for the museum's security cyborgs.

Seconds later, every cyborg in the museum could be seen on the video monitors abandoning its broom or mop or dust rag. Some of the cyborgs left the building to link arms with those that Margo needed Beckett's help getting past, forming an even more secure barrier against visitors.

Cyborgs surrounded the Structural Safety officers conducting their investigation, forming rings of four or six cyborgs around each officer, then ushered the officers out of the building. The officers' attempts to resist were useless. Most knew this and went along calmly with the cyborgs. Those who fought back only slowed, but could not halt, their forced march out of the building.

On the monitor showing a view of the rooftop, Margo saw that O'Keefe had his arms wrapped around something. At first she thought it was his cyborg's arm. But the cyborg's arm was free. The thing O'Keefe's arms were wrapped around wasn't attached to anything. The thing looked like a gun.

Her first reaction was shock that O'Keefe somehow had gotten hold of one of Warhol's laser rifles. But the thing wasn't a laser rifle. She squinted at its blurry image. And she realized what it was, and as she watched six security cyborgs surround O'Keefe and his cyborg in order to force them down the stairs and eventually out of the museum, she was even more horrified than she was when she thought he had a laser rifle.

It was a squirt gun—probably the squirt gun contaminated with goblin polyp spores.

O'Keefe would be squirting and sloshing and generally making a mess with the contaminated water during his entire descent down the museum steps—and, eventually, he would bring it outside.

Thinking this, Margo hardly noticed that she, Beckett, and Spreck's cyborg also had been surrounded by a half dozen security cyborgs intending to forcefully escort them from the building for their own safety.

Margo ducked her head and dashed between two of the cyborgs.

To her surprise, they didn't catch her.

On tired legs, she ran up the museum steps toward O'Keefe.

TWENTY-THREE

LATER

The leeches were afraid of heights.

Margo had taken one of the Pest Control Department's hover cubes. Thorsten had offered it, over Cola's objections. "You're letting her leave?" she'd said. "You're going to let our only chance to save the Bublinaplex just walk out the door?"

"You think we should hold her here against her will?" Thorsten replied pointedly.

Cola shook her head. "She's a fugitive. You let her go, and Community Safety will catch her. She won't be saving anyone from inside the Asylum, and we won't have the leeches."

"We don't have the leeches now, Cola." Thorsten was almost shouting. "Margo does. She's not giving them to us. And we're not going to take them by force. So yes, Margo out there, trying to fix this mess, is way better than her twiddling her thumbs in one of our cells or one of Community Safety's cells."

Margo spoke up just to remind them she was still in the room, listening to their conversation about her. "I no longer have thumbs," she said.

Now Margo was piloting the hover cube up to the highest point in the center of the Bublinaplex, where the mile-high tube of material was supposed to funnel the spores out through a hole in the dome, and where Structural Safety workers were being too overcome with hallucinations to complete the task.

She wasn't quite sure what she was going to do when she arrived at top of the tube, but she felt so relieved to be getting away from Cola that not having a plan didn't much bother her.

But the leeches were almost as anxious about this upward escape route as they were about Cola.

They had been fine when the hover cube started to make its slow ascent. But then it was as if they suddenly became aware of how far from the ground they were, they started writhing and wriggled and coiling themselves around anything they could find and then uncoiling themselves and coiling back up again. Margo immediately understood what was happening. The leeches were throwing a temper tantrum.

She tried to will them calm. That didn't work—unnervingly their ability to influence her was far stronger than her ability to influence them. Thankfully they did eventually settle down of their own accord by the time the hover cube was almost halfway to the top of the dome. But by then the leeches were clearly exhausted, and so was Margo.

Once the leeches calmed down, Margo realized she was getting hungry. She thought it was actually quite rude of Thorsten and Cola not to offer her anything to eat, especially considering what they'd attempted to ask of her. She made the sudden decision to forgive Thorsten—for not feeding her and for everything else. And then the pang of regret for not trying harder to find Jasper in the Fungus Wasteland reappeared. She'd have to forgive herself too.

Margo liked the idea of getting past her grudge and seeing Thorsten for no reason other than just to hang out.

She shook her head. Hanging out was impossible now that she was a fugitive. She'd survived the Fungus Wasteland, but she soon probably would be banished. Even if the Executive Designer did say via the cyborg that came for her in the wasteland that she wouldn't be banished. Why should she trust the Executive Designer?

At least she could imagine sitting with Thorsten and watching a movie and the fantasy seemed so much more reasonable, so much more real, compared to her thoughts of becoming a hunter-gatherer with Jasper. So what if when Thorsten asked her to pass her the popcorn his attention temporarily would veer away from the movie to the parasites that now served as her arms?

Meanwhile the hover cube continued its ascent. Now Margo could clearly see the top of the tube and the torn flaps where it was supposed to be sealed. And she could see the four-cornered safety net dangling like an enormous hammock just under where the Structural Safety workers had been working.

She saw that a worker was caught in that net right now. He was trying to free himself. He looked like a helpless insect. Margo felt bad for the worker but trusted that rescuing him was someone else's job. The hover cube proceeded up and past the worker. She knew he was trying to get her attention and she tried not to look.

Finally, the hover cube reached the open flap at the top of the mile-high tube. Immediately when she opened the hover cube door she noticed the air outside had the unmistakable smoky, earthy smell of fungal spores. She couldn't help breathing it in.

The spore-dense air started changing her mood at once.

She felt a gleeful lightness and a sense of deepened awareness that was not there before. A kind of tangy tartness tickled the back of her tongue. She braced herself for the hallucinations.

But the hallucinations didn't come.

She looked down the length of the mile-high tube—and the leeches threw another tantrum.

They squeezed themselves flat against her sides and coiled themselves around her body. They writhed and wiggled in a panic she was sure was going to make her lose her balance until, of their own volition, her suction cup hands latched onto the inside of the cube and held fast.

For more than an hour she tried willing the leeches to relax—first mentally, without speaking, and then eventually by yelling at them in what eventually built up to a tantrum of her own.

Her yelling changed nothing. All she was doing was wearing herself out, so she tried a different tactic. She tried to force herself to relax while at the same time looking downward at the various districts of the Bublinaplex, marveling from this vantage at the enormity of the feats of engineering that allowed the city to exist.

Eventually, the leeches relaxed.

Now Margo could get to work. Her first idea was to stretch the leeches out of the hover cube door as far as she could, but when she tried stretching them out the door and almost reached the first snaps, probably ten feet away, the cube tilted slightly and the leeches, spooked, snapped back to her sides.

Another half an hour or so passed before the leeches let her try again. This time she quickly whipped the leeches up so they grabbed on to the top of the hover cube, then used them to pull herself up on top of it. Several terrifying, dangly seconds followed. The leeches trembled with apparent fear, but they did not disobey. Margo was relieved. Disobedience would have meant the three of them plummeting into the net below.

As she clung to the roof of the hover cube, her breaths came short and shallow. Soon she crouched down to brace herself for her next step, then stood up, first with the leeches stretched out, still connected to the roof. She then coaxed them with a combination of soothing, reassuring words and mental willpower into relaxing their grip.

She looked at the snaps she would have to snap shut. Thinking she wished the people whose job was to fix this had fixed it without her needing to intervene, she looked down with annoyance toward the hallucinating worker caught in the net.

He wasn't there.

An instant later the hover cube listed suddenly to one side and Margo stumbled. She heard the hover cube's engine hum to life and click into gear. Regaining her balance, she glanced down quickly enough to see the hallucinating worker's legs hanging out of the hover cube door.

He was stealing her ride.

The hover cube lurched sideways.

Then she fell.

Immediately the leeches snapped upward, reaching farther and faster than she thought they could. Her suction cup hands reached the surface of the dome and grabbed on.

She dangled from the surface of the dome like some unfortunate berry and she looked down to see the hallucinating thief make his escape in her hover cube. She kicked her legs. She lost a shoe and watched it fall.

Suspended a mile above the city, she released a suction cup hand and then quickly reattached it to the dome a couple of feet closer to the open flap she'd come to close. She then released the other suction cup hand and reattached it closer to her other suction cup hand. She continued like this, walking along the inside of the dome with her suction cup hands until she reached the flap.

At the flap, while one leech kept her attached to the inside surface of the dome's ceiling, she used the other to reach down and grab one side of the snap. Carefully she brought it with her suction cup hand up to the other side's snap, shepherding the two together in a suction cup hand, which she closed like a mitten to snap them together.

The next snap must have slipped from her suction cup hand more than a dozen times before she succeeded in snapping it shut.

None of the rest were as easy as the first.

Not long after she finished she watched the blur of the sun set, its brightness and brilliant colors dulled through the grimy glass of the dome. The way the sun shrank and disappeared over a horizon she saw as where the smudge of the sky met the smudge of the earth, it was easy to imagine the sun never coming back.

She snapped the final snap. The tube was repaired. The spores would be expelled.

The Museum of Genius was saved, she told herself. The Bublinaplex was saved. Her success did not feel especially momentous. No, it felt just like giving up, but at the right time.

Soon the artificial stars on the inside of the dome were twinkling to life around Margo.

She willed the leeches to let go.

The safety net caught her, and in that immense hammock under the false stars and nearly a mile above the ground, she relaxed and fell fast into a deep, dreamless sleep.

TWENTY-FOUR

"Ghost heads in my eyes!" Margo heard O'Keefe shrieking down the stairwell from above. "Ghost heads in my mouth! Ghost heads under my fingernails!"

Margo was running up the stairs, straining her short legs to take two steps at a time. Her muscles ached. Her lungs burned.

She stepped up onto a landing at the same time as O'Keefe and his cyborg escorts rounded a corner. "Get their teeth out from under my skin!" he howled while using the squirt gun to fire streams of water into the air. Margo guessed its tank must hold at least a half gallon. It looked heavy and awkward as he wheeled around, firing in all directions at imaginary enemies. The six cyborgs surrounding O'Keefe meanwhile completely ignored what he was doing. They continued to push him down the steps.

Margo called out to him: "Sub-Chief!"

He did not hear her. She called him again. She waved her arms in the air. She called him again and finally his eyes met hers. "Drop the gun!" Margo said. "Please, Sub-Chief. Drop the gun."

He stared at her with frightened animal eyes. "Get out of here, Inspector Chicago!" he shouted. "Save yourself!"

"I'm the one trying to save you!" said Margo. "Drop the gun! Please!"

"Drop the gun?" said O'Keefe, seeming utterly perplexed by the idea of such an object as a gun, of such an action as dropping.

"Yes!" Margo was walking down the stairs backwards now, holding the railing. The cyborgs pressed O'Keefe forward. She wanted to keep talking to him and she wanted to keep a safe distance between herself and the contaminated water. Her hallucinating boss was squirting it everywhere.

"No," said O'Keefe. "I can't surrender. Not now. Not with the air filled with these biting ghost heads. Here comes one now!" He shot a stream through the space between two cyborgs toward Margo. She jumped back, lost her balance, and fell backwards a few steps down the stairs. She landed on her elbows and against the wall on the marble floor of the next landing down.

The fall hurt but she was fine. She was losing her patience.

When she stood up she noticed a work of art on the wall beside her. It was a pointillist assemblage or something like that, a picture made out of hundreds of billiard balls, golf balls, tennis balls, ping pong balls, and baseballs as well as deflated basketballs, footballs, soccer balls, beach balls, and volleyballs, all set against a background of marbles that filled the spaces in between. Together the assembled balls made a picture, more clearly visible the farther back the viewer stood, of a pair of testicles. The piece was titled "Balls." Of course it was.

O'Keefe and his cyborg escorts were coming closer. She reached up to the work of art and yanked a tennis ball off of it. It was like what she imagined plucking fruit from a tree must be like. She then lobbed the ball as hard as she could at O'Keefe. It bounced off the square head of one of the cyborgs and smacked against O'Keefe's pointy nose. O'Keefe, seeming to think the ball was one of the ghost heads terrorizing him, freaked out. He screamed and fired the squirt gun in every direction.

Margo felt a few drops of water splash on her face. The front of her shirt felt cool. She looked down. She was wet. She took a deep breath and told herself the front of her shirt was wet because she'd been sweating so much. She told herself if she'd been contaminated with spores, she could deal with that after she stopped O'Keefe's descent.

She tore some marbles and golf balls off of "Balls" and threw them one at a time at O'Keefe's hands. She was trying to hit a knuckle or something to make him drop the squirt gun.

"Ouch," he said, giving her a wounded look when she did manage to strike his hand with a large marble. But he did not loosen his grip.

O'Keefe and the cyborgs joined Margo on the landing. Their descent seemed unstoppable. Margo felt flustered and frustrated. She had to keep trying.

In desperation, she tore a deflated beach ball off of "Balls," then charged at O'Keefe, who was still looking sadly at her between shots in the air at "ghost heads." She broke through the ring of cyborgs. Up against O'Keefe, she threaded the empty ball around the squirt gun, between the gun and O'Keefe's body, and pulled as hard as she could to dislodge it from her boss' grip. O'Keefe fought back. He lost his balance, and so did Margo, again. So did four of the six cyborgs.

They all tumbled together onto the marble floor. Margo found herself at the bottom of that pile of bodies. And she was completely drenched.

The squirt gun was flimsier than it looked.

O'Keefe stood up, and as he did the gun fell from his lap in dripping plastic pieces that clattered on the floor. Margo sat dripping in a puddle.

She looked around.

One second, everything was normal.

The next, everything turned into melting rainbow sherbet.

The screen-face of one of the cyborgs became the enormous balloon version of Margo's face from Warhol's installation. The face filled the stairway. It turned and looked at Margo with bulging compound eyes. With a great twirling tentacle nose it grabbed hold of O'Keefe and then delivered him screaming into its fang-filled jaws.

The balloon leered at Margo. It spoke, and as it spoke its eyes sunk back into its skull and its teeth stood up on its gums and the teeth performed a nightmarish dance on the thing's forked tongue to a rhythmic bleating that blared out of its nostrils.

The balloon was trying to tell her something but she couldn't understand what.

Waterfalls of purple blood erupted from the balloon head's ears and from the holes in the gums where the teeth had popped out from before they started dancing.

As Margo strained to listen to the balloon, the cyborgs surrounded her. She saw that the cyborgs were not cyborgs. She didn't know what they were, then she did. They were crumpled piles of burning paper. Purple flames licked up from the burning paper piles as they tried to stop her from speaking to her own balloon face. She stabbed at them with the pitchfork she hadn't realized she'd been carrying. They didn't stop trying to stop her from understanding the balloon face, which was now speaking from its eye sockets, which had become two mumbling mouths with fat tongues lolling out.

And she understood now the mouths were telling her the Bublinaplex dome was the shell of an unspeakable mollusk. All of humanity was living on this massive creature and the creature was in danger.

The mollusk was trying to escape from something that wanted to kill it but it was weak and slow. Even its mighty shell, which had protected it through the eons, was not strong enough to save it.

Margo didn't know if the balloon wanted her to be happy or sad about the mollusk, or if she was supposed to save it or kill it.

The more the balloon spoke, the less it seemed to matter.

Whatever was going to happen was what was going to happen. The only difference was that Margo now knew.

The burning piles of paper became burning fingers as Margo realized the six cyborgs made up a strange hand that carried her down the stairs and out of museum.

Being outside of the museum relieved Margo for a moment, but still she couldn't stop thinking that she wanted to get farther out. Out. Out. Out. The word repeated in her head like a chant. She was standing in the crowd surrounding the Museum of Genius and she had to get out. She was shrinking or the crowd was growing, the people were growing or climbing up on top of each other, becoming a wall or a wave of bodies. She was sure she'd drown underneath.

A big hand grabbed her shoulder and squeezed, hard.

It was a Community Safety officer. He wasn't even looking at her. His head was turned on its tree stump neck toward someone else. "This the one?" said his coarse voice to the someone else.

Then Margo saw the someone else: Chief Austen. She had a patch over one of her eyes and her body was blending into its surroundings like a shadow on a dark day.

"Yes," the Chief said. "Her."

All Margo could think was Out. Over and over again it kept repeating in her head. Out. Out. Out.

She tried wriggling free of the big hand. Its grip only tightened and then another big hand came down on her other shoulder. "Let go!" Where was that pitchfork? She tried to wriggle free. Her eyes searched the crowd for Beckett or O'Keefe or anyone who might help.

Out. Out. Out.

In the crowd, the sound of someone screaming momentarily drew Chief Austen and the big officer's attention.

The crowd parted. A woman with terror in her eyes and blood all over staggered through. One of her arms dangled from her shoulder on gory threads of muscle and skin. Entrails cascaded out of a gaping wound in her stomach. She dragged the innards along between her feet, then tripped on them and fell. She screamed again.

Throughout the crowd, people started screaming.

Then a blood-covered man appeared. He dragged a dead leg behind him. A great gash across his head exposed his brain. Cerebral goo dripped out and one of his eyeballs dangled from its socket.

Margo realized the officer's hands had disappeared from her shoulders.

She saw him disappear into the crowd, presumably to face whatever horror was ripping these people apart. Confronting that horror, he must have judged, was more important than dealing with Margo. Chief Austen was gone, too.

People backed up to make space for to the bloody man and woman dying face down in the grass. Then, together, the bloody man and woman sat up. A sound was coming out of their throats. For a moment Margo supposed that was what the last gasp of breath from dying lungs sounded like. The sound from their throats grew louder and louder.

Margo realized the man with the dangling eyeball and the woman who tripped on her guts were laughing. Hysterically. They were having trouble breathing, they were laughing so hard.

Another bloody, half-dismembered person flopped down in the pool of blood beside these two. And then another. And then another.

Before long, all of them were laughing hysterically.

And the attitude of the surrounding crowd had changed from shock and terror to anger, bemusement, and admiration of the craftsmanship that went into creating the fake gore and rubber body parts.

Dadaists, Margo figured. Anti-art performance pranksters. They must have planned this bloody spectacle for inside the Museum of Genius, once Hazard no. 457 opened, to make other viewers think Warhol's installation had mangled their bodies. They must have grown impatient. The crowd outside the museum must have been too tempting.

It wouldn't be long before that Community Safety officer with the large hands realized he'd been fooled. Margo heard the roar of a river of blood. She knew it wasn't real. Still it compelled her: Out. Out. Out.

She turned and ran as fast as she could away from the museum.

Out. Out. Out.

In Liminal Park she saw a Pest Control officer using an electric prod on a clutch of tardigrade hatchlings. He was nudging them into the cylindrical bed of the vehicle he would use to transport them.

Margo glanced back toward the crowd. A pair of Community Safety officers were following her. One was a round-faced, athletic young man. The other, an older, thicker-set man who could have been the younger man's father. Margo saw their bodies continually fusing together and then coming apart rearranged and mixed up, then fusing back together again, and in that moment what she feared most was that they would try to force her to fuse with their bodies.

She ran behind the Pest Control vehicle. The Pest Control officer was in the driver's seat now. He started the engine. The Community Safety officers were fast approaching on dozens of stilt-like spider legs. She thought she heard one call her name. The vehicle started lurching away and she hopped onto the back of it. Its bumper provided enough of a ledge for her to stand on. She held on tight to the cylindrical bed, her face against the cool metal spiral shutter that caged the tardigrades behind its metal sphincter. Like the hover cube, this vehicle didn't move quickly either.

The Community Safety officers jogged after the vehicle. It was easy for them to keep up with its slow pace. "Inspector Chicago," one said again. She thought he said more, too, but she couldn't hear it over the engine noise.

The younger officer trailed just a pace or two behind. When he closed the distance between himself and Margo, he lunged forward. He grabbed hold of her pant leg. She kicked back, though what she was kicking at, she wasn't sure. One second the officer was flesh and the next he was made of some sand-like substance and the next something like pebble flesh, then back to normal again.

Margo wouldn't let them take her to the Community Safety Asylum. Her compulsion to get out—whatever that meant—was too strong. Just the thought of being locked up made her feel suffocated.

The older officer was now grabbing for her other foot. Still kicking, Margo pulled herself up. She lost her grip. She almost fell off the back of the vehicle, tried to regain her balance, then started to fall into the mouth of the cylinder that contained the tardigrades. She kicked as hard as she could. The officer who had got hold of her pant leg let go.

The vehicle stopped abruptly. Margo lost her balance. She slipped forward and through the metal shutter and all the way into the cylinder.

It was dark. The startled baby tardigrades squeaked with alarm at Margo's sudden intrusion. Inside the cylinder the air was damp and close. The musty, mossy smell of the tardigrades' bodies filled her head.

There was barely enough room for her to turn around and find the way she'd come in. The tardigrades scrambled to the far end of the cylinder, instinctively assuming she must be something coming to eat them. She ran her hand along the inside where the opening had been. What had opened from the outside was from the inside hard, solid, and completely sealed.

Margo pushed against it. She had to get out. It didn't budge. Mindlessly, desperately she clawed with her fingers at where the opening had been until they bled. She must get out of this darkness, out of this cylinder. Out. Out. Out.

The vehicle was moving again. Thorsten appeared to her in the dark. He was a baby tardigrade. Margo was too confused to speak. Thorsten the tardigrade said he wished they could be friends again. He told Margo that he missed her and that he'd do anything to get her back into his life. He crawled toward her and closed his mouth on her still damp sleeve and began to suck at the moisture. Disgusted, Margo pulled back her arm. Undaunted, the Thorsten-tardigrade put its mouth on the end of her pant leg. Margo kicked it.

"I'm sorry Margo," said the Thorsten-tardigrade. "Goblin polyp spores are irresistible to us tardigrades. They're so delicious, we just can't help ourselves." It tried putting its mouth on her clothes again. She kicked it again. "Your clothes are saturated with soggy deliciousness," it said. "Just another taste— "

Margo started screaming.

"I know you want out," it said. "Remember what I told you about what happens to creatures captured inside the Bublinaplex."

She remembered. Pest Control would hold some creatures in the kennel for further study. And some were immediately expelled back into the Fungus Wasteland.

If the baby tardigrades were to be expelled, she would too.

Basically, she would be banished.

The Thorsten-tardigrade, understanding her understanding, nodded its little head. "Out. Out. Out," it said.

Margo knew the thought should frighten her.

In the dark, Margo and the Thorsten-tardigrade made up, went back to fighting, then made up again.

Time passed, maybe an hour. The tardigrades were no longer afraid of Margo. They snuffled and sniffed at her with their curious little heads. They sucked the spore-seasoned moisture from her clothes. Then the cylinder shook as it rammed into something hard. The far end of the cylinder clicked open. Blinding sunlight burst inside. The cylinder tilted. Margo and the tardigrades were being poured out.

She tried to grab hold of the smooth metal inside the cylinder but she could not. Then she was falling. She couldn't tell from how high. Higher than she would want to fall from. She inhaled. The foul air of the Fungus Wasteland burned her lungs.

When finally she landed, it was on top of the baby tardigrades. They squeaked and plodded away, their pudgy, grubby bodies lengthening and shortening as they sought hiding places within dense patches of undergrowth.

Margo stood up. Her body was bruised and her clothes were smeared with the filth of the Fungus Wasteland. She looked around. It was morning. Diffuse daylight through purple clouds cast dreamlike light on the monstrous landscape and the outside of the Bublinaplex dome.

She was out.

She started running.

She ran for a long time. Then she stopped to catch her breath. Then she ran some more. Her body ached and her lungs burned but she couldn't stop.

She ran until she tripped and fell and bumped her head on a stone. She would black out in the muck of despair.

When she awoke she would allow a pair of sludge leeches to take her arms and then she would use them to save herself.

TWENTY-FIVE

LATER

Margo awoke in a cell in the Community Safety Asylum.

How long was she lying there unconscious in the net above the city? She didn't know. She only vaguely remembered a pair of Community Safety officers strapping her into their hover cube and bringing her here. The leeches made the officers uncomfortable. She could sense their reluctance to touch them as they ushered her in.

Why shouldn't they have been reluctant? If she'd wanted to she could have grabbed the officers by the fronts of their shirts and tossed them out of her way like dolls.

At least they didn't ask many questions. They'd known who she was. For that she was thankful.

In the Asylum cell there was a gray bed with gray blankets, a gray pillow, and a little plastic table with a plastic chair. They gave her shapeless but clean and comfortable long-sleeve white pajamas to wear. There was a window in the cell that let in light but was too high up to look out of, kind of like the window in the kennel cell. On the wall was a flat, bodiless cyborg head she could use to watch broadcasts. Several paintings and drawings, all depicting scenes in the Fungus Wasteland, decorated the wall. Some of them were not very accurate. One in particular she thought was supposed to show a lobopod lunging after a slime grazer looked like it had been drawn by someone who had never seen either.

Her first meal in the Asylum was breakfast. An officer brought her an austere plate of egg spheres and oatmeal. As the officer delivered it he tried to make it sound awful: "Blind eyes and gruel," he called it.

But Margo thought the meal was lovely—the egg spheres were buttery and soft and the oatmeal was neither too watery nor too thick. Lunch was "lizard slivers on loaf"—a sandwich of some kind of salami between two slices of warm bread. That was delicious too.

When dinner came—"Curdled regurgitation with bowel scrapings and maggot eggs"—and it was a kind of green curry with cubes of soft cheese over rice, Margo was sure that coming up with these revolting names for the dishes must have something to do with her guard's creative pursuit.

The worst thing about the meals was how frustrating it was to try holding a fork or a spoon or a knife with her suction cup hands.

Between meals, she sat and thought. Considering she was locked in a cell with a pair of enormous parasites attached to her, she felt like she should be more upset about how things had turned out. She wondered whether this overall sense of well-being was because of the leeches. Or had everything she'd been through, her life-and-death struggles with muck and lobopods and nimos, make her more easily contented with surroundings that lacked weird predators?

She decided it didn't matter. She was alright now and she could face whatever came next. She could face it and she knew she could handle it.

Inside the cell she felt safe. There was no risk of falling or being devoured or being experimented on. She had no mission. There was just the cell. She'd almost forgotten what safety felt like. It was glorious, not worrying, though now there was a part of her that couldn't stop thinking of all those hostile things in the Fungus Wasteland and what would happen if they got into the Bublinaplex.

The existence of those things made her sense of safety feel a little bit like a lie. Wasn't that something Lorcan Warhol told her?

What happened to Warhol anyway? Did the video evidence from Beckett's surveillance cameras set him free? Or was he here in the Asylum too? He could be her next-door neighbor and she wouldn't know. And Spreck, was he still hiding out in her apartment? Or was he captured and maybe that's part of why she was locked in a cell now?

No, Margo understood the system well enough to know that both of them almost certainly would be held responsible for the goblin polyp crisis. When it came to the destruction or near-destruction of the Museum of Genius, the Administration would not be forgiving. She was sure they would be charged with High Recklessness. She was sure she would too. Ultimately, that would mean banishment.

Maybe the three of them would be banished together. She laughed out loud at the thought. That would be fitting punishment, wouldn't it? The Recklessists and the safety inspector, wandering in the Fungus Wasteland. How long would those two last? How many times could she resist the temptation to just let some predatory thing eat them?

For the moment she wasn't afraid or angry or even annoyed at the injustice of the prospect of her own banishment. She was just tired, and now she could get that much-needed rest she was supposed to be getting before Spreck showed up and ruined everything.

Cuthbert visited in the afternoon. He was a weepy mess. He was allowed inside the cell and he put his big arms around Margo and hugged her like he didn't even notice the leeches and she hugged him back like she didn't even notice the front of his shirt was sopping with tears. "Everything will be alright," he said. "Everything will be alright."

For some reason hearing Cuthbert say everything will be alright made Margo surer everything wouldn't.

Cuthbert sat down in the chair beside the little table. He seemed tired. He looked at Margo. Though her sleeves covered the leeches, for the first time she felt self-conscious about them.

He started crying again.

Now it sunk in to Margo what a tragic case she must seem. She had leeches where her arms should be and she was locked in a cell and she'd never crochet again and no one would take her safety inspections seriously anymore and there was an immense mockery of her face on top of the Museum of Genius and now she was probably going to be banished.

She loved Cuthbert but she hated how he was seeing her and that how he was seeing her was changing the way she saw herself.

She tried talking to him but the right words didn't come. When he left, he didn't even say goodbye—he just gave a little nod and wiped his nose.

Afterward, Margo cried for the first time in a long time.

The next day he came back more composed.

"Your boss, O'Keefe, he wanted me to tell you he's alright," Cuthbert was saying as he sipped tea with Margo in her cell. "He says he wants to visit you himself but because of what passed between you and his boss, Chief Austen, he thinks he better not. He said, and I quote, he feels like a 'paper popsicle wrapped in wet socks.' Do you have any idea what that means?"

Margo chuckled. No, she did not. And they chuckled together. It was, for a brief moment, lovely.

"I also spoke with your friend Thorsten," he said. "The way he tells the story, you saved us. Everyone. The whole Bublinaplex."

"Is that right?" she said. She couldn't help smiling.

"He didn't say how, specifically. Just that you were able to fix that big tube over the museum. Now of course I believe him, but there's been nothing about what you've done or the tube needing repair on any news broadcasts. And throwing you in here is an awful way to say thank you. All I know about what happened, what anyone seems to know, is that the museum was contaminated and a guy who works there, Beckett I think his name is, came up with this idea to shoot the contamination out through the big tube, and I guess that's working, though the Recklessists are livid about Warhol's exhibit still not being opened yet."

"They would be," said Margo.

"That reminds me," Cuthbert went on. "Thorsten gave me something for you. Something he wanted you to have." He reached into his messenger bag and pulled out a flat, square package. Margo unwrapped it.

Inside was a hand-drawn comic book, "LEECH GIRL LIVES." The drawings were obviously Thorsten's. They were drawn in ink and colored with pencils. On the cover was a hero, clearly modeled after herself, leaping forward, maybe executing some kind of martial arts maneuver, into a tsunami of fierce-looking lobopods. She wasn't drawn with exaggerated boobs or made skinny or dressed in some weird bathing suit costume. It was just her, short and stocky as she was, in a somewhat stylized version of her yellow and black Art Safety uniform. And though the style was unmistakably Thorsten's, the drawings were actually not bad.

Inside the comic book were illustrations of Leech Girl fighting lobopods and tickle swarms and nimos and other monstrous things Margo was pretty sure had come from Thorsten's imagination. There was a story, but only just barely. Mostly it was just cool drawings of fight scenes.

Margo thought it was awesome.

Her one quibble was the diminutive "Girl" in the name. She was almost thirty. She was not a "girl." But whatever. She could call Thorsten out on that when she saw him. After the way Lorcan Warhol had portrayed her with that grotesque, inflated caricature over the installation, she loved seeing this flattering, semi-accurate representation of herself.

She cried again. "Tell him to come see me," she told Cuthbert. "Tell him I said I'll try to stop holding what happened in the past against him."

The next day, Margo had no visitors. She was disappointed, but it passed quickly anyway as she read and re-read "LEECH GIRL LIVES." Yes, she recognized herself in that hero. It was a better version of herself, one that didn't think about killing herself or giving up. There were times in her life when she would have found being held to such a high standard depressing. Today, it was inspiring.

The next day seemed like it would be another without visitors. Then, at about the time dinner usually was served, Belga appeared.

Margo had been lying in bed, thinking. Belga entered the cell and stood at her bedside. Belga's cyborg, clothed in a crisp white uniform, followed. She put a cool hand on Margo's cheek. "Are you awake?"

"I'm not asleep."

Belga stepped toward the center of the room. "Get up," she said gently. "Let's talk."

Margo sat up in bed. "What do you and I have to talk about?" she said. She was surprised by her own anger, which she knew was partly because of Thorsten's failure to visit. So what if she took it out on Belga. What was Belga to her now, anyway? What concern of Belga's was Margo's predicament now? "You broke Cuthbert's heart."

"Come with me. Let's take a walk."

"I'm not wearing pants," said Margo. "And I'm locked inside this room."

Belga glanced around the room and found Margo's pajama pants on a chair. She picked them up and tossed them toward her bed. "Here," she said. "The door is open. Let's go." Margo pulled her pants on. Together they left the cell, with Belga in the lead and her uniformed cyborg following behind Margo. A guard standing in the hall outside gave them a curt nod of acknowledgement.

They walked down the Asylum's brightly lit corridors, past scores of cell doors identical to her own. Margo couldn't tell if the cells were empty or occupied. The guards they met along the way seemed to pretend not to see them, as if a prisoner out of a cell was merely an embarrassing observation that no one minded so long as no one spoke of it out loud.

Margo wondered where she was being taken but didn't ask. She was afraid of what the answer might be. She knew Belga worked as a "courier" for the Executive Designer but she never understood what that meant. All she knew was that Cuthbert never wanted to talk about it. Maybe her job was delivering Asylum inmates to the Shame Administration. Maybe her job was delivering those guilty of High Recklessness into banishment.

The truth was, Margo loved Belga like a Mentor. Even if she was pissed off about how Belga was treating Cuthbert, it was the kind of pissed off you feel only at people you love when they let you down.

They approached an unguarded cell door at the end of the hall. Belga opened it, then placed a hand on Margo's shoulder to guide her inside.

Through the door was a balcony and on the balcony was a cafe table with an open bottle of white wine, two wine glasses, and two chairs.

Belga took a seat and poured the wine. "Are you comfortable?" Her sharply-dressed cyborg stood behind her chair. At Belga's invitation, Margo took a seat too.

"That depends, I guess," Margo said. She looked at the semi-sphere of her glass, then met Belga's eyes. She looked worried.

Margo thought a sip of wine sounded nice, but hesitated when she remembered the leeches. She didn't know if she was even capable of holding a wine glass without dropping it. "Are you going to banish me?"

Belga knitted her fingers together. "That decision rests with the Executive Designer. It doesn't look good, and I'm afraid there's nothing I can do about it."

"So why are you here?"

"Two reasons, one official reason and one unofficial. The official reason is the reason I'm here on the Administration's behalf: to make sure you are comfortable." She picked up her glass and took a sip. "So. Are you comfortable?"

Looking at Belga reminded Margo of when she was young, when sitting across from her at the dinner table with Cuthbert was a highlight of the day. The company was so loving and the home-cooked food was so satisfying and meanwhile Margo the teenager was only just becoming comfortable in her own skin, just overcoming her self-doubt. It was talking with Belga, seeing her confidence about what she liked and her blunt indifference to what she didn't that demonstrated to Margo the kind of person she wanted to be. And even if she never did fully become that person, she was at least somehow more herself than she'd ever been.

"I've been comfortable enough here in the Asylum I guess," she said. "But I'm not very comfortable right now."

Belga's face pinched into a look of concern. "Is there anything I can do?"

Margo took a deep breath. Was she about to cry? She'd never been a crier. Now it seemed like she was crying all the time. It was a change she didn't think she could blame on the leeches. She thought Belga must be able to tell and that she must think she's just like Cuthbert. But Belga had loved Cuthbert for years. Why hold back?

Margo held up her suction cup hands. "I've got giant fucking leeches for arms," she said. "I have to use these fucking suction cups for hands. That glass of wine looks awesome. But I don't think I can pick it up without dropping it or spilling it all over myself." Her voice cracked. "And that's kind of bumming me out, you know? That's kind of making me think, jeez, I don't really want a can of soda with a curly fucking straw sticking out of it but that would have been better, I wouldn't have gotten all upset over that and I probably could have drank it without any trouble. Do you understand?"

Belga snapped her fingers. Her cyborg leaned forward over her shoulder. "Get Margo a straw," she said. The cyborg straightened up, then hurried out. "Sorry about that oversight," Belga said to Margo. "I thought this little setup out here on the balcony might be nice. Theatrical perhaps, but nice. My cyborg will fetch a straw from the commissary for you."

They sat in silence for a moment, Margo staring at her glass, Belga lifting hers for the occasional sip. "So," Margo said, "What happens next?"

"Well, now that I know you're reasonably comfortable, or will be soon, I'll move on to my unofficial reason for being here." Belga arched an eyebrow. "Which is to tell you something you're not supposed to know."

"About what?"

"About banishment," Belga said. "Because I think you're going to have to face the fact that you will be banished. I think I owe it to you to let you know what you're in for."

Margo was stunned. Would she really be forced to walk down that terrible aisle in the Temple of Shame? The possibility of banishment was only just now becoming real to her. Though she'd been through the Fungus Wasteland, the thought terrified her.

"Number one," Belga said, "Contrary to popular belief, banishment is not a death sentence."

Margo gave Belga a skeptical look. "You mean all the banished people are surviving somewhere out there in the Fungus Wasteland, living on mushrooms and fighting off lobopods?" She shook her head. "I'm sorry, Belga. I've been out there. I know what it's like. I can't see how it's possible."

"You're right," Belga said. "There is no way people would survive out there. It's actually quite amazing that you survived long enough to get back inside the dome, albeit not unharmed."

"Then how can you say that banishment is not a death sentence?"

Belga folded her hands together. The cell door behind Margo opened with a clatter. It was the cyborg with a straw. The cyborg dropped the straw into Margo's wine glass, then resumed its post behind its master.

"What I mean," Belga said, "is that no one who is banished actually sets foot in the wasteland. I mean the whole idea that the punishment for recklessness is to be sent out into the wasteland to die like a sick slime grazer pup is a lie. Yes, that is what you and everyone else who grows up inside the Bublinaplex is taught, probably since before earlier than you can remember. But it's just not true."

Margo thought of Cuthbert and all her other Mentors who taught her about the justice system. She thought of Chief Austen and all the higher ups in the Tower of Safety—of everyone whose job it was to fight recklessness.

"But the Temple of Shame," Margo said. "And the whole ritual with people throwing useful things at the person being banished. And the Shame Administrator—how can all of it be a lie?"

"It can be," Belga said, "because it is." She poured Margo more wine. "It's all a performance. It's all theater. It's also not the only thing in this city that's false but presented as fact, but it's the only one of these falsehoods you need to hear about today."

Margo leaned forward and took a slurp of wine from her straw. She leaned back. "Why should I believe you?"

"Just think about it. And think about what happened to Jasper. Doesn't condemning someone to death because he leaves the dome—leaves to try to save some kid's life even—seem, I don't know, excessive?"

"I don't know," Margo shrugged. "People died. I mean, I know it wasn't Jasper's fault. Everyone knew that. So I guess you're right. I'm just so used to thinking of it in a different way, the way that I was taught to think of it, so it's hard to understand."

"You're used to thinking that perpetrators of 'High Recklessness' deserve banishment. Hell, it's been your job. So I can see how this is hard."

"No. I guess I've always thought it was excessive. But it never occurred to me that the system being excessive meant that it could be wrong. I always thought there must be a good reason for it the system to be excessive and brutal and remorseless. That maybe it's excessive by design. As if maybe our survival relies on the system's excessiveness."

"Yes Margo, the Bublinaplex does rely on the system's appearance of excessiveness, even brutality. But it doesn't actually have to be those things to be effective. It's for safey's sake that you're led to believe our penal system is so unforgiving. The lie prevents recklessness—you, as the top Art Safety inspector, should understand how important that is for the Administration. And the truth is, the people who run the Bublinaplex would say they need the people who are banished—just not in the same way that it needs those who live out their whole lives inside the dome."

Now Margo was angry again. Angry and confused. Had so much of how she thought about the world really been built on lies? And Margo realized there had been some comfort for her in knowing what happened after you're banished. You were sent out to the Fungus Wasteland, where you'd die. But if you're not banished to the Fungus Wasteland when you're banished, where do you go?

And what had happened to Jasper?

Margo's eyes met Belga's. "So then what happens when you're banished?"

Belga raised an eyebrow. "You're sent ... elsewhere. Somewhere where you still can be useful."

"Belga, please. Where?"

"It isn't really a question of where," she said. Her cyborg started to make a buzzing sound. "It's more like when." Then, seeming to read the thought foremost in Margo's mind. "And when you are banished, Jasper could very well be waiting to greet you on the other side."

Belga turned toward the cyborg as it bowed to show her who was calling. She frowned. "I'm sorry," she said. "I can't ignore this." She stood up. "Please excuse me." And Belga walked out into the hallway with her cyborg. "Belga Breugel speaking," she said before shutting the door behind her.

Belga was out in the hall for several minutes. Meanwhile, Margo's imagination had been lit up in a confusion of possibilities and puzzles. She repeatedly asked herself what Belga could have meant when she said "more like when." Time travel? That didn't make sense. But if the banished were no longer in the dome but not out in the wasteland either, what other answer was there? And wherever or whenever Jasper is, could Belga's insinuation that she could be reunited with him after she's banished possibly be true?

Margo thought hard. Belga could have been lying. Maybe what Belga was saying seemed too good to be true because it wasn't true. Maybe banishment really was just a death sentence, and maybe Belga's real creative pursuit was telling stories to people who were about to be banished in order for the process to run a little more smoothly. In order for those who are banished to go willingly. That seemed more plausible than time travel.

Belga and her cyborg returned to the balcony. Margo was about to ask her more about what "more like when" meant. If time travel was truly what Belga was insinuating, she would insist on proof. Maybe a cat. A living, breathing cat might prove to her that time travel was possible. Otherwise she would have to convince herself Belga was lying. She would have to convince herself there really was no chance of surviving banishment or seeing Jasper ever again.

Then Margo saw the worried look on Belga's face. "That was Executive Designer Fash's office," she said.

"So it's official," Margo said, unable to stifle a small smile.

"I'm going to be banished, aren't I?"

And in that instant, she decided to go back on everything she'd decided the instant before. To hell with the cat. If banishment was inevitable, she would let herself believe what Belga had said about it not being a death sentence. It was a chance to be with Jasper again. So what if it was a lie. She would believe it. Wasn't the choice she now faced between one world of lies and another? Believing Belga meant believing she'd been lied to all her life. Not believing Belga meant clinging to a hopeless truth.

"No," said Belga, shaking her head, "You're free to go."

TWENTY-SIX

Belga led Margo out of the Asylum. Belga's cyborg followed. As they waited on the ground floor for Margo's paperwork to be finished, Belga explained to Margo what the Executive Designer expected from her in exchange for her freedom.

Margo's ugly, insubordinate attack on the Art Safety Department's Chief Austen would be forgiven, at least as far as the Administration was concerned. Her willingness to selflessly put herself in harm's way for the people of the Bublinaplex had been noted. Her death-defying repair job to the spore tube was, in the Executive Designer's words according to Belga, "nothing short of heroic."

Now Margo's help was needed on a different matter—a dire situation the Executive Designer ominously called the "tardigrade apocalypse."

"Tardigrade apocalypse?" Margo repeated back to Belga.

"The Executive Designer says huge tardigrades are gathering outside of the dome and trying to climb up onto it. Pest Control says they're attracted to the plume of goblin polyp spores being siphoned out of the museum, which are now erupting from the top of the dome. Tardigrades love to eat goblin polyps, apparently."

"So why is it an 'apocalypse' then?"

"The Administration believes there are enough big tardigrades out there that if even a tiny fraction of them are able to climb up onto the dome, the dome will collapse." Belga took a deep breath. "It could be the end the Bublinaplex."

"The end?" Margo had only been half paying attention. She was still ruminating on the idea that banishment might or might not be what she'd always thought it was, and that much of what she'd supposedly known about the world was based on lies. Now Belga was asking her to confront the idea that her world—founded on lies or not—faced imminent destruction. She felt sick. They stepped outside.

"I know no one worked harder than you to stop the goblin polyp spores from spreading, and to eject them from the dome." Belga pointed upward. On the dome there was an irregular blotch like a black cloud. "See that darkness overhead? That's the polyps growing on top of the dome."

"The tube that was supposed to funnel the spores out," Margo muttered. "Oh god. They botched it. And I helped."

Belga nodded. "If that dome comes down, everything you encountered out in the Fungus Wasteland will take hold inside the Bublinaplex. First the predators, then the fungus. Everyone will die. Everything you've ever loved, every work of art, every place, every person, destroyed." She hugged herself as if she was cold. "This is not how it's supposed to happen."

At that moment the sun must have come out from behind some clouds. An abnormal, diffuse brightness shone down from overhead from around the fungus blotch. The leeches withdrew into the long sleeves of Margo's inmate pajama top. "And the Executive Designer thinks I can somehow stop this from happening?"

"Apparently."

Margo felt overwhelmed. She'd made Lorcan Warhol's installation safe. She'd fought for her life in the Fungus Wasteland. She'd been imprisoned and told to expect banishment, she'd been told banishment as she knew it was a lie, been given hope she might live and once again meet the man she loved and thought was dead.

And now she was being asked to save humanity from extinction.

"It would be crazy for me to say 'no'," said Margo.

"This way," Belga said, gesturing toward the Imagination Cultivation Administration building, just visible at the east end of Liminal Park. Most people referred to the building as "the Grapes." Dozens of red, bulbous sections, each of which roughly corresponded to a department, made up the building. The sections would routinely shift and slide and move around so different departments within the Administration were beside each other at different times, a design supposedly intended to reflect the non-hierarchical nature of the Administration's work. Of course, everyone knew that it didn't matter if the Executive Designer's office was on the top floor or the ground floor or somewhere in the middle. He was in charge.

"Right," said Margo, and they started toward the Grapes.

Then as soon as Margo sensed Belga wasn't paying attention, she turned in the opposite direction and started running fast as she could.

From behind she heard Belga yelling something unintelligible. Seconds later, Belga's cyborg was giving chase and getting close.

Margo stopped. Her leech arms unfurled from her sleeves. She reached out with them and shoved the cyborg, hard. She heard something crack as it hit the ground. It tried to get up but it couldn't. It kept trying, like a half-crushed bug.

Margo and Belga stood looking at each other across the distance between them. It was far enough that Margo couldn't clearly make out Belga's face. She half expected Belga to chase after her now. But it was hard for her to imagine Belga exerting herself like that—running, sweating, panting, her heart pounding. Such bodily activities seemed in Margo's mind somehow below Belga. And she did not move.

Margo turned and ran again.

She ran until she reached a public restroom stall at the edge of Liminal Park. She ducked inside. She didn't need to use it. This particular stall was a place where when she was younger and feeling depressed she would lock herself away. She hadn't thought of it at all for a long time but she remembered thinking of it then as her fortress.

But with Belga telling her that banishment could mean a reunion with Jasper, then telling her she wouldn't be banished at all and instead was needed to get back to work saving the Bublinaplex and she wouldn't have any choice in any of this, something snapped. She could handle being a selfless hero. She could handle being Leech Girl. But being a hero who did what she did simply because she was told to do so? Because she was expected to be obedient, like a cyborg? No. She was no cyborg.

Now she actually wanted to be banished. That was the problem. She wanted to see Jasper and she wanted to get away from Belga and Community Safety officers and the Executive Designer. She was confused. She was tired. She was sick of it.

The toilet seat was painted chrome. Fragrant chemicals in the stall masked any bathroom odors. The smell was the same as it was years ago, and this familiarity comforted Margo. The stall was cool and its walls were dense with graffiti. For a minute she sought familiar graffiti, then remembered she'd seen the stall wall of her youth on display in a gallery. This wall and this graffiti must have been new.

There was a ventilation slit to Margo's right and a magazine holder to her left. Sitting on the toilet she could look out through the slit and watch games of Field Pretend being played on a hilly section of the park twenty yards away.

Belga's words looped over and over again in Margo's head: "It isn't really a question of where. It's more like when. And when you're banished, I bet Jasper will be waiting to greet you on the other side."

What did she mean "when"?

What did she mean "the other side"?

She didn't care if Jasper was underground or on another planet or in the future or in the past. Finding him seemed like the most important thing she could do. She wanted to be where he was. But even the simple act of entertaining the idea felt to Margo like a deeply subversive act.

She would have to find out more. She should've pressed Belga for answers. She could have insisted her help saving the Bublinaplex was conditional on more information.

But Margo honestly didn't really want to help. She was tired of helping, especially considering her reward last time she tried to help was a stay in the Community Safety Asylum.

Maybe refusing to do what the Executive Designer wanted her to do was the easiest way to get herself banished. But she couldn't really want to get banished. Could she? Were her thoughts and feelings being manipulated by the leeches again? Did they think banishment meant a return to the Fungus Wasteland? Had they not been paying attention? Why would they want to go back out?

Margo went back and forth like this for a while. Through the slit in the bathroom stall wall she watched a game of Field Pretend being played outside. The story being made up for the game was being performed by two teams, one wearing formal suits that made their wearers look like archaic English bank clerks or something and the other dressed up like large flightless birds. Some of the suit-wearers were attacking some of the birds. Some of the birds appeared to be trying to have sex with some of the suits. Some of them pantomimed the act of eating one another, complete with oversized plates and prop forks and knives for carving whomever was playing at being eaten.

Margo could not tell who which team was supposed to be the protagonists or which the antagonists. She thought she'd seen this arrangement played out before. "Dodo Revolt," she remembered it was called. If either team was winning, she couldn't tell.

She looked into the magazine holder. Usually there were catalogues from the Fashion District and copies of weekly gossip rags containing event listings about upcoming gallery openings. There was one publication she thought she recognized and she grabbed it with a suction cup hand and pulled it out.

She looked at the cover: LEECH GIRL LIVES.

She stood up and charged out of her stall to look in the magazine holders in the other stalls. Each one contained a glossy-covered copy of LEECH GIRL LIVES.

Cursing Thorsten, she returned to her stall. She wanted to scream. How dare he? She'd thought the comic was just for her. The hand-drawn version Cuthbert had given her was obviously just the original. She'd thought it was an intimate gesture. She thought Thorsten was telling her alone that she was a hero. That had seemed nice. That had seemed thoughtful. But no. Apparently he meant to tell the world she was a hero. Her mind raced as she tried to put her anger into words.

She thought of the *Venus de Milo*, that poor armless statue. As a Mentee she'd asked repeatedly, "Who is she?" She couldn't remember anything about the Quinary Mentor giving the museum tour that day except his inability to give her a satisfying answer. He said she was Venus, the goddess of love.

"No," Margo had replied, "I mean the woman, who is she?" He then offered some half-hearted words about "some woman" in ancient Greece. He went on to say that nothing also was known about the artist who created her, so "of course" nothing was known about the model.

Now Thorsten had done to Margo what had been done to the woman who was the model for that statue. Who she really was didn't matter anymore—what others would see now was the character she'd become, the idea she represented. Somehow, this hurt more than Warhol's balloon-faced caricature of her, which was so ridiculous and grotesque, of course it didn't really represent her. But Thorsten's comic made her into a hero and being a hero came with expectations. She *knew* she would disappoint.

Margo sat with the leeches bent on her knees like elbows and rested her head in her suction cup hands. For a while she sat there like that, alone in the bathroom stall, thinking.

When she sat up she noticed a flurry of hearts sketched on the door in front of her. They were not the hearts she'd drawn on this stall wall years ago, but they reminded her that drawing hearts on the old stall wall was something she'd done.

She remembered the day she'd drawn hearts in the stall. It was the day she and Jasper first met.

She was sixteen. A Tertiary Mentor whose name Margo now could not remember had invited Jasper to speak in front of her class about ways the Bodily Safety Department took care of people. Jasper was fifteen, but already he had been helping out with various tasks at Bodily Safety for years.

Jasper talked about ways of getting hurt that had never occurred to any of the twenty or so other Mentees in the room, even the SafetyPunks. He talked about chemical burns from art supplies and out-of-control infections requiring amputations and transplants. With detached wonder, he described cancers that devoured a patient's innards and radiation treatments that nearly killed patients while the physicians attempted to cure them.

She remembered him seeming so confident and sincere, the way his young, serious face set itself to convey such hard truths, the way he hardly moved his arms and legs at all as he spoke. She was fascinated by how he expressed his passionate interest in safety so dispassionately. It was as if the harms being described were completely inconsequential for the people in the room, as if the Mentees need not worry about even being harmed in the ways he described, the same way someone might describe flaws in an obsolete model of hover cube.

Thorsten was in the room too. Margo remembered him asking questions about victims of animal attacks. He asked, "Have you seen what a tickle swarm does to a person?" and "Have you seen what a lobopod can do?" and "Have you seen what a nemo can do?" The room's patience with Thorsten wore thin, but Jasper gave succinct but graphically thorough answers to each question.

Jasper surprised the classroom with an anecdote about the worst animal attack injuries he'd ever seen. A man had tried to catch a tardigrade cub that somehow wandered into his studio. The official explanation for the man's actions was that he'd been afraid the tardigrade would tip over a particularly brittle sculpture, the man's work in progress. The creature was only about the size of a large loaf of bread. He thought he could grab the animal and shove it away from his art. But the cub was stronger than he thought. Its attempts to wriggle free after the man picked it up resulted in permanent disfigurement from the two-inch claws at the ends of each of the tardigrade's eight nubby legs, which it raked across the man's face, chest, and stomach.

As Margo sat in the bathroom stall remembering Jasper, she watched a broad-shouldered suit-wearing player on the Field Pretend field wearing a big fake paper maché head swinging an enormous fake sword. In her head, Margo named him King Suit. King Suit's opponent was a giant flightless bird puppet containing at least four people, Margo guessed. She called it King Bird.

Margo wondered how Jasper would react to the leeches. Would they disgust him? Probably. She looked at them. Reggie and Leroy. Rita and Lola. Whatever. They were part of her now. They'd saved her life. They made her not want to give up.

If Jasper cared about her he would understand: the leeches were part of her now.

But if he didn't understand, what then?

King Bird meanwhile was trying to bite King Suit's butt. The bird was defending an egg, and out of the egg hatched a person wearing a costume, a guitar with arms and legs. The guitar with arms and legs was playing a saxophone. At the end of the scene, suit-wearers hanged themselves with their ties as triumphant birds squawked in their nests, bracing for an attack by the hanged suit-wearers, who had become zombies.

Margo was wondering how the next scene would begin when several hover cubes landed on the field. The cubes bore the red and black stripes of the Structural Safety Department. The crowd of Field Pretend players and spectators dispersed.

A long vehicle also bearing the Structural Safety Department's stripes rolled onto the field. Behind the long vehicle was a metal container at least twice the size of the house Margo had grown up in. The container opened. The mechanical thing inside looked like a compact tangle of steel girders. With a hiss and whir of hydraulics, it started moving. Slowly, the thing was stretching itself out like an immense accordion.

Little by little, the immense metal accordion stretched from the ground all the way up to the dome. The base of the container sunk down into the ground. Dozens of impossibly long, telescoping metal extensions unfurled from the thing in every direction. Margo watched it complete its task, and was impressed.

It was a mobile buttress, a support meant to reinforce the dome—presumably an attempt to hold it up under the tardigrades advancing up the side.

Margo stepped out of the bathroom stall and saw that the buttress on the field was just one of dozens around Liminal Park newly extending from the ground to the dome.

How long could the supports hold up the dome? How many mountain-sized tardigrades could they bear? Margo wondered. She also wondered what part of the dome would be the first to collapse and whether the people living underneath would try to evacuate or if they would understand evacuation would be useless.

Margo remembered raising her hand to ask Jasper a question. She was as deep into Art Safety at sixteen as Jasper was into Bodily Safety at fifteen, and she was especially furious at the growing trend of Recklessism in art.

"Weren't those people who died just being reckless?" she asked. "Didn't they, in a way, deserve what they got?"

Jasper thought for a minute, then replied: "If you saw these patients suffering in their beds, bleeding and crying while friends and Mentors gathered around, I don't think you'd say anyone deserves that. When people panic, they become reckless. They can't help it. The Bodily Safety Department's job is simply to help them. Not judge them."

Margo could not predict how Jasper would react to the leeches. He might accept them. He might hate them.

But she thought she could predict how he'd react if he learned she'd joined him in banishment because she'd refused to help save the Bublinaplex.

He'd never forgive her.

She wouldn't give up on getting banished. But if she was going to be banished, she wanted it to be because of something she did recklessly trying to save the Bublinaplex, not because she refused.

So she would help. But she would be reckless about it.

She kicked open the restroom door, then walked up to the Structural Safety workers standing near the base of a buttress. They were looking up through binoculars toward where it touched the dome. Hover cubes piloted by their colleagues floated around the connection points.

"What are you guys doing?" Margo asked.

"Trying to stop the tardigrade apocalypse," said one worker.

"You think these buttresses will work?" she said.

"I think they'll buy us time," said the worker.

"Time for what?"

"Time for all of us to kiss each other goodbye," he said. "Or time for some hero to figure out how to save us," he said.

"So you need a hero," Margo said.

The worker lowered his binoculars. He looked Margo in the eye. "We sure as hell need something."

TWENTY-SEVEN

Margo hijacked the Structural Safety worker's red and black hover cube.

It was easy. She just unfurled the leeches and pried open the door and tossed out the supervisor who'd been dozing in the passenger seat. And then she was off.

She steered the hover cube toward the Museum of Genius. Teeth clenched, she ruminated about how pissed off she was at Thorsten and Belga and the Executive Designer and Warhol and Spreck. They all needed her to save them? FINE. Maybe she'd make them regret it. Maybe she'd make them wish they hadn't fucked up so much that they now needed saving.

She'd be their hero alright. But she'd destroy as much as possible in the process of saving everyone's life.

It would serve them right.

When she got to the museum she crash-landed the hover cube into the line of cyborgs guarding the front door. None were harmed thanks to the inflatable cushions that popped out of the bottom of the cube, but still, she thought it was a hell of an entrance. A hero's entrance. Whatever.

She leapt out of the hover cube and hurried toward the doors. The nearest cyborgs got up and tried to stop her. She looked up. The dizzyingly high tube of of material covering the building was a mile high, all the way up to the inside of the center of the dome. Cyborg hands were closing around her ankles and shoulders. The museum doors were locked. She grabbed hold of one using both suction cup hands. Teeth clenched, she ripped it from its hinges then used the part of the door that came off in her suction cup hands to beat back the cyborgs.

The inside of the museum was a wind tunnel. Massive fans roared all around to blow out the goblin polyp spores. A purplish-gray coating of fungal slime coated the atrium from floor to ceiling. The actual spore-bearing stalks of the polyps must have been blown out by the fans. The wind was blowing so strong that it was hard to stand in one place.

Margo's plan for stopping the tardigrade apocalypse was simple: she would use brute force.

Turning away a few tardigrades trundling along on top of the dome would be easy, she reasoned, since she'd already defeated two lobopods and an arachnimonite. Sure, there supposedly were a lot of tardigrades. Dozens, hundreds, she didn't know. And, of course, there was the issue of their hugeness. That didn't bother her. She wasn't in any hurry. And when she used her leech arms, she hardly felt like she was exerting herself at all.

The question of outwitting the beasts didn't even cross her mind. Of course she could outwit them. People had a saying in the Bublinaplex: "The only thing dumber than a tardigrade is a tardigrade egg."

On her way to the stairs she stopped in the atrium and looked around. Standing in that room she couldn't help thinking about the night of The Tragedy and the final inspection of Warhol's installation that she never performed. She remembered wanting to stop Warhol, Spreck, and the rest of Warhol's assistants from being blamed for The Tragedy. In a way, she supposed she still did, even if they did still probably deserve to be banished.

At least believing as she now did that banishment probably wasn't a death sentence made her feel less guilty about Warhol's imminent banishment.

She ran up the stairs. Somewhere around the landing beside what was left of the "Balls" picture, she realized that running up the steps was not exhausting her the way it did the last time. Were the leeches responsible for this strange stamina? No other explanation made sense. She wondered for a moment if they might also have a hidden drawback. No, she reassured herself. Having big leeches attached to her forever probably was drawback enough.

When she reached the museum rooftop—the space now filled by Warhol's installation, Hazard no. 457—she found Oliver Beckett blocking her way.

In his hands he held a long, shining metal sword. It was an old creature-killing weapon in the style of those once made by Smitty the weaponsmith. "I knew you'd come looking for me sooner or later, Inspector Chicago," he said, holding the sword out in front of him. "Or should I say, LEECH GIRL? As soon as I heard you'd survived the wasteland and come back, I knew."

Margo was confused. And annoyed. She was busy saving the Bublinaplex from the tardigrade apocalypse. She didn't care about what Beckett was doing, she wasn't looking for him, and she certainly didn't have time for this. "I don't know what you're talking about," she said. "Can we talk about this later?"

She started to go around him. He thrust the sword at her. "Watch it," Margo said, still sounding more annoyed than threatened.

Beckett pointed the sword at her like it was a gun. "You've never read Lorcan Warhol's *Recklessist Manifesto*, have you?"

"What?" Margo said, her annoyance turning to anger.

"Warhol's manifesto says almost nothing on display in this so-called 'Museum of Genius' deserves to be here. And if you worked here every day like I do, you'd know Warhol is right. There are halls upon halls here of sentimental landscapes, narcissistic portraits, pretentious abstractions, and childish scribblings. They're not works of 'genius'. They're gravestones marking utterly insipid moments in the history of our obsolete, self-centered ancestors."

He jabbed the sword toward Margo, forcing her to hop backwards. She regained her footing, then dryly replied, "No, Oliver. I've never read the *Recklessist Manifesto*."

Beckett raised his chin. "But you must at least be aware of the utter stupidity of the things our artists can't help but create under the influence of the 'works of genius' in this building," he sneered. "They make paintings of imagined pastoral scenes, of trees and mountains, of parasol-carrying aristocrats. When they do portray our synthesized food or Field Pretend games or Pest Control officers, they do so as if there is some dignity in it, which there most definitely is not. They slop colors and images and 'found objects' around to express feelings that would be better kept private. 'Genius'," he spat the word with the bitterest contempt. "Please."

As Beckett spoke, he held his sword alarmingly close to Margo's chin. "But look," she said. "Look around you. We're standing in the middle of Warhol's 'genius' installation. I remember what a big fan of his you are. His art, honored here, that counts for something, doesn't it? As soon as this mess with the goblin polyp spores is cleaned up, everyone is in the Bublinaplex will line up to witness the brilliance of your favorite artist— "

"Favorite artist!" Beckett shrieked and stomped his foot like an angry toddler, the sword blade quivering in his trembling hand. "You know as well as I—probably better than I—that Lorcan Warhol is a fraud and a hypocrite. That was your secret, the secret between the two of you. You thought you could get away with it. But I figured it out." He lowered his sword. Then he raised it again, shouting, "But you figured it out that I figured it out! So now here we are."

Margo understood that Beckett was completely unhinged but she had no idea what he was talking about. Still, she played along, hoping it might distract him long enough for her to sneak past him and deal with the tardigrades. "You're right," she said. "And now here we are. Face to face. Finally."

"Finally indeed," said Beckett, smiling the way one might smile to endure pain. "You know I realized what was happening up here with Hazard no. 457 while Warhol was working on it. I saw on my surveillance monitors how he and his assistants were politely removing everything unsafe about what should have been a masterpiece of truly genius Recklessist recklessness. And so, before anyone else, I saw Hazard no. 457 for what it was: a sham. There was nothing truly unsafe about it. Warhol wasn't trying to sneak anything past your safety inspection efforts. He was giving you what you wanted—and in so doing, betrayed everything he'd made himself seem to stand for. Hazard no. 457 was nothing more than pre-chewed baby food for the masses.

"Don't think I didn't try to let Warhol know how I felt. I tried. But I never got close enough to speak with him. The tall fellow, Spreck, he at least was willing to listen. Spreck accepted the goblin polyp spores I arranged to have delivered to him by some incompetent Pest Control worker. Those alone would have been enough to redeem Hazard no. 457's recklessness. But then YOU found out." Beckett was pacing back and forth, holding his sword high like a medieval sentry.

"I had to think fast. The Pest Control officer who was supposed to deliver the spores mentioned to me that even the small amount their lab kept for study drove their caged baby tardigrades wild. He told me the polyps don't make tardigrades hallucinate, that the tardigrades just find the fungus and spores irresistibly delicious. Then I had an idea, the idea that was the germ of a creation truly worthy of being called a 'genius' work of Recklessism." He gestured with his sword up toward the mile-high tube of fabric. "Behold!"

"The tube to funnel away the spores was your idea?" Margo said. She'd risked her life to fix that damn tube. But its purpose wasn't to save the museum. The point all along was to destroy the Bublinaplex.

And she, unwittingly, had risked her life to help make it happen.

"That's right," Beckett said with a chuckle as he saw the realization on Margo's face. "After you used the museum's cyborgs to evict everyone from inside the museum, I organized a meeting with Structural Safety and Pest Control and the Administration to decide our next move toward re-opening the museum and, of course, ensuring its safety. Executive Designer Fash failed to join our meeting and the two department chiefs were in a panic. Without their leader, they couldn't decide what to do. Pest Control's chief wanted to trap and contain the spores. Structural Safety's chief had ideas for filters and containers and things. I held firm. I opposed their suggestions. I said they would create an 'unsafe concentration' of the spores. Better to let the spores disperse 'naturally' out into the air, outside the Bublinaplex, I said. Apparently, my argument was persuasive."

Margo set her jaw. "And now tardigrades are stampeding onto the dome," she said through her teeth. "And you call it art. Art that could kill the last of humanity!"

"You think you know so much," Beckett said. He laughed. "You think you can prevent humanity from going extinct? I've got news for you: we're already extinct. This bubble over our heads doesn't change that." He jabbed his sword up in the air. "I wonder, has no one told you what this place really is? Or do you have all the information, but are just too stupid to put it together."

Margo said nothing. Her eyes narrowed.

"Right then," said Beckett. "You don't know. Really, it's rather sad that you're supposedly the best inspector in the Art Safety Department and the secret has been kept from you."

"What do you mean?" she asked. "What secret?"

In reply, Beckett smiled, a genuine-looking smile this time, and slashed at one of her leech arms with his sword. The blade grazed the leech. It recoiled, wounded, while the other leech whipped forward and struck Beckett full force in the gut. The blow knocked him on his knees before Margo fully realized what had happened.

She decided that whatever "secret" Beckett was talking about would have to wait. With Beckett stunned and coughing on the floor, she dashed toward a metal basket beside the ring of squirt guns. She'd noticed the cables running up from the basket and inferred (correctly) that there were associated with a kind of pulley system that could carry her up the tube.

From behind, Beckett lunged at her.

Margo felt no pain, only a strange sort of pressure. Beckett's sword had passed completely through the left leech. The leech recoiled and writhed in agony. Beckett withdrew the sword and prepared to lunge again. The violence of the wounded leech's movements made Margo lose her balance and she fell to the floor. She saw the thick, crimson liquid spurting from the leech and knew it was her own blood coming out.

The right leech twisted around toward Beckett and lashed out, knocking his feet out from under him. He fell backwards. The back of his head hit the floor with a dull thud. The sword clattered down beside him.

Margo was not sure if she was willing the leech to do what it was doing or if the leech's will was imposing itself on her. Margo's suction cup hand grabbed and lifted Beckett by his leg. He was going to say something but he didn't have time. Margo's leech threw his limp body toward the stairwell, where he tumbled down at least one flight and was silent.

Margo didn't hesitate. She leapt into the basket and started the automatic pulley system. It carried her up the tube toward the dome. It moved much faster than she'd thought it would.

For a second Margo stood eye to eye with the balloon caricature of her face. This time it didn't embarrass or terrify her. She could admit that how it looked was sort of how she looked. In another sense, it didn't seem like it was her at all anymore.

The face she saw caricatured in the balloon was Inspector Chicago. But she wasn't Inspector Chicago anymore. She was coming to terms with that. Who she was, what she was, was something else. Maybe she was just Margo. Maybe she was Leech Girl.

She decided who she was didn't matter. She was going to save the Bublinaplex and she was going to get herself banished and she was going to find Jasper, whoever she was, whatever anyone called her.

Blood oozed from the wounded leech. Yet it was Beckett's well-being Margo was worried about. Had she seriously injured him? Had she killed him? She realized either was possible and the realization horrified her. She wanted to be reckless enough to get banished while she was saving the Bublinaplex, but she didn't want to kill anyone.

Margo reminded herself she was doing what she was doing for safety. Only by reminding herself that the entire Bublinaplex—the entire human population of the world—was still at risk was she able to move past her concern for the traitorous jerk who'd stabbed one of her leeches.

She was somewhere between the balloon with her face on it and the top of the tube when she looked down and saw she was being followed by a hover cube. It had to be Beckett. He was alive. She was at once relieved and irritated. If he was following her, he would attack again. If he attacked, she might almost kill him again. She just wanted dealing with him to be done.

The higher Margo rose up the tube, the more densely the goblin polyp spores were concentrated in the air. When she took a breath she could taste the spores and feel a tangy tingle in the back of her throat. She squinted to keep the particles out of her eyes. She took short breaths to avoid gagging. Before long she started feeling the dulled effects of the spores, the wooziness and sense of distance from her own movements. It was distracting but not debilitating.

The mechanical basket stopped about five feet shy of where the top of the tube opened to the toxic air outside the Bublinaplex. She reached up with the unharmed leech and used it to pull herself up and out through the hole. She stood up on the top of the dome.

The hole she'd come through was wide enough to fly a hover cube through. Great.

Outside, the familiar stench of the Fungus Wasteland mixed with the spore-dense air funneling out of the hole, making breathing the thin air somewhat easier. Overhead, clouds swirled pink, black, and lavender. A waist-high thicket of goblin polyp tendrils already covered the top of the dome around the hole. The sticky, spongy stuff made moving forward annoyingly difficult.

An eastward darkening of the cloud-thick sky told her night was coming. From that same direction, she could hear the snuffling and scraping and bellowing of unknown numbers of tardigrades.

The dome creaked and groaned under their weight.

She followed the tardigrade sounds, slowly at first where the goblin polyps had grown dense and waist-high, then quicker farther down where the fungus was only as deep as her ankles. The wounded leech attached to her left shoulder continued to flop and writhe but with less vigor.

She saw the tardigrades. She stopped.

The tardigrades were like living mountains. The slow movement of their trunk-like legs and the scraping of their claws against the glass and one another's backs called to Margo's mind footage she'd seen of flowing lava. How many were there? Hundreds of large ones, certainly, and countless juveniles. The smaller tardigrades seemed to have the most success reaching the goblin polyps. They scrambled around their gigantic kin, gorging themselves on fungi and avoiding being trampled. Among this mass of hungry creatures, Margo could tell a few truly enormous specimens were present just by the way the climbing pile heaved and shifted.

Could she really turn them back on her own?

She heard the hum of a hover cube approaching her from behind. Sure enough, Beckett had followed her. Now the cube was climbing higher and higher into the sky.

After flying through the dense concentration of goblin polyp spores in the tube, Margo realized he must have been reeling from their hallucinogenic effects.

He probably didn't know the difference between what was real and what was not. He probably was completely out of his mind.

Margo turned to face the tardigrades. A small one, about twice as big as herself, had come snuffling up to her. She ran toward it and applied the full force of her body weight toward shoving it away.

The tardigrade dug its claws into the layer of fungus and grime covering the dome. Though its claws barely gained purchase, it didn't budge.

She then ran toward a larger one. The wounded leech hung limply on her side as she ran. One of the large tardigrade's feet alone was the size of the small tardigrade she'd failed to move. She extended her good leech arm and wrapped it around the beast's foot. With all her strength and all the leech's strength, she pushed and pulled and strained to change its direction through sheer force of will.

It didn't work.

Now Margo was starting to feel exhausted. She sat down beside the tardigrade's foot and tried to catch her breath. The tardigrade turned its head toward her. It seemed to look at her with a sort of dull curiosity. She stood up and yelled at it. "MOVE, YOU STUPID THING! MOVE MOVE MOVE MOVE MOVE!" She ran toward the edge of the mass. Dozens of the creatures faced her. "TURN AROUND! GO AWAY! AAAAARGH!" Some of the animals seemed to notice her. Most did not.

She screamed herself hoarse. The tardigrades did not care. The small angry thing posed no threat to them.

She sat down again. Her face twisted in an expression of disgust. She'd sat in goblin polyp filth. Then she looked up. There was Beckett's hover cube again, high in the air directly above and descending fast. Faster than hover cubes were supposed to be able to move. As fast, she supposed, as the cube might move if gravity alone was propelling it downward in freefall.

She saw that the inflatable safety cushions that were supposed to open up on the bottom of the hover cube were missing. She saw the vehicle's metal frame, its exhaust system, the bottom of its electric motor, and other mechanical parts exposed underneath, coming down fast toward her.

She inhaled, about to scream. The good leech wrapped itself around her head.

The hover cube crashed.

TWENTY-EIGHT

Margo felt the muck of despair oozing up her nose and into her mouth. It crept along her gums and ran down her throat. The muck intruded under her clothes and against her skin. Its pseudopods reached hungrily for her lungs and dragged her deeper and deeper down within itself. She felt it burning away under her fingernails and toenails and sucking at her scalp, consuming her alive.

And she was thinking she would have survived if she'd allowed the leeches to take her. If she'd just been strong enough to sacrifice her arms to those parasites, there might have been something left of her in the end.

With a flash of lightning outside the window, Margo awoke. It was a rare storm that sent lightning and thunder and torrents of rain forcefully enough against the dome for it to be heard inside the buildings within its protective shell. Tonight's storm was exceptionally loud and bright, even among those rare storms.

She sat up in the small bed. Medical equipment, most of which was no longer attached to her body, cluttered the room. An exception was the intravenous tube running between a sack of fluid hanging from a hook beside her bed and the bandaged stub of partially-digested flesh and bone that remained of her left arm after the dead leech had been removed.

With her living but half-crushed right leech arm she poked at the bandage. She felt nothing.

Thorsten appeared in the doorway and turned on the lights. His hair was a mess and his clothes were rumpled from sleeping in a cot in the hall. "Is everything alright?" he asked, as he always did. "Is there anything I can do?"

Margo was still breathing hard from the nightmare. She let her head drop back onto the pillow. She told him she was fine. "Go back to sleep," she said. "See you in the morning."

Thorsten turned out the light. Margo lay in bed, staring in the dark up at the ceiling and trying to distract herself from the rotten, sweet taste of the muck still lingering in her mouth. She sat up again and leaned toward the nightstand where she'd left a glass of water with a straw sticking out. She sucked up the melted ice at the bottom, then spat it back into the cup.

She'd been unconscious for days, then woke up screaming here in the Pest Control Department's animal attack ward. That was over a week ago.

The physician who'd examined her told her she was lucky Beckett's modified hover cube hadn't killed her. His best guess for how she survived was that the leech must have taken the brunt of the impact. Still, she'd suffered a severe concussion, several broken ribs, a cracked clavicle, and enough internal bruising to immobilize her for at least a month. The right leech still had enough life in it despite its being half crushed to fend off Cola or anyone else interested in removing it while Margo was unconscious.

Margo mourned the left leech. Whole days after she first regained consciousness were spent sobbing into her sheets. She couldn't help but wonder if her sorrow wasn't caused by chemical manipulation by the surviving leech, or some trace of the dead one. But the depth of her sadness made moot the question and dissipated any doubts she had about the authenticity of her feelings. To her, her sadness was real enough. She would have to endure her depressed state regardless of the cause—dumb manipulations of a hungry parasite or not.

Among the get well cards and hand-crafted flowers and other things she found when she first awoke (things that morbidly reminded her of tokens left outside the Museum of Genius in remembrance of victims of The Tragedy) was another copy of LEECH GIRL LIVES, this one containing a handwritten note from Thorsten. "I don't expect you to forgive me," it read, "And I know I don't deserve it. But please try. Please."

To be honest Margo felt she lacked the energy to continue her grudge. She never came out and told him she forgave him, but when he came to visit she smiled at him and they sat quietly alone together in the room for a long time. She let him hold her suction cup hand. The leech didn't protest either.

Beckett didn't survive the crash.

Soon after Margo regained consciousness, Belga visited. "I'm glad you're alright," she said. "But I can't believe what you did. The Executive Designer, he was livid when he heard you escaped."

"Does that mean I'm going to be banished?" Margo asked, her voice creaking weakly.

Belga chuckled and shook her head. "No, I don't think so. I think you're safe." She sighed. "I should have been more clear with you about how the Executive Designer wanted you to help. The Administration and Pest Control, they'd already come up with a plan to turn back the tardigrades. It was Doctor DuBuffet—Cola, I think her first name is—who came up with the idea to dump salt on the tardigrades to make them shrivel up into their inert, dormant state. After that, all that needed to happen was for cyborgs to roll away the tardigrades and clean up the goblin polyps.

"What the Administration wanted from you was for you to supervise the tardigrade removal and goblin polyp cleanup process. Because of your immunity to the spores, no one but you could have done that."

"Wow," Margo said. "Now I feel like an idiot."

"It's all taken care of now," Belga said. "Don't worry about it. Sub-Chief O'Keefe volunteered to do the job. Doctor DuBuffet used the dead leech they removed from you to make an experimental antidote to goblin polyp spores' effects. So far, O'Keefe is fine and the project is proceeding as planned. That is, somewhat slowly and somewhat tediously, but it's proceeding."

Margo felt even worse. O'Keefe was cleaning up her mess, again. Exposing himself to goblin polyp spores because of her, again. And Cola was proving that Margo really should have just let her take a leech instead of running off and trying to deal with everything as if she really were some kind of a hero. As if Leech Girl was who she really was and not just some story Thorsten made up so she would feel less shitty about herself.

"I'm sorry," Belga said. "I'm upsetting you. I should go." She stood up to leave.

"Wait," Margo said, realizing she was about to once again miss the opportunity to press Belga for more information about banishment. "Tell me Belga, where do the banished people go? Or when? Tell me, where is Jasper?"

Belga looked to the open door out to the hallway. Bodily Safety workers, nurses and doctors, were making their rounds. Quickly, she closed the door and returned to Margo's bedside. "I'm sorry," she whispered. "I've already told you too much. Hopefully some day you'll understand. But not here. Not now. I need you to trust me Margo, and I need you to forget it. And I need you to not speak a word of what I said to you to anyone, not even Cuthbert. Do you understand?"

Margo gave Belga a tired, skeptical look.

"Listen to me," Begla said. "Don't say anything. People will die. Understand? If you do, people will die."

Margo was more confused than ever but she nodded. She'd made the mistake of not trusting Belga before and regretted it. She'd keep her mouth shut. "You're sure the Executive Designer isn't going to have me banished?"

"I'm sure," Belga said, and apologised again before kissing Margo's forehead and leaving the room.

One day late in Margo's convalescence, Thorsten brought a bottle of champagne into her room. He smiled his small funny smile as he popped the cork and then poured the foamy beverage into paper cups. Margo asked if he remembered a straw for her and he said yes.

He'd also brought a tray loaded with hot hors d'oeuvres—finger food she easily could pick up with her one suction cup hand.

And he'd brought something else too: a box. It was so large it had to be wheeled in on a cart. It shifted and jumped. Whatever was inside it was alive.

As soon as Margo saw the box she thought she knew what was inside. When Thorsten opened it, what she saw did not surprise her. What surprised her was the excitement she felt.

It was a leech.

The now mostly healed leech attached to Margo's right shoulder extended itself into the box. It seemed to greet its new companion. Could these things communicate? The idea was absurd. But both Margo and Thorsten confessed later that they thought they'd witnessed a kind of uncanny recognition pass between the creatures. The new leech reared up from the box and Thorsten jumped back. He was a little frightened that the thing might find one of his arms more appetizing than the scarred nub of Margo's shoulder. But it seemed to know what was expected of it. Promptly it reached out and clamped its circular jaws on where the dead leech used to be attached.

After finishing their second cups of champagne, they started drinking from the bottle. As Margo attempted to take a celebratory glug it slipped from between her suction cup hands. Foam gushed over Thorsten as he caught it. She had far less control of the new leech than the other, but it was only a matter of time before she and it adapted to one another as well as she and the older leech had.

She didn't feel embarrassed about the leeches around Thorsten and they didn't seem to bother him.

"I made this for you," he said, handing her a newly drawn comic book page. "Brace yourself," he said. "It's awfully cheesy."

The comic was titled "LEECH GIRL CONQUERS MY HEART." Margo rolled her eyes. She agreed. She said thank you and he said he loved her and then there was an awkward silence. They kept drinking.

When Cuthbert visited, he was a mess, as expected. He insisted she come back and stay with him after she was discharged. She didn't argue.

Sub-Chief O'Keefe wrote. He sent his best wishes in a card signed by everyone in the Art Safety Department except Chief Austen. There was no mention of Margo returning to work.

Weeks after Margo had arrived in the animal attack ward, she was finally released.

Margo didn't return to the Art Safety Department. Community Safety never bothered her again. Neither did Cola. Neither did Executive Designer Fash.

She tried to crochet, but the leeches made it impossible.

She didn't get a new cyborg.

She almost never saw Thorsten. Almost everyone in the Bublinaplex loved Thorsten's LEECH GIRL LIVES. His Creative Potential score rose so high he hardly had to go to work at the Pest Control department at all anymore.

And much to Margo's chagrin, a schism occurred within the Recklessist community between self-described "Nihilist" Recklessists—those who continued to follow Warhol and some of whom attempted to make aesthetic justifications for Beckett's actions—and "Purposist" Recklessists—those who insisted that recklessness was commendable when it was done for a reason. They tried to use the threat of physical harm to represent hard choices, emotional pain, or to criticize their violence-for-violence's sake of their peers' creations.

Their inspiration, these Purposist Recklessists claimed, was Leech Girl.

TWENTY-NINE

The day of Lorcan Warhol's banishment arrived less than a year after The Tragedy.

Cuthbert was out with a new crop of Mentees, giving a tour of the sculpture garden at the edge of Liminal Park.

Margo was at his house by herself.

Neither she nor he had seen or heard from Belga since Margo left the animal attack ward.

With a piece of graph paper and a red marker, Margo sat down to write Cuthbert a letter. With practice she'd taught herself how to hold a pen by closing her suction cup hand around it like a pincer.

The letter was an apology.

She wrote that she was sorry for not saying goodbye in person. She wrote that she'd be okay, and that she'd put a lot of thought into what she was about to do.

As she was writing she realized it read like a suicide note.

And she realized the only way to write the note without betraying what she'd learned from Belga was if it read like a suicide note the whole way through. Cuthbert should think she was dead or as good as dead for as long as she might survive in the Fungus Wasteland.

"I'm sorry and I love you," she wrote. "There's nothing you could have done to stop me. Please don't feel guilty about this. You're awesome."

She wiped her eyes with her leech arm.

She had to hurry. She had to go now if she was going to go. She folded the note and placed it in the middle of the kitchen table.

And she got the SafetyPunk costume out from its hiding place under some dirty bath towels and old wrinkled pants in the closet in her old room, the room where she'd practically grown up, the room she'd hardly come out from over the course of this past year.

She removed her pajamas and strapped on the kneepads. She picked up the heavy, smelly shoulder pads and pulled them over her head. The elbow pads were especially annoying since she didn't have elbows. She put on one and then tightened its strap using her teeth. She put the other elbow pad on and pulled it tight, then noticed that it was not quite lined up with the other elbow pad on her other arm. One elbow looked higher, one looked lower. So she fussed with that for a while until finally she gave up and put on a shirt made of inch-thick foam.

She felt like the padded shirt was suffocating her. The inflatable SafetyPunk pants were just as bad.

Luckily the boots were made to be easy for someone wearing everything she was wearing to put on. She thought by themselves the SafetyPunk boots actually could have been kind of cute and comfy. Anything less practical and she wasn't sure how she would have made it into the next room let alone the nearly two-mile trip across the entire Bublinaplex.

The helmet was the most important part of her costume. It looked like the head of a giant bug with balloons for eyes. It would mask her identity. She put it over her head and was pleasantly surprised she was still able to breathe with relative ease, even if it did take away her peripheral vision.

She'd thought people obsessed with safety would have made being able to see their surroundings a priority. But maybe that missed the point. Maybe those who routinely wore SafetyPunk outfits such as this had the luxury of not caring about their surroundings. They knew nothing was going to hurt them, not even anything or anyone they accidentally bumped into or stumbled over because they couldn't see where they're going.

It was a point of view Margo didn't plan on getting used to.

She completed her SafetyPunk ensemble with a pair of oven mitts that she slid over her suction cup hands. With the oven mitts on she thought they could pass for normal hands, even if her lack of thumbs meant her suction cup hands were basically useless inside the mitts.

She waddled in her unwieldy padding out of Cuthbert's house toward the Temple of Shame.

The walk to the nearest pneumatic tube station was tedious. When finally she took a seat in the capsule and caught her breath she looked out the window and scarcely had the energy to consider she was seeing her city for the last time.

In the distance she could see the balloon with her face on it floating over the Museum of Genius. It was facing away from her.

Mercifully the Temple of Shame was closer to the nearest pneumatic tube station than Cuthbert's house had been, and even a little downhill. Margo felt drained from the effort of the cross-town trek. She was sopping with sweat inside her costume, but seeing the temple restored her sense of purpose for this clumsy quest. She pressed on.

The temple was a long, narrow building. At the far end was a curved, pointed steeple. It looked like a long black boot with its toe pointing up in the air. Outside the main entrance was a line of people waiting to take their places inside.

Some of the Bublinaplex's most respected authorities were among those standing in line. Margo recognized Gustav Glass, the head surgeon from the Bodily Safety department. He was having a chuckle with Nann Borromini, a curator from the Museum of Genius, and Emmanuel Andrès, a senior administrator in the Grapes.

Margo was careful to steer clear of Chief Austen, who she saw standing near the doorway, looking surly and munching on roasted nuts from a paper bag. If anyone would see through Margo's disguise, it would be her.

Once Margo reached the door, a hostess suggested she make her way all the way to the front of the "sanctuary" for the best view.

The air inside was hot and damp from the lights and the bodies standing in the cramped space. Wrought iron barriers lined the recessed walkway that bisected the nave.

Awkwardly large inside her disguise, Margo shoved her way between the iron barrier and the crowd to get as near as possible to the empty dais at the far end of the room. The SafetyPunk shoulder pads and elbow pads and the foam shirt made her feel huge and she kept shoving people and but not saying she was sorry out of fear someone might recognize her voice. She got a lot of nasty looks and a few shoves back that, thanks to her padding, she hardly felt.

The ceremony was exactly the same as it was when Jasper was banished.

First the Shame Administrator appeared. He began his "Shame, shame, shame," chant, quietly at first, then louder and louder. "Shame. Shame. Shame. Shame." The crowd joined in the chant. Some stomped their feet to the terrible rhythm.

Lorcan Warhol appeared at the end of the recessed walkway. He was naked. Without clothes he looked like a much smaller and much older version of the man Margo remembered meeting. He looked cold, the way his arms crossed over his sunken chest, and he looked weak.

Cyborgs draped a tardigrade-hide blanket across Warhol's shoulders, then strapped a gas mask over his face. Warhol began his slow march through the chanting crowd.

People in the crowd started throwing things. A pair of pants landed on top of him. Now he had this pair of pants on him with one leg over his head and the butt on his shoulder by his face. Some rubber shoes barely missed him and landed on the floor in front of him. Then he tripped over the shoes and landed on his face. Before standing up, he stopped to gather some of the canned goods and clothes that had landed beside him on the floor. More objects were landing on and around him every second.

Margo had hated Warhol for a long time, but she took no pleasure in this. What must he be thinking? Having things thrown at him as he advanced in his walk of shame toward the Shame Administrator, expecting to die in the Fungus Wasteland, she felt like he must have somehow convinced himself that this punishment was what he deserved. Otherwise he would be trying to get away. Naked, he would attack the cyborgs and Safety Administrators and the Shame Administrator with his teeth and fingernails. Instead, he trudged forward, toward what he must believe was his doom.

Margo realized that was the genius of this punishment. He seemed to think he deserved it. The spectators, even those who must know the true nature of his punishment, seemed to think he deserved it too. Everyone seemed to agree that this was what justice was supposed to look like.

Margo didn't think it looked like justice but she wasn't sure she'd know justice if she saw it, either.

Warhol stopped at the front of the Temple. In his trembling arms was a haphazard assortment of food and survival gear.

It was just like when Jasper had stopped at the front of the Temple.

It was time for Margo to make her move.

The Shame Administrator raised his hands. The crowd went silent. "You, Lorcan Warhol, have been found GUILTY of HIGH RECKLESSNESS," said the administrator in his high-pitched, grating voice.

Margo removed the oven mitts from her suction cup hands by grabbing the mitts between her knees and pulling them off.

"FOR SHAME!" cried the administrator, and the chanting resumed. The Helmet of Shame was placed on Warhol's head. The Shame Administrator raised his club, then brought it down hard. Warhol collapsed to his hands and knees. All of the things he was carrying in his arms clattered to the floor.

Using her helmet and shoulder pads as a wedge, Margo shoved the people standing in front of her out of the way. They pushed back and made annoyed noises. It amused Margo how much etiquette seemed to matter at an event the high point of which was throwing things at another person. She ignored them and pushed through to the front row, where she wanted to be.

The Shame Administrator raised his club again and brought it down.

Margo braced herself. She would have to move quickly.

As the third blow fell on Warhol's head, the administrator and the spectators cried out "SHAME!"

The trap door opened under Warhol. He screamed. In an instant, he was gone and the sound of his scream cut off.

With her suction cup hands, Margo grabbed the top of the barrier between the crowd and the recessed walkway, then vaulted herself over. She fell sideways toward the trap door and on top of the scattered clutter of things. She was thankful for all the padding.

The Shame Administrator cried out, "STOP! STOP THIS RECKLESSNESS AT ONCE!"

Community Safety officers and their cyborgs vaulted the barrier and made their way toward Margo.

All around, spectators murmured excitedly. Nothing like this ever had happened as far as anyone could remember. What could this SafetyPunk possibly be doing?

Margo cursed as the trap door where Warhol fell closed before she could reach it.

The Community Safety officers and cyborgs were closing in.

On top of the trap door, Margo got down on her knees and searched with her suction cup hands for a latch or a knob or a lever or anything to grab onto. There was nothing.

Now the Community Safety officers and cyborgs were on top of her. She attached her suction cup hands to the flat surface of the trap door and pulled. The officers took hold of her shoulder pads. Cyborgs reached for her padded pants. She clenched her teeth as if she actually could feel the effort the leeches were exerting, but really she felt nothing except the racing of her heart as the parasites demanded more blood for more strength to do what she wanted.

She grunted and pulled, and the officers pulled too, her inadvertent assistants. The trap door buckled on its hinges, then ripped away to reveal a gaping hole. Margo, the officers, and the cyborgs fell backwards, the officers and the cyborgs on their backs, Margo on top of them. The heavy trap door landed on her.

The officers let go of her costume as they tried to get up.

Margo stood up and tossed the trap door aside. She headed for the hole.

The hole was a black, empty pit. For all she knew it was bottomless.

She took a deep breath. She closed her eyes.

She took the risk. She jumped in.

The feeling was nothing like falling. It was nothing like moving at all. She was immersed in something and whatever it was, it was as if it was alive. She immediately knew wherever she was, she was far, far away from the Temple of Shame. Wherever she was, it was fundamentally elsewhere. And after seconds or hours or days she was instantly dislodged from that in-between place.

She was somewhere else again. The nausea was overwhelming.

Then it was dark.

She awoke in a clean bright room. On the other side of the room, sitting in a pile of canned food and survival equipment, was Lorcan

Warhol, stark naked. She took off the SafetyPunk helmet. He started laughing.

BOOK TWO: THE PAST

THE SPEECH, PART TWO

The leader of the revolution looks out over the ragtag assembly of her followers. There are hundreds of them. They are all braced for action. They are all prepared to advance their great purpose.

There are men and women she'd known for years. There are men and women she'd never seen before.

There are some who look far too young for this and there are others who look far too old. She wishes she could stop time and one by one excuse them from this task. She wishes she did not need them but she does.

Her eyes scan up to the balcony. Could that be Margo up there? Impossible.

This is what the leader of the revolution says next:

"Many of you were taught to believe in the inherent inferiority of slum dwellers. Many of you learned early that your life and the lives of everyone around you are disposable.

"None of you can forget the first time you heard about someone you know surrendering their life to the Machine.

"That this has become common enough for so many to accept as the way things are and always must be is a crime that cannot be forgiven. It is a crime rooted in a fundamental misunderstanding of who needs who in our society. It is a crime committed by the corporate republic in order to keep itself and the elites it serves in power.

"It is a crime. And it is up to us to deliver justice.

"In the rulers' cruel language, 'parasite' is a slur we've all heard. A man in a suit will use it as he kicks away a homeless woman asking for bread for her children. A police officer will use it as she leads her armored squad into a community of cardboard dwellings. A child of privilege will use it most contemptuously, as if what that child can call his or her own by luck of birth was somehow earned and not stolen.

"The irony of course is that it is not we, the workers and slum dwellers and strivers, who are draining the life from our society until it is a sick, half-alive thing.

"It is THEY who take from us all and return nothing but suffering and disease as they fill their bellies and secure themselves against the worst.

"It is THEY who have created a system that feeds their children by starving ours.

"It is THEY who, once cut out of our sick society, will not be missed.

"This belief in their own superiority—and the rightness of their damnable creation, the Bublinaplex—is the real parasite. And if humanity is to survive, this thief of blood and flesh and life must be destroyed.

"And in order to exterminate this parasitic belief, those who are carrying it must be made to understand its nature."

THIRTY

Margo's eyes adjusted to the brightness. She could not see any lights anywhere. It was as if the harsh white light emanated from the walls.

Warhol was now sitting crosslegged on the floor on one end of the strange circular room. He chuckled to himself. "What the hell are you doing here?" he said. His Helmet of Shame and gas mask were off. His once-spiky hair was plastered flat against his head and stubble covered his jaw.

What was she doing? For a second she forgot. Then she remembered: Jasper. The point of this was to find Jasper. That, of course, was none of Warhol's business. Unsure of how best to reply, she dropped the SafetyPunk helmet on the floor and said, "Don't worry. We're not being sent to the Fungus Wasteland."

Warhol replied with shrill peals of laughter. He rolled on the floor. When finally he caught his breath, he continued to chuckle to himself until he started hiccuping. "I'm sorry," he said eventually. "Your face. You're so damn serious." He sniffled and wiped his nose with the back of his hand and looked up at her. His eyes were red and she noticed he was more well-fed-looking than he was when she'd met with him in the café nearly a year earlier.

"Thanks, Leech Girl. Golly you really are an expert on the Fungus Wasteland, aren't you? I'm sure only a very intelligent person who has gone through your extensive training and singular experiences would be able to tell the difference between that stinking land of rot and filth from the Cog City antechamber at the end of a transchronological portal—where we're now, relative to the Bubinaplex, in the distant past."

Apparently Warhol understood their present situation better than she did. So what? She didn't want to let him have the satisfaction of explaining it to her further. The important thing was that Warhol didn't seem afraid of whatever he expected to happen next. She sat down on the floor and scowled across the room at him. The leeches wriggled excitedly in her sleeves.

A few minutes of awkward silence passed. Warhol started doing what looked to Margo like yoga poses. Finally her curiosity got the best of her. "How do you know so much about where we are?"

"The Shame Administrator gave me an information packet. I read it before the ceremony. Well, that, and this is where I'm from originally."

Margo wanted to ask more, but a door hissed open where a moment before there had been no sign of an opening. A pale woman wearing a black uniform and a little black hat stepped into the room. "Welcome, Mister Warhol, to the Independent Republic of Cogworks Incorporated." Her voice was the voice of someone who spent a lot of time practicing speaking. She handed Warhol a floor-length white terrycloth robe.

She didn't acknowledge Margo. "I'm Margo Chicago," she said. "I've been banished too."

"No you haven't," the pale woman said.

"Well, but I'm here."

"Yes. I'm well aware of that," she said. "Your family is coming to collect you. But you'll have to wait." She gestured dismissively toward the door. "Leave the chamber now. It will need to be cleaned." She then turned to Warhol. "Are you comfortable, Mister Warhol?"

"Very."

"Good. Follow me." They left the circular chamber and entered a cavernous control room. The outside of the chamber was encrusted with buttons, switches, valves, pipes, and digital display screens. In the dim light of the large room, what Margo and Warhol noticed first was the curved, ceiling-high windows that looked out onto the night and the sprawling city below. They'd fallen down a hole in the ground and arrived at what looked like the top floor of a skyscraper. The sky was black save for a sliver of moon and faint glimmers of real stars, the first Margo had ever seen.

The columnar buildings nearby were speckled with squares of light. Office windows. Far below, rows of street lamps lined the city streets. Cog City, Warhol had just called it. In the distance, a row of towers resembling the posts of an impossibly high fence surrounded the city. The towers seemed to be swaying like reedy fungi in the breeze.

Only after she spent a minute taking this in did she realize what the pale woman had said: Your family is coming to collect you.

Who did she mean?

Before she could ask, a hoarse voice shouted "Hello?" from the dark end of a nearby corridor. Breathing heavily, a large sweaty man wearing a slightly too-small suit and tie charged in. He placed a greasy hand on the window and caught his breath as he eyed the pale woman, Warhol, and Margo.

"Ah," he said with a nod toward Margo. Then, with a nod to the others, "Pardon me. Official Abbotzo family business." He turned back to Margo and gave her a short bow. "Miz Abbotzo. Delighted to make your acquaintance. Pascal Tromscratt, at your service." He offered her his arm. "We must hurry, the chopper is waiting."

Confused, Margo looked to the pale woman. All she said was, "Go on. You're his problem now."

Margo tried to protest, "But my name, it's not— "

"Tromscratt knows better than you do what your name is. Now go."

She took Tromscratt's arm. With the padded shirt still covering the leeches, he didn't notice them. "Call me Margo," she said.

"Or Leech Girl," called Warhol from behind them as they started down the corridor. He'd been looking out the window. "She answers to Leech Girl, too."

Tromscratt hurried Margo deeper and deeper into the building. She was grateful for this man, whoever he was. He was not hostile like the pale woman, but also not especially chatty. Together they eventually reached a mirrored elevator. Inside, Margo flinched when she saw her reflection. Her hair was half smashed against her head, half sticking out in all directions. Her face was as shiny as plastic from sweating. And she was still wearing the ridiculous padded SafetyPunk shirt and pants with the shoulder pads and knee pads and her elbow pads had slid down to where her wrists should be on her leech arms. When the elevator door closed, she realized she reeked of body odor. She avoided meeting Tromscratt's eyes in the mirrors.

He pushed a button to send them down.

When the door opened, Tromscratt hurried her through a series of hallways with tile floors and plain gray walls. Eventually, they passed through a set of doors that led outside and onto a kind of large, unfurnished balcony. The helicopter was waiting for them there. Margo gasped. The air was bracingly cold, colder than any she'd ever felt other than what came out of an open refrigerator door. The leeches withdrew and scrunched themselves as deep as they could into her sleeves.

As Tromscratt gave Margo a boost into the back seat of the helicopter, she asked, "Where are we going?"

"Home," he said. He climbed into the front and strapped himself in. The engine roared to life. The noise of the spinning propeller blades made further communication impossible, though when Tromscratt yelled back to Margo to buckle up, she understood and obeyed.

As the helicopter rose from the helipad, she realized she'd forgotten to ask how to find Jasper. She thought for a moment that maybe when the pale woman referenced her "family" it was Jasper she was talking about, and that all this Tromscratt person was doing was delivering her to him and as soon as she arrived there would be an explanation that would make everything make sense. She had the thought but she was too smart to believe for a second that finding Jasper actually would be as simple as that.

And then they were flying. The speed terrified Margo. The leeches were terrified too, she could tell, but instead of throwing a wriggling and writhing temper tantrum they shot out from her sleeves so her suction cup hands could latch onto the first surfaces they found inside of the helicopter—the right leech, the floor and the left leech, a window.

Looking back she could almost take in a full view of the building they'd just departed from. She saw that there were many structures like the helipad sticking out from midway up the building like the petals of an immense, misproportioned flower. Above the petals the building thinned abruptly into a tower that grew narrower and narrower until terminating in a sort of bulb shape at the top—the location, she guessed, of the antechamber where she and Warhol first arrived.

Far below, the city passed under the helicopter too quickly for her to make more than the most basic observations. Shining skyscrapers clustered near the flowerlike tower. Surrounding these was a ring of low metal and brick buildings where industrial fires flared and chimneys bellowed brown fumes. Then taller buildings with rows of windows, probably apartments. Then the fence-like ring of moving tentacle-towers.

After the towers, the buildings passing by below were too small to see clearly. Margo guessed that the countless tiny window lights spreading out in all directions indicated a kind of residential district, the scale of which she found hard to comprehend. From one end to the other, the Bublinaplex was just two miles across. By comparison, this city seemed to stretch out endlessly—and the factor by which the number of people living down there must have dwarfed her domed city's population astounded her imagination.

That she was now in a place where people were so numerous—and not, apparently, on the verge of extinction—brought to Margo an unexpected joy. With so many people to help each other and to work to avert the crises that must inevitably challenge humanity, the odds seemed to favor people's ability to overcome any threats they encountered.

One downside to the densely populated world occurred to her: with so many people, finding Jasper might be even harder than she anticipated.

Soon the lights of homes and roads gave way to an unlit, indistinct landscape. In the darkness, Margo could make nothing of it. She closed her eyes. Then Tromscratt was shouting at her again.

When she opened her eyes he was pointing straight ahead. He was pointing toward a house and bringing the helicopter down.

The house was immense. Its appearance called to mind a cross between a castle and a cabin. As they descended she saw the house was nestled in a field of brown grass—grass!—dotted by great branching oaks and pines—trees!

The helicopter touched down in the field. The leeches relaxed enough for Margo to let go with her suction cup hands and withdraw the parasites into her sleeves.

Tromscratt cut the engine. He turned in his seat and shouted, amid the quieting roar of the slowing propeller blades, "Here we are! I can't say you were exactly expected, but I hope you feel welcome."

From the direction of the house Margo could see a woman approaching in the helicopter's lights. "Who's that?" she asked.

"That?" Tromscratt turned. "Oh, well that would be your mother. Missus Fayette Abbotzo."

THIRTY-ONE

Fayette Abbotzo was a small, stout woman. She wore a white turtleneck sweater and a long black skirt. A pair of thick-lensed glasses made her eyes look huge. Her dyed black hair was done up in a beehive. Her wide smile displayed perfectly white false teeth.

Margo met her in the ankle-high brown grass halfway between the helicopter and the house. The leeches once again had withdrawn into Margo's padded sleeves to get out of the cold. Tromscratt followed close behind.

"Well here you are," Fayette said. Her hands were clasped together in front of her. "I suppose we'll just have to make the best of it. Good, Pascal," she said as Tromscratt arrived by Margo's side. "Come show our guest to her room." To Margo she said, "I'm sure you're exhausted. We can get to know each other better in the morning." She turned and led them toward the house.

Countless questions came to Margo's mind. Was this woman really her mother? Did that mean she was born in the past? And who then was her father? And what was the relationship between the Bublinaplex and this past world where she'd arrived?

For now she kept her questions to herself. Maybe this woman—her mother, supposedly—or Tromscratt could help her find Jasper. At the very least their hospitality would make it possible for her to get her bearings. She would begin her search in earnest tomorrow.

Tromscratt hurried ahead to open the front door. Before Fayette could lead Margo inside, something gray and furry and fast darted out of the house. Fayette turned and yelled, "Duchess! Get back here Duchess!" Then to Tromscratt, "Well don't just stand there. Go get that cat." Tromscratt nodded, then dashed after the animal.

Margo couldn't believe it. A cat! A real live cat!

"You have a cat," she said.

Fayette turned and stepped over the threshold. "If Pascal can catch her, I do," she said. "Come in. I'll tell you where you need to go."

Margo joined Fayette inside. The orange glow of a fireplace lit the two-storey great room. It was almost unbearably hot. The walls were made of stacked stone and a wooden staircase curved upward into the unlit second floor. Paintings on the walls depicted nature scenes—dense forests, snow-capped mountains, rocky cliffs, and rushing waterfalls. It struck Margo as a sort of shrine to places where people were absent.

"Right up there," Fayette said, pointing up the stairs. "Turn right at the top. Follow the hall until you reach the fifth door on your right. Go on in. Pascal will be up to assist you shortly. Now, please excuse me." She ducked into doorway behind the stairs and disappeared into it.

Exhausted, Margo followed the instructions. Behind the fifth door she found a room lit only by what little moonlight entered through a large window. Dusty sheets covered the bed, armchair, and chests of drawers. The room had a musty smell and it was cold—apparently too far from the great room fireplace to enjoy any of its heat. Piles of odds and ends and boxes of various sizes had been shoved against the walls.

This, she thought sleepily, was a place for putting away things that didn't belong anywhere else.

She pulled away the sheet that covered the huge bed. Underneath she found overstuffed pillows and a quilted blanket. She removed her boots and collapsed onto the bed and passed out almost immediately.

Some time later she suddenly awoke. She didn't know where she was and there was something moving in the dark. The leeches whipped out a full ten feet from her sleeves and with her suction cup hands she pinned the intruder against the wall.

Pascal Tromscratt whimpered incoherently.

Margo released him and withdrew the leeches. He backed away toward the door. He'd dropped a lump of something on the floor.

"What's that there?" she asked.

He continued to whimper. Margo still couldn't understand what he was saying. Was he crying?

"What did you drop on the floor?"

"Pajamas," he managed. "For you, Miz." He bowed and scrambled out the door and slammed it shut behind him.

Grateful to finally get out of the stinking SafetyPunk costume, she changed into the pajamas, a frilly nightgown with long sleeves and a baggy pair of cotton pants. The pajamas must belong to Fayette. She was too tired to feel bad about scaring Tromscratt. She realized she should have asked him where she could find a shower—her own body odor at this point was far worse than the musty smell of the room.

Before she fell asleep, she wondered if Judy Chicago was still alive and if, after everything was sorted out, this Fayette woman might someday introduce her to her.

In the morning Margo discovered there was a bathroom with a shower attached to her bedroom. She had to move boxes of junk that were stacked on bathroom floor to get to the shower, but the important thing was that the shower worked.

She closed her eyes and let the hot water stream through her hair and run down her face and shoulders. When she spoke with Fayette and Tromscratt she would ask for their help getting back to Cog City. Jasper could have been anywhere, but he must have at least passed through Cog City to get to wherever he was now.

Where would she start? The city was vast and strange and she didn't know anyone. Then she remembered the pale woman. Maybe she'd greeted Jasper the same way she greeted Warhol. She'd return to the flower-shaped building and hunt for that woman. She was the key.

After her shower Margo put the pajamas back on since she had no other clothes besides the SafetyPunk costume and she wasn't getting back into *that*. She stepped up to the window and pulled aside the thin curtain. What she saw outside amazed her. The yard in front of the house sloped downward into a forest. The trees were yellow and red and orange, not at all the simple green she'd expected. She was sure she'd seen trees depicted in this way in paintings. She'd supposed they'd been artfully exaggerated.

There was a knock on the door. "Yes?" she said.

It opened just a crack. "Missus Abbotzo is waiting for you Miz Abbotzo," Tromscratt said without even peeking his head inside. "Come on out and I'll show you the way."

Margo noticed Tromscratt sneaking glances at her suction cup hands as he led her through the house. Something about her situation now made her feel unusually self-conscious about the leeches. She was relying on their hospitality, so of course what they thought of her mattered more than what people had thought of her in the Bublinaplex. There, she could always withdraw into the loving and judgement-free shelter of Cuthbert's house. Having no such shelter now, she was actually going to have make an effort to get these people to like her enough to want to help her. Except this Fayette woman was supposedly her biological mother. Maybe that changed things. Margo wasn't sure.

After leading her down the stairs and through a number of hallways to the opposite end of the house, Tromscratt motioned Margo through a door. On the other side was an indoor patio decorated with potted palm trees and exotic flowers. The patio was encased in curved glass that reminded her of the glass of the Bublinaplex dome.

Fayette was sitting at the end of a long table, reading a book and slurping from a mug of coffee. "Sit down, Margo," she said without looking up.

Margo sat at the table. Fayette said nothing more for a moment or so and Margo found herself gazing through the glass and once again marvelling at the multicolored forest outside. Tromscratt soon reappeared by her side. He poured her a mug of coffee from a hot carafe.

"Cream? Sugar?" he asked.

"Yes." He plopped a cube of sugar into her coffee and poured in a little cream, then stirred it for her. She felt like she should make conversation with him. "It's strange," she said, "being served by a real person. I'm more used to being served by cyborgs. Don't you have cyborgs here?"

Fayette put her book down. She frowned. Tromscratt hurried back into the kitchen. "No," said Fayette. "Keeping cyborgs here, or almost anywhere outside of where you're from is … " she paused to search for the right words " … is not considered appropriate."

Margo inwardly scolded herself. Her choice of topic was apparently taboo. Why would it be inappropriate to have a cyborg? It didn't make sense to Margo but it didn't matter. She'd have to do better. "I like your trees," she said, rather lamely.

This comment seemed to please Fayette. "Thank you," she said. "I can't stand to be away from them. They are my oldest friends. They are like my family." She sipped her coffee. "There aren't any trees where you came from, are there?"

"No," said Margo. "Just mushrooms." Margo wasn't sure what to say next. "I'd always thought I was born in the Bublinaplex," she said.

"I can assure you, you were not."

Tromscratt reappeared with breakfast. "Frittata a la provenzal," he said as he placed the plates in front of Margo and Fayette. "With rosemary sausage and fresh-baked croissants. Bon appetit." He gave a little bow and withdrew back into the kitchen.

Margo picked up her knife and fork and immediately started eating. It had taken weeks of practice at Cuthbert's dinner table for her to master the art of using silverware with her suction cup hands. But Cuthbert had offered seemingly endless encouragement and Margo had been determined. By the time the day of Warhol's banishment had arrived, she'd even mastered chopsticks.

Several mouthfuls into her breakfast, she realized Fayette was not eating. She was watching Margo eat and she had an odd look on her face. "Something wrong?" Margo asked.

"Those... appendages of yours."

"It's a long story."

Fayette nodded and pursed her lips. She did not want to hear the story. Soon she turned her attention to her food and started picking at the triangular piece of egg on the plate in front of her.

Tromscratt cleared the plates when they finished, then quickly returned with champagne flutes. "Mimosa?" Neither Margo nor Fayette objected.

"I need to get back to the city," Margo said after taking a sip. "Cog City, I think it's called."

"The Republic?" Fayette replied disdainfully. "Now that you're here, there's nothing for you there."

"I'm looking for someone, someone I care about very much who passed through, from where I was before and to this place, now, about two years ago."

"What makes you think this person is still in the Republic?" Fayette asked. "It's not a place where people stay, except perhaps those that have no choice." She lifted her coffee mug, looked like she was about to take another sip, and then, after peering inside, set it back down. "Though I suppose he must be one of those who has no choice."

"What do you mean about having no choice?"

Fayette looked at Margo as if through her, then allowed her gaze to drift downward until she was staring openly at Margo's leech arms and suction cup hands. "Pascal!" she called, still staring at the leeches.

Seconds later, Tromscratt was back at the table. "What can I do for you, Missus Abbotzo?"

"My daughter is looking for someone who arrived in the Republic from the bubble about two years ago. You're going to help her."

"Yes, Missus Abbotzo."

Fayette looked Margo in the eyes. "What's this person's name?"

"Jasper," Margo said. "Dr. Jasper Bearden. He has brown hair and wide-spaced eyes and he's not especially tall or short."

"Do you think you can find him?" Fayette asked.

"I'll do my best," Tromscratt replied, then returned to the kitchen.

"There," Fayette said to Margo. "No need to go back there. Tromscratt knows the city. He knows where to look, who to ask. And you can stay here. Spend some time relaxing. Spend some time with the trees."

"Thank you," Margo said, somewhat taken aback. She didn't want to seem ungrateful for the help, but she felt perfectly capable of looking for Jasper herself, even if she didn't know anything about this place or this time. What was, the time, anyway? "I'm sorry," this is going to seem like a strange question—"

"I'm sure you have lots of questions."

"What year is it?"

"2055. Which probably doesn't mean much to you. What year did they tell you it was when you were where you were before?"

"200,055."

Fayette chuckled. "That's clever, I suppose. Keeps things easy to remember."

"So you don't think the Bublinaplex—where I was before—was not precisely one-hundred and ninety-eight thousand years ahead of today."

"No. The place you're from is more like eighteen million years ahead of today."

She wasn't sure why, but this piece of information made Margo nauseous. "I think I'd like to go back to my room now," she said and stood up.

She was so far away from everything she'd ever known. Too far. Everything was so strange. Everything was so different. And so much of what she'd thought she'd known was turning out to be lies. "I need to lie down. And I think I need help finding my way back to my room."

"Pascal!"

Tromscratt returned.

"Show my daughter the way, please."

"Of course Missus Abbotzo."

With Tromscratt beside her, Margo started back toward the doorway. In her dizzy state, she almost leaned against Tromscratt. Tromscratt recoiled away from Margo and her leech arms the instant she seemed about to veer toward him. She stumbled and almost fell, then caught herself and continued.

They were about to step out of the patio when Fayette said from behind them, "There's one thing I'm surprised you haven't yet asked about."

Margo turned. She fixed her glassy eyes on Fayette. "What's that?"

"Your father."

Margo sighed. Was it strange that she didn't ask about her father? Was it strange that, despite Fayette's insistence upon bringing it up, this was a subject she still was not particularly curious about? There was a man who'd had sex with this woman in this distant past place and then apparently had nothing else to do with her. End of story. Cuthbert was as much of a father as she'd ever need, she was sure. As much of a mother for that matter too. Margo knew on an intellectual level that biological parents were an important part of peoples' lives before there were Mentors.

She'd read the old stories and watched the old movies. Despite her sudden illness, she still felt she should make an effort to seem interested in this subject if for no other reason than this woman who was providing her food and shelter wanted her to be. "I'm sorry," she said although she didn't feel sorry at all.

Fayette smiled. "There's a portrait of him hanging just out in the hallway there, if you want to take a look."

"I'll do that," Margo said, feeling thankful that she at least would not have to go out of her way to satisfy the obligation of her host's request.

With Tromscratt at her side, she stepped out into the hall. Only one portrait was hung on the wall in that hallway. It was impossible to miss. She was surprised she hadn't noticed it on her way in. The frame was at least five feet high and four feet across, and the figure posing triumphantly inside was familiar. She recognized him instantly.

It was Executive Designer Fash.

THIRTY-TWO

Life at the Abbotzo estate took some getting used to for Margo.

Fayette was a mystery. Days went by and Margo would not see her, and when she did see her, her host might not say anything at all. Or if she was in the mood to speak, it would be to make some brusque comment about Margo's "appendages" or to point out her lack of knowledge about things that were perfectly obvious to people who had not grown up in "the bubble."

Thankfully, solitude and isolation suited Margo just fine. On rainy days, she explored the house. There were rooms upon rooms where dusty piles of old clothes, paintings, furniture, and books were piled precariously close to the ceiling, and there was an office with a tremendous oak desk and a TV set.

With some effort, she got the TV working. To better understand this time and place, she tried to cultivate an interest in current affairs. These efforts generally were not successful— the programs that weren't strictly for entertainment usually contained huge gaps in information. Mostly they just added to her confusion.

An ongoing theme of the news programs was the clashes in Cog City between the Republic Police Force and a group of armed insurgents called Saboteurs. She inferred that the police were something like the Community Safety Department, except with clubs and guns, and that the Saboteurs were something like Recklessists, except without making art. Margo didn't understand the motive for the insurgents' attacks. In an interview, a Cogworks spokesman said the Saboteurs "hate our productivity, our industriousness, and our vision." Margo found herself shouting at the screen "BUT WHY?"

Instead of answering, the program would cut to a commercial.

Duchess remained a gray blur despite Margo's best efforts. She would spend hours trying to coax the cat from its hiding places and still it refused to come near her. "Those appendages," Fayette said while witnessing Margo attempting to lure Duchess out from underneath a wooden cupboard in the great room. "She doesn't trust them. And I can't say I blame her."

She spent most days outdoors wandering in and out of the woods and marvelling at her surroundings. Hours passed as she watched squirrels and chipmunks foraging and crows and sparrows gorging themselves in preparation for their migrations. Sitting there, so silently and for so long, she saw a deer once, maybe twice, she wasn't sure. One morning she somehow wandered into a flock of turkeys, which, as soon as they became aware of her, became an alarming storm of flaps and gobbles as they retreated into the darkest hollows of those woods.

Despite Fayette's frequent absence, Margo was never completely alone. Tromscratt was always there, ready and waiting to serve. Margo went out of her way to avoid asking anything of him. He never forgot about being attacked by Margo's leech arms that first night. He always kept his distance. He was never much company.

The exception to Tromscratt keeping his distance from Margo was his weekly reports on his search for Jasper. Sometimes there was progress, most of the time there was not. One week he would describe his plan to follow a lead he was sure would direct him straight to Jasper, and then the next week the lead would turn out to have been false. One week he would have a plan to make inquiries in places where those who had been banished from the Bublinaplex were known to frequent and then the next he would be asking Margo if she was sure his name really was Jasper and if his appearance was as she'd claimed to remember it.

"This is him," Margo would say as she once again showed Tromscratt the photo of Jasper she'd brought with her from the Bublinaplex.

Tromscratt would shake his head. "You say this is him some three or four years ago. He could look like a completely different person now."

Diego Leon, Fayette's personal chef, was Margo's favorite person on the estate. A week or so after she'd arrived she noticed him taking a cigarette break outside the kitchen and decided to introduce herself. His skin was dark and his clothes were white and he had large, expressive brown eyes. She'd just finished eating her dinner alone on the patio, a satisfying dish of braised pork with mashed potatoes and beet salad. He offered her a cigarette. She declined. "That meal was amazing. I grew up around good food," she said, thinking of Cuthbert. "Thank you. It reminded me of home."

"You're welcome," he said, then took a drag. "You grew up in the future, right?"

"That's right," Margo said timidly.

"What was that like?"

Margo started to answer, but it was soon time for Diego to return to the kitchen. Margo only had time to say just a little about Cuthbert, his cooking, and the comparatively small house where she'd grown up. Diego was fascinated. "Will you meet me out here at the same time tomorrow and tell me more?" She did. Soon it became their routine.

"I'm going shopping for groceries tomorrow morning," he said one day. "Want to come with me?" A sly smile crossed his lips. Fayette had instructed Margo not to venture off of the estate grounds for her own "safety and protection," and Diego knew it.

Margo met Diego outside the kitchen at dawn. "Hey let me see the leeches," he said. "Do you mind? I want to see what has Pascal so freaked out."

Margo shrugged and pulled back one of sleeves of the trench coat she was wearing. Her leech arm snaked out and she held it up. "High five?"

"Holy shit!" Diego said. He slapped her suction cup hand with his palm. The other leech, apparently perceiving the slap as a threat, immediately lashed out of her other sleeve. It shoved Diego to the ground and pinned him there.

"Oh, no, I'm so sorry …" Margo said. She willed the leeches to withdraw. In a few seconds, they'd disappeared into her sleeves.

Diego was laughing as he got up from the ground. "That's crazy!" he said. "How did this happen?"

They sped toward the grocery store in Diego's miniature pickup truck. Margo told him an abbreviated version of her story. She didn't say anything about Thorsten's LEECH GIRL comic. Nevertheless, Diego said, "Wow. You're like a real live superhero."

"Do you ever go into Cog City?" she asked as she watched the scenery zip past.

"Never," he said.

"Why not?"

"It's an evil place. The people there, they are either desperate or taking advantage of those who are desperate. Out here, away from that place, there are rules, you know?"

"There are no rules in Cog City?"

"Not exactly, it's just that the place, the 'Independent Republic of Cogworks Incorporated,' is what's called a corporate state."

"What does that mean?" Margo fiddled with the buttons on her trench coat sleeves. Fayette had arranged to have an entire new wardrobe delivered for her within a week of her arrival. Some of the clothes were things she would never wear, but she wore the trench coat almost every day.

Diego sighed. He kept his eyes on the road. "It's like this. The city used to belong to everyone, in a way. Not really, because there were always rich people arranging things so they could get richer and there were always poor people trying simply to exist. But still, on paper, it was as if the city belonged to all the people. The people got to pick their leaders, the people whose job it was to make the difficult decisions, the people got to say their piece if the leaders made bad decisions, and so on. Does that make sense?"

"Sort of."

"Anyway the leaders made lots and lots of bad decisions based on bad advice from Cogworks, the company. Bad decisions that made the city poor but helped make the company rich. Tax breaks and stuff. Soon the city was broke and so in debt to Cogworks that no one thought it would be possible for the city to repay. So Cogworks bought the city, then seceded from the country. Now everything that happens in the city is completely under the company's control. Now the poor people don't really have any choice—if they don't fit into the system, the company finds ways to force them into it. I don't exactly understand the details, but it was the transaction between the indebted city and the company that made your parents rich. And it was some part of this arrangement that put your dad in charge of that place in the future, the 'bubble,' as Missus Abbotzo calls it."

They passed an abandoned farm. There was a rotting fence that surrounded the remains of a half-collapsed barn on a hill. Sharp tufts of dirt brown weeds gone to seed stuck out from under the rusted skeleton of a tractor. "Do you think that's why Fayette doesn't want me to go into the city?" Margo said as she looked out. "Do you think she wants to hide these things from me?"

Keeping one hand on the wheel, Diego fished a cigarette out of his coat pocket. He put it between his lips and lit it, then took a thoughtful drag. "My opinion is, I think she's hiding these things from herself. That's why she's up in that house, no newspapers, no Internet, practically no TV. I once left a newspaper lying on a table where Fayette could find it, and old Pascal snatched it up and stormed back to the kitchen and threw it in my face. 'How dare you!' is what he said. 'How dare you!' Didn't make any sense to me until I saw that the front page had something about Cogworks experimenting on people by combining them with machines. Horrible stuff, like prosthetics gone too far. Anyway Fayette, I think she has to hide all this from you if she wants to keep hiding it from herself." They rounded a corner. Ahead was a straight stretch of road lined with shops and restaurants. "Here we are," said Diego, turning into a plaza.

Margo loved the grocery store. "It's like a huge piece of installation art that says, simply, 'you should eat some food'," she said. Piles and piles of neatly stacked produce was something she'd never seen before. For some reason she found the onions especially fascinating. The meat counter left her feeling somewhat traumatized. Then there were the rows upon rows of boxes and cans in the soup aisle. "This part is like a food library," she said. All the food in the Bublinaplex was synthesized, she explained to Diego, so seeing such a quantity of food—food that had been grown from seeds or born or hatched from mothers—was an entirely new experience for her.

Diego filled the shopping cart as they wandered the aisles. Despite Margo's enjoyment, she started turning over in her head the thought that Fayette was hiding things from her in order to hide them from herself. The thought made her wonder if she was depending too much on Fayette's hospitality.

She'd let the warm bed and new clothes and delicious meals lull her into a routine.

Maybe, she thought, it was time to break out of it.

Margo had an idea as they loaded the groceries into the truck. "Let me drive," she said.

"Have you ever driven with a stick shift before?"

"I've driven hover cubes."

"You've driven what?"

"Never mind. Let me help you out with those bags."

"No, we can give it a try."

Diego pointed out the gas, the break, the gear shift, and the clutch. Margo asked what the clutch was again and Diego tried to explain again. Margo pretended to understand. She tried to make the truck go forward. It made a spasmodic lurch, then stopped. Diego held tight to the grocery bag in his lap (it contained the eggs). Margo tried again. The truck lurched again. On her fourth try she got the truck moving forward, then it stalled when she attempted to shift up to second gear.

They were still in the parking lot when Diego said, "Let's switch. At this rate, the milk will be spoiled before we get back."

Margo nodded glumly and got out of the driver's seat. In the truck she'd perceived a potential means of escape. She didn't think it would come to that, but it would be nice to have the option. If an escape was possible, staying felt voluntary. In practice, that would mean she wouldn't mind staying a little longer.

Now she just felt frustrated. Now she was ready for a way out.

For dinner that night Diego prepared a simple dish of pasta with pepper and cheese and a side of bitter greens. As usual, Margo ate alone. Tromscratt appeared and suggested a twelve-year-old sangiovese to go with the pasta. Margo thought it was perfect. Before she knew it, she'd downed half the bottle. On her way out she hollered into the kitchen to Diego and Tromscratt that the rest was all theirs if they wanted it. She didn't understand why they refused to eat with her. She supposed it was another of Fayette's odd rules.

Now that she was full of wine and pasta her eagerness to leave the estate had dulled. She told herself she'd have another chance to try driving the truck, and she told herself there surely were other ways of disentangling herself from this comfortable but lonely existence.

She remembered the muck of despair and chuckled quietly to herself. She'd been stuck before in far worse circumstances. The leeches had saved her then. Could they save her again?

In the hallway she came to the portrait of the man who was supposedly her father. Tipsily, she regarded him. He was pictured from the waist up. He wore a vaguely military-looking uniform with epaulettes and decorations on his chest that could have been medals or badges, or they could have been a series of very small abstract expressionist paintings—Rothkos, to be precise. His unruly hair and thick eyebrows were gray in the portrait, not white, and his craggy face was clean-shaven. His dark eyes were half-closed, as if the portrait painter had caught him nodding off.

Executive Designer Fash's real name, she learned, was Xerxes Abbotzo. Where the hell was he? Fayette said she didn't know. He could be in the future. He could be in the past. The present, Margo corrected herself. She wasn't sure if she believed Fayette about her ignorance of his whereabouts.

If he were present, she wondered, would he offer any more insight into how things really were than her mother had? She told herself he would have to. He was the Executive Designer, after all. His position of power would require him to know all about how this past world related to the future world and why she'd wound up in the future despite being born in the past and so on. Fayette refused to discuss it. So did Tromscratt, though Margo was sure he knew the story.

Maybe her father would come back to this place. Maybe he would find out that she was here and come to meet her. Maybe when he did, he would show Margo where to find Jasper.

If that was the case, all she needed to do was wait.

Margo yawned. As she followed the dark but now familiar route back to her room, she decided she could wait. She could try again to crochet using her suction cup hands. That would pass the time.

What would she make? Not cats. Duchess had turned her against them.

Tardigrades, perhaps.

Yes. It was decided. She would take up crocheting again and tardigrades are what she would crochet.

THIRTY-THREE

By the middle of winter, Margo had mastered crocheting tardigrades.

She crocheted lobopods and slime grazers and nimos too. And because old habits die hard, she even crocheted some cats, though none that resembled Duchess. Coincidentally, once the weather turned cold and hostile and the snow started coming, Duchess warmed up to her—though the cat did have the annoying habit of swatting at the yarn when she was trying to crochet.

She convinced Tromscratt and Diego to dine with her sometimes. When Fayette occasionally descended from wherever she spent most of her time in order to eat at the table, it was always a surprise. Tromscratt and Diego would scramble to resume their respective subservient posts and Margo would be left at the table feeling more like an awkward host than an awkward guest. She was determined to learn from these encounters as much as she could. She did not learn much.

"Where is my father?" Margo once asked.

Fayette sat up from the soup she was slurping. She smiled and chuckled. "I find myself asking the same question."

"I'm not really related to Judy Chicago, am I?" Margo asked another time.

Fayette rolled her eyes. "What do you think?"

Tromscratt's search for Jasper meanwhile had taken a bureaucratic turn. He claimed to know for a fact there was a basement full of archival records in one of the Republic buildings and that he was sure the most fruitful course of action was to access these records. The task, he claimed, required acquiring a full understanding of the bureaucratic channels and going through a formal process and allowing various administrative officers an opportunity to approve or deny the request, then appeal the inevitable denials when they came, and so on.

Margo tried not to let her frustration show. She didn't have any proof but sometimes she suspected Tromscratt's "search" for Jasper was an elaborate ruse, something Fayette put him up to in order to keep her at the estate. But she didn't want to accuse him of anything in case he really was trying and the task really was as hard as he made it out to be. And if he really was lying to her, well, she'd rather let him think she believed him. That way it was she who was doing the fooling. That way he'd be taken by surprise when she set off to find Jasper herself.

Snow blanketed the estate. Its beauty astounded Margo, the way the minuscule flakes fell and formed drifts in the yard and gathered on the trees. She wanted to know what it felt like so she went outside in it, but her leech arms refused to leave her sleeves. Eventually she lost her patience. She got down on her knees and put her face in the snow, then immediately sprung back up from the shock of the cold, then put her face back down in the snow again.

Diego found her like that. "Margo?"

"Oh, hi Diego," she said as she stood up, rather clumsily because of the leeches' refusal to help.

He shook his head and sighed and a mix of mist from the cold and tobacco smoke escaped from his lips.

"Finished clearing the driveway?"

"Yes," he said. "For now." He'd attached a plow shovel to the front of his truck.

She'd noticed him using it to push the snow into neat piles. "How about another driving lesson?"

"I don't think so," he said. "You could hit a patch of ice. You could crash into a snowbank."

She asked again and again over the next several weeks.

He refused again and again. "In the spring," he would say.

Margo didn't want to wait for spring. She'd ask again in a few days, maybe if the snow melted, maybe in the supermarket parking lot during the next grocery run.

*

One night Margo awoke in her room to a high-pitched electric buzzing sound. She felt oddly groggy and slow, even for the middle of the night, and when her eyes opened she was surprised by harsh white lamplight shining over her head. She couldn't see and she didn't understand what was happening.

A metallic bang against the wall and the clatter of metal things falling on the floor drew her attention to her left. What was going on? She tried to focus. Something wasn't right. Was she drunk? How many vodkas had she had that night? No more than two. Didn't matter. She wasn't drunk. This was something else.

The scene came into focus. Her left leech arm had reared up and was poised to attack a man who for some reason was cowering in the corner of her bedroom. He wore a long white coat and with one arm he was covering his face and in his opposite hand he held what looked like a gun. This gun-looking thing was what was making the buzzing sound that woke her up. He was pointing it at her left leech.

"I think she's waking up," she heard Tromscratt say from the opposite side of the room. She turned her head to see Tromscratt, his eyes wide with fear, standing in the doorway. He looked like he wanted to turn and run. Fayette stood next to him. Her face wore a sour expression. Her arms were folded across her chest and she was wearing a mauve pantsuit, which Margo hazily thought to herself as an odd thing to be wearing in the middle of the night. Her right leech arm, she realized, was stretched out toward the two of them, also rearing up and ready to attack.

Margo willed the leeches to snap back to her sides. "What's going on?" she said.

The man in the white coat stood and ran toward the door. He shoved past Tromscratt and almost knocked down Fayette.

"Well that was stupid, wasn't it?" said Fayette.

"What?" said Margo, coming to.

"Dr. Green was finally going to get rid of those parasites from the future for you."

"WHAT?" Margo stood up. The agitated leeches writhed by her sides.

Fayette and Tromscratt exchanged glances. "It was supposed to be a surprise," she said. "It was supposed to be the first step toward making you normal." Fayette took a cautious step forward. "Don't you want to be normal, Margo? I know I want a normal daughter..."

In Fayette's hand Margo saw a syringe. "The FUCK is THAT?" Margo said as she whipped a leech arm out and slapped the syringe onto the floor where it rolled against a wall.

Fayette stepped back. She had a hurt look on her face and she was rubbing her hand. "Only something to help you sleep dear," she said. "Don't you want to go to sleep?"

"LIKE HELL I DO." Margo's heart pounded. If she had fists they would be clenched. She no longer felt groggy. She was livid, mostly with herself. She'd been too trusting. She'd let her guard down. The only thing saving her from becoming a captive amputee was a lucky mistake by the doctor who apparently had given her an inadequate dose of sedative. She stormed toward the doorway where Fayette and Tromscratt stood.

"MOVE."

Tromscratt scuttled off somewhere into the darkness of the hallway. Fayette didn't move. "You disappoint me, Margo Abbotzo," she said firmly, fearlessly. "I wish you could see I only want what's best for you."

Margo stood with her face close to her mother's.

"You don't know anything about me," she said. "You have no idea what's best for me. And if the normal life you're scheming to arrange for me is anything like this lonely life you've arranged for yourself, well, you can shove it up your ass."

She pushed past Fayette and walked out into the dark hallway. Tromscratt was nowhere in sight.

There was only one thing she could think of that she could do right then. She didn't know if it would work, but it wasn't the first time that was the case.

She made a beeline for Diego's room.

The servant quarters were on the opposite end of the estate. Margo had never even been to Diego's room, but she knew roughly where it was. She ran down the stairs and followed the hall and turned right and then left and then right again and followed another hall to a door. It was unlocked. On the other side of the door was the hall with to the rooms where servants slept. She was pretty sure there was only Diego and Tromscratt now but there were enough rooms for many more. The walls in that hallway were painted white and had no decorations.

Margo opened every door she came to. The first three were empty. The fourth was locked. Behind the fifth, she recognized Diego from the sound of his confused, mumbling voice when she opened his door.

"Diego, wake up!" She stepped inside. In the scant light of a digital clock she could see his room was tidily arranged and that he was buried under a mountain of blankets. Diego mumbled again. She strained her eyes to scan the room for his keys and found them on top of a bookshelf near the door. "It's not safe for me here anymore," she said. "I'm taking the truck."

Diego sat up. He wasn't wearing a shirt. "What? No no no no Margo. You can't do that."

"I'm sorry," she said. "There's no time to explain. I'm not asking. I have to go now."

"I'll drive you," he said. He stood up and pulled on a bathrobe and reached for the place on the bookshelf where he'd left his keys. They were gone. Margo now held them in her suction cup hand.

"I'm sorry," she said. "I can't trust you. I can do it myself."

She let the keys jingle and he reached out to take them from her. She blocked him with a leech arm and knocked him down to the floor. "I mean it," she said.

"I need that truck," he said. "It's all I've got."

"I'm sorry," she said again and left, closing the door behind her. She found the nearest exit. Outside, the cold was shocking. She was still wearing her sleeveless pajamas. The leeches had nowhere to withdraw so they bunched themselves up like thick little logs. She jogged to the lot behind the kitchen where Diego usually parked.

There was the truck.

She got in, stepped on the clutch, and turned the key. The engine rumbled. She flipped on the headlights. They lit up the plastic garbage bins lined up against the back of the house. The glowing eyes of an opossum peered out curiously from behind one.

She attempted to shift into reverse. To her surprise she succeeded on the first try and zoomed backwards faster than she meant to. Suddenly Diego was out there with her, standing in the light of the truck's headlights making pleading gestures and calling, "Stop! Wait! Please!"

A sudden jolt in back of the truck. She checked the mirror. She'd hit a tree. The truck stalled. Now Diego was running towards her. She locked the doors and started the engine and shifted into first gear. The truck lurched forward and Diego had to jump out of the way. The gears grinded as she shifted into second.

Diego was running beside the truck now. He was shirtless still and he had something bunched up in his hand. Margo rolled down the window. "I'm sorry," she said again. She was sure he wouldn't be able to hear her. The engine was roaring now because she was trying to accelerate but for fear of stalling again she didn't dare shift gears out of second. He threw the thing bunched up in his hand into the open window and as she tried to recoil away from it she turned the steering wheel hard and almost swerved into a ditch.

His bathrobe landed in her lap.

She pulled it over her shoulders as best she could while driving. In the rearview mirror she could see Diego recede into the darkness as the truck tumbled into the forest-lined stretch of driveway.

She followed the route Diego usually took to the grocery store. She slowed down but did not stop for stop lights. She glanced in the rearview mirror over and over again. No one was following her. At an intersection, instead of turning east onto the highway toward the plazas and shops where she and Diego ran errands, she turned west.

On the four-lane highway, she passed a road sign that said "The Republic" was 33 miles away.

She shifted the truck into third gear.

The dashboard clock said it was 2:45 a.m. She wasn't tired anymore but her eyes felt raw as if she hadn't blinked since she'd woken up to discover her leech arms fending off the attempt to amputate them while she slept.

There were times, Margo was certain, when the safest course of action was getting the hell away from wherever you are as fast as you possibly can. This, she was equally certain, was one of those times.

Now as she stared out onto nothing but miles of straight highway and darkness, she thought about everything Tromscratt had ever told her about his search for Jasper and wondered if any of it was useful or true.

Trusting him—and Fayette—had been a mistake.

She was done letting others do the work of finding Jasper for her.

She decided then that she would find him herself or not at all.

THIRTY-FOUR

Driving about 30 miles per hour on the highway, Margo felt like she was going faster than she should. Even so, cars raced past, startling her every time. Huge trucks like buildings on wheels would loom in the rearview mirrors and seem about to crush Diego's truck before veering around at the last second, sometimes with a hostile horn blare.

Ahead, the jagged city skyline was visible through the ring of moving towers. A thin fog had settled over the landscape. When she rolled down her window for fresh air, a sulfurous stench stung her nostrils. The smell reminded her of the Fungus Wasteland, except there was something thoroughly alive about the air in the wasteland. In this place, the air smelled dead. She rolled the window back up.

A road sign told her the next ten exits would take her to "The Republic." She didn't know which to take but she wanted to get off the highway, so she took the first off-ramp that appeared.

The ramp twisted down onto a warped street where the remains of woody weeds erupted out of cracks in the pavement. Crumbling brick houses, many with boarded up windows, lined the street, their dead lawns wild with brown tufts and tangles of weeds. On some lots were clusters of lean-tos made of corrugated metal, planks of scrap wood, tarp, and cardboard amid the ruined buildings. What few cars she saw in driveways and along the streets were mostly half dismantled and missing their wheels.

The city skyline, Margo realized, was now behind her. She made a left, went past a burnt-down structure, then made another left, which she followed down another ruined street that she thought should lead her back toward the city. After several blocks the remains of houses gave way to hulking, angular apartment buildings. Small trees sprouted from the broken windows of some but there were more signs of life here than among the houses. Clothes were hanging out to dry. Toys were strewn around impromptu playgrounds. Bicycles were locked into bike stands. Dawn was fast approaching but if she stopped to look up at the buildings she could see light coming from some of the windows. Curled up in doorways she noticed shapes she thought might be people sleeping. There were some cars and trucks parked along the streets that looked drivable but none on the road.

Several blocks later, the road ended. Where it stopped there was a low, fenced-in building with a concrete pit in front that might once have been a fountain. Margo yelled and smacked the steering wheel, then turned the truck around. She would have to backtrack. The fuel gauge indicated about an eighth of a tank was left. She couldn't afford to waste gas. She'd have to find someone to ask to tell her the way.

So much for finding Jasper without any help.

She made another series of turns and thought for a moment that she might be headed the right way. She followed another street over a bridge. Then she came to a T in the road. To the right about a block ahead she could see someone walking. Whoever it was was walking away.

She turned right and pulled up beside the person. It was a woman with dark skin, like Belga. She wore a long, puffy blue coat. Margo rolled down the passenger-side window. "Can you tell me the way into the city?" she asked. The woman walked on as if she'd heard nothing. Margo lurched the truck forward several feet. "Excuse me," she said, louder this time. "I'm trying to find the way into the city. Where the skyscrapers are. Can you tell me?" Again, the woman ignored her and walked on.

Margo stopped the truck and watched the woman. Her pace was constant, mechanical almost. Maybe she was wearing headphones that were too small to see. Maybe there was something wrong with her.

Now that the sun was coming up Margo supposed more people would soon be out for her to ask. But she decided to try one last time to speak to this woman. She got out of the truck.

The woman turned to cross the street. She was too far ahead for Margo to get her attention without shouting. She wanted to avoid a confrontation—always a possibility when accosting a random stranger—so Margo sped up to catch up to the woman without taking her by surprise.

Two blocks later the woman walked out onto an empty lot. What was she doing? Margo saw then that the lot was not entirely empty. On the edge was a twenty-foot spiral staircase. The staircase led up to nothing. To Margo's eyes it looked like a piece of abandoned playground equipment, except as she got closer she noticed the grass around it had recently been mowed and the staircase didn't look abandoned at all. It was white and shiny, not peeling or rusted like everything else she'd seen in this dismal place outside the city.

The woman stepped up onto the staircase and climbed up to the top.

Margo thought she saw her take a quick look in her direction. "Hey!" She called toward the woman. "Hey, I'm trying to —"

"I don't give a fuck." The woman said, loudly but flatly.

Margo jogged up to the staircase. "I'm lost, I just need some help—"

"No help for the lost here," said the woman. "You're on your own."

"I'm trying to find my way into the city, The Republic, can you see from up there if there's a way to get in from this road here?"

"If you were smart you'd keep your distance from Cog City, lady." The woman looked down. "What the hell are you wearing?"

Margo realized now that the woman was much younger than she'd realized. She couldn't be more than twenty-five. And in the sunlight, talking to a stranger, she realized that yes, her bathrobe and pajamas outfit looked even more ridiculous than it had at night. "Hey, I'm getting tired of shouting, I'll come up and we can talk up there."

"Don't come any closer, crazy bitch!" she said, and Margo stopped. "It's coming now, I can see it." The woman looked down at Margo. She took off her long, puffy blue coat. "You look cold," she said. "Here," and dropped the coat down.

"What are you doing? You'll freeze up there without your coat."

The woman laughed. A puff of vapor escaped her mouth. "You sound like my mom used to sound. Or my sister."

Then Margo saw it. A long shadow. A building was falling on them. No. What was it that she was seeing? A building-sized metal snake? A metal tentacle?

The building didn't fall on them. It had bent itself down so it became a huge arch, with one end hanging over the woman on the spiral staircase and the other originating in the ring of moving towers. That's what it was, it was one of those moving towers. The end that had bent down toward the woman on the staircase was narrow, not much bigger around than a person, and at the very end of it was what looked like a kind of glass eye. The eye was perfectly black.

Margo could tell the woman's eyes were closed and her lips were moving, but she couldn't make out what the woman was saying.

A ring of curved hooks snapped out of the metal tentacle from around the eye. They latched onto the platform at the top of the staircase to form a cage around the woman. She didn't make a sound.

Then the moving tower quietly lifted the woman in the cage high into the air, then arched inward toward the city. At least half of the other moving towers she could see also had bent into arches that dipped down toward the city. She thought they looked like a herd of long-necked dinosaurs sharing a desert water hole she'd once seen in an illustration of prehistoric life.

What the hell had just happened?

Margo put the woman's coat on over Diego's bathrobe. She must have been much taller than Margo. The bottom of the coat almost touched the ground. Were these metal tentacle towers a form of transportation? Maybe all she needed to do to get close to the skyscraper where she'd arrived, where she wanted to start her search for Jasper, was climb these steps and let the tower take her.

She ascended the staircase. The leeches seemed somewhat anxious about the height. Inwardly she scolded them. It couldn't have been more than thirty feet up. Nothing compared to the inside of the middle of the Bublinaplex dome. They relaxed and she took in the view, which gave her a better sense of her whereabouts.

She looked toward the black skyscrapers rising out of the center of the city and the row of swaying towers. Smoke from nearby factories framed the scene with a brownish haze.

She waited for the tower to bend toward her.

And waited.

And waited.

She put her suction cup hands in the pockets of her new coat. One of the pockets had something in it. She took it out.

A folded paper menu for a place called Magarac's Diner.

After an hour of waiting she had to admit to herself that she was hungry. And the diner's address was on this same street. She checked the street number of the diner against the street number of the nearest building and judged she'd have to walk back past where she'd parked Diego's truck. The diner should be a couple of blocks after that.

Disappointed in her unsuccessful attempt to use the tentacle towers for transportation, she climbed down. As she walked she searched the rest of the puffy blue coat's pockets. She found a wadded up tissue and less than a dollar in change. She understood very little about money but she knew the change didn't amount to much. She hoped she had enough for just a little something to tide her over.

It was cold outside but under her layers of clothes she was getting hot, which meant she soon would get sweaty, which meant she soon would start to smell. It was bad enough that when she found Jasper she would have leeches where her arms should be. Did she have to stink too? When she got to Diego's truck she stopped and took off the coat and bathrobe and put the bathrobe inside.

Close to where she thought the diner should be, she heard someone crying.

Soon she saw the diner and the source of the crying. A little boy, no older than ten, was screaming and wailing inconsolably and standing on the roof. A woman wearing an apron over a sweater and jeans was trying to talk with him from the ground below. Both the boy and the woman had the same dark complexion as the woman on the staircase.

Margo approached the woman. "What's the matter?"

The woman in the apron looked at her. "His momma took the tentacle," she said, then looked Margo up and down. "Looks like you found her coat."

The boy wailed and sat with his legs dangling off the rooftop. The woman turned her attention back to him. Margo didn't think the fall was high enough to kill the boy if he went off the roof, but he'd almost certainly break a leg or whatever part of him hit the ground first. "Walter," she said. "Don't do anything stupid now. What your momma did, you know she did because she thought she had to."

"She didn't have to!" the boy sobbed.

The woman shook her head. "I know," she said quietly, then shouted up to the boy, "She made her decision. It can't be unmade. Lord knows I hate it too, Walter. I hate it more than anything."

"I'm gonna take the tentacle too," said the boy.

"Oh no you're not. You're my responsibility now. You know how bad you feel right now? You'll make me feel ten times as bad if you go, because if you go, I won't have anyone. Right now, you and me, we've got each other, okay?"

The boy said nothing.

Margo didn't quite understand what was happening but she wanted to help. "Would you like me to get him down?" she asked the woman in the apron.

The woman gave her a look that said she doubted there was anything she could do to help. "Did I ask for your help? Does this look like any of your business?"

Margo took a step back. She wanted to say "Fine, have it your way," and walk away. Instead she said, "Let me try to reach him."

"Reach him?" the woman balked, and Margo was aware woman probably thought she meant metaphorically.

The boy started to cry again. Margo stepped forward and stretched her leech arms toward him as long as they could go. The woman gasped and when Margo grabbed hold of the boy, he screamed. A second later she was lowering him gently on the ground. The instant his shoes connected with the gravel of the parking lot, he was running. Margo let him go. He turned and watched with wild eyes as the leeches withdrew into Margo's sleeves.

He screamed again, and then disappeared down the street.

The woman yelled after him. "Walter!" she said. "Don't go far, darling. You're all I've got!" She then turned and regarded Margo with her tired brown eyes. "Some trick."

"Aren't you going to go after him?"

"Let him go," she said. "He needs to grieve. He'll be alright. And if not, there's nothing you or I can do. Anyway I've got customers inside wondering where their eggs are at. Coffee?"

*

Margo sat in a corner booth. The woman brought pancakes and bacon along with the coffee and left Margo while she tended to her customers, a family of four at one table and a trio of old men at another.

Eventually the woman joined Margo at the table. She yawned and rubbed her eyes. "My name is Kay," she said. She apologized for her "mean-ass" tone when Margo first offered to help.

Margo took a bite of pancake. "All is forgiven," she said.

"So what's the deal with your arms?" Kay asked. She was watching her eat. The way Margo used one suction cup hand to hold her fork and the other to hold her knife seemed to completely fascinate her.

Margo couldn't help but give a wry smile as she answered. She knew how her story sounded. "I used to live in the future. Giant leeches ate my arms and then replaced them. Under the circumstances, this actually was a good thing. Anyway now I'm here and I'm looking for someone else from the future."

Kay didn't react as if she thought Margo's story was especially unusual. "So you came from the bubble." She shook her head and sighed. "Thought so." She started to get up. "Well, enjoy the rest of your breakfast."

"Wait," Margo said. "Please, I need to ask you something. Earlier, you said the kid on the roof— "

"Walter. My nephew."

"—right, Walter, you said his mother 'took the tentacle.' He threatened to do the same. Now I saw that thing, the tower that bends over and picks people up, picked her up. I tried to use it to get closer to the center of the city. I climbed those steps and I waited and nothing happened. I didn't see any buttons to push or anything. What did I do wrong?"

Kay frowned and gave Margo a hard look. "You're from the future," she said as if trying to solve a puzzle out loud. "And you tried to take the tentacle?"

"That's right."

"For transportation?"

"Right."

Kay sighed heavily. Suddenly she looked very old. "You really don't know what it's for, do you?"

Margo took a sip of coffee. "I saw it take Walter's mother."

Someone in the restaurant coughed. Kay craned her neck to see the other tables. "I'm sorry dear, I'll be right back," she said, then got up to tend to the customers. When she returned she sat down. Firmly she asked, "You're not pulling my leg? You really don't know what the tentacle is for?"

"I only know what I saw."

Kay shook her head in disbelief. "I really thought you, as someone from the future, would know." Several seconds passed. Kay seemed to have made some kind of decision. "I won't bullshit you, I don't know either. I've heard rumors but I'm not sure if I believe them. So I'll tell you what I do know, specifically about Walter's mother. My sister. Norlene.

"She was an addict. Harmless, supposedly, in theory, if it weren't for Walter. And the overdose. I don't know where Walt's daddy is or if he left them or if they left him. The feeling I got when the subject came up was always that it was better they were apart, but I guess that's more I don't really know about. They've been living with me here above Magarac's. Walt's a smart kid, sensitive, which I guess is a little bit of what you saw. Loves his mama. Took care of her." She waved a hand in Margo's direction. "Probably him who bought that coat for her.

"So anyway she overdosed. This was a few months ago. Nasty scene, seizures and foaming mouth and everything. She must have fallen and concussed her head on the floor, blood all over. Walt came and got me. We both rode in the ambulance with her, there was nowhere else for him to go. They took good care of her in the ER, gave her something that stopped whatever was happening inside her. Kept her there in the hospital for almost a week.

"When she got out, she truly seemed better." Kay sighed heavily. "Her eyes got that yellowness out of them. She started taking better care of herself, taking regular showers, that sort of thing. She didn't look like an addict anymore.

"Then a few weeks later she got the hospital bill, $50,000 or something. Some ungodly amount. And I flipped. Norlene don't have that kind of money. I knew I'd be the one stuck paying that bill. Her goddamn habit, her overdose, and I'm stuck paying for it. I said I'll probably lose the restaurant because of her and I said if she so much as thinks about that junk again I will kick her ass out of my home for good."

She gave Margo a pleading sort of look. She wanted desperately for Margo to understand.

"Tough love," she said. "I was just trying to give her some tough love. I'dve done anything for that girl and I thought she knew it. I wanted her to know it wasn't okay, what I was going to have to do for her. You know what it's like to be pissed off at someone you love, don't you?"

Margo thought about Thorsten. She nodded. She knew what it was like.

Kay let out a long sigh. "My theory is, she must have started thinking about the junk again. They say you never stop being an addict. She must have thought I wouldn't help her. That I wouldn't even try to understand." She looked down at the table. "Sad thing is, she might've been right. Dumbass that I am. I never thought she'd take the tentacle. Never thought that she would in a million years."

For a minute Kay said nothing. Margo asked, "What does it mean for someone to take the tentacle?"

Kay's eyes met Margo's. "You climb those stairs. If you're there at 5 o'clock in the morning, it comes for you. You saw that?"

"Yes. That's when she gave me her coat."

"It takes you, and you're never heard from ever again. And then a few weeks later, maybe a month, your next of kin gets a check from Cogworks for $300,000."

"She was worth more gone than she was if she stayed."

"I don't agree, but that's the idea. Her being here for that boy, even if she was struggling with drugs, you can't put a price on that. Now her bill will be paid and I'll be able to pay off the restaurant. For Walt, if he gets past this, maybe there's a chance for him to go to school. And I hate it. I hate that I know all of this right off the top of my head and I hate that it is, in fact, true that our lives will be better in some ways because of what Norlene did."

There were parts of Kay's story that were difficult for Margo to follow. She didn't quite understand what it meant for Norlene to be in debt because of the medical treatment she received or what it meant that the money Kay expected could be used to send Walt to school. "What will he do if he doesn't go to school?" she asked.

Kay was getting up. "Probably wind up like his momma," she said, then glanced toward a group of customers that had just entered, two men and two women, all wearing grimy shirts and soot-stained trousers. "I need to seat these people. They just clocked out off the shop floor, they're gonna be hungry. Get mean real fast if they don't get a seat and something to eat quick. You stay here, don't leave yet. I have some of Norlene's clothes upstairs that'll likely do you more good than they'll do her."

Margo waited. She looked out the window beside the booth and saw more filth-covered workers out on the street. What had they been doing that made them so dirty? They looked exhausted. Some were talking animatedly with each other. Others trudged along all alone. What kind of tasks could they be doing that lead them to look like animated dead things? Nothing she'd ever seen in the Bublinaplex prepared her to understand how some people lived in the place.

And that poor woman who "took the tentacle." Margo knew what it was like to feel desperate, to run out of options and be willing to risk everything. It was how she felt before she followed Lorcan Warhol through the time portal and into this place. Maybe the woman who Margo saw taken away, Norlene, had better information than her sister did. Maybe she was fine. Maybe, if she could find no other way to get inside the city, Margo would risk taking the tentacle too.

But she would wait until she ran out of options.

When Kay returned to the booth she asked Margo to follow her. Kay took her through a door in the back of the restaurant and up a dusty stairway into an apartment. "Home sweet home," said Kay, dryly reading the words of a framed needlepoint decoration hanging by the door. The walls were wood paneled. The main room was crowded by a yellow corduroy couch and a large television on a low table. It looked cramped but comfortable.

"Norlene's room is the second one down the hall," Kay said. "Bathroom is at the end if you need to use it."

"I have to ask," Margo said. "If what you said is true and Norlene isn't coming back, why aren't you more upset?"

Kay sighed. "I guess it hasn't completely hit me yet. In my mind, I'm devastated. In my heart, I'm still expecting her to come home carrying a bag of chips and a can of soda in a plastic bag. And anyway I have customers down there right now expecting me to feed them. I have tables to clean and dishes to wash. I have Walt to deal with when he gets back. I'd love to take all day to cry about Norlene being gone, think about how much I'm going to miss her. But I can't. What I'm doing is, I'm helping you, the white lady who showed up in her coat, because I couldn't help her. Now I've got to go downstairs and you've got to get yourself changed." She went to the door. "Don't leave without saying goodbye," she said before closing it.

Alone in Kay's apartment, Margo suddenly felt tired. She was only just barely beginning to understand how this society worked, how different the way people lived here was from how they lived in the Bublinaplex, and it made her certain that this mission that had seemed so simple when she was escaping her mother's estate was a complicated labyrinth with no clear path forward. And her search for Jasper had hardly even started. What would she do next? Where would she go?

She entered Norlene's room. The space was like a large closet with a mattress on the floor with a tangle of blankets on top. Beside the mattress were some magazines and an ashtray containing a single cigarette butt. At the far end was a narrow door that opened into a truly tiny closet where clothes were stacked and hung neatly. There she found an oversized flannel shirt and pair of sweatpants that seemed like they would be reasonably comfortable even if they didn't quite fit. She also found a pair of boots and tried them on. They might have been a half-size too small. She took them.

After choosing an outfit, she looked at the mattress again. Would it make a difference if she stayed and took a nap and continued her search for Jasper in the evening? Kay might have good advice for what she should do next. Margo didn't want to exploit Kay's hospitality to such a degree that her host might regret helping her.

She decided instead to take a quick shower in Kay's bathroom. When she was clean and dressed, then she would go back down to the restaurant and ask about sleeping just for a couple of hours in the empty bed.

After showering and putting on the fresh clothes, Margo felt revived. By the sink she found an array of colorful creams and scented oils. On a whim she rubbed some of lavender-scented oil onto the leeches. Maybe they look ghastly and maybe they'll repulse Jasper, so why not make them smell kind of pretty? Anyway despite feeling better, she still meant to take a nap. The scent, she thought, might help her relax.

The boy, Walter, opened the door to the bathroom. Margo, surprised, let out a startled shriek. He screamed and ran out of sight.

"I'm sorry—" Margo started to say, following out him into the living room.

The boy reappeared holding a sort of aluminum club that Margo recognized as a baseball bat. He was shouting at her now. "What are you doing in our house? What are you doing wearing my momma's clothes? What the hell kind of a weird-ass freak-arm lady are you?"

"Calm down," Margo was saying, and she held out her leech arms and suction cup hands in a way that, if they were normal human arms, would be a gesture of harmlessness. The gesture didn't work. The boy swung the bat. Margo pulled her arms back to show she wouldn't hurt him but one of the leeches lashed back and grabbed threateningly for the bat. "No!" she yelled at the leech. "He's just a boy! He doesn't understand!" Through sheer mental exertion she was able to will it back against her side.

The boy's eyes went wide with fear. He was panting. Then his eyes locked on Margo's and his jaw set and he leapt forward and swung the bat at her head. Both leeches whipped forward. One suction cup hand caught the bat mid-swing and flung it through a living room window, shattering the glass. The other balled itself into a fist and punched the boy in the stomach, knocking him to the floor and rendering him a coughing, sputtering heap. He began to cry again, the wail of a terrified, orphaned child.

Margo put on his mother's coat and picked up his mother's boots, not stopping to put them on, and ran as fast as she could down the stairs and through the restaurant and out the door.

Kay's sharp, confused voice shouted after her.

Filthy, tired-looking workers now filled the streets. In response to Kay's shouting, several moved forward to block Margo's path.

THIRTY-FIVE

The workers surrounded Margo.

There was a short one, about Margo's height, who said, "Whoah, slow down miss." Margo guessed he was fifty-ish. He was bald and had a gentle face.

"I need to go," said Margo, backing up, eyes wide with panic. Who were these people? What terrible purpose could they have been working on all night? And when they found out she'd attacked Walter, what would they do to her? And the leeches, sensing the threat to her when they attacked—what would they do to the workers?

"You'll need to wait until we iron out the misunderstanding between yourself and Miz Magarac, got it?" said the gentle-faced man. "We look out for each other here in the Periphery. Now I don't know for sure, but I think you're a stranger here." His eyes darted to her suction cup hand holding Norlene's boots. "I don't recognize your face."

Walter was screaming and crying outside now. Kay was holding him back, trying to understand. It wouldn't be long before they understood what Margo had done.

Not sure what else to do, Margo sat down on the ground in the middle of the growing crowd and put on the boots. As she tied the laces, a woman with a loud voice leaned in and yelled even though she was just a couple of feet from Margo, "Eeew, what's the matter with your hands?"

Still sitting on the ground, Margo held up her suction cup hands and said in a deadpan voice, "Deadly parasites from the future. Better stay back."

Hushed murmuring spread through the crowd. She heard them repeat "from the future" more than once.

The gentle-faced man knelt down to face her. "You're from the bubble in the future?"

"You could say that," Margo said.

"What the hell are you doing here?" he asked, shaking his head.

Before she could answer, the crowd parted. Kay stepped forward with Walter by her side. Kay shook her head. "I helped you," she said, loud enough so others could hear. "And this his how you thank me? By smashing my window and beating up this poor boy here whose momma was just taken by the tentacle."

"I'm sorry, I— "

"No," Kay said. "You ain't sorry. These fine folks here. Maybe they'll make you sorry." Hushed murmuring from the crowd again. "Maybe they'll introduce you to the Saboteurs. Pampered scum from the future like you, they'll make you sorry you were ever born."

The gentle faced worker spoke so only Margo could hear. "I'm sorry," he said. "You're a perfect hostage. If you want to live, you'll cooperate."

A large, grim-faced man in dirty black coveralls stepped forward. He had a square, clean-shaven jaw and large expressive eyes. He looked like he thought he was going to enjoy what was going to happen next. He stepped behind Margo and grabbed her roughly by the shoulders.

"Don't do this," Margo said.

"Why not?" the man growled.

"Because you'll regret it." Her leech arms extended. She opened and closed her suction cup hands like a pair of weird throatless mouths.

With a horrified look on his face, the man released her and stepped back. "What are you?" The man asked. He was backing up toward the crowd.

"I'm Leech Girl."

Margo watched him closely—too closely, perhaps, because she didn't see the woman rush out of the crowd behind her and jam a taser into her back. Margo screamed as a feeling like a million red-hot needles piercing her spine paralyzed her. She collapsed, and as she fell the woman dropped the taser. Margo's head hit the ground and in one quick gesture the leeches reached back and picked up the woman who'd tased her and chucked her at least 10 feet away as if she was a doll. Taser woman landed mostly unharmed, caught by a few surprised workers when she landed on top of the crowd.

The workers gathered around Margo saw the act of self-defense as an attack. Together they rushed forward to restrain her. Two of them grabbed one leech arm and three grabbed the other. Margo stood up and used her leech arms to fling the workers back into the crowd. Some bounced back and returned to her side immediately and others moved forward to replace anyone who wanted to back down. "Stop the freak!" she heard someone shout. Someone tasered her again and the several workers trying to restrain her also fell. Minutes later they were all up and trying to wrestle Margo down to the asphalt.

There was a pistol shot. Everyone stopped. A hush fell over the crowd. The crowd parted away from a thin man who stood about five paces from Margo. He was pointing a revolver into the air.

"Enough!" he said.

Margo stood up and caught her breath. She held the leeches out from her sides, ready to fend of the next wave of attackers.

"Let's talk about this," said the thin man. He put the revolver inside his jacket. Carefully, with his hands up, he started to approach Margo. "I think we may be able to reach an understanding."

Another pistol shot, and the man who thought an agreement was reachable had a bullet hole in his head.

Margo stared in horror as his body hit the road. He was on his back. A puddle of blood quickly formed under his head.

A voice through a bull horn followed by a sound like horse's hooves against the pavement followed.

"THIS IS THE POLICE. DROP YOUR WEAPONS. DISPERSE IMMEDIATELY."

Seconds later, gunshots were being exchanged as most of the crowd fled. Many workers took cover in Magarac's or some other nearby building.

In the middle of the melee, Margo stood, unsure of where she should go or what she should do. She was still disoriented from being tasered. She couldn't stop looking at the thin man's body and the blood pooling under him.

Trying to talk with her was the last thing he ever did. Were it not for her, this would not have happened.

A sudden nausea overcame Margo and she threw up right there on the street.

Then the police came into view.

There were five officers. All wore heavy body armor and helmets with visors covering their faces. They carried black batons. Rifles were slung over their backs. And they were riding on the backs of things that Margo at first didn't quite understand.

The things were like horses but they didn't have heads. Instead, their necks ended in a piece of machinery that was nothing like the correct shape of a horse's head. Shiny black plastic covered their bodies.

And then Margo understood. She was seeing cyborg horses.

An officer rode up to Margo. "Are you alright?" he asked in a mask-muffled voice.

She looked up, too dazed to answer him.

Nearby, a worker who'd been shot in the leg and was lying on the ground replied, "Is SHE alright? This freak robbed the woman who runs the diner and attacked her poor nephew."

The officer lifted his visor. Bright blue eyes gazed coldly out from under his heavy, furrowed brow. "This freak, as you call her, is Margo Abbotzo. Do you really expect me to believe that someone whose family owns practically every piece of property in the Periphery has any reason to commit petty crimes against slum-dwellers like you?" He turned back to Margo. "So, I ask again. Are you alright?" He reached a gloved hand out to her.

Margo nodded. Not thinking, she gave him her suction cup hand. He recoiled. "What is that?"

"Sorry!" she shouted so he could hear over the noise around them. "These are what I've got for hands!" The officer fixed her in his cold gaze, then nodded as if he understood. He offered his hand again, then helped Margo climb up onto the cyborg horse's back.

She grabbed hold of the officer's armored vest. "I take it you've never ridden an equiborg," he said. "There are handles on its hips. Hang on. I'm taking you to safety. My partners can finish with these rioting Sobs."

He murmured a command Margo couldn't hear into the machinery at the end of the equiborg's neck. From behind it looked like a miniature control console like the dashboard of a hover cube or Diego's truck.

The equiborg launched into a gallop. Under the nearly uniform bright gray of the overcast sky they raced down cracked roads between dilapidated buildings and makeshift hovels.

Margo couldn't stop thinking of the man she'd seen shot. The shame of feeling responsible for causing the confrontation that led to his death mixed with an arresting fear of the officer who rescued her. She had been wrong to liken the police in this time/place to the Bublinaplex's Community Safety officers. Protecting the public was not the primary purpose of the officers here. How could it be? You couldn't shoot people to protect people.

No, she realized, the purpose of these officers was not protection. It was control.

Of course the people here surely had not grown up with the daily safety lessons that made people in the Bublinaplex place such a high value on human life, and they certainly could not have been raised believing their immediate community was the sole human population on Earth. So maybe the people here were dangerous to each other, maybe more dangerous than anything threatening to creep out of the Fungus Wasteland, and maybe the officers here using deadly force against the people they were supposed to be protecting actually did protect people by stopping them from tearing each other apart.

Margo considered this, the foreign-to-her idea that the threat of violence was what was used here to keep people safe, and she missed the Bublinaplex more than ever.

She told herself finding Jasper would make it worth it, but even this she was beginning to doubt. Images of awful things that could have happened to Jasper since his arrival had started seeping into her imagination. For the first time since she'd leapt through the portal into the past, she seriously considered the possibility that he could be dead. He could have been dead all along, not devoured by a tickle swarm or a lobopod, but shot by a police officer or attacked by rioting workers or who knows what else?

She imagined the expression on the face of the man she'd seen shot, the sudden absence of life in his eyes and the slackening of everything and the collapse, the sudden transformation of a person into a heap of person-shaped meat. She imagined the same expression on Jasper's face. She nearly threw up again off the side of the equiborg. Looking down she tried to focus on the blur of the road but could not.

She closed her eyes. She told herself to stop freaking out. Jasper was fine. That's what she would have to believe. She would believe it until it was proved otherwise. To go on, she had to.

And even if she would never again see the Bublinaplex, she thought that maybe reminiscing with Jasper about the Bublinaplex once he and she were reunited would be almost as good as going back.

She opened her eyes.

Over the officer's shoulder she saw the black wall marking the end of the Periphery rising out of the scorched grass. The wall was higher than the skeletal trees growing on either side of the triangular gate in front of them.

"Where are you taking me?" Margo asked the officer.

"Into The Republic," he said. She strained to hear him through his helmet and visor. "Your family reported you missing. I reported you found. There's a man with a helicopter waiting at Security Headquarters to take you home."

Shit, thought Margo. Tromscratt.

"I'm not going anywhere with that man in the helicopter."

"Beg your pardon, Miss," he said. "But I have strict orders—"

"To hell with your strict orders," said Margo as they passed through the triangular gate. It closed behind them with a mechanical click and she fell silent. On the other side, the officer brought the equiborg to a halt.

From the ground, Cog City's gleaming skyscrapers and narrow streets had the feel of a forest made of metal. The buildings cast shadows that enveloped the close streets in nearly permanent darkness despite the gray daylight high above. Black-uniformed workers hurried on foot up and down the streets. Equiborg-mounted police patrolled among them.

Composing herself, Margo resumed, "I'm an adult."

She swallowed.

"An important adult. Clearly, I'm fine. The Abbotzos will be grateful to you for finding me and rescuing me from the mob. But you can't just return me to my mother's toady like a piece of lost property. I'm here for a reason, and I'm not going to turn away from that reason just because my mother would rather I not leave her house."

She caught herself holding her breath, then inhaled and exhaled. For all she knew, the officer could very well be required to return her to

Tromscratt exactly like a piece of lost property. She would have to seem very sure of herself to get someone like this officer to break protocol. She would have to seem entitled to his assistance.

Apparently, it worked. The officer sighed. "Where should I take you then?"

"I don't know. Take me to where I can get help finding someone from the same time slash place I'm from. An archive?"

"I don't know anything about an archive," said the officer. "At least not any archive that will be useful for you. But I think I know where you might find help." The officer leaned forward and spoke into the equiborg's machinery-head. "HR." Immediately it began to trot forward and veered into a path to their right.

"HR?" Margo asked.

"Human Resources."

"I don't understand."

"Cogworks' Human Resources Department. They have a file on everyone who works here. And everyone who comes here after being banished from the bubble works here. Everyone except you, of course."

"Oh," said Margo. "I didn't realize that."

"I gather there's a lot that you don't realize about The Republic."

Margo ignored the slight. "Thanks."

The officer shrugged. "You're on a mission. I get the feeling that if I refused to help you, I'd find you a couple of hours from now in the middle of another riot. As you say, you're an adult. Maybe you'll find who you're looking for and maybe you won't, but at least you'll have tried."

They came to an angular, crystalline building the color of smoke. "Here you go," said the officer, looking at the equiborg screen. "Good luck."

Margo dismounted, then turned to thank the officer. She gave the equiborg's flank a pat with her suction cup hand. "It never occurred to me that cyborgs could be grown in non-human shapes. But why would it make a difference? Growing one animal in a lab is like growing any animal in a lab."

The officer gave Margo a funny look through his open visor. "I don't know anything about growing cyborgs in labs," he said. "For years, old Josie here was as reliable a mare as I'd ever ridden. Raised her up with the rest of our police foals. But we got the orders from above that the horses would be Processed through the Machine. When the orders came, I honestly was surprised they hadn't come sooner. Don't get me wrong, I loved that animal. But sentimentality doesn't do anyone any good, especially not in this line of work. I guess even the most reliable mare can be unpredictable, and, of course, severely lacking as far as built-in digital maps are concerned."

Margo backed away from the officer on his equiborg. She hoped her face did not betray her horror. She forced a smile. She should be grateful to this man. She must have misunderstood what he was saying. Or maybe it was he who misunderstood what he was saying. He couldn't mean a perfectly beautiful, healthy horse was decapitated and turned into the part-animal, part-machine thing he now rode. Or if he meant it, he had to be wrong. Maybe the Cyborg Laboratory in this time/place was a secret for some reason. Maybe she knew something that he did not.

"Thank you," she said, then quickly turned and jogged up the crystalline building's stairs and passed through its opaque glass doorway.

She looked back through the door. The officer was still sitting on the equiborg at the bottom of the steps. His visor was down and he seemed to be muttering something into the machinery where the creature's head should be.

THIRTY-SIX

The building was cold inside. Sparsely geometric paintings like grayscale Malevichs decorated the lobby walls. Margo stepped forward cautiously. Her footsteps clacked against the green marble floor. Barely audible clarinet music warbled out from hidden speakers. For a moment her solitude seemed absolute.

"Can I help you?" said a voice from an alcove Margo hadn't noticed. She whirled around as the leeches withdrew to the safety of her coat sleeves.

Before her sat a small woman behind a very large wooden desk. All Margo could see of the woman was the top of her head and her eyes, which were almost hidden in the bangs covering her forehead. Something about the size of the desk intimidated Margo. She took a step toward the alcove, timidly at first, then, remembering the air of confidence she assumed when asserting herself here and reminding the people of this time/place that her last name was Abbotzo, with self-assured strides.

"Yes," she said. "My name is Margo Abbotzo. I'm looking for someone. I was told HR could help me find him. He was banished from the Bublinaplex almost two years ago. Can you help me?"

When she reached the desk she looked down at the woman. The woman's large eyes met Margo's. Her face wore a practiced expression of expressionlessness. Something about the way she looked out from the wooden desk surrounding her on all sides reminded Margo of a captive animal, something that has been taught for years to fear punishment and whose quick movements anticipate the sudden need to hide or retreat. The woman turned to the computer monitor on her desk and her fingers tapped a rapid rhythm on the keyboard in front of her.

"Yes, Miss Abbotzo. Of course." She didn't look away from the screen. "What is the employee's name?"

Margo felt a swelling of hope in her chest, and anger. Could finding Jasper be so simple? Had Tromscratt—and Fayette—truly have been lying to her all the long months of their supposed search for him?

"Dr. Jasper Bearden," she said. "At least, I think that's his name. My name isn't the same here as it was in the Bublinaplex, so I don't know if his might have changed too ..."

"I understand, Miss Abbotzo," she said, typing as she spoke. "My records include both names. And ... yes. Here he is. Jasper Frick. Here since November 17, 2052. Hmm ... I need to make a phone call. Can you please wait a minute?"

"Yes," said Margo, barely able to believe what she was hearing. "Yes, of course. Do whatever you have to do." Then, after a pause. "Are you calling him? Can I talk to him?"

"No. A Senior Manager flagged Jasper's record. I'm required to contact the Senior Manager if anyone comes looking for him. Please wait." Anxiously, Margo watched the woman make her phone call.

"Hello, Mr. Vargas," she said. "I'm calling about the Jasper Bearden-slash-Frick record you have flagged in the employee database. I have someone here who would like to see Jasper."

At this, the woman looked up at Margo and offered a reassuring smile. "Yes," she said into the phone. "Of course. Of course. Thank you Mr. Vargas. Thanks. Goodbye."

"Well?" said Margo after the woman hung up.

"Mr. Vargas is coming down for you. He'll help you find who you're looking for. Please wait. He said he'll just be a few minutes."

Margo couldn't believe it. After everything she'd risked and everything she'd suffered, she was finally going be reunited with Jasper.

He was here. He was alive. He would see her and she would see him and maybe things could be something like the way they were when they had each other in the Bublinaplex.

Yes, maybe he'll be repulsed by the leeches. But maybe not. She was too euphoric at her success in finding him to let herself dwell on that possibility. And if the leeches became the sole obstacle to their reunion, maybe she could bring herself to have them removed. Maybe if she had a choice and the opportunity to think through the implications of the surgery Fayette had tried to force on her, she could go through with it. Maybe there's a way to do it that doesn't harm the leeches.

Yes, that's what she would do. She decided right there that she would be willing to have the leeches removed for Jasper. She would see that the removed leeches were unharmed and attached to some animal with missing limbs, a dog or a goat or something. The animal would be her and Jasper's pet. He'd help her take care of it and she'd learn to use her toes to do whatever she needed to do, turning door knobs and opening books and maybe even holding her crochet hooks. She knew in that moment she was willing to do anything she could to make it work with Jasper in this new time/place. She refused to entertain the possibility that she might lose him again.

Margo had started pacing back and forth as she thought. She was at the faraway end of the lobby when the elevator doors across from the alcove opened and she heard the woman behind the desk say, "Hello Mr. Vargas."

Margo stopped and turned, and started walking quickly back toward the woman and Mr. Vargas. From far away she could see he was a slight man wearing a tailored suit and tie.

As she got closer she noticed something about him was uncannily familiar.

A few steps closer and she stopped. He was familiar alright.

He was Lorcan fucking Warhol.

No fake beard this time. His thin hair had been shorn down to his scalp. But there was no mistaking him.

For an instant she questioned whether finding Jasper would be worth once again dealing with Lorcan fucking Warhol.

"Inspector Chicago!" he said as he approached. "I feel like I should welcome you to Cog City, but this isn't your first time here, is it?" He extended his hand and didn't flinch at the leech Margo timidly offered in return. He took her suction cup hand in his and shook it vigorously—so vigorously that Margo was a little afraid the leeches might attack. Not that attacking Warhol was something she was opposed to. "I guess Missus Abbotzo and her creature Tromscratt finally gave in and sent you here to meet with me. It's about time. I was starting to get impatient."

"Hi," Margo said flatly. "I was definitely not expecting to meet with you when I got here. And if Fayette and Tromscratt know where I am, it's because the police told them."

"The police?" Warhol/Vargas feigned a look of shock. "Oh dear!"

"Let's just say I had an interesting encounter with some 'Saboteur' types and the police sort of helped me out of a difficult situation. Anyway, you're here to help me find Jasper, right?"

"Sobs! My oh my. Walk with me. Tell me all about it," said Warhol/Vargas, ignoring her question as he started toward the exit. "Did they say anything interesting to you?"

Margo hurried to walk beside him instead of behind him. "Not much to tell. They threatened to kidnap me, I fought them off, one of them fired a gun into the air, and the police shot the guy who fired the gun."

"What an adventure!" he said. The contempt in his voice was so thick Margo hoped he might gag on it.

As they stepped out onto the street, Margo asked Warhol/Vargas what she should call him.

"Vargas is fine. It's my real name, the name I grew up with. This place—this time—is where I'm from. Of course it's where everybody's from. Some of our elites, the billionaires, the powerful, get to send their kids, kids like you, to the Bublinaplex when they're too little to remember being here. That way the kids grow up without witnessing the embarrassing mess of what their parents did to the world."

Vargas stopped walking and looked Margo in the eyes.

"That's what this whole project is about: making it so the rich can protect their offspring from the truth. It's the closest thing that you'll ever see to an expression of their shame for killing the world. And that, just so you know, is why safety is so important in the Bublinaplex. Cogworks must be able to reassure its customers of their children's absolute safety in the Bublinaplex."

"Hold on. You're telling me the Bublinaplex is basically a colony of rich peoples' kids sent to the future. For what purpose?"

They started walking again. "Maybe you haven't been here in the past long enough to notice, but the planet is dying. The temperature gets hotter every year. The oceans are rising and swallowing up the coasts. Medicine-resistant diseases are rampant. Crops rot before they ripen, let alone produce seeds. A miasma of desperation hangs thick in the air, and terrorists like the Saboteurs lie waiting for their chance to accelerate the decline.

"For a time, it seemed like the collective resources of the richest countries, corporations, and individuals would devote everything they had to salvaging the world. Then someone discovered it was possible to open portals into the future. The portals always led to the same time, the same place—the Fungus Wasteland—some who-knows-how-many-million-years hence. No one could imagine any use for that place. But when people saw it, what they saw was the fate of the world, what it looks like after The End, and they were filled with despair.

"And then your father had the idea that would become the Bublinaplex and Cogworks Incorporated embraced it. He persuaded the rich that, instead of fixing the mess they had made of the world, they could skip ahead and start fresh by colonizing a new world with a new society where war and economic strife were ancient history and creative self-expression—and safety—were the organizing principles. Before long, the Bublinaplex business was booming and the projects meant to salvage the world for those of us who can't afford to send our descendants into the future withered away. They've been replaced by a sad sort of hospice care for what remains of the possibility for a dignified life here."

It was a lot for Margo to follow.

This time seemed so full of life. The oaks and squirrels and birds and flowers thrived just fine along the edges of the Abbotzo estate. How could giving up on all of that life and starting over in the Fungus Wasteland make sense to anyone? Where did Jasper fit into all of this? She had so many questions. Between buildings she saw a tentacle-tower slowly undulating in the sky.

"What about people who get picked up by the tentacle-towers around this city and never come back?" Margo asked. "Are they given a way to travel to the Bublinaplex too?"

Vargas laughed. "You're not completely wrong. What I want to make sure you understand right now—and this is probably why Fayette refused to send you to me—is that the entire reason I was sent to the Bublinaplex was to give you something to do."

"Wait, what?"

"Ever since you were very young, Executive Designer Fash, your father, was disappointed by your lack of interest in the fine arts—"

"What do you mean?" Margo said, knowing perfectly well what he meant. All her life, she'd been given hints at the perceived inferiority of her plush creations compared to the poems, paintings, sculptures, and symphonies that her peers spent their time on.

"I made my crochet cats..."

"Crafts!" Vargas snapped. "It was embarrassing for him when the children of others showed so much promise. He had the expectation that you, the daughter of the Executive Designer, would grow up to create exceptionally important things. So when he became aware of your precocious, if odd, interest in making art safe, he turned the two-person Art Safety team into a whole department at the top of the Tower of Safety. And when he realized there really wasn't enough work for an entire Department of Art Safety, I, a mere administrative assistant here at Cogworks Incorporated, invented Recklessism.

"Day and night, I'd been wasting my time, time I should have been able to spend pursuing my creativity, on menial office work for your father. I'd been biding my time, seeking my opportunity to find a way into the Bublinaplex, and this was my chance. At first, I pitched Recklessism to him as a joke. I brought it up several times a week as he picked up or dropped off reports from my desk. The idea must have stuck. He took some persuading that I was actually the right person to execute my own idea—what an insult it would have been if it had been given to someone else. Ultimately, I prevailed. I was sent through the portal into the future and named Lorcan Warhol. You know the rest."

The revelations hit Margo like blows to the face. They made perfect sense, and they were utterly devastating.

The Bublinaplex was not a place where the last of humanity survived. It was a protective bubble where the elite of the past—the present, she reminded herself—shielded their children from the harsh realities of this dirty, dying world.

The Department of Art Safety did not serve an essential function. It was set up by her father to keep her occupied so her time could be filled with an activity that was less embarrassing to him than crocheting cats.

She was not the best Art Safety inspector. How could she be? No, she was given so many assignments and so much encouragement from Sub-Chief O'Keefe because it was the best way to keep her distracted. Entertained, even. She was special only because her father secretly was in charge of the system and he could adjust the system to accommodate her. Now she knew, and everything was ruined. The idea that she was especially talented at anything was suddenly replaced by the suspicion that everything positive she ever believed about herself must be a lie.

And Warhol! Or Vargas. Now she understood why Warhol's "genius" installation came out the way it did, with that monstrous balloon with her face on it now permanently attached to the museum. It was all just to keep Margo busy. His popularity in the Bublinaplex, it was a sham too, orchestrated by her father. Except Vargas didn't seem to mind. Was the public enthusiasm for Recklessism in the Bublinaplex entirely a creation of this man walking beside her and her father, or had the philosophy espoused in the Recklessist Manifesto really caught on to some degree and taken on a life of its own? Certainly there were some Recklessists who took Warhol/Vargas' ideas seriously despite their insincere source. Like Beckett. His devotion to Recklessism led him to destroy himself and almost destroy the Bublinaplex and everyone in it.

And all apparently because Margo's father thought his daughter should occupy herself with something besides crocheting cats.

"Ah," said Vargas. "Here we are. The factory."

The building was a gray box away from the other buildings. It had no windows. A squat smokestack like a brick-and-mortar volcano bulged from the roof of the near end but no smoke came out. It was, Margo thought, almost aggressively dull-looking.

"This is where Jasper is?" she asked.

"Right," Vargas said with a nod. "This way."

They approached the fence that surrounded the building. A section of the fence slid open for Vargas when he stepped up to it and Margo followed him through. A concrete sidewalk led the way to the factory entrance.

Inside was a vast shop floor where row after row of white tables were lined up between bulky machines. Some of the machines ran the length of the building; the smallest were the size of cars. Workers in white smocks stood at the tables, focused intensely on mysteriously minuscule tasks.

What were they making? Margo didn't want to ask Warhol/Vargas. He seemed to be enjoying lecturing her a little too much. He was getting on her nerves and she was not interested in inviting another round of horrifying revelations. Despite herself, his cynical description of the Bublinaplex and how it fits into this world was eating away at her, forcing her to see the place she'd always loved in a light that made her feel ashamed. At the same time, everything he said made too much sense for her to deny, and though she never before had any way of knowing any of the things Warhol/Vargas was telling her about, still, her ignorance made her feel embarrassed.

She told herself it would be worth it once she saw Jasper.

She would try to keep it together.

She would try to stay cool.

She would not invite further lectures from Warhol/Vargas.

On a long table against a wall she saw something she recognized.

"Cyborg heads," she said, pointing them out to her guide.

"Yup," said Vargas. He smiled. It was an ugly expression. She looked away from him and back to the cyborg heads and was reminded of the officer's words about his equiborg.

"We got the orders from above to that the horses would be Processed through the Machine. ... I guess even the most reliable mare can be unpredictable, and, of course, severely lacking as far as built-in digital maps are concerned. She suppressed her suspicions and reminded herself of the cyborg lab in the Bublinaplex. She'd seen it with her own eyes, the semi-formed bodies floating, lit by strange lights and growing in their nutrient baths. So what if their heads were made here?

She followed Vargas toward a metal stairway. On a landing halfway up, he started lecturing her again. "Cyborgs are Cogworks' signature product. They're produced exclusively for the Bublinaplex. In fact, if you ask the Executive Designer, he'd say cyborgs are the key to the Bublinaplex's success. They're not merely machines for doing work. No, their purpose is to produce time. Time for those privileged Bublinaplex citizens to focus on their creative pursuits without having to worry about the menial, everyday tasks that threaten to overwhelm life with tedium and make true creativity completely impossible. All the things that require two hands but not a brain, the cyborgs are there to do."

Margo found herself nodding along with Vargas' speech as she followed him up the stairs and then across a catwalk over the shop floor. She could feel the leeches' hesitation at the height—they were fifty or so feet up—but she was able to will herself forward without any resistance. She was reminded that when Jasper saw her it would be his first time seeing the leeches and she didn't know how he would react. She would do her best to keep them retracted in the sleeves of her bulky coat, at least at the very beginning of her encounter. He was a good guy and she wasn't ashamed of the leeches but she figured seeing her would be shocking enough and that softening the blow about how she had changed was the considerate thing to do.

Down below, she noticed the white-smocked workers buzzing around at their workstations between the machines. None of the workers looked up from their tasks or gave any indication that they were aware of Margo and Vargas traipsing through the factory. They seemed to be constantly moving. Margo found the relentlessness with which they worked surprising. She couldn't help but ask Vargas, "Who are these people, anyway?"

"They are the banished, of course," he replied. "This is what they do, day in and day out in ten, sometimes twelve-hour shifts. This and other essential, if repetitive, jobs that are necessary for keeping the Bublinaplex going. There," he pointed to a tall figure threading wires through one of the nearly-finished cyborg heads. "You recognize him?"

Margo strained to see the worker's face. She couldn't make it out, but his height gave him away. "Spreck Purcell?"

"Né Spreck Heinz."

Margo watched Spreck. There was something reassuring to her about seeing another familiar face. Seeing him so hard at work, she felt a surge of pity for him.

As if he sensed her thought, Vargas said, "Don't feel too bad for him. Remember, it's the work that he and others do here that make life in the Bublinaplex possible. Cog City is full of the banished, all hard at work supplying the Bublinaplex with clean air and water, food, building materials, and, of course, art supplies. Everything there comes from here. Of course, eventually some people are working toward the goal that the Bublinaplex will one day become self-sustaining city, able to exist independently after humanity here in the past or present, drive ourselves to extinction."

"Are you one of those people?"

Vargas chuckled. "No. I think it's as doomed as the rest of us."

They came to a locked circular door at the end of the catwalk. On the door was written "DIS / ASSEMBLY." Vargas knocked. The shadow of someone inside passed in front of a narrow slit in the door. Someone inside was looking out at them.

The door creaked open. "Lorcan," said the weary voice from inside. "This is a surprise. Can I help you?"

Margo instantly recognized the voice: JASPER.

"You have a visitor," said Vargas.

Jasper opened the circular door a little wider and Vargas pushed his way inside and past Jasper to the far end of the room.

Then it was just Jasper and Margo facing each other through the door.

He had aged. There were lines around his eyes that weren't there before. There were flecks of gray in his hair.

After a few seconds of incredulously staring at each other, Margo stepped into the room and embraced him and pressed her lips against his. Tears streamed from her eyes now and his too, and each felt the cold trickle of the other's tears on their cheeks. As she hugged him she was careful to keep the leeches hidden in her coat sleeves. There would be a time to show them to Jasper soon, but right now was not that time. Their faces separated and they stood forehead to forehead, holding each other.

"I missed you," said Margo.

"I missed you too," said Jasper. Then, "What on earth are you doing here, anyway? How did you get yourself banished?"

"I wasn't banished. I came here looking for you."

They stood there quietly feeling one another's closeness while the mechanical hum and rhythmic churning sounds of the factory surrounded them.

Suddenly there was another sound that broke through the mechanical din. It sounded like someone crying, and it was coming from inside the DIS / ASSEMBLY room Jasper had come out of. There were groans and sobs and pitiful, incoherent utterances, and they became louder and louder and louder.

Margo pulled back from Jasper. "Does someone in there need our help?"

"Ignore it," he said, more sharply than Margo was used to hearing his voice.

She took a step back. "Please Jasper. I love you and I've missed you so much, but if your job here is to help someone in pain, please, you have to go to them."

"Trust me," he said. "Ignore it."

The sobs became shrill, desperate wails.

Lorcan Vargas opened the circular door. "Hey Margo, you're not going to want to miss this. The show's just about to start."

Margo shot Jasper a confused look.

"Don't go in there," he said.

Margo went in there. Jasper tried to stop her by grabbing her arm. He must have felt something off about the way it writhed inside her sleeve because he immediately let go.

The room was a cramped space. Monitors showing what looked like medical data, heart rates and breathing rates and brain activity and so on, covered the walls. A stool on wheels stood at the far end of the room amid an array of dials and buttons and knobs. A large window took up most of the wall above this control panel. Whoever was crying was on the other side.

Vargas stood next to the window. He tapped it with his finger. "Right here," he said.

"You're an evil fucker," said Jasper, then turned to Margo. "Please listen to me. Don't look through that window."

She searched his face for an explanation. She was confused and frustrated. She'd spent so much time and energy missing him. Now here he was. He made her heart beat faster. She loved him. But he was acting strangely, being oddly pushy in a way she'd never heard or would have tolerated before, and it made her afraid. He was hiding something. What was he hiding? What was he doing here in this factory? Why was someone crying on the other side of that window in the room where he was working?

The vehemence of his attempts to dissuade her from looking only guaranteed that she would have to look. Both of them knew that.

Suddenly Vargas was talking on a mobile phone. Jasper stepped toward him and gestured frantically for him to stop, but it was no use and Jasper stopped short of anything physical. A sinister smile crept across Vargas' face. Margo was reminded of how he looked that day in the SafetyPunk hangout seconds before he revealed Hazard no. 457 to her.

"Yes, right," Vargas said to whoever he was on the phone with him. "Process them now. Start the Machine."

"No!" shouted Jasper. "Goddamnit, no." He crumbled to the floor and covered his head with his hands. "Did you have to? Did you have to right now?" He was on the verge of tears. "Oh please don't look through that window Margo. Please!" he was groaning.

The sobs and wails coming through the window became screams. Margo ran to see.

At first, all she saw was a tangle of mechanical parts—hydraulics and belts and nodes and joints, all fitted together in a mass with little space in between. Parts flexed and hummed, gears turned. Then she saw past the wires to a row of chairs where ten men and women sat facing away from the window. The chair on the end was moving away from the seated group as if on a conveyor belt.

The chair turned a corner on its path through the dense machinery and now Margo could see the face of the woman sitting on it. And a new rhythm emerged from the metal cacophony. The noise was like marching and it was like chewing.

It was the woman who'd given Margo her coat.

She remembered her name. Norlene.

Norlene stared at nothing in front of her. Her jaw was set. She was not the person who was screaming. Margo saw her wrists and ankles were bound to the chair with leather straps. From the neck down, some kind of baggy black material covered her body.

For an instant Margo's eyes locked with Norlene's and she realized she could see her too, and even though she did not understand what was happening, she felt ashamed and afraid and angry and appalled all at once, and she had to look away.

The Machine grew louder. Marching. Chewing.

She looked back to Norlene. Norlene was still staring at her. Glaring at her.

And then from every side mechanical arms tipped with claws and surgical knives and lasers descended around Norlene and neatly removed her head.

The mechanical arms moved in rapid succession. They extended and retracted like spindly insect legs. They cut and lifted and twisted and cauterized.

They were finished before Margo could look away.

An arm pulled the head up into the machine and out of sight. Its eyes blinked rapidly.

On the chair the body moved forward. A large tube came up from the floor, completely covering it. Seconds later it withdrew and the baggy black material covering her had shrunken to become a layer of plastic skin against the body.

Now the next chair was moving, carrying a man with thin hair and bloodshot eyes to where the mechanical arms would descend on him. He struggled weakly against his straps and when his eyes caught Margo's he mouthed the words "Fuck you" at her.

Then the arms came down and removed his head.

She looked back toward the headless woman. Her body was moving away now. The back of her chair slid away and another pair of arms descended. In rapid succession they connected a set of tubes to her body like an extra backbone along her spine. The ends of the tubes hung limply where the back of her head once was.

The large tube came up from the floor again, engulfing the thin-haired man.

The woman's body approached the end of the conveyor belt. Her chair stopped and a metal shield came down from the ceiling, covering her from the shoulders up. Flashes of light and sparks came out from under the shield. Seconds later, the shield was lifted.

In place of the woman's head on her shoulders was the familiar, rectangular head of a cyborg.

The leather straps fell free from the cyborg's wrists and ankles. It got up and walked to the wall on the opposite side of the room and stood facing the Machine that had made it what it now was, devoid of thought and feeling and will.

THIRTY-SEVEN

Margo was shaking.

She picked up the sole chair in the room and before Jasper or Vargas could stop her she was beating it against the window. She was trying to break the glass. There was nothing Jasper or Vargas could do to stand in her way. Safety—protecting others from harm—was what she'd long ago devoted her life to. She couldn't just stand there and let the rest of the eight or so people strapped into chairs on the other side of that window be decapitated. She couldn't stand there and just look—though just standing there and looking was presumably a significant part of what Jasper did here in Cog City.

"I'm supposed to make sure the Process is painless," Jasper was pleading. "It was the only chance I was given here to use my medical background, you've got to understand Margo—"

"I understand alright. I understand that you are complicit in murder," she heaved the chair once more at the glass. The chair bounced off, the window was clearly something stronger than ordinary glass, and it came back and hit Margo in on the side of her head. She yelped as it knocked her to the floor. She started weeping. Jasper reached for her. She swatted him away, then stood up. "I'm leaving."

Vargas blocked the doorway. "And where do you think you're going?"

"Anywhere but here," she said. "Anywhere but this horrible 'Cog City'."

"Oh no," Vargas tsk-tsked. "I'm afraid I can't let you leave the city. Not after seeing what you've seen. No, you have to stay. And here I thought you'd never again want to leave Jasper's side."

Margo looked contemptuously at Jasper. He was still on the floor, hugging his knees. "I never want to see Jasper again." Then she turned toward Vargas. "And you," she said, allowing her leech arms to snake out from her sleeves. "I'd like to see you try and stop me."

"Oh, we have ways here to make you stay put," he said, producing a taser gun. And you may not have noticed, I'm not the only one you must deal with. He stepped aside to reveal a half-dozen laser-carrying cyborgs gathered outside the DIS/ASSEMBLY room door. "This isn't the Bublinaplex. Anything happens to me, these cyborgs won't hesitate to kill you."

Margo let out a frustrated growl. "Goddamnit Warhol," she said, not caring if the name she used was not the correct one. "Why the hell did you bring me here?"

"Because you asked me to."

"No. I asked for Jasper. You could have brought me to him when he wasn't working. You could have—"

"—spared you the truth?" Vargas suggested. He returned the taser gun to his pocket. "Let's go. There's someone who might take you in."

"Margo, don't go," whimpered Jasper from the floor.

Wordlessly, Margo exited the room with Vargas. Two of the cyborgs with laser guns followed them.

"Why did you bring me here?" she asked again as they walked back across the catwalk.

Vargas stopped. "I brought you here because your father fucked me over. He used my ideas, my inspiration, my art to give you something to do. It was humiliating, really, to know the only reason my creations were going to see the light of day was because it so pleased his royal highness the Executive Designer who simply wanted to entertain his spoiled brat. But in exchange for my willingness to debase myself and my art, he promised me a life of luxury and creativity when I returned here after my banishment from the Bublinaplex. We had an agreement. An understanding. But he wasn't happy with how I'd executed some of my ideas. And he was furious about your friend Beckett's attempt to crush the Bublinaplex under a pile of tardigrades. He blamed me for that. So, to punish me, your father, instead of giving me the freedom he promised, made me a 'Senior Manager.' Now I'm forced to do the dirty work of overseeing his empire. Now I'm not much more than a self-aware cyborg, which might be worse than actually being one of these can-heads."

"I see one big difference between you and a cyborg," Margo muttered as they proceeded down the steps.

"Oh?" called Vargas back to her. "What's that?"

"You are capable of exacting some revenge for what's been done to you."

When they reached the exit, Vargas told Margo to wait. The cyborgs with laser guns waited with her as Vargas walked out onto the shop floor. When he returned, he had Spreck by his side. Though in the Bublinaplex Spreck had been Warhol's assistant, the only other time she'd seen the two of them together was on the video footage from Spreck's cyborg of the night of The Tragedy. Seeing them together now gave Margo an uneasy, uncanny feeling of being in a kind of scrambled alternate universe that was populated by the same characters as the ordinary universe but with the characters all cast in different roles.

"Spreck here has agreed to take you in for the night," Vargas said. "We'll furnish quarters for you here soon enough."

"I'm not staying," Margo said flatly.

"You don't understand," replied Vargas. "No one who has seen what you have seen is permitted to leave Cog City. The Executive Designer does not even allow himself to leave for fear he might be captured by the Saboteurs and tortured into confessing the truth of what happens to the Applicants who are taken by the tentacle-towers. Your confinement here will deeply disappoint him, I'm sure. But, in the end, he won't mind. And he won't make an exception for you to let you leave."

Margo looked at Spreck, who used his great shoulders to shrug sympathetically. "Sorry," he said, seeming more timid than he'd ever been in the Bulinbaplex.

"Don't apologize," Vargas snapped. Then, to Margo, "I'm finished with you for now." He turned and started to walk back onto the shop floor. "Take her to your rooms and make her feel at home Spreck," he said, then turned. "Make her understand that, were it not for the work we do here, there would be no Bublinaplex."

*

The building where Spreck lived was narrow, rectangular and brown. It stood about twenty stories high and was filled with cramped apartments.

Margo and Spreck had said nothing to one another during the entire twenty-five minute walk to the building. Now Margo was sitting on the vinyl sofa in Spreck's living room, staring at the blank TV screen and Spreck was in the kitchen, trying to find some kind of snack to offer.

"I don't have much," he said. "I take most of my meals in the cafeteria across the street." Margo didn't respond. He brought his offerings out to her. "Stale corn chips or cheese cracker crumbs?"

Margo continued to stare.

"I can turn that on for you if you want," he said with a nod toward the TV.

Margo's stare became a scowl.

"Or not," he sighed. He reached into the corn chip bag and pulled out a handful of the pale chip crumbles. He brought his hand up to his face and licked them from his palm like an animal. After chewing them up and swallowing he said, "How about a drink? Water? Wine? Whiskey?"

Margo said nothing.

"Well I'm getting myself a drink." He returned to the kitchen. "Coffee?" he said when the suggestion occurred to him. When he returned to the living room, Margo was lying on the couch, staring at the ceiling.

"Why don't you take off your coat? I can get you a blanket if you're cold. Or maybe you want to take a shower, change into something fresh? Nothing of mine will fit you of course but you're welcome to try. I might have some sweatpants that shrunk in the wash—"

Again Margo fixed a scowl at him. "I'm not going to sleep with you," she said. "In case you have any—I don't know—ideas."

"I don't want to sleep with you Margo," said Spreck. He sat down on an ottoman. Because of his height his knees were bent like a grownup sitting in a child's chair. He took a sip of coffee.

"Oh," she said. "So you think the leeches are disgusting."

"Margo," he said, resting a large hand on her shoulder. "Of course I think the leeches are disgusting. That doesn't matter. I'm gay. With or without the leeches, I don't want to sleep with you. So I don't know if you think you're picking up on some kind of tension between us and, yes, this situation where you are kind of being forced to spend the night here in my quarters is awkward, but please try not to read anything into my trying to be nice. I know you've been through a lot. I'm just being nice."

"Oh, sorry, I didn't know that."

Spreck's brow furrowed. "Well, why should you know anything at all about me? Let's not act like we're best buds or anything."

At this, Margo burst into tears. Spreck realized his mistake. She sat up and Spreck joined her on the couch and put his arm around her. "After Jasper was gone, I wanted to die," Margo sniffed. "And then when I found out he might not be dead after all—the hope of finding him alive again, it was everything."

"And now you've found him," said Spreck. He was petting her head as if she was a large cat.

"I found him alright. I found him complicit in mass fucking murder," she said. "I saw the woman who gave me this coat, the woman who all these clothes used to belong to, put through that Machine. She looked at me. She remembered me." She'd become uncomfortably warm at this point and pulled back from Spreck's embrace to remove her coat. The relieved leeches unfurled.

Spreck inched away but pretended he wasn't repulsed. "Margo," he continued gently. "Everyone in the Bublinaplex either owns a cyborg or depends on the work that cyborgs do to keep the place running. Everyone from the future is ... complicit. They just don't know it. That's just how it is. But listen, those people you saw put through the Machine, it's not like they don't volunteer, and it's not like they aren't compensated ..."

"That woman has a family. A son. If she thought she had a choice, and if she'd known what the choice meant when she made it, do you really think she would have made the choice she made?"

Spreck stood up. He was shaking his head and looking pityingly at Margo. "I'm going to go get us something to eat. You should get some rest. Get some rest and consider all the problems you're dealing with and all the problems of the world. And how about this: think about how what happens to Applicants in the Machine is kind of a way to opt out of all of that."

As Spreck stood in the doorway about to leave, Margo called his name.

"Yes?" he said, returning to the living room.

"What happens to their heads?"

"What?"

"The people who go through the Machine. What happens to their heads?"

Spreck fidgeted impatiently. He itched his ear. "Honestly, I'm not sure. I think maybe they're incinerated. I think that's what the smoke stack is for, the incinerator." He turned away. "I'll be right back," he said.

She was amazed that Spreck could know what went on in the Factory but not wonder what happened to the heads.

And she was amazed that she had owned a cyborg almost all her life and never wondered how it came to be.

The Cyborg Lab in the Bublinaplex must have been designed specifically to stop people like Margo from wondering about the source of their cyborgs. The lab itself must have been a recycled B movie set. The scientists must have been actors. Were they people from the Bublinaplex whose creative pursuit was acting, or were they brought in from the outside like Warhol/Vargas to put on a show for the ignorant children of the elite?

Margo felt like a fool for devoting her life to safety and for caring so much about the Bublinaplex that she'd risked her life to save it. And for caring so much about Jasper that she never stopped to consider the possibility that he might disappoint her profoundly.

But how could she have known? There must have been hints. But no. She told herself she mustn't be so hard on herself for her inability to predict the future, or, more aptly, know what happened in the past. She'd thought Jasper was dead. The truth was that he was some kind of quality control functionary for a monstrous decapitation machine. She closed her eyes. Could she will herself back to that headspace where she could once again think of him as merely dead?

No. Because when she'd thought he was dead, she missed him.

Now she felt nothing.

No. Not nothing. There was a rage in her now that had not been there before. And a hate.

Yes, Vargas/Warhol was capable of taking revenge against those he thought had wronged him and the cyborgs were not. But maybe there was a way for her to take revenge on their behalf.

Spreck returned with a bucket of fried chicken and a tub of macaroni and cheese. "Eat up," he said. Margo was ravenous. She took her fair share and then some and ate. When she was done she sunk into the couch, relishing the post-meal torpor.

Restored, she turned to Spreck and asked, "So how do I get out of here?"

"You don't," he said, still nibbling on a chicken bone.

"There must be a way," Margo insisted. "Please, think. I have to get out. I have to do something about what happens here."

"You want to 'do something,' huh?" He dropped the bone into the bucket, now empty except for the leftover breading and bones. He carried the bucket into the kitchen and smushed it into the garbage. "Maybe I don't want 'something' to be done. Maybe I'm perfectly okay with things here the way they are. I do my work and it keeps the Bublinaplex going. Generations of artists can fulfill their creative potential. That's a beautiful thing, right?"

"The Bublinaplex is a lie, Spreck," Margo said. "The work you do here props up that lie. I might have been willing to die for it before I knew it was a lie, but I'm definitely not willing to kill for it now that I know the truth." She stood up and put on her coat and pulled the zipper up to her chin. "I'm leaving Spreck. You can't stop me. But you can help me by telling me where to go."

"Fine," he said. "I truly do not know. But go to the building next to this one, 5545 H Street and find Room 833. Someone there might know."

"Thank you," she said, heading for the door.

"Oh, and Margo?"

"Yes?"

"Thank you for helping me back in the Bublinaplex. Obviously, I didn't get away. But just know that you're always welcome here with me if whatever you're trying to do doesn't work out."

A young woman with short red hair and glasses answered the door of Room 833 at 5545 H Street. When Margo asked her if she knew the way out, the woman said, "I truly do not know. But go to the building across the park from here, 4444 G Street and find Room 109. Someone there might know."

The woman closed the door. Margo thought it was an odd coincidence that she'd phrased her directions almost identical to the way Spreck had phrased his until the dark-eyed man who opened the door to Room 109 told her, "I truly do not know. But follow the road outside until you reach the intersection of 20th Avenue and E. Find the building with the pink marble stairs. That's 20372 E Street. Go to Room 721. Someone there might know."

For the next few hours, she trekked from apartment to apartment, asking the same question—"How do I get out of here?"—and received almost identical answers from the people she met, all directing her toward different buildings and different rooms. Sometimes it seemed like she was making progress and that the directions led her in a particular direction, but then she'd be directed back and had to retrace her steps past buildings where she'd already made her inquiry to buildings she'd originally passed by.

Until finally she knocked on the second door on the ground floor of 9595 B Street. She didn't know what time it was except that it was the middle of the night and she was extremely tired.

No one answered. Frustrated, she tried the knob. The door opened.

The room inside was dark and full of dirt. She took a step forward and a dank, musty smell wafted up around her. Her eyes adjusted and what she was seeing became clearer. There were mushrooms sprouting in clusters on the dirt floor. In the middle was a dark, cavernous pit with a packed floor sloping downward into the ground.

She closed the door behind her, careful to leave it unlocked, and descended into the pit.

THIRTY-EIGHT

After walking the damp, lightless tunnel for what seemed like hours, Margo stepped out into the muted moonlight.

Almost immediately, she was set upon by four men who jumped out from the winter-bare shrubs that grew on either side of the opening.

Margo didn't fight them, and she forced her leech arms to hold back. She was too tired and anyway she understood that these men who had been stationed on this end of the secret tunnel out of Cog City were not her enemies.

They were not so sure of her. Two of them locked her in the back of a rusted old police car. A wire cage separated the front seats from the back. The men took their seats in the front and proceeded to transport her somewhere.

The driver didn't speak. The man in the passenger seat told her they would take her to their headquarters and decide what to do with her there. "Probably you won't be going anywhere anytime soon," he said. "Not if our leader wants to use you as a hostage." He turned around and faced forward. "I hate this kind of thing. Sorry. I know it's wrong. But it's a wrong to right a worse wrong. A bad for the greater good."

"Would you just shut up?" snarled the driver.

"Whose headquarters?" Margo asked groggily. "You mean Saboteur headquarters, right? You guys aren't the, um, official police, right?"

"You'll see soon enough," said the driver.

The car traveled to the edge of the Periphery, where in the dawn light Margo could see small trees and thickets of brambles and vines quietly consuming this part of the city. They parked the car behind a huge stone structure, a church. From the outside it looked like a ruin. The men brought Margo inside. Aside from the stained glass windows, any religious statuary and art had been stripped away along with the pews. A lectern stood where there might once have been an altar. Candles and oil lamps lit the inside, giving the place an air of ancient holiness.

"Up here," said the man who had been the driver. He was pointing to a stairway that led up to a balcony. He led the way while his partner followed after Margo. On the balcony were a half dozen rows of intact pews with cushions. "Get some rest here," the driver said, more a command than an offer. "We'll decide what to do with you when the leader arrives."

Margo carried herself to the closest pew and collapsed.

"Don't try anything funny," she heard him say. "We'll be here, ready to stop you, just in case."

And though she did not know what would happen to her at the hands of these men or whether they represented the Saboteurs or sympathizers or a cult or some other sort of rag-tag collective of the desperate, she felt content. The most important thing for the moment was that she had escaped from Cog City. Warhol and Jasper were behind her, and so were the police and Fayette and Tromscratt.

She fell into a deep dreamless sleep almost before her eyes closed.

When she awoke she had to squint in the light from the gold, blue, and red stained glass windows on either wall. The church was full of people now, except for the balcony, and the crowd's hushed murmurs were a dull roar. One of the men who'd captured her stood at the top of the spiral staircase leading down from the balcony. He was looking out over railing into the packed floor below and sipping something steamy from a ceramic mug.

It took Margo several seconds to remember where she was and why she was here. Her legs ached from the previous day's journey. For a moment she felt grateful for the excuse for not trying to go anywhere that being held captive provided.

Then she remembered the Factory. The Machine. The Process. She thought of Jasper. She was so used to thinking of Jasper. She felt a pang of regret and insisted to herself she should feel nothing.

She stood up and approached her guard. She wanted to tell him about the things Warhol/Vargas had forbidden her to talk about. But when she started to speak, he shushed her. He shook his head and pointed down to the front of the church. "Our leader is about to speak."

Irritated, Margo looked down where the guard was pointing. A hooded figure wearing a tattered brown cloak stood a few paces behind the lectern in the front of the room. Large guards stood on either side of the figure. One stepped forward and raised his hands and said, "Silence!" and the crowd obeyed.

The hooded figure stepped forward and pulled back the hood. The leader was a woman.

And then Margo realized she recognized the leader. She couldn't believe it. The short black hair. That serene, determined brown face.

Belga.

She gave the speech.

"All of us who grow up in the so-called 'civilized' world are taught to believe human sacrifice is something that happened only in the distant past," she began.

*

By the time she was finished, Margo knew this cause was hers as well. She was ready to follow Belga into any danger anywhere.

Belga walked offstage and into a private room in the front of the church. After members of the crowd finished cheering and applauding, the guards that had flanked their leader stepped down to help arrange the gathering of hundreds into groups and each of those groups into a rough queue. Most of the individuals already seemed to know where they were supposed to be and the guards' role seemed simply to be to inspect how the people had arranged themselves.

Soon it was clear that all were now simply waiting for a signal, and at that signal, what they all were now waiting for would begin.

A guard had come up from the floor and was talking with Margo's guard. Margo looked at the new guard and he waved his hand for her to come closer. "You've been summoned by the leader," he said. "Come with me."

She followed him down the steps and through the crowd to a narrow door that led to a backstage area.

And there was Belga, sitting alone at a card table and typing furiously on a portable computer. Except she wasn't entirely alone. Margo was surprised after hearing her speech to see a cyborg standing behind Belga. If this was the cyborg that had followed Belga in the Bublinaplex, it had undergone a profound transformation. Its black plastic outer skin had been removed to reveal the scarred human skin underneath. On its screen-face was the static image of a man's smirking face.

Belga sat back for a moment and rubbed her eyes. Then she noticed Margo and she smiled. The smile was genuine but strained. "I thought that was you up there Margo," Belga said, her voice clear and commanding even in conversation. "It's good to see you. But I'm sorry to tell you, you can't stay. Look." She turned the computer so it faced Margo.

There on the screen was the familiar face of Executive Designer Fash. His white eyebrows and stubble and his deeply creased features were arranged in an expression of absolute sorrow. Belga pressed a button and the video began to play.

"The Saboteurs have sunk to a low even I didn't think they were capable of," said the Executive Designer. "They have attacked my family. My only daughter," he said with a sniffle, "They've taken my only daughter. And I will not rest until she is found and the Saboteurs' reign of terror is brought to an end—"

Belga stopped the video. "He goes on like that for a while. He says he's unleashing 'elite forces' to find you. We can't have them barging in and discovering you here. Not today."

"You know I've never even met the man," Margo said. She was still standing near the door.

Belga shook her head. "We can offer you safe transportation to where you want to go," she said and cracked her knuckles.

"I want to go where the people out there are going," Margo said with a nod toward the door. "I want to join you."

Belga stood up and stalked across the room. Margo thought there was something almost liquid in the way her cloak hung off of her thin frame. She turned and held a mug in the air. "Coffee?"

"Please," said Margo.

"Black okay?"

"Yes."

Belga carried two steaming mugs back to the card table. "Come. Sit." Margo joined her at the table, still in awe of this woman she'd looked up to her entire life. She noticed that the cyborg did not make any move to help Belga get the coffee.

Margo breathed in the steam. "So, I have to say it seems weird after the speech you gave out there that you have a cyborg back here," she said.

"That's Billy," Belga said. She looked down into her coffee and reached a hand back so her hand gently touched the cyborg's hand. "The Saboteurs who have been with us for any amount of time know he's back here. I usually keep him out of sight. Seeing him upsets people."

"But why do you have him back here?"

Belga closed her eyes and took a deep breath. When she opened them they met Margo's curious face. "Billy was my brother. Is my brother. I want to keep him comfortable."

"I'm so sorry Belga, I had no idea—"

"Don't." She gave the cyborg's hand a loving squeeze. "Now tell me, did you find Jasper?"

Margo nodded. "He operates the Machine."

"I know." Belga took a sip. "I'm sorry Margo. I didn't realize when I mentioned him, when we spoke so long ago. I shouldn't have told you about banishment not being a death sentence and I shouldn't have said anything about a possibility of a reunion with him. I was being selfish. I'm sure I wanted to find a way for you to join me, to join us here. And Jasper too."

Margo let out a sad little chuckle. "It's a nice thought."

"When did you find out? About Jasper and the Machine?"

"Yesterday."

Now Belga was looking at Margo hard. "So you came all this way just for him, through time and over and under every barrier that came your way, and now you see what he does, the sort of cog in Cog City he has become, and you won't forgive him?"

The question surprised Margo. "I might forgive him some day," she said. "But I'll never love him again. Not after seeing what I saw."

"But it's not as if you know any of these slum-dwellers who wind up being Processed through the Machine, right? Yet you feel more loyalty to them than you do this man who might love you till you're old and gray?"

Now it was Margo who was looking hard at Belga. These questions Belga was asking, Margo realized, were the same questions she'd asked herself when she'd left Cuthbert. They were the same, she and her. Belga realized it, and she was inviting Margo to realize it too.

"All my life," Margo began, "I've been devoted to protecting people. That's what an Art Safety inspector does. I put safety before everything else. And now I can't help but think about the pointlessness of putting safety before everything else from inside the Bublinaplex. I mean, there I was, doing things like stopping an artist from making a plinth the wrong way because someone might stub a toe on it, and meanwhile the whole city's existence depends on an army of decapitated slaves—"

"The cyborgs," Belga interrupted. "We call them the Executed."

"My point is, my whole purpose in life has been, up to this point, a lie. So I want to make it true. And the best way I can see right now to save people is to join you Saboteurs and destroy the Bublinaplex."

"You once risked your life to save the Bublinaplex."

"I was WRONG."

Belga reached her hands across the table. She did not flinch when Margo unfurled her leech arms and accepted Belga's long fingers into her suction cup hands. "No. You were right. You saved Cuthbert and thousands of others like him."

"Does Cuthbert know? About this place and where cyborgs, the Executed, really come from?"

"No, I don't think he knows."

Margo sighed, relieved. She didn't think she'd be able to handle it if Cuthbert was somehow complicit in the system behind the Bublinaplex.

"And I have to tell you," Belga continued, "We, the Saboteurs, do not intend to 'destroy' the Bublinaplex. We intend to raise awareness."

"Oh."

"Don't get me wrong. If we successfully pull off what we're trying to pull off today, the Factory will no longer function. But it will very much still exist. The inside of it, at least. That's part of the point."

Margo withdrew her leech arms and gave Belga a puzzled look.

"You'll understand soon," she said, then reached down into a box under the card table. "Here." She held up a spray can and tossed it to Margo. "Take that and join the others."

Margo eyed the can. It had no label and its metal surface was cool to the touch. "What is it?"

"Kronozoa," said Belga, smiling like someone in an advertisement. "In a can."

"Huh?"

"Kronozoa. Time-traveling microbes. They're what create the portals between this time and the future time of the Bublinaplex. The trick is getting enough of them to jump through time simultaneously. That's when they can carry a person along with them. They're sort of like salmon, if you know about salmon."

"I know salmon are fish," said Margo. "But I don't see what they have to do with time-traveling microbes."

"Salmon survive by dividing their lives between two faraway places— inland streams, where they are born and where they ultimately return to mate and die, and the ocean, where they live most of their lives. The kronozoa in your can are like that. They travel to the future, no one quite understands how, where they mate and lay eggs and die. The hatchlings then return to this time. The span between the two points in time is always precisely the same, a zillion years and five months and eleven days and two hours and 44 minutes and three seconds or something like that."

"So the idea is that we spray this stuff on something and it gets sent to the future by these time-traveling germs?"

There was a knock on the door. "Come in," called Belga. One of the guards, a man wearing a flannel shirt and camo pants, stepped in and bent down to whisper something in Belga's ear. "Good," she said. "Good." The man left. Belga stood up and pulled open the blind of the room's single window. "Come here," she said to Margo. "Let's see if our diversion is working."

Margo joined Belga by the window. Half-collapsed houses and dense tufts of brown weeds and small trees surrounded the church building, which Margo now realized stood on the side of a small hill. In the distance, one of the tentacle-towers swayed.

"The kronozoa in your can are defective," she said without turning away from the window. "Cogworks had a warehouse full of them. They were supposed to be destroyed. Some workers who are loyal to us thought they might be useful and instead of destroying the cans, took them."

"How are they defective?"

"It's hard to explain. Basically, the kronozoa in the can you're holding, they travel through time but they don't quite make it. They somehow mate and lay their eggs while still lodged in time. And if you would try to send something through time using them, that something would be lodged in time as well, still visible from the vantage point of the future, but not quite present physically."

"I'm not sure I follow."

There was the sound of an explosion off in the distance. The church shuddered under their feet. "That'll be the demolition crew with their diversion. There's no more time to explain. Look." In the window they watched smoke and dust rise into the air around the base of the visible tentacle tower. It arched and writhed, then fell to the ground with a thunderous boom. "Go," said Belga. "Hurry!"

Margo couldn't stop watching the chaos of smoke and fire now surrounding the place where the tentacle tower once stood.

"Go now!" Belga gently pushed Margo away from the window. Margo opened the door and bumped into a guard before she could make any progress. She apologized and wandered toward a group of men and women who stood leaning against the interior wall. An older woman with silver hair drawn up in a tight bun nodded in her direction. "I think we have a new recruit," she said toward no one in particular in the rest of the group. Then, to Margo: "I'm Hemlen. Are you here to help?"

"Yes I am," Margo said. "Thank you."

Another explosion rattled the church. Hemlen turned to the rest of the group. "That's our signal. Let's move!"

Together they surged out of the church and into the parking lot where a row of school buses that were painted black waited. They crammed into one of the lead buses. Packed in with the anxious, sweating bodies, Margo found it hard to breathe but she was feeling too exhilarated to care. This time, she was sure she was doing something right.

Almost immediately the bus started rolling toward Cog City.

Almost immediately Margo wondered if she had made the right choice. She recognized in the grim looks on the faces of those around her that these people were prepared to die for this cause. It dawned on her that the Cog City authorities would be prepared to kill to defend their atrocious Machine.

She knew she could not do what Belga had done. She could not mobilize a militant group such as this, even if their cause was just, even if all involved understood the risks.

But she was grateful Belga had done it. She forced away her doubts.

The Machine did not hesitate when it removed peoples' heads and turned them into cyborgs.

Margo would not hesitate either.

THIRTY-NINE

Black buses full of Saboteurs approached the entrance to the secret tunnel into Cog City.

Three of the tentacle-towers had been destroyed, all on the opposite side of the city. Sirens blared. Plumes of gray smoke rose up from the ground where they once stood.

A thin layer of frost covered the ground and the world outside of the buses seemed to wait in hushed anticipation for what would happen next.

On a bus, Margo sat next to the old woman Hemlen and got to know a few of the others. There was Min Fang, who pointedly asked Margo who she was and what she was doing. He insisted that someone he'd never met before could not possibly be trusted on a mission like this. The mission required a true understanding of what the Saboteurs were up against, he said, and he claimed reaching this true understanding was "impossible for someone new." Margo resisted slapping him with a suction cup hand. She reminded herself they were on the same side and offered a tight-lipped smile and the assurance "I understand just fine" in response.

Hemlen tapped Min Fang on the shoulder. "Tell me," she said in her calm, creaky voice. "Do you understand how your spray can full of dormant kronozoa works? How they are kept in a state of near-frozen suspended animation until they are released when you simply remove the cap and press down with your finger on the nozzle?"

"Not exactly, but—"

"It's okay," she said with an arch glance toward Margo. "I invented canned kronozoa. But I'll allow you to use it."

"Excuse me," said a dark-skinned man with braided hair who was seated behind Margo and Hemlen on the bus. "I overheard you talking. You're Hemlen Mattoo, right?"

"That's right," said Hemlen.

"I'm Tito Jefferson. It's an honor."

Hemlen turned in her seat and extended her hand toward Tito. He hesitated, then brought up his hand. It was large and clawlike and had only two large deformed fingers and a thumb. Hemlen grasped his hand and shook it. "Delighted," she said.

Margo stared at Tito's hand then shifted her gaze upward to the man's face, which had turned toward her. He offered her his hand in turn. "Go ahead and stare," he said. "I'm used to it."

Tentatively, Margo allowed a suction cup hand to emerge from her sleeve and accepted the Tito's hand into it. His grip was warm and dry and looser than she expected. And now he was staring at her suction cup hand. "Now there's something you don't see every day," he said. "Bet there's one hell of a story behind that."

"Bet you're right," said Margo.

Hemlen was staring at the suction cup hand too. "You're from the future," she said matter-of-factly. "You traveled here somehow, from the future to your past, and now you're here, on our side, with us."

"Wait," said Min Fang, turning to give Margo a hard look. "You're from the Bubble-zoid or whatever? The place where all the rich babies get Executed slaves as birthday presents?" He glanced at Hemlen. "And you don't have any problem with her being here with us? You're okay with this?" Then he glanced at Tito. "And you're okay with this?"

Tito shrugged. "It raises some questions ..."

"Damn right it raises questions," said Min Fang. "It raises some very serious questions. For example: why the hell are we not stopping the bus to give this person-from-the-future a hearty heave-ho so that there is zero chance that she'll mess up our mission?"

Margo was annoyed, but she refused to back down from the argument. "You're afraid I'm going to sabotage the Saboteurs?"

"Yes." He nudged the blonde-haired woman beside him. "Don't others share my concerns?" The woman had been looking out the window, apparently trying very hard but ultimately failing to avoid being dragged into the debate.

"Sure," she said with an unhappy glance in Min Fang's direction. "Sure."

"Tell you what," said Hemlen, "I'll vouch for her." She reached over and squeezed Margo's leech arm affectionately through her sleeve. "If she proves untrustworthy—and she won't—you can put the blame on me."

Min Fang let out a heavy sigh but did not protest any further. His companion returned to looking out the window. Tito's face remained a solemn, expressionless mask. He closed his eyes and seemed to retreat into himself. "Let's all calm down now," he said. "This mission is supposed to be easy. If we're quick and coordinated, we'll be in and out before anyone in Cog City has any idea what we've done. Just think about the all-you-can-eat brunch waiting for us when we get back." He opened his eyes. "That will be a glorious brunch."

"Thank you," Margo said to Hemlen. "I don't know who you are, but I can see why that man in front of us was honored to meet you."

"Think nothing of it," Hemlen said. "I am in many ways a very fortunate person, and in other was a very unfortunate person. Some people give me credit for creating this group. This movement. That's why they listen to me."

"Oh wow, I see. I thought Belga was your leader."

"Belga is our leader. All I did was put up the money to make what she does possible. Or no. That gives me too much credit. Let's say the money just made it possible on a more accelerated timeline."

"It sounds like you've been very generous," Margo said.

"It does sound that way, doesn't it? Except I wouldn't have any money at all if I hadn't discovered how to can kronozoa. You see, I sold the patents to Cogworks. And they took my invention and used it to create a slave trade. So, from another point of view, I suppose I can take additional credit for making the mistake that made the Saboteurs necessary. But if more of our friends thought about it that way, I suppose they wouldn't listen to me, would they? Anyway, I can't say I have no regrets. And today I finally have a chance to use my invention to undo some of the harm it did. That's why I'm here. How about you?"

During the rest of the ride Margo told Hemlen about her connection with Belga, her dedication to safety, her disappointment with Jasper and, ultimately, her wish to avenge the people being made into cyborgs—and the people of the Bublinaplex who are unwittingly implicated in Cogworks' murderous system.

The bus stopped. Its door opened and one by one the Saboteurs filed out. As they stood up to leave, Hemlen said, "Your story is quite reassuring."

"What do you mean?" asked Margo.

"Once you learned the truth behind the Bublinaplex, you decided to fight back. So if others inside the Bublinaplex respond anything like you did after we complete our mission today, I think we'll be able to call what we're about to do a success."

Hundreds of Saboteurs poured into the secret tunnel Margo had followed out of Cog City. They were sort of jogging and sort of marching, and they took a winding underground route that seemed different to Margo from the route she'd taken through just a few hours before. Just as dark of course, but windier and hillyer, and she realized she should be thankful she had not taken a wrong turn when she'd walked these tunnels alone.

At first, Margo was anxious that Hemlen, old as she was, would not be able to keep up with the group's vigorous pace. But it was her own stamina that started to flag before the old woman's. The fact was, she still needed more sleep. She pressed on, occasionally reminding herself of the victory brunch Tito had mentioned, which in her imagination blossomed into a mountain of eggs, bacon, pancakes, waffles, and fruit waiting back at the dilapidated church.

The Saboteurs' trek through the tunnel ended at a twenty-foot ladder. One by one, they ascended. And when they emerged, they came up through a hole in the Factory floor. Once inside, they dispersed to every corner of the building to wait until the last person up the ladder gave the signal to begin.

Margo went up the steps and across the catwalk toward the circular "DIS / ASSEMBLY" door. The room where she learned the truth about Jasper and witnessed the Machine at work was the place she wanted to send into the future.

Fuck that room, she thought.

When she pulled open the door she saw three people were already inside. She was disappointed. Three people were already too many to be crowded in that tiny room, working on spraying the walls. She would have to find someplace else to send to the future.

Then she realized there was something wrong with one of the people in the room.

The person was dead. What she was seeing was a body dangling from a bundle of cables attached to the low ceiling.

The body was Jasper.

Margo shoved her way inside and told the two Saboteurs in the room to back off. Yes, it was definitely Jasper. She reached up with her leech arms and grabbed hold of the cables around his neck with her suction cup hands and gave them a good yank to dislodge them so she could lie Jasper's body on the floor.

There was a note taped to the window through which Margo had watched the Machine. It was written on Cogworks Incorporated letterhead:

Dear Executive Designer Abbotzo,

I no longer want to be what I've become. I never should have let it happen. I can't undo what I've done.

So: I quit.

Jasper Frick

P.S. Send my love to Margo. My last wish is to hide from her what's become of me, if possible. Just don't tell her I'm anywhere where she might think she could follow me. Because you and I both know that she just might try and if she tries, she'll probably succeed.

Margo started backing out of the room.

The two Saboteurs were standing by the door, whispering. "... we could strap the body onto the Machine," she overheard one say. "We could let it take his head off so the people in the future will fully understand what they're seeing."

She stepped back into the room and picked up Jasper's body with her leech arms, then carried him out. To the whispering Saboteurs, she spat, "He was a fucking person."

Carrying Jasper, she backtracked across the catwalk and found a stairway leading upward. The Factory was crowded with Saboteurs now, all waiting for the signal. Margo squeezed past them, indifferent to the stares at the dead body and the parasites she used to carry it. She climbed the stairway as far as she could go and on the top floor, which seemed to be occupied exclusively with dust-covered storage boxes, she found a maintenance ladder that led to the roof. With some difficulty (owing more to the smallness of the space than the heaviness of Jasper's body) she ascended the ladder, opened the small latched opening that led to the roof, and hoisted herself along with Jasper's body up and out into the cool air.

It was snowing and uncannily quiet. On the other side of the city all that remained of the smoke was a brownish yellow smudge slowly dissolving into the surrounding sky. The fires around the fallen tentacle towers must have been extinguished.

She carried Jasper's body to the edge and then dropped it by her feet.

She forced herself to look at the body and look carefully. She believed it was her fault Jasper was dead.

His face was gray. His wide-set eyes were half shut. His tongue was sticking out. His neck was black from the bruising.

She shouldn't have come to this place.

She shouldn't have been so quick to judge.

She could have gone easier on Jasper.

She could have made an effort to accept what he did here.

Or she could have pretended she didn't mind and then coaxed him away slowly.

Or she could have kidnapped him.

There was no coaxing or kidnapping that could bring him back from where he was now.

There was no point in doing anything for him.

There was no point to anything she'd done, for him or for anyone else.

What good was it to try to save anyone? To protect anyone? To try? If this was what was going to happen, what good was any of it?

Margo stood on the roof for a long time, looking at Jasper but not looking at him. Maybe she would go back to Fayette and Tromscratt. And Diego. She did actually miss Diego.

Or she could find Xerxes Abbotzo. Her father. Could he continue to keep himself hidden from her, after all she'd been through? Would he just put her to work alongside the others who'd been banished from the Bublinaplex? Would she simply be tasked with rebuilding what the Saboteurs were about to destroy?

She could think of nothing she wanted to do besides stand in the snow and watch the flakes slowly cover the surface of Jasper's cold face.

From the building below, she felt an odd sort of rhythmic rumbling. She listened.

The signal.

Tito taught her the signal when the bus had stopped and they were waiting to get out. He'd stood up in the aisle, hunched and smiling, and performed what looked like a silly, stompy little dance. "The important thing is the stomping," he said. "You stomp twice with your left foot, pause, then stomp three times with your right foot, pause, once more with your left foot, pause, then three times with both feet. Watch me one more time." The bus rattled and swayed as others crowded into the aisle to join Tito.

The signal meant the last of the Saboteurs had entered the Factory and that it was now time for them to take their positions and start spraying the frozen kronozoa.

And then in precisely eighteen minutes and forty-four seconds, the thawed microbes would begin their migration. They would take everything they touched along with them to the future, or the odd space that was visible from the future but not quite actually the future, if Margo understood correctly.

And, for the first time, the people who live in the Bublinaplex would see the true origin of the cyborgs they so thoughtlessly use.

Margo took out her can of frozen kronozoa and looked at it, then dropped it on the roof beside Jasper's body.

She looked out over the dead grass and fence surrounding the Factory. Through the thickening snow she could just make out rows of laser-carrying cyborgs marching toward them. Police on equiborgs and stranger things, a whole zoo of animals with mechanical devices where their heads should be, marched among them. Under the officers Margo thought she recognized the bodies of big cats, buffalo, ostriches, elephants, and apes.

Those that had been executed by the Machine had been summoned to defend it.

Below, the stomping sounds of the signal ceased. A few seconds passed. Cog City's grotesque defenders advanced in eerie silence.

The Saboteurs should be just beginning to spray the inside of the Factory with kronozoa.

And then, from below, Margo heard screams. She was frightened and alone, and she didn't know what to do. She waited.

Minutes later she could hear someone climbing toward her on the ladder. She braced herself for anything.

It was Hemlen. Her face and clothes were splotched with some kind of rust-red substance. "Margo," she cried. "We need you." With surprising nimbleness she threw herself up on the roof and ran toward Margo. "Oh god," she said when she saw the body. "Did you know him?"

Margo looked down. "I think I thought I knew him. And now ... "

"I'm sorry," Hemlen pleaded. "But there isn't time. Please—" She grabbed Margo's sleeve.

Margo stood her ground. "What happened?" she asked. "What's that red stuff?"

Hemlen sighed. "The Saboteurs have been sabotaged. It's the cans. Someone tampered with the kronozoa cans. When everyone started spraying after hearing the signal, the cans, some of them blew up and some sprayed in multiple directions. The kronozoa, they're in people's eyes and on people's faces, it's horrible ... Please. You must come help."

Margo saw the anger in Hemlen's eyes. "How?"

"Your leeches," said Hemlen. "If you're willing to sacrifice your leeches for this mission, you can stretch them out and use them to spray the Machine so that the most horrifying part of the Factory is destroyed and exposed to the people of the Bublinaplex. You won't be able to avoid getting kronozoa on the leeches, and when the kronozoa start their migration, they'll take anything they touched along with them."

The request shocked Margo. "I can't do that," she said. "The leeches are a part of me now. I don't even know if they'll let me."

"There are people down there who are covered in kronozoa. When the kronozoa start to migrate, they will take those people and entomb them in the not-quite-future where we were supposed to send the inside of this building. The lucky ones have just a few splashes on their faces. But once the kronozoa start to migrate, the microbes will create deep wounds, many probably fatal."

"No," Margo insisted. "I don't think you understand, I can feel what the leeches feel, and the leeches, they have their own desperate will to live ... "

Hemlen put a hand on Margo's shoulder. "I understand," she said. She bent down and pulled the pant leg of her trousers up to where her knee should be. Instead of a leg, there inside her pant leg was the deep green, segmented body of a sludge leech.

"What... how?" Margo stammered, staring.

"I already told you I discovered how to can kronozoa," she said. "Did you think someone who put the work into creating a portable portal through time would be able to resist trying it out herself? And, of course, you know what I found on the other side."

"The Fungus Wasteland."

"And all the fascinating and awful things that live there. So listen to me Margo. The people downstairs, Tito and Min Fang and the rest, they need your help. If you don't help, their mission—their sacrifice—will have been meaningless. I'm not asking you to do anything I'm not willing to do myself. Everyone here today is going to lose a part of themselves. I'm sorry. It's not fair. But it's what we must do."

Margo nodded. "But what about them?" She gestured toward the advancing army of the Executed.

"My god," said Hemlen, seeing for the first time the quietly advancing, semi-mechanical, mostly headless mass. "We have to go. We have to go now." She took one of Margo's suction cup hands in her hand. With Margo's other leech arm she picked up Jasper's body by partially coiling the leech around him. Once they'd descended the ladder, Hemlen started stomping a signal. It was a different pattern than the signal to start spraying. She pounded her left foot, the boot-clad suction cup foot, on the ground three times, paused, then stomped with her still-human right foot twice, paused, stomped with her left twice, paused, then jumped to pound both feet simultaneously again four times. "It's the signal to retreat," she told Margo on the way down as the Factory filled with the din of others repeating the dance, conveying the message.

The area around the Machine was splattered with rust-red kronozoa spray. Spray cans littered the floor alongside the bodies of mannequins, models that were supposed to be strapped into the Machine and posed in different stages of being turned into a cyborg. Hemlen and Margo arranged the mannequins and removed some of their heads and balanced cyborg heads on top of their plastic torsos.

Hemlen pulled down her kronozoa-splattered sleeve to look at her watch. Her hand, Margo noticed, was covered in the red stuff and the color of the splotches on Hemlen's face and clothes were changing color, becoming shimmery and slivery, as were the splotches that were already on the Machine and the floor and walls. "Less than five minutes until the kronozoa on me start migrating," she said. "We have to hurry. I won't be much use to you once that begins."

Margo picked up a spray can from the floor with each of her suction cup hands and reached out her leech arms as far as they could stretch while still holding up the cans. She aimed the cans as best as she could at a mannequin strapped into one of the Machine's chairs and tried to press down both nozzles.

Her suction cup hand refused. "I can't," she said. "The leeches know what I'm about to do will hurt them."

"You have to insist that you are in charge," replied Hemlen. "Let them let you know they don't want to do what you're trying to get them to do. Lie to yourself, convince yourself no harm will come to them. Insist. Insist. Insist."

Margo nodded and cleared her mind. She told herself everything would be okay and quieted the part of herself that knew what she was about to do was self-destructive.

She pressed the spray can nozzles. A red mess spattered in every direction, covering the mannequin and soaking everything within a four-foot radius, including Margo's suction cup hands. Her leech arms dripped with the stuff, but her face and body were safe. She emptied the cans, then picked up another two to continue the sloppy spray-job as quickly as she could.

Hemlen meanwhile had dropped down to the floor beside Margo and took off her shoe. She picked up a spray can with her suction cup foot and stretched her leech leg as far as it could stretch, then set to work spraying the Machine with Margo.

They were not quite halfway through their task when Hemlen stopped suddenly and gasped in agony. Her spray can clattered to the floor and her leech leg whipped back toward her, apparently wanting to fight off the hidden enemy attacking its host.

Hemlen twisted and writhed and curled up on the ground in fetal position, head down on the floor and hands over her head, as the confused leech leg whirled around, found Margo, and, mistaking her for the threat, shoved her as hard as it could, sending her tumbling backwards across the floor.

As soon as Margo righted herself, her leech arms lashed back at Hemlen's leech leg. Hemlen was screaming in pain and Margo was yelling "STOP IT STOP IT STOP IT" at her leech arms, but it was no use, they'd found their enemy and together tried to coil around their attacker. Hemlen's leech leg slipped away from their grip and looped itself into a kind of lasso in an attempt to restrain both of Margo's leech arms at once. It failed. Margo's leech arms attacked Hemlen's leech leg from both ends, its head, where it attached to Hemlen's thigh, and the suction cup at the end, and pinned it down.

Margo realized Hemlen wasn't screaming anymore.

The writhing leech leg flipped Hemlen's body over. Almost the entire right half of her head was gone. It was like a piece of fruit with a rotten spot that had sloughed away.

Hemlen's hand was the same—entirely gone except for a glistening, irregularly shaped nub of tissue and bone. And there were neat little holes in her clothes anywhere the kronozoa had landed during that first spattering when the Saboteurs started spraying the Factory.

And there were now great, irregularly shaped gaps in the walls and the parts of the Machine. All through the building, holes were appearing where the kronozoa had taken it with them too the future. The structure, suddenly unstable, creaked and groaned under its own weight.

Margo picked up two more kronozoa cans and continued spraying. She didn't have time to mourn Hemlen. She had to finish covering the Machine with kronozoa before what happened to Hemlen's head happened to her leech arms.

There was a crashing sound below, on the ground floor. Margo stopped and listened. She tried to place the rhythmic sound. The sound reminded her of the Machine at work, what she'd heard before she saw it take Norlene's head. Except this sound was not as steady. The rhythm stayed the same. But it grew louder and louder.

And then she realized: The army of the Executed was inside the building.

Hemlen's leech, meanwhile, had released its grip on its dead host's thigh and wriggled out of her pant leg and pulled itself across the tiled floor, suction cup end first.

Margo didn't notice it. She was too busy trying to spray the Machine's various insectile parts before the surge of cyborgs found her. But her left leech arm noticed it and veered off at a right angle to where Margo was trying to aim a sloppily spraying can and shoved the can toward the hungry thing's mouth. Unencumbered by a host, the third leech was agile enough to dodge the attempt to clog its throat and then spring toward Margo's left foot. It slurped its way up past her knee in seconds, boot and pant leg and all.

Margo cursed and tried to stomp through it from the inside. It was no use. All three leeches were now starting to shimmer with the awakening kronozoa that dripped thickly from their segments. The Machine shimmered too.

With a tremendous boom, two cyborg-headed gorillas smashed through the steel doors that had separated her from the attack from below. Helmeted police officers rode on both gorillas, and both officers had already drawn and started firing their laser rifles.

A hot red beam sizzled into Margo's side. She cried out in pain and a shimmering leech rapidly whipped the officer off of the cyborg ape.

The other officer fired rapidly into the leech, severing half of its length from Margo. The suction cup that had been her hand twitched as the other leech tried to slap the weapon out of the officer's hands. It too was burned in a burst of hot red fury from the end of the officer's weapon.

The pain Margo felt from the damage to her leech arms was already too much when the kronozoa began to rip the rest of what was left of them into the almost-future.

She gasped and collapsed. The cyborg apes, now accompanied by their masters and what seemed like dozens of cyborgs, cornered her against the wall as the shimmering Machine faded out of existence from the present.

Margo saw that on the screen-face of every single cyborg was the image of her father.

He spoke: "I love you. I don't want to have to hurt you, Margo. Surrender. Join me. I only want what's best for you. I'll make everything alright. I love you. I don't want to have to hurt you, Margo. Surrender..." The message looped over and over again.

As she backed away the wall behind her buckled and a sound like an explosion rippled through the room.

Margo lurched forward on the bloody remains of what was left of her leech arms.

The police and cyborgs surrounding her seemed, for the instant, to hesitate.

She gasped and groaned against the agony of her dismemberment and the loss of Hemlen. Yet she let herself recognize the Machine had disappeared and released a euphoric whoop to celebrate this victory.

The wall behind Margo collapsed. Freezing air and debris burst into the room as an enormous hole was ripped into the building.

And through the hole came another cyborg.

The cyborg reached for her. Margo shook her head and decided she would use the last of her strength to fight. She would bite and kick and run until they aimed a laser gun at her head and killed her. She would cede nothing.

And then she realized there was a face on the cyborg's screen-face. For a moment it confused her and a wave of despair threatened to pummel her further because she misunderstood and thought the face of the person on the screen was the person that the body had belonged to and she thought, "Not you, not you." And then she recognised the cyborg. Its scarred skin was exposed to the air instead of hidden under black plastic.

"Try to get up," said Belga through the cyborg. "Try to let Billy's body carry you away."

She did not get up but she let the cyborg with Belga's face on its screen pick her up and carry her.

The army of the Executed stood still. The looping recording of Executive Designer Xerxes "Fash" Abbotzo stopped. The army's screen-faces went blank. Then the Executive Designer's face was back in an apparent live feed. "Don't go, Margo," he said. "Everything I've done, I've done for you."

The cyborg with Belga's face on its screen stepped out through the dusty hole in the side of the building. They were at least forty feet up. The cyborg's foot rested on something firm.

Margo started to laugh and she couldn't make herself stop.

The cyborg that held her was standing on a tentacle tower that was bent in half like a black metal rainbow. It had not been destroyed in the earlier attack. It had been released.

Carrying the cyborg that carried Margo, the severed tentacle tower listed and pitched as one end of the arch lifted away from the ground and then came to rest farther from the remains of the Factory. Then the other end of the arch took a step. The tentacle tower walked toward the Periphery and Margo imagined this was what it must feel like to float in a vast and turbulent sea.

EPILOGUE: THE SPEECH, PART THREE

Belga clenches her fists. She tries to focus her inner anger. The anger demands expression as wordless violence.

She refuses the demand and attempts to articulate herself. Her followers must understand why they are about to do what they are about to do.

She unclenches her fists and opens her mouth and this is what she says:

"Many have said that it is our creativity that makes us human, that our ability to make new things is the single most important quality that makes us different from animals.

"We experience the creations that others have made and we in turn are inspired to create new things—and as long as our children and our children's children are experiencing the creations of others and becoming inspired and creating new things on and on into the future, there is hope that humanity might go on.

"It was this hope that inspired the creation of the Bublinaplex. It was this hope that drove those who could afford it to colonise the future by buying their children one-way tickets to what must have seemed to some like an actual utopia.

"The rich people sending their children off to the Bublinaplex knew all-too-well the reality of this dying world. It is they who are most responsible for its death.

"The Bublinaplex became their chance to protect their children from the dying world by sending them into the future where a new world could be reborn.

"All of you now poised to end this abomination must understand, at least a little, that the deep-seated drive to protect their offspring, together with their profound shame from having ruined our world, have combined to blind these people to the viciousness of the system they are responsible for creating and which, unchecked, they would allow to go on forever.

"You must understand it, but you must not let it soften your resolve to destroy this system utterly and for good. You must not let it make you hesitate.

"Because the moment they perceived the possibility that they could save their own children while allowing the rest of us to suffer the apocalyptic consequences of their shortsightedness and greed, they did not hesitate. They did what they told themselves they must do in order to save their descendants.

"And the moment they realized that the rest of us surviving in this hopeless world would do anything we could to save our children too, anything at all, again, they did not hesitate. They saw our desperation and they exploited it. They saw our fathers' and mothers' and sisters' and brothers' willingness to sacrifice themselves and they accepted the sacrifice—their bodies, their minds—so that we, the children of the poor, might have a little more security and stability against the plagues and the storms and the hunger and the filth that are fast consuming what's left of this dying planet.

"Make no mistake. Death is consuming this planet faster every day. And every day, more of everything that is beautiful and pure and unpoisoned and worth saving is being torn up by its roots today so it can be sent to the future for the children of privilege.

"And I can't help but wonder: would the wealthy have so fully abandoned our present day if there were no far-future colony where the children of privilege live in an as-safe-as-can-be artists' retreat?

"And I can't help but wonder: would these children of privilege accept what their parents have done, the sacrifice of peoples' lives and the very Earth upon which we live, if they were forced to look at it? If they knew the truth, that they live as they do because they are so fully sheltered from their past?

"Today, we find out.

"I believe the change will come. Seeing the Bublinaplex from both sides is what has inspired me.

"Let us act now in faith that seeing the true origins of the Executed will ignite the spark.

"Let us act now in faith that this revelation can lead to revolution.

"Let us act now in faith that the revelation alone is not enough—and that the degree to which our action can be called a success will depend on whether it works as a physical barrier against further crimes against us.

"Let us act now in faith that the elite's attempt to create a society rooted in devotion to imagination and creativity worked—and that these children will join us in imagining and creating a better world.

"Let us act now in faith.

"We who have seen the future must find a way to believe it still can be changed. We must believe we truly do not know what will happen next.

"We must believe we can win.

"We must believe that what we are about to do will change the world, even in the face of overwhelming evidence that it will not."

Acknowledgements

Enormous thank yous to all who offered feedback on, entertained my ravings about, and/or quietly tolerated my years-long obsession with writing this story. In particular, I want to thank early readers Glenn Simpson, Stanley Stepanic, Gavin Mueller, Judy Ruszkowski, and Lena Pons; my editor Amanda Hardebeck; my publishers Nate Ragolia and Shaunn Grulkowski; my Public Citizen family; my actual family, especially the person who specifically asked not to be acknowledged; and everyone I forgot to mention (sorry!). You are all weird heroes and I love you all.

About the Author

Rick Claypool is a writer and activist who lives in Pittsburgh. He works for Public Citizen, a nonprofit organization that fights corporate power. He has a master's degree in popular culture from Bowling Green State University. He grew up in a small town in western Pennsylvania called Leechburg. *Leech Girl Lives* is his first novel. For more about Rick, visit rickclaypool.org.

About the Publishing Team

Amanda Hardebeck has been a sci-fi & film addict since birth. When her older brother handed her a copy of *Dune* for her birthday 20 years ago, her passion for science fiction took off. She is a roller derby referee for her hometown team and is Chief Editor for Spaceboy Books LLC.

TJ Stambaugh received several commendations for his bravery as a battalion commander in the Meme Wars. After the war, TJ retired to Catonsville, MD, where he paints, enjoys movies you have to read, and is Art Director for Spaceboy Books LLC.

Learn more about Spaceboy Books at readspaceboy.com

Made in the USA
Lexington, KY
27 August 2019